THE APPROACH TO KINGS

Books by Patrick Anderson

THE PRESIDENTS' MEN
THE APPROACH TO KINGS

THE APPROACH TO KINGS

Patrick Anderson

DOUBLEDAY & COMPANY, INC.
Garden City, New York
1970

*All of the characters in this book are fictitious, and any re-
semblance to actual persons, living or dead, is purely coin-
cidental.*

For my mother, with gratitude and love

Honor hath three things in it: the vantage
ground to do good; the approach to kings
and principal persons; and the raising of
a man's own fortunes.

SIR FRANCIS BACON: "Of Ambition"

BOOK

I

A Day in the Life

1

The story was on the front page, with a good picture—the President hunched over his desk, frowning; Dave whispering intently in his ear—and a good headline too:

DAVID HYER EMERGES
AS KEY NEWFIELD AIDE

No quarrel there. Dave read the story again, slowly and approvingly, as he sipped his breakfast coffee. Eleanor sat across the table, her long blond hair tied back with a blue ribbon, looking cool and lovely. She was ignoring the newspaper story and he was ignoring her. Neither of them had forgotten the night before, and they had not spoken that morning. To hell with her, he told himself, and put the matter from his mind.

Sally wandered in, a glowing miniature of her mother, and Dave started to show her his picture in the paper, but decided against it. He knew that if he did, Eleanor would say (or think, which was the same, for they read each other's thoughts) "That's right, show your daughter what a big man you are; tell her that's why she hasn't seen you for an hour in the past month." So he put the paper aside and called to the child, "From there to here, from here to there . . ."

"Fun-ny things 'r everwhere!" Sally cried happily and raced around the table. Dave grabbed her and put her on his lap and they talked about her preschool class until his car arrived in front of the house. He slipped on his coat, picked up the paper and his briefcase, kissed his daughter, and hurried out to the black Mercury for the twenty-minute drive to the White House.

It was a gorgeous Friday in early April. Along the George Washington Parkway, lilac, redbud, and dogwood waved to the passing motorists like girls with bright scarves; as they crossed the glittering, polluted Potomac, the pink blur of cherry blossoms could be glimpsed in the distance. But David Hyer had no eyes for the scenery. He sank back into the Mercury's soft upholstery, ignoring the rush-hour traffic, studying the *Post* article intently, evaluating it on several levels.

First, at the level of sheer ego, he enjoyed the article immensely—it flattered him. Immodesty was among his vices— how else would he be where he was, without a king-size ego? —but he tried to keep it out of sight, like an alcoholic who only drinks at home.

At another level, in another part of his mind, he was studying the article quite coldly, quite without ego, trying to compute how well he had presented himself to this writer, this Catherine Quinn, and what good or harm it might do him. All in all, he had no complaints. She called him a complex mixture of politician and intellectual—that was obvious. She said he did some of the President's dirty work for him—well, someone had to do it. Yes, he supposed his critics called him an empire- builder—empire-building was the name of the game. Yes, he knew that people sometimes found him impatient, even arro- gant—there wasn't time for all the amenities. (A mental note: stress patience and humility in future interviews.)

In sum, it was a fair article, generous to him, more perceptive than most about the way government worked. Its most important paragraph was this one:

"In the six months since Bernard Newfield succeeded the late Milton Osgood as President, his most intimate all-around adviser has been David Hyer, a thirty-one-year-old, Texas-born lawyer. Few people know the new President well, but David Hyer knows him very well, from the four years he served Newfield when he was Governor of Tennessee. Hyer was New- field's emissary to the now-famous all-night bargaining session at which Democratic party leaders put together the Osgood- Newfield when he was governor of Tennessee. Hyer was New- convention. Today, from a base as the President's top speech- writer, Hyer has extended his influence into domestic affairs, congressional relations, even foreign policy. Veteran policy- makers can grumble about his youth and inexperience, but one White House insider sums it up this way: 'The guys in the cabinet call Dave for advice, he doesn't call them. That ought to tell you where the power is.'"

Dave smiled ruefully. That would ruffle some feathers, in the cabinet and elsewhere, but it was true. And Dave was worrying less and less about ruffled feathers. There was only one man he had to please, the President, Barney Newfield, and he was ninety percent sure Barney wouldn't mind the article. He'd growl a bit about Dave's press clippings, but not mind. It wasn't that Barney was a modest soul, anxious to share his glory, not at all. As Brenda once put it, "My husband's ego is so big it casts its own shadow."

But the article made the administration look good, and the girl had included several quotes wherein Dave heaped lavish praise on the President, who never objected to lavish praise. So Dave expected no kickback from his boss. The only thing that bothered him was that the girl had found out somehow that he opposed U.S. intervention against the guerrillas in Caravelas. But that didn't really matter, for the whole Caravelas debate was going to surface that afternoon at the NSC meeting.

Meanwhile, throughout Washington (and the nation, for the article was syndicated) other men of the political world were studying the article, making their own computations. Dave's stock was high that morning. He was the President's man. Perhaps in the days ahead senators would confide in him more fully, cabinet members weigh his judgments more respectfully, bureaucrats resist his orders less fiercely. It was a pleasant thought, and Dave was smiling as his car paused at the White House gates. From the sidewalk, three early-rising tourists peered in at him—a prune-faced man with a camera hung around his neck, his plump wife, and their daughter, a bow-legged girl in an orange miniskirt—wondering who this privileged young man might be. He looked at them and through them, then the Mercury shot out of their world and squealed to a halt in front of the West Wing. Dave jumped out, a tall, slender young man, swinging his briefcase, whistling a Lennon-McCartney tune. It was eight o'clock, springtime danced in the air, and all seemed right with the world, or as right as it ever was.

"Who's dying to talk to me?" he asked Mrs. Gill.

"Russ Boesel's three minutes from collapse."

"Call him in two." He skimmed through the morning's CIA report while Mrs. Gill got his coffee. The report on Caravelas gave nothing new—Rivera and his men had not been heard from since their attack on an army outpost a week earlier. Dave reached for another pile of papers—yesterday's unanswered phone calls, today's early mail, old reports, new memos. The mayor of Boston had called again about his brother, who aspired to a diplomatic career. The AEC had sent another memo urging a resumption of underground testing; Dave and Leon Kerkelot, the national-security adviser, had thus far persuaded Barney not to resume testing. Dave smiled and put the AEC memo on the bottom of his pile.

Mrs. Gill brought coffee and the news that Russ Boesel was on the line. Boesel was an assistant to the director of the Public Health Service, a very bright young man, and he had interested Dave in a proposed treatment center for skid row alcoholics in the District, hopefully the first in a national program. The problem of course was money: PHS claimed to lack the necessary five million and Congress had been cool to the idea.

"Russ, how's it coming?"

"Spingarn's committee meets at four this afternoon on the budget. Either we get the money then or we don't get it."

"Did you talk to Spingarn?"

"Briefly. He says the government has no business sobering up drunks. So I guess it's up to you."

Dave promised to see what he could do. He hung up the phone wondering just what he *could* do. Call Senator Spingarn? No, the old bastard would tell him to go to hell. Ask Barney to intervene? No, he wouldn't go to Spingarn on anything this small. Dave decided to call the Majority Leader for suggestions. Of course, he could let the matter drop—it was not his responsibility. But it was a good idea; besides, he wanted ideas and information from men like Boesel, and for their cooperation he had to serve, from time to time, as deus ex machina for them.

Ethyl Gill returned with more messages. She was a plump, motherly woman. For that reason he had almost not hired her, despite her glowing references; then he'd noticed on her résumé that she'd worked at Defense when McNamara was there. "I guess you saw a lot of generals over there," he'd said, making small talk, and she'd replied sweetly, "Yes, we used them for office boys." He decided Mrs. Gill would do just fine.

"Professor Fleishman has been camped in my office for two days," she said. "I'm running out of excuses."

"I'll try to see him after the staff meeting. And try to get the Majority Leader. And about ten, call Cathy Quinn, that reporter."

"That was a nice story."

"It was all right. Now, get me Commissioner Stumblebum."

He returned to his memos. There was one from Justice about the draft resisters who were about to be imprisoned; Dave was trying to persuade Barney to pardon them but this was not the day to pursue the matter.

Mrs. Gill had Commissioner Stubblefield on the line. Dave let the commissioner hold while he glanced again through a folder on one Horace Rice, Stubblefield's chief counsel. Dave had met Rice once; he was blond, round-faced, pleasant, very bright. Dave picked up the phone and said what he had to say:

"Have you taken action yet, Commissioner? . . . Yes, I know he's a good lawyer . . . No, it isn't a discretionary matter. If he's had one relationship like that, he'll have another . . . It comes to this, Commissioner, either you fire the man or I will, and it's not my job to fire him."

Stubblefield was upset. Dave was impatient. What was he supposed to do? They were running a government, not a daisy chain. He listened to the commissioner's complaints for a moment, glancing at the bed of bright red and yellow tulips outside his window, and when he had a promise of action he hung up. It was almost time for the staff meeting. He stepped into the small bathroom off his office and combed his hair, studying his face for a moment as he did. It was a good face, a useful face. The darker passions within were not reflected there; the face was open, pleasant, handsome in a youthful, American way. The hair was dark brown, a little long by Washington standards. He had high cheekbones, a long nose, gray-green eyes beneath thick brows, and a small, triangular mouth. It was a face in transition. Since childhood it had been thin, almost gaunt, the skin stretched tight between cheekbones and chin. Now, in the past year, with too much good food and drink, and too little exercise, his face was filling out, broadening, blurring the line of his jaw. The result was not unattractive —he looked older, more mature, more handsome. Yet he was vaguely troubled to see the familiar visage fade so fast; he remembered what Orwell had said, that at forty every man has the face he deserves, and he wondered what he might deserve by then.

"Mr. Secretary, this just ain't the time for you to show yourself on *Meet the Press*. Honest, pal, after that oil-lease case, you better lie low for a while. Yeah, I know how you feel . . ."

The press secretary, O. B. Perkins, was on the phone, as he often was. The phone was cradled between his ear and his shoulder, he was signing some papers with one hand, and he waved Dave in the door with the other. "*Be right with you, Dave,*" he stage-whispered, so the man on the other end of the line could hear. That, Dave knew, was the Secretary of the Interior, an Osgood appointee who wasn't destined to be Secretary of the Interior much longer.

Dave leaned against the doorway and watched the press secretary, a stocky, sandy-haired, sleepy-eyed man who was a legend among newspapermen. In city rooms across America, ambitious young reporters imitated O. B. Perkins' skeptical, bemused expression, his way of gesturing with his thumb and calling everyone "pal." O.B. was a plumber's son who became a police reporter for the Chicago *News* and at thirty became famous by singlehandedly cracking the biggest murder case of the decade. He'd bribed a judge, blackmailed a prostitute, broken into an insurance company's files—and for his enterprise he'd won his Pulitzer. The next year he'd become his paper's city editor, and two years later he'd managed a young lawyer's successful race for the Senate. When Milton Osgood ran for President, he recruited O.B. as his press man, and when Barney entered the White House he'd gladly kept him on.

O.B.'s interests did not stop with press relations. He was a shrewd political operative, on first-name terms with hundreds of politicians, and Barney increasingly sought his advice. All this bothered Dave a bit. He wished he knew what goals, if any, motivated his endless wheeling-dealing. But he knew almost nothing about him—not even what those damned initials stood for.

"Gotta get off the phone, pal," O.B. told the Secretary, with a wink at Dave. "The President's waiting on me." That would depress the Secretary, who hadn't seen the President in two months.

"Hey, pal," O.B. called to Dave, "I read in the paper where you're the second most important man in the whole mother-loving government."

"That was a mistake. They meant the second most important man in this corridor."

"Some story. Who is that girl?"

Dave shrugged. "Her name's Quinn and she works for an outfit called National Newsfeatures. The *Post*'s been carrying her stuff. She wrote that piece that cut up Bartle."

"Well you sure came out like a rose, pal. What'd you do, love her up a little?"

"Just boyish charm." Dave guessed O.B. was miffed because he hadn't told him about the interviews, but he wasn't about to start clearing things with O.B. They left the Press Office and walked briskly along the corridor that led from the West Wing to the White House proper.

"You know, those twelve draft resisters are going to prison in a couple of weeks unless the President intervenes," Dave said.

"Serves the bastards right," O.B. replied.

"Maybe so, but it'll stir up demonstrations and protests, just when things were starting to settle down."

O.B. frowned and asked a few incisive questions about the President's pardoning powers. As much as he disliked draft resisters, he disliked bad publicity more, and Dave suspected he'd come around.

At the elevator they met Leon Kerkelot, the national-security adviser, a formal and ironic man, very much the European intellectual. At precisely 8:45 the three of them marched past a watchful Secret Service man and into the bedroom of the President.

"Come in, gentlemen, come in," Barney roared. He was propped up in his huge, canopied bed, eating breakfast off a silver tray.

A Negro waiter hovered nearby with coffee. Barney had spent some of his best years in foxholes and Dave knew that, however much he joked about it, he gloried in the sheer elegance of the presidency. He was wearing white silk pajamas and a sky-blue robe. The curtains were pulled open so the dazzling spring sunlight flooded the room.

Seated on the edge of the bed, as if to heighten the President's splendor by his own striking inelegance, was Eddie Gooch, presidential crony, jester, and (officially) appointments secretary. Eddie was a moon-faced, sweaty man, possessed of a raucous charm and a good measure of cunning. He was wearing his usual shapeless brown suit and red bow tie.

"Come right in," Barney called again. "You especially, Mr. David Hyer, you young tiger you. We've been reading about you in the papers and we're mighty proud to be associated with you."

Dave grinned helplessly, as was expected. "I lucked out, Mr. President."

"Don't be modest, boy. I'm glad to find out about your talents. Me, I don't know shit from Shinola about this government. You run it and I'll take me a vacation. Right, Eddie?"

"Right, boss! You and me can buzz off to Pay-ree for the *Folies Bergère*." That was good for a laugh, for legend had it that in 1946 Barney and Eddie had started a brawl—trying to kidnap a chorus girl—that had closed the *Folies* for a night. The banter continued while the Negro poured coffee for the newcomers. Dave was pleased; Barney apparently didn't mind the newspaper article.

After a while Barney signaled to Eddie to begin the morning's business.

"First off," Eddie said, "is a meeting at ten-thirty with the governors of Washington, Oregon, Idaho, and Montana. Dave set it up."

"Yeah, this is that New Cities problem," the President said. "Dave, fill in O.B. and Leon."

"There've been rumors spreading in the Northwest that the New Cities are going to bring the black hordes to God's Country," Dave said, "and the governors are feeling the heat. So the President has to hold their hands a bit."

"Will there?" O.B. asked.

"Will there what?"

"Be black hordes?"

Dave shook his head. "The fact is, although we can't tell them this, that if we build a New City on the West Coast, it'll surely be in California, not in the Northwest."

"Okay, Dave, you sit in on that one," Barney said.

"Do you want Elias to come too?" Dave asked.

The President frowned.

O.B. said, "That little monkey gets on people's nerves."

"That little monkey is holding the New Cities program together," Dave shot back.

"Okay, pal, he's a genius," O.B. said. "But he gets on people's nerves."

The President laughed. "Yeah, I can't have Elias giving that evil-eye of his to the governors. You come by yourself, Dave. Eddie, what's next?"

"At eleven-thirty, Leon's got two professors coming in to talk about China," Eddie said.

"God damn, Leon," the President said, "I been talking about China so much lately my eyes are starting to slant."

The others laughed, but Leon Kerkelot remained perfectly straight-faced. "I think you'll find these men most useful," he said.

"At one o'clock," Eddie continued, "the National Security Council meets."

"Mr. President," Dave interrupted, "a couple of writers are in town I'd like for you to say hello to, just before the NSC meeting."

"Friendly writers?"

"I think so. A poet and a novelist. I'll send you a memo on them."

"Okay, I'll talk to anybody. Now, Leon, what about this NSC meeting—you following my rule?"

In some administrations, NSC meetings had grown to include thirty or forty government officials, but Barney insisted that his be kept small—it was his joke that NSC stood for Nobody Stupid Comes.

"Mr. President," Leon replied in his crisp, ironic tones, "I have ignored many piteous pleas, and thereby limited today's convocation to eight—the Secretaries of State and Defense, the Chairman of the Joint Chiefs, the Director of Central Intelligence, Dave, O.B., and I from your loyal staff, and of course yourself."

Barney nodded. "Everybody's ready to talk about this Caravelas business?"

"Mr. President," Leon said, "some of the participants have been talking of little else for weeks."

"Okay, what's next, Eddie?"

Eddie Gooch was unconcerned about strife in Caravelas—his full moon of a face glowed with delight as he studied the appointments schedule. Next, Dave knew, was a courtesy call from the Duchess of Cornwall, who was visiting America on a goodwill trip.

Eddie announced her as "the Duchess of Cornhole." It was the sort of barracks humor Barney loved and he laughed until his bed shook. The others laughed, too; Eddie's a crude bastard, Dave thought, but he *is* funny.

"You be careful, Eddie," the President said, still choked with laughter. "You be careful or you'll get us in trouble."

"Boss, would you believe I tried that line on the chief of protocol and he just about crapped in his striped pants?"

"I believe it, Eddie, but you be careful. Okay, what's next?"

"At four, there's the swearing-in ceremony for Tubby Walton in the East Room." General Thornton Walton, an old Army friend of Barney's, had been his choice as Deputy Secretary of Defense, and he was being honored with a full White House ceremony upon assuming the office.

"Okay, I want to do this thing right for old Tub," Barney said. "This speech they sent over from Defense ain't worth a diddly-squat. Dave, how about you knocking out something I can use?"

"Sure, any special subject?"

"Well, talk about Tubby being an old comrade at arms, that sort of stuff."

"You'll need a news peg to get any national coverage on this," O. B. Perkins reminded them.

"You could follow up on the Princeton speech," Dave said.

"Give some specifics on how military resources can be used to meet domestic needs. I've got some ideas on that."

"Okay, but let me see it before the NSC meeting," the President said. Dave nodded his agreement, and as he did, Barney sprang from his bed to stand beside the large window overlooking the dozen-acre panorama of the White House lawn. Three gardeners in blue overalls were working in the tulip beds beneath the window; farther on, the collie, Ace, chased a squirrel past the turquoise circle of the fountain; in the distance, above the green cascade of elms, the Washington Monument was poised like a great sword against the sky.

"And Dave, get something in the speech about the springtime. My God, will you look at those flowers!"

The President asked O.B., Leon, and Dave what business they had that day.

"About all I've got," the press secretary said, "is a lot of heat on when your next news conference will be."

"When I'm damn well ready," Barney snapped. He was still angry because reporters had asked what he considered loaded questions at his last press conference.

"Right," O.B. said.

"Listen, what're you going to do about that bastard Willingham and those wise-ass stories he's been writing about me?" Barney demanded of the press secretary.

Dave spoke up: "Why don't you forget to invite his boss, old man Evans, to that dinner for the Southern publishers next month? I'll bet he'd straighten out his hotshot Washington correspondent fast."

"Good idea," Barney said. "You do that, O.B."

"Sure," O.B. said. "I've been thinking about that." He looked sharply at Dave—O.B. didn't like anyone else advising the President on press relations.

"You got anything else?" the President asked.

"One other thing," O.B. said. "Our friend Governor Ellsworth wants you to be his special guest at the Derby next month."

"Shit," Barney snapped angrily. "People are starving in this country and he wants me to come watch those rich bastards run their fucking ponies."

He stared moodily out the window and the others waited in silence.

"What about this?" he said after a moment, thinking aloud. "What if I went to Kentucky on Derby weekend, but I went to see the folks in the hollows and the men down in the mines? How would that be?"

"It'd make a lot of people mad," O.B. said quickly.

Barney, his anger cooling, nodded uncertainly. Dave had often seen him like this, poised between his own wonderful instincts and the dictates of political caution.

"It'd make a lot of people happy, too," Dave said. "I'll get up a memo on places you could go."

"Okay," Barney said. "There's time to think about it."

Dave was satisfied—the door was still open on the trip. You had to fight the nay-sayers every inch of the way.

"Okay, Davey, what's the news from the Hill?"

A month earlier, Barney had put Dave in charge of the four-man Congressional Relations staff. That responsibility, on top of his others, was almost more work than Dave could handle, but the alternative, he feared, was for O.B. to get the job and he didn't want to see O.B. with that much power.

Dave gave his daily summary. The first New Cities hearings had been scheduled. The usual fight was shaping up over foreign aid. He mentioned his problem with Senator Spingarn on the alcoholic-treatment program, but no one had any suggestions.

"What about that hospital bill?" Barney asked.

"It goes up tomorrow," Dave said.

"What's it called?"

"The Family Health Services Act."

"Come on," Barney groaned. "You can beat that. Sex it up."

O.B. spoke first: "How about calling it the Mother and Child Health Protection Act?"

"Beautiful," Barney said. "I want to see the son of a bitch who'll vote against that. You got that, Dave?"

Dave had it—score one for O.B. But a moment later O.B. and Leon clashed on the degree of candor Leon should use in briefing some senators on China policy. Leon and O.B. were natural antagonists—the Harvard professor and the police reporter—and Dave did nothing to reconcile them. The more they cut each other up, the stronger it left him.

And so it went, endlessly, he thought as he glanced out the window at the gardeners working in the flowerbeds. Aides argued with other aides; aides argued with the cabinet; the cabinet argued with bureaucracy; the bureaucrats argued with one another; civilians argued with the military; the military argued with the diplomats—on and on and on without end. He knew the Secret Service was divided into bitter cliques, that Mrs. Gill was feuding with Eddie Gooch's secretary, that his driver wasn't speaking to the chief of the motor pool. In an instant's daydream he imagined he saw them all, the whole damned government—the cabinet, the generals, the bureaucrats, the secretaries, the FBI men, the gardeners—all out there on the White House lawn in a wild free-for-all, kicking and scratching and pounding one another with rakes and wastebaskets and coffee mugs, as in some mad, uncharted circle of Dante's Inferno. Your government in action.

Leon gave his dry, dispassionate report on the state of the world—a coup was possible in Algeria, a CIA man was missing in India, there were signs of discord in the East German cabinet—and when he finished the President had something to say:

"Okay, it's seven months now till the congressional elections, and I expect you guys to have those elections on your mind all the time. Eddie, maybe I'll start seeing more of the big contributors. O.B., you keep those damned reporters happy. Leon, you keep the Russians quiet. Dave, maybe we send up a few bills we know can't pass, to put the other side on record against motherhood and apple pie. All of you write me a memo on what you can do to help. Okay? Then the meeting's adjourned."

As the four aides started toward the door, the President called to Dave, who returned and stood beside a chair. Barney slipped off his robe and pajama tops and began his morning push-ups. He ripped off twenty-five, then stopped to rest a minute. His body was brown and hard, and he had an ugly, jagged scar, the size of a fist, to the left of his navel.

"I meant to ask you about the gun-control bill," Dave said.

That was not entirely true; he hadn't wanted to bring up the bill in the staff meeting with O.B. there to argue against it.

"Forget it."

"There's got to be some way to make the sportsmen understand it's not their weapons we're after."

"You're too logical," Barney said. "Talk about gun control and those characters think you want to cut off their peckers. Forget it."

Dave didn't forget it, but he dropped the subject. Barney flopped to the floor and did ten one-armed push-ups, five with each arm.

"Let's see you do a couple kid," he said when he arose. "One-arm."

"You know I can't cut that," Dave said, trying to laugh his way out.

"Come on, maybe all that publicity this morning put some lead in your pencil. Hop to!"

You didn't argue past a certain point, so Dave slipped off his coat, eased himself to the floor, lay on his left side with his left hand flat beneath his face, and pushed. Nothing happened, except that his arm hurt, and after a second he lost his balance and fell over onto his back.

"Come on," Barney said scornfully. "You're not trying."

Dave got back on his side, pushed harder, and rose an inch or two off the floor before he felt a sharp pain. His elbow buckled and he fell to the floor.

"God damn," he said, "I think I pulled a muscle." He sat on the floor rubbing his arm.

"Jesus, what a weakling," Barney declared. "Okay, do some regular push-ups. We got to build you up."

Dave managed twenty conventional push-ups before he gave out.

"That's better," Barney conceded. "But somebody your age ought to be able to do fifty. You start exercising. A man's got to keep in shape, so he can drink all day and fuck all night."

"I don't get many chances to do that any more," Dave said. He was still sitting on the floor, trying to catch his breath.

"Me neither," the President admitted, "but you got to be

ready when opportunity knocks. Okay, get up and tell me what's happening about that Northcutt race."

"I think I've got it worked out," Dave said easing himself into a chair. "To begin with, I found out that the old Judge, Atkins, needs money—he's got a sick wife. So I persuaded your good friend Sam Hillary to offer him a big-paying job as chief counsel with one of his corporations. That opened up the judgeship. Next there's Finlay, who wants to serve humanity, and would rather take a sure-thing federal judgeship than risk getting beat in a Senate race. With him out, we're free to support young Sistora or not, depending on whether Northcutt plays ball with us on the New Cities. You with me?"

"I'm way ahead of you," the President said. "What does Hillary get?"

"I offered him Switzerland but he says he doesn't like snow."

"See if he likes spaghetti," Barney said. "Maybe we'll give him Rome. Now, what else is on your mind?"

"Caravelas," Dave said. "Caravelas is on my mind."

"You still feel the same about it?"

"I still think it could be another Vietnam," Dave said.

"Oh, hell, Dave, we could send a hundred good men in there and finish off Rivera."

"That's what they told Kennedy about Vietnam."

"So what do I do? Hand the damned country over to Rivera? Have me another Castro taking over in South America just in time for the elections?"

"You talk sense to the people. Nobody wants us to police the world. Vietnam was enough."

"Yeah? Well it wasn't enough for a lot of senators and publishers and corporation presidents I talk to. They say if Caravelas goes red, you and me are out of a job."

"I'm just telling you what I think."

"Well, you better keep telling me your side of it, 'cause there's one hell of a lot of people telling me the other side."

"I will."

Barney executed a neat about-face and marched into the bathroom for a shower. Dave hurried back to his office. It was 9:25.

2

Just outside his office, Roger Fleishman, the Consultant for Cultural Affairs, was grimly studying the New York *Times*.

"Roger, I'll be right with you. Mrs. Gill, come in here a moment." In his office, he told her: "I need forty-five minutes to write a speech. Where do I get it?"

"You'll have to cut the two writers."

"Damn. Okay, Fleishman can handle them. I'll see him next. Right now, take a rush-up memo to the President."

Norman Mailer and Wallace Waldhorn were lecturing in Washington and Dave had arranged for them to see Barney. Dave had looked forward to meeting them, but the President's speech had top priority. The memo he dictated was on the two men's writing. He was sure Barney hadn't read Waldhorn's poetry, and he should at least know about *Freedom Songs*. Barney probably had read *The Naked and the Dead*, but Dave dictated a plot summary lest he confuse it with *From Here to Eternity*.

Dave rose and greeted Fleishman warmly.

"Sit down, Roger, and tell me what I can do for you."

Fleishman's bulldog face was as tired and rumpled as his old tweed suit. He sighed audibly before replying.

"Dave, it's about the President. I just don't understand what he wants from me. I send him position papers on vital issues and I get no reply. I call and he never calls back. Perhaps this whole thing was a mistake. Perhaps I should resign . . ."

Dave let him talk; it was the best therapy. Fleishman knew what the trouble was but didn't want to face it; he had come seeking not confirmation of his fears but encouragement for his hopes. Fleishman was one of Dave's mistakes. Some visiting college presidents had urged Barney to appoint an intellectual-in-residence. Dave had interviewed Fleishman and been impressed, and Barney had hired him. Now Dave realized that his first impression had been mistaken; the professor had an easy, worldly manner, but in fact he was a political innocent, given to brave stands on principle, scornful of the ultimate horror, compromise. After hearing Fleishman's views on a congressional problem, Eddie Gooch had cracked, "That guy fits in this joint like Mary Poppins in a Tijuana whorehouse." Barney agreed, and ordered Dave to "Keep that windbag out of sight." So Dave had invented chores for the professor, looking all the while for a final solution to the problem.

The problem was two-edged. Dave wanted to spare the professor's feelings, and he also wanted to avoid any unpleasant incident with the academic community. Thus far, the intellectual world had regarded Barney as something of a noble savage. Dave knew Barney was neither as noble nor as savage as it often pleased him to appear, but he did not want to rob the intelligentsia of its illusions—and an ugly incident with Fleishman might do just that.

So Dave nodded his way through as many minutes of the professor's monologue as he could spare. Then he spoke gravely of the terrible demands on the President's time; he recited compliments Barney had allegedly paid to Fleishman's wisdom and devotion.

"Roger," he said finally, "the President and I have discussed a very significant project we hope you will undertake. We want you to write a short history of the Osgood administration, with full access to the people and records involved. While the trail is fresh, so to speak. A really unique history."

Fleishman's eyes had widened—it was a marvelous idea. He began to ponder the possibilities aloud, and Dave listened contentedly. This would keep Fleishman busy until he was ready to return to his university. And Dave could see no dangers to it. There were no skeletons in the closets of Milton Osgood's brief administration; there were hardly any closets. Fleishman was beaming, his mind already gamboling through the green fields of the Osgood administration, as Dave guided him to the door.

"One other thing, Roger. Mailer and Waldhorn are coming

in at noon, and I think it'd be better if you talked to them instead of me."

Fleishman protested, Dave insisted, Mrs. Gill was called to arrange details—and it was done. The professor departed with a satisfied mind.

"I have the Majority Leader," Mrs. Gill announced. Dave sought the Majority Leader's advice on how Senator Spingarn might be persuaded to approve the money for the alcoholism treatment program. The Majority Leader was dubious. The Majority Leader would ponder the matter. Dave thanked the Majority Leader profusely but he did not think the future looked bright for the nation's alcoholics.

The President's meeting with the four Northwestern governors went well, very well. It went well because Barney was a man of ups and downs, and at this particular meeting, on this particular subject, the New Cities, he was very much up. The New Cities bill was his biggest legislative proposal. With luck, it would pass Congress by the end of the summer. The question now confronting the administration was the exact shape the New Cities should take. How big should they be? Located where? For whom? To the four governors, the biggest question was racial—would the New Cities transport unwanted blacks to their part of the country?

Dave briefed the governors and fielded most of their questions. Barney did exactly what he was supposed to do: listened sympathetically, spoke reassuringly, but avoided specific commitments. Then, near the end of the meeting, he began to speak to them in a soft voice:

"You know, I remember when I was a boy, visiting my father's people in north Alabama, down below Muscle Shoals, places where they'd never seen an electric light. I remember going there one summer and then going back the next, after they'd installed the TVA power lines, and it was like those people had been taken out of chains and given a new life."

He was leaning back in his chair now, his arms folded across his chest, gazing over their heads at the picture of FDR on the wall opposite his desk.

"Some columnist was writing about the New Cities the other

day, saying they would be the biggest job any country had taken on since the pyramids. Hell, what's a pyramid? A pile of rocks with some old bastard's bones inside. That doesn't impress me. But TVA impresses me—that's a monument that'll last a thousand years, because Roosevelt and Norris had vision and guts. I tell you, these New Cities can mean as much to America as TVA did, even more. They can do for people in the slums what TVA did for the country folks down South. Sure, there'll be problems—with Congress, with the bureaucrats, with the construction people, with the blacks—but that's why I'm here, to solve the problems.

"And I'm going to solve them, with your help, and Dave here, and a lot of others, and when all this is past, and you and me are old men, we'll look back at these New Cities, the millions of people they gave a good home, the kids who got their first decent school, who went on to make something of themselves, we'll look back on that and by God, we'll know we left a monument behind us!"

There was nothing more to be said, and they all knew it, so the governors shook the President's hand and filed out of the office. Dave left with them, and as he shut the door he had a final glimpse of the big, inscrutable man standing at the window, staring out at the future, brooding on the new world he would build for his monument.

When Dave got back to his office, Mrs. Gill had the Quinn girl on the phone.

"I wanted to thank you," he told her. "That was a flattering article."

"For Pete's sake, don't tell anybody I flattered you," she said. "You'll ruin my reputation." She had a Boston Irish voice, sharp and high-pitched, with a hum of humor in it, and the clamor of distant slums.

He didn't remember much about her. She'd interviewed him twice, each time for an hour or so, but then she'd been less a person than a challenge, an equation to be solved. He remembered that she'd done her homework, that her questions had been sharp, that she'd refused to accept bullshit replies.

Once he'd seen she was a serious writer, he began giving her serious answers, and the interviews had gone well.

Now, the challenge past, he tried to remember Cathy Quinn. He remembered that she was small and young and not pretty. He recalled various imperfections—eyes too narrow, nose too large, mouth too wide, breasts too small, legs too thin—and yet there had been something proud and defiant about her, a spark, a stubbornness, a verve, that lingered in his memory and made him smile into the telephone.

"Okay, it wasn't flattering," he said. "I'm really that great. But anyway I appreciated it, and I want you to call me if there's ever anything I can do for you."

"I'll do that," she said, and he remembered that wide, funny mouth.

He started to say goodbye, then said, "Look, we're swearing in the new Deputy Secretary of Defense at four today in the East Room, with the Marine Band and a reception and all. Why don't you come?"

"I'll be there with bells on," Cathy said.

"I'll listen for you."

He cut off all calls and began writing the President's speech. A month earlier, in a speech at Princeton, Barney had called for the use of military skills and manpower against domestic problems—"to fight the wars at home." That had been a lofty generality, but now Dave hoped to pin him down to some specifics—the use of the Corps of Engineers in New Cities planning, the use of the military's medical corps in a national health program, a new draft policy whereby qualified men could substitute work in the New Cities for Army duty.

Dave knew he was not just inventing pretty phrases—he was proposing national policy. If Barney spoke these words that afternoon, the U. S. Government would be committed to a new policy; throughout Washington and the world men and governments would respond. At the Pentagon, as well as the domestic agencies, some men would dig in for bitter-end resistance, while others scurried to satisfy the President. On Wall Street, cool-eyed speculators would estimate how this public policy would affect private interests, and the stock market would reflect their calculations. America's editorial writers would variously hail the new Utopia and damn the erosion of national security. Halfway around the world, Russia's leaders would make their calculations.

Dave pounded away on his old Royal, the rest of the world temporarily tuned out. He did not enjoy speechwriting—it was hard as hell—but it was the base on which his power rested. He had captured, as no one else ever had, the peculiar style, the rough-textured prose with which Barney Newfield liked to address the world. The style was neither as elaborate as Kennedy's nor as folksy as LBJ's. It was perhaps closer to Harry Truman's than any President in memory: a straightforward, almost defiant prose that seemed to say: "Here's what I think and if you don't like it, go to hell!" It was, Dave knew, the style of a shrewd and complex man who wanted very badly to be regarded as a simple man.

He finished his second draft and gave it to Mrs. Gill to type. Barney might revise it, or reject it entirely, but Dave had done his best. His batting average was fairly high. Barney knew he was pushing ideas on him—so were plenty of other people—and if Barney had not had a basic receptivity to Dave's ideas he would have found another bright young man by now.

"Walt Kroeger wants you to call," Mrs. Gill said. "Some political problem."

"Okay."

"And Sharon Flatt has been in twice to see you."

"Who?"

"She's one of the President's typists." Mrs. Gill's right eyebrow was discernibly arched.

"The redhead? With the ponytail?"

"Right."

"What does she want?"

"It's very mysterious. But she must see you."

"Oh God, all right. But nobody after her. I've got to get ready for the NSC meeting."

He took the call from Walt Kroeger, an Assistant Secretary of Labor.

"What's the problem, Walt?"

The problem was that the Department's manpower experts were holding up a $10,000,000 grant for a job-training program to the city of Denver. The mayor of Denver, who had worked hard for the Osgood-Newfield ticket, was threatening a direct appeal to the President. Kroeger's question: Should he buck the mayor or buck the experts?

"Walt, what have these experts got against the project?" Dave asked impatiently. "Is the mayor going to pocket the money? Are they going to train the people to be safe-crackers? What is it?"

"Just professional points. A weak staff. No plans for evaluation."

"Can't all that be fixed?"

"In a few months. But the mayor won't wait."

"He can't wait. He's got a tough primary on June fifth. Look, this is a friend of ours, and we help our friends. You make that damn grant and screw the experts—they're your worry. And when the grant is ready to be announced, you call me and we'll have the mayor in for a ceremony with the President. Okay?"

Kroeger said okay and Dave hung up, annoyed. He wanted to deal with people who knew what decisions to make for themselves, and this was twice that Kroeger had been wrong.

"Oh, yes sir, I love my job," Sharon Flatt said as she settled into the chair beside his desk, her eyes downcast demurely, her ample breasts, less demure, pushing against her thin blue blouse. She was a pale, pretty, wide-eyed girl of twenty, blessed with the face of a choir singer and the body of a chorus girl. He guessed she was from West Virginia, as most of the White House secretaries were. The state's main export seemed to be girls like Sharon who were voluptuous, good typists, and (according to the Bureau, which had studied such things) vigilant anti-Communists. It was a matter of record that no West Virginia girl had ever violated national security.

Sharon had been ill-at-ease when she entered his office—as well she might for it was a very big office, embarrassingly big, bigger in fact than the President's—but he had put her at ease and now she was chattering happily.

"Gosh," she was saying, "when I think that a year ago I was still back in Charleston—it's like a dream."

"Dreams sometimes come true, Sharon. Now tell me what's on your mind."

"It's about the President, Mr. Hyer. I hate to bother you but everybody says you know him best and . . ."

"What about the President, Sharon?"

"Well, the other night I took some papers in for him to sign and we talked for a while—he was real nice, he said how pretty I was and he'd always liked red hair."

"You are a pretty girl, Sharon. I'm sure the President just wanted you to know how much he appreciates the work you're doing."

"Yes sir. And then he sort of patted my hand and said he'd like to buy me a new spring outfit, and if I'd tell Mr. Gooch he had a charge-a-plate I could borrow."

Dave nodded but said nothing.

"What I want to ask, Mr. Hyer, is if you think it's all right. I mean, clothes cost a lot of money, but I don't want to make him mad or anything. I just don't know what's right."

The girl, he saw, was as dumb as she was desirable. She had to be dumb, not to understand Barney in the first place, then to come in here and put him on the spot. What was he supposed to do—tell her the President was a nasty old man? This was one of Eddie Gooch's recruits, all right; the trouble with having a dumb procurer was that he'd probably procure dumb girls.

"I'm sure you can decide this for yourself, Sharon. Perhaps, if you think a dress or a suit costs too much, you might get a hat or some gloves or something that isn't expensive."

"Oh, that's perfect," she said, clapping her hands in delight. "I *know* that'd be all right. I was afraid I'd have to write Mother and ask her what to do."

"Well, that won't be necessary now, will it?" He guided the joyous girl to the door. She was, he reflected, the happiest individual to leave his office since Professor Fleishman, who also wondered about the President's intentions toward his person.

But the Sharons were no joking matter. Barney's attitude toward the opposite sex was gloriously uncomplicated: he would screw anything that walked. He had pursued this policy since age twelve, and over the years he had bestowed his favors on hundreds of women of every size, shape, age, race, and political persuasion from Fifth Avenue to Singapore. Dave had coexisted with Barney's affairs since he had first gone to work for him in Tennessee, and to him the situation had long since ceased to be a moral issue and become simply a logistical problem: sometimes Barney couldn't be reached for a few hours; sometimes there were angry scenes between him and Brenda; sometimes the Playmate of the Month would decide she no longer had to perform her office work. Dave kept as far from these affairs as he could. Barney, sensing his disapproval, rarely mentioned them.

Or perhaps it was not so much disapproval as a sullen jealousy. Dave was a normal American male, which is to say he rarely glanced at a woman between fifteen and fifty without contemplating the joys to be found astride her and the prospects for getting there. But in recent years he had rarely had the time or audacity to pursue his inclinations, as his boss so vigorously did. In this, as in so many things, there was something superhuman about Barney.

Barney's appetites had caused no political problems. Other politicians considered him a hell of a fellow. Nor were their wives offended by his reputation—on the contrary, they buzzed about him like bees to honey. No doubt some citizens would have objected to their President's wicked ways, had they known of them, but here Barney was protected by the curious morality of the press, which rarely hints at a politician's extracurricular sex life.

Barney was not entirely indiscreet. He believed the old axiom that you shouldn't screw the help was wrong—you shouldn't screw anything but the help. Not your friends' wives; not the society girls who dabbled in politics (although he'd broken that rule a few times); certainly not the lobbyists' call girls. Instead, he filled his office with attractive young women and let nature take its course, and thus far he had never suffered for his sins. Even his discarded mistresses never caused problems; he had a genius for sending them away happy. Sometimes, to ease a separation, he would get a girl a better-paying job elsewhere, or even get her father or (when she married) her husband a job.

Barney wasn't the first politician—nor the first President—to like girls, nor would he be the last. Still, as Dave watched Sharon Flatt's flame-colored ponytail bounce out of view, he had an uneasy feeling that even Barney's luck might not hold forever.

3

"Gentlemen, the enemy is in these mountains," declared General James B. Boswell, Chairman of the Joint Chiefs of Staff, tapping with his mahogany pointer against a large map of Caravelas. The general was a lean, deeply tanned man, a fine-looking man. He wore no medals on his uniform but the seven men watching him knew he had them all.

"The enemy is in these mountains," General Boswell repeated, "moving about at will, coming out each day or two to attack government positions or to inflict terror on the civilian population."

The National Security Council was meeting in the President's dining room, on the west end of the second floor of the White House, a lovely room, a wonderfully bright and airy room in which to be discussing a dirty jungle war. Yet, all around them were reminders of an earlier guerrilla war—Washington and his generals on horseback, grateful citizens cheering them, Redcoats routed in battle. Dave looked from the wallpaper back to General Boswell.

"I believe we are all aware that the ROC government has asked U.S. military assistance in meeting this threat," the general continued. ROC, pronounced rock, was Pentagonese for Republic of Caravelas, the name the ruling junta had given itself. "Colonel Molina, president of Caravelas, has asked our assistance because the guerrillas are supplied and controlled by the Castro regime."

"That point is somewhat in dispute, General," Leon Kerkelot injected.

"The evidence, as presented by the Director of Central Intelligence, strikes me as overwhelming, Professor Kerkelot," Boswell said. Dave noted the exchange appreciatively. The general wasn't going to breeze through this one unchallenged.

"My purpose this afternoon, Mr. President, is to outline a solution to the problem in Caravelas. In brief, the Joint Chiefs believe that a five hundred man strike force, with ten helicopters, could put down this disturbance within two to three weeks."

"Do you mean combat troops, General?" Dave asked.

"Yes. That is our first preference."

If the general disliked being questioned by a civilian half his age, he did not show it. He had been dealing with Presidents and their staffs since the Truman administration.

"Then there could be American casualties?" Dave persisted.

"Our mobility and superior firepower would hold casualties to an absolute minimum."

"What's your second choice, Jim?" the President asked.

"Should it be deemed politically undesirable for U.S. forces to engage the enemy, we could make helicopters available to the ROC army and send counterinsurgency teams to train an elite force of ROC Rangers."

"That would of course take longer?" Leon Kerkelot asked.

"Yes. It would be a matter of months before the ROC force would be prepared to attack the enemy stronghold in the mountains."

"General, there's one thing I find it hard to understand," Dave said. His tone was most respectful. "The junta has a five thousand man army, which we've been supplying for many years. That army spends about a third of the Caravelian national budget. Why can't this army march fifty miles into those mountains and defeat a small guerrilla band without our help?"

Dave stole a glance at the President, whose opinion of banana-republic generals was not high, but his face was impassive. General Boswell, too, remained cool.

"One reason is that much of the ROC army is now engaged in civic-action programs throughout the country. Another reason, as has been said, is that the rebels are extremely well supplied, thanks to their foreign allies."

Dave had studied the situation in Caravelas rather closely and he would have described it differently. He would have said

that Caravelas, a small, poor nation on the northeast shoulder
of South America, had long been ruled by a corrupt military
regime, possibly the second most repressive government on the
continent, and that its people now supported a six-month-old
guerrilla uprising led by a Caravelian lawyer, Alberto Rivera.
He would further have said that the junta's army had no
stomach for a fight, that the guerrillas seemed only weeks away
from victory, and that the junta now desperately sought U.S.
troops to save itself.

The President broke in with some questions about the military
aspects of the Joint Chiefs' proposal. Dave relaxed a moment,
letting his eyes sweep around the room.

The President was at the head of the table, hunched forward,
his elbows on the edge of the table, his chin resting on one
fist, his eyes alert, his face expressionless. He was flanked by
Dave and O. B. Perkins, whose chairs were a few feet back
from the table in deference to their status as staff men. Leon
Kerkelot, as Assistant for National Security Affairs, sat opposite
the President, his pale blue eyes glittering behind steel-rimmed
glasses.

General Boswell, standing to Leon's left, answered the President's questions crisply, indicating locations on the map with his
mahogany pointer, a picture of self-confidence. To Leon's right
was Phillip Drummond, the CIA Director, a short, stocky man,
a retired utilities executive, who had opened the meeting with an
intelligence report and not spoken since. Drummond knew he
was scheduled for early replacement and he had ceased to
work at his job. As a result, his career underlings, who after
all were plotters by profession, had been pursuing their various
schemes and counterschemes at a hectic pace. One of the more
impressive plotters was the Assistant Director for Latin American Operations, a young man named Rod Sinclair, who earlier
in the week had told Dave that almost everything the director
would report in this meeting—that Castro was supplying Rivera's
band, that Rivera had arms from China, that Rivera's men were
committing atrocities against civilians—was untrue.

Warren Cutliff, the Secretary of Defense, was on the President's left, looking like a beardless Santa Claus. He was a
jolly, jowly man who was said to have made a million dollars

without making one enemy. His career had been a spectacular truimph of personality. A Mississippian by birth, son of an itinerant preacher, he'd started out selling kitchenware from door to door, made his way to North Carolina, switched from pots to insurance, become president of his own company at thirty, a millionaire at forty, governor of North Carolina at fifty, now Secretary of Defense at sixty.

Cutliff combined limitless goodwill with limited ideology, and the result was a genius for bringing other men together. That was his assignment at Defense, to coax the generals into accepting budget cuts, and he was having considerable success. Cutliff was also a noted raconteur, a great teller of tales and drinker of bourbon, and he had become one of Barney's favorite companions.

Cutliff brought to the table an aura of goodwill; the Secretary of State, Charlton MacKenzie, seated in the position of honor at the President's right, brought an aura of dazzling success. A tall, strikingly handsome man, as graceful in middle-age as he had been as an Ivy League tennis champion three decades earlier, MacKenzie's life had been an unbroken series of successes. He'd gone from Princeton to serve with distinction in the Second World War, then to the Yale Law School, where he'd edited the *Law Review*, then back to practice in his hometown in upstate New York, from which he'd been elected to Congress at thirty. But Congress moved too slowly for MacKenzie. It satisfied neither his political nor his financial ambitions, and after two terms he left to open a law office in Washington. He rarely saw the inside of a courtroom, but he enjoyed spectacular financial success. His specialty was advising corporations on their dealings with the government, and soon half a dozen firms paid him $100,000 annual retainers. For more than a decade his success snowballed; the richer he became, the more politicians respected him, and the more politicians respected him, the richer he became. He advised leading Democrats and contributed to their campaigns, and his talent for problem-solving led many politicians to think him wiser than the more ideological men who worked for them. President Milton Osgood was among the politicians who valued MacKenzie's counsel and he proved his esteem by making the lawyer his Secretary of State. When Osgood died, the new President valued MacKenzie as highly as had his predecessor. Barney did not consider him an equal—he did not consider anyone an equal—but MacKenzie came as close as anyone. It is hard not to respect a man who had earned twenty million dollars not by selling a product—oil or automobiles or houses—but by selling only his thoughts, his ideas, his judgments. The question now, in Dave Hyer's mind and numerous others, was what the elegant Charlton MacKenzie's judgment would be on Caravelas.

Completing the circle, dominating it, making even as commanding a figure as MacKenzie pale by comparison, was the President. He was a big, rugged, brooding man, his face craggy and lined, a shade roguish when he smiled, a shade cruel when he did not. He was an intensely physical man, with an aura of power, of restlessness, of violence about him. This hint of violence was not all illusion. Dave remembered a time in Memphis, when a rightwing crowd surrounded Barney and his wife, and a drunk grabbed at Brenda. Barney broke the man's jaw with the flat of his hand.

Because he was big and jovial, sometimes crude and not outwardly intellectual, there were those who even now dismissed Barney as a clown, a big clown with amazing luck. Dave knew how wrong they were. From the first there had burned in Barney a fierce ambition that had driven him on toward his unknown destiny. In 1942, he had been a sophomore at West Point, a football star but no scholar, and at Christmas he had quit to enlist in the Army. A year later he won his commission on the battlefield, and when the war ended he'd re-enlisted and made the Army his career. When his twenty years were almost up, and his fellow officers were planning their retirements in Florida, Barney enrolled in night law school. Upon his discharge, he returned to Nashville, his birthplace, to practice law. Two years later he ran successfully for state attorney general. He cracked down on bootleggers, led some well-publicized raids on gambling houses, and next was elected governor. During his second term, he stormed the Democratic National Convention and convinced his party's leaders that his vigor, liberal record, and border state geography provided an ideal balance to Milton Osgood's advanced years, conservatism, and New England roots.

Dave knew Barney as well as anyone, and he didn't pretend to understand him. He did know that all Barney had wanted from life he had gotten, one way or another. His path was strewn with men who had underestimated him, from the five Italian soldiers who thought it would be no trouble to disarm a lone GI, and were gunned to pieces for their error, to the American politicians who thought it would be no trouble to outmaneuver him for the attorney generalship, or the governorship, or the vice-presidential nomination. Barney was a hard man, and shrewd, and he learned very fast.

He said to Dave, one night over a drink, "Those newspaper guys, they think I spent twenty years charging up a hill with a machine gun on my hip. That ain't the way it is. I spent an hour or two doing that, and the rest of it was politics. The Army's the most political place on earth. Every minute, you're either kissing somebody's ass, or stabbing somebody in the back—or somebody's kissing your ass or stabbing you in the back. When I fell in with those courthouse pols in Tennessee, it was like taking candy from babies."

The President had finished his exchange with General Boswell, and Warren Cutliff had a question.

"I'm wondering, gentlemen, if we've really done all we can to get those fellows together down there? Maybe we could work out one of those coalition governments." Like many Southerners, Cutliff pronounced it gum-ment.

"Warren, the ROC government has made every possible effort to negotiate with this man Rivera," said Phillip Drummond, the CIA chief. "He's set on revolution."

This, too, was untrue, according to Dave's source at the CIA, but he said nothing. He could talk to Barney later.

"What about you, O.B.?" the President said. "You got any pearls of wisdom for us?"

The press secretary looked bored, but Dave knew that O.B.'s looks were deceptive. His was a fine, if limited mind, beautifully attuned to what he took to be the realities of American politics.

"Mr. President," O.B. said in his soft, con-man's voice, "it

looks to me like we should either stay out of this place entirely, or get in there fast and win it. Either way's okay, but
if you send in twenty men this week and fifty men next week,
the leftwingers will be taking to the streets again."

"I wonder, O.B.," said Leon Kerkelot, "if we went in and
won it fast, as you suggest, if they might not still take to the
streets?"

O.B. shrugged and a faint smile crossed his face.

"I'll tell you, pal, I used to cover all the executions in Cook
County, and sometimes the ACLU types would be out picketing
for some guy who was about to fry. But they never picketed
for anybody after he was dead."

The talk was drifting away from where Dave wanted it.
"Getting back to your proposal to send combat troops, General,"
he said. "You predict that a few hundred Americans can end
this uprising in a few weeks, but isn't that what some of your
predecessors were telling Kennedy in 1961? How can we be
sure we aren't getting into another Vietnam?"

The general sucked in his breath sharply. His voice was
perceptibly cooler.

"The analogy fails, Mr. Hyer. One nation was halfway around
the world; the other is virtually in our backyard. Today we
have techniques and equipment we lacked ten years ago. In
Vietnam we moved too slowly; in Caravelas we have an opportunity to put out the fire before it spreads."

For several minutes he explained why Caravelas was not
Vietnam. Dave listened with grim pleasure. He felt rising inside
him a hot, furious hatred, not for this one general but for all
the generals, for the military mind, for the evil they had done
and would do again if they could. Go on, he thought, keep
talking, talk your way out of Vietnam, make us forget those
40,000 men, make us forget Khesanh and Hamburger Hill,
make us forget all the rosy predictions you brave generals made.
Talk your way out of it, you son of a bitch.

A picture burned across his mind. A young girl, holding her
baby, the hot Texas wind rippling her black dress and veil,
weeping helplessly as the box was lowered that contained her
husband, a kid named Billy Reese, who'd had his guts blown
out in the Mekong Delta. An Army honor guard stood beside

the grave and a bugler played taps while the casket was laid down, as the girl wept and pressed her child against her. Dave had begged her not to let the soldiers come, to keep them away from this, at least, but she had said no, that Billy would have wanted it this way.

He could not forget and he could not forgive. He could not forget that a few years earlier, other men had sat around this very table and made the decisions that sent all the Billy Reeses to be slaughtered. He knew the men who had made those decisions. They were still around, writing books, making big money, trying to wangle invitations to the White House. He knew them and he knew their rationalizations and he hoped they rotted in hell.

He could not forget, either, that there were men sitting at this table with him today who would make the same decisions again if they were given the chance.

"General," he said, when Boswell finished, "you say it will be simple to crush this guerrilla movement, but the fact that Rivera moves about the countryside at will suggests to me that he has widespread popular support. The experience in Vietnam and elsewhere has been that foreign armies can't defeat popular uprisings."

The general was gripping his pointer now until his knuckles showed white.

"Mr. Hyer, this is a purely military question. Rivera has a certain number of men and we know we can eliminate him with a certain number of our men."

"But I'm suggesting, General, that the Pentagon and the CIA made similar estimates in the past decade that were wrong and that were costly, from the Bay of Pigs to Vietnam. Many of us, General, think that this nation, under President Newfield's leadership, stands at the threshold of a golden era, and that the only thing that could stop us is to become bogged down in another Vietnam."

Vietnam. Vietnam. Vietnam. The word was his weapon, and he would beat this man to a pulp with it. The general did not reply and there was a momentary hush. Dave glanced down and saw his thumb bleeding. As he talked, he had picked at a hangnail until the flesh was torn. He slipped the hand into his pocket.

"Mr. President, perhaps I might make a few comments," said the Secretary of State, Charlton MacKenzie.

"Fire away," Barney said.

"We can all agree that we must avoid another Vietnam," MacKenzie said. "Yet we must also avoid an oversimple approach to foreign policy. I would suggest there are clear distinctions between Southeast Asia and Latin America. Militarily, there are the shorter supply lines, and other factors General Boswell has mentioned. Politically, there is the fact that great powers are understood to have spheres of influence. Russia has hers, China hers, and we ours. Vietnam may or may not have been in our legitimate sphere of influence, but Caravelas clearly is."

MacKenzie had a wonderful voice, a musical, reassuring voice, the voice of a classical actor—or a multimillionaire lawyer.

"But a sphere of influence for what, Mr. Secretary?" Dave asked. "Does proximity give us the right to dictate what kind of government these people must have?"

MacKenzie fiddled with a pair of horn-rimmed glasses that he rarely wore. A ray of afternoon sun caught the diamond in his cuff-link. He looked at Dave with a gaze that seemed not unfriendly.

"That could depend on whether or not we are prepared to see a Communist government established on the mainland of South America," he said.

There it was—the unspeakable. Dave was annoyed, but he kept his voice as dispassionate as MacKenzie's.

"I think we have to get past this 'Communist' bugaboo. Instead of talking about Communists and anti-Communists, let's talk about who'll do the most good for the people of that country."

"Which people, Dave?" MacKenzie asked.

"The ninety percent of the people who now exist on incomes of less than fifty dollars a year, while twenty-one families control two-thirds of the land in Caravelas. Colonel Molina's regime has been in power for six years and they've done nothing about land reform, nothing about illiteracy, nothing about medical care . . ."

"No one claims that Colonel Molina's government is perfect," MacKenzie said affably. "But it has brought stability to the country, and it is one I think we can work with effectively."

It crossed Dave's mind that this might be his most important moment in six months in the White House. It was not that he expected to change MacKenzie's thinking, any more than MacKenzie could change his. Both were really talking to the President, for he was the only man whose opinion mattered, and as far as anyone could see, his mind was still open on Caravelas.

"If I understand you, Mr. Secretary, you're suggesting that we accept the junta and try to push it toward reform. But I don't see that the experience we've had with the Francos and Diems and Parks and Batistas of the world makes that approach seem very hopeful. I don't see any evidence that the rich in Latin America are going to give up anything voluntarily."

"Not many folks do," Warren Cutliff injected, and several of the men laughed.

"No sir, they don't," Dave continued. "And when they don't, there's revolution. What I'm suggesting is that we grab hold of this revolutionary fervor in Latin America, try to use it for our own ends."

Cutliff shook his head. "I'll swear, we didn't have much luck trying to woo that bandit in Cuba."

"I don't think we tried very hard," Dave said. "But let's look at Rivera. From all I've heard he's a smart politician, a practical man. He knows we can ruin him economically. If he takes power, I think he'd be ripe for a modus vivendi with us. I suspect there could be arrangements to protect U.S. investments, at least from outright seizure. I suspect he'd welcome U.S. technical help. Our dealings with him could start a new era in U.S. foreign policy. Instead, we're here today talking about sending U.S. soldiers to kill Rivera and his followers. I just don't see that this is an enlightened policy, a humane policy, a realistic policy, or a policy with any chance of long-range success."

Warren Cutliff's face wore an unaccustomed frown. The general and the CIA chief were grim-faced. O. B. Perkins continued to look bored. Leon Kerkelot's eyes darted back and forth across the table. The President remained impassive.

MacKenzie smiled his warm, winning smile.

"Dave, even if I agreed with everything you've said, and I don't, I would still have to raise one hard political question. Will the people of the United States support an administration that stood by idly while Communist guerrillas planted their flag on the soil of Latin America? I think not."

"And I think, Mr. Secretary, that the only good result of Vietnam was that the American people finally understand that we can't police the world. If President Newfield explains to our people why we've kept hands off Caravelas, I think they'll understand. I think they'll be damned glad of it, in fact."

Dave was enjoying this exchange. He did not dislike Mac-Kenzie. He thought MacKenzie's thinking was typical of his generation, the generation of the Second World War, and he thought it not impossible that MacKenzie might in time change his views on Latin America. Not today, but in time. MacKenzie was a pragmatist.

"I must say that is a very risky prognosis for the President to act upon with crucial elections coming up this fall," Mac-Kenzie said.

There it was. If Vietnam was the stick Dave would use to beat the interventionists, the elections were the stick they would use to strike back.

"There are always elections coming up in this country, Mr. MacKenzie," Dave said with a trace of annoyance. "But if I'm right, and our policy needs to be changed, then there's no better time than now to begin."

"If you're right," MacKenzie replied with a smile.

Both men were silent. Dave thought he had pushed as hard as he should. To speak out at all had been a risk, for there would be leaks, distortions, counterattacks. But to keep silent was to grant the initiative to the military, to imply there was something unmanly, something shameful about preferring peace to war. Dave thought he was right, thought the President could be convinced he was right, and he wanted this battle fought and won out in the open. Still, he wished Leon had given him more help. He wished Barney would give some sign of his thinking. But the President was silent, all of them were silent, and suddenly an army officer hurried into the room and handed a cable to General Boswell.

The general read the message quickly, then jumped to his feet and addressed the President:

"Sir, the discussion is no longer academic. Rivera's men have bombed our embassy in Caravelas!"

The President spoke first. His lethargy of the past hour was gone. His voice was sharp and his eyes burned with excitement. A line from *Coriolanus* crossed Dave's mind: "Let me have war, say I, it exceeds peace as far as day does night." The thought was not pleasing.

"Tell us what happened, Jim," the President said.

"This is a first, fragmentary report," the general said. "The explosion went off within the past half hour. There were some injuries, how many is unclear. Two suspects were captured at the scene and are believed to be members of Rivera's band."

The President nodded to Leon, who had half-risen in his chair, and the national-security aide quickly left the room to check his own sources in Caravelas.

"Mr. President," General Boswell said, "I submit that the time has come for action against these terrorists. If you'll say the word, we can have men in Caravelas in three hours."

Dave broke in. "Mr. President, we need more information. The timing of this explosion, if there has been an explosion, is damned suspicious. It may be that the junta set off the blast hoping to stampede you into sending troops."

"That's uncalled for," Boswell said angrily.

"It's happened before," Dave snapped back.

"Where would your men come from, Jim?" the President asked the general.

"From the Canal Zone. I can move five hundred men, or five thousand, in there by nine o'clock tonight."

"Okay," the President said. "Put a thousand men on alert. But not one plane leaves unless I flash the go-ahead. Right?"

"Yes sir," General Boswell said, and hurried to the next room to telephone. The President lit a cigarette, and a moment later Leon returned from his call.

"Okay, what've you got?" the President demanded.

"It was a small charge of dynamite," Leon said, "placed at the rear of the building, beneath a kitchen window. A cook and a waiter were cut by flying glass. Neither seriously. Two young men, students, were arrested on the street. I spoke with Ambassador Ball and he says business will continue as usual."

"I'll want to talk to him later," Barney said. "Okay, now I want to hear what you men think. You first, O.B."

The press secretary chewed his lower lip for a monent. "It's gonna look bad if somebody bombs our embassy and we don't do anything. Maybe we could send some men down there, make a show of it, then bring 'em back in a few weeks."

"Dave?" the President said.

"The trouble with what O.B. says is that it's easier to send troops into a country than to pull them out. They put down roots. Mr. President, let's get more facts. We don't know that Rivera's done this, and even if he did that's not necessarily cause to send troops. Let's not overreact."

"Leon?"

Leon was calm, professorial, almost pedantic. "Mr. President, it's very easy to start wars and very hard to stop them. If we want to send troops, we can do it tomorrow or the next day, but first let's get the facts and consider the alternatives. Let's act by calculation, not in the heat of anger."

"Drummond?"

The CIA Director pulled himself upright in his chair. "Mr. President," he said, "I'll confine myself to an opinion on the intelligence aspects of the matter. It has been suggested that Rivera did not set the bomb. I must say, however *liberal* one might think fancy oneself, that to ignore that Rivera is a guerrilla leader, a terrorist, a Communist, a committed anti-American, to ignore these facts and suggest that our allies bombed our embassy, is a form of self-delusion that borders on lunacy."

General Boswell returned and the President called on him next.

"Jim, I guess we know what you think," the President said.

"I think you do," Boswell replied. "I have felt all along that it was necessary and desirable for us to end this guerrilla uprising, and now the enemy has given us a splendid justification for doing so. If we do not act, there will be other bombings and other uprisings, encouraged by our inaction, all over the continent."

"Warren, what do you say?"

The Secretary of Defense looked troubled. He was a man who lived by compromise and he saw no easy compromise in this situation.

"I wonder, Mr. President, if it might not be possible to send a few men, just a handful, to guard the embassy. Just enough to show the flag."

"The difficulty there, Mr. Secretary," General Boswell said, "is that we can't send a force into potentially hostile territory that is too small to defend itself."

Cutliff's jolly face faded into a frown, then after a moment the accustomed smile returned.

"You know, Mr. President," Cutliff said, "it may sound a little far-fetched, but this business reminds me of a fellow I knew down in Culpeper County a long time ago. He married him a banker's daughter and after the wedding her pa gave them a fine-looking horse and carriage. Well, the young couple got in the carriage to start their wedding trip, and after they'd rode about a mile, the horse stumbled, and the fellow just said, 'That's once.' They rode on another mile or so and the horse, he stumbled again, and the fellow said, 'That's twice.' Then—would you believe it?—the horse went and stumbled again, and the bridegroom says, 'That's three times,' and he climbs down and pulls out his pistol and shoots the poor horse dead.

"Well, you can imagine, the wife starts raising cain. 'What do you think you're doing?' she says. 'My daddy gave us that horse and now we're stranded out here and . . .' And the fellow, he just looked at her sort of quiet like and said, 'That's once.'"

Their laughter broke the tension and when it died Cutliff added: "I guess what I'm saying, Mr. President, is we may have to shoot that horse down there, but maybe we ought to give him a couple more stumbles before we do."

The President laughed again, then called on MacKenzie.

"I think, Mr. President, that if Rivera has bombed our embassy, it is a most serious offense," MacKenzie said. "But I agree with Dave and the others who have said we need more information before any military action is taken."

"I'm glad you two finally agreed on something," the President said. "Anybody got anything more to add?"

No one did.

"Okay, here's what we're going to do. This ain't Pearl Harbor. General, you keep your troops on alert, but only on alert. Chuck, you tell that ambassador he's to make a full investigation. I may send somebody down from here to help him. Drummond, your intelligence people should go all out on this investigation. Leon, you ride herd on this and keep me posted. O.B., you tell the press I'll make a statement on this at the swearing-in ceremony this afternoon."

"For live TV?"

"Right. Dave, looks like I postpone that speech you wrote me."

"Can I help on the new one?"

Barney shook his head. "I'll talk off the cuff. Okay, I want this same group here at two tomorrow to keep on top of this. That's all for now. Meeting adjourned."

The President marched from the room, with Leon at his heels. The others followed in ones and twos. Charlton MacKenzie fell in beside Dave.

"Well, this proved to be an exciting session, didn't it?" he asked in his elaborate, solemn tones.

"It did indeed," Dave said.

"I'm glad we found ourselves in agreement on this bomb incident," MacKenzie said.

"So am I, Mr. Secretary."

"But it disturbs me," MacKenzie continued, "that we are in such sharp disagreement on broader questions of Latin American policy."

"It's a subject on which reasonable men differ."

"If we discussed it further, Dave, we might find we agree on more than we disagree on. Perhaps you could join me for dinner some evening."

"I'd be happy to, Mr. Secretary."

Come into my parlor, Dave thought. But he did not fear MacKenzie. To the contrary, the Secretary fascinated him, and he would look forward to an evening with him. And however distasteful MacKenzie's politics might be, his cuisine would surely be excellent.

They descended the stairs to the North Portico. A hundred yards away, across Pennsylvania Avenue in Lafayette Park, Andy Jackson stood tall in the saddle, waving his hat in eternal triumph.

"Oh, Dave," MacKenzie said, as an afterthought, as he stepped toward his waiting limousine, "I understand you're having a bit of difficulty getting Sam Spingarn's cooperation for a project of yours. I know the senator rather well. If you like, I could speak a word in your behalf."

"Please do," Dave said. What else could he say? He needed all the help he could get.

4

A dozen new calls and messages were waiting at his office. Commissioner Stubblefield had left word that Horace Rice was resigning quietly. Dave dialed Jerry Drucker at the Bureau to report the resignation. He had never seen Drucker. The man was only a name, a number, and an amazing repository of information. He told Drucker about the resignation, then added on the spur of the moment, "Jerry, see what you've got on a girl named Catherine Quinn, a reporter for National Newsfeatures." He knew the Bureau had files on most Washington reporters; these guys had files on their mothers.

Drucker left the phone, and Dave skimmed a memo from the director of the Bureau of Prisons. Dave had asked them for a report on homosexuality in federal prisons, and now he had it, with this conclusion: "The urgency of the situation points up the need for additional supervisory and psychiatric personnel within the federal prison system." In short, more money. Dave scribbled in the margin: *Haven't conjugal visits helped in several states? Please report.*

"We haven't got much on this individual," Jerry Drucker said. "Born in Boston. Father a longshoreman. I can give you plenty on the longshoremen."

"Just the girl, Jerry."

"Public schools. Boston College. Had a scholarship. Couple of years with the Boston *Globe*. Came here last summer with this newsfeatures outfit. Been writing a weekly feature, usually on a political figure. Some pretty leftwing stuff. You want a full check?"

"No, that's plenty." He felt dirty, as if he'd read someone else's mail. But knowing things was his business.

"I hear Roy Hailey's back in town," Dave said.

"You hear right."

"What's he up to?"

"Organizing."

"Organizing who?"

"You name it," the agent said. "Maids. Car-wash boys. Colored cops."

"He'll be over organizing you guys next."

Drucker was not amused. "We're already organized," he said. "Against bastards like him."

Dave called a friendly reporter at the *Times* and briefed him on the NSC meeting. He assumed that General Boswell would give his version to the Chicago *Tribune* and one or two others. He hoped that the *Times*' vaguely attributed story the next morning, raising the possibility of U.S. military intervention in Caravelas, would scare liberals and thus stir up some anti-intervention pressure on the President.

Dave dialed a number from a notebook in his desk drawer. He was in luck—Roy Hailey answered.

"Roy? How's the kid?"

"How the hell you get this number?"

"I've got all the numbers. How are you?"

"I've been worse. I saw your picture this morning. You're getting up there."

"Never had my picture on *Time*'s cover, like you."

"Never had your teeth kicked in in Mississippi, either, but you ain't missed nothing. What's on your mind?"

"Just this, Roy. As long as you stay within the law, I'll give you any help I can. We don't want trouble in Washington, and if you start any we'll be all over you. So you decide."

"No, Dave, the people will decide. You ought to listen to the people sometime."

"You listen to me. Don't cause any trouble here this summer."

"The trouble is already here," Hailey said. "Come around some-time and I'll show you." He hung up.

Dave put down the phone and almost immediately the buzzer under his desk went off. He grabbed the other phone and heard the President's voice, loud and angry.

"Dave, call that son of a bitch Duffey and get him off my back. He's been calling here all day. Something about a monk."

"Yes sir," Dave said, and called Donald Duffey immediately. Duffey was Secretary of Housing and Urban Development. He was also the most audacious, most successful publicity hound in Washington, a Barnum among bureaucrats.

"Dave, thank goodness you called," Duffey said. "I've got the Monks right here in my office . . ."

"The what?"

"The Merry Monks. The quartet. I'm sure you've heard *Sunshine in the Vatican*—twelve weeks in the Top Forty. Well, the Monks are right here with me. They just sang for our Go-Go Citizens Award Luncheon. And a little bird told me you might like them to come perform at General Walton's swearing-in this afternoon."

Dave thought: And I'll bet that little bird told you you'd get your picture taken with the Monks and the President, you transparent bastard.

"I'll check it, Mr. Secretary," he said. Then he told Mrs. Gill to call Duffey's office in ten minutes and say the swearing-in program couldn't be changed.

Charlton MacKenzie called at three-thirty.

"Dave, I spoke with Senator Spingarn and I believe some agreement can be reached about that program for alcoholics."

"Wonderful."

"There is one additional point," MacKenzie continued. "The senator has a valued friend, a Mr. Lester Sisk, who he would very much like to see named regional director for the Post Office in the Alabama-Mississippi region."

The spot was open, and Spingarn's man would be a leading contender in any event. "That's possible if he's qualified," Dave said.

"Oh, I'm told he's a leading businessman," the Secretary of State said.

"I'll check with the Postmaster General."

"There is one difficulty," MacKenzie continued. "It seems that Mr. Sisk once killed a man."

"Oh good God," Dave said. "Who? A Negro?"

"No, a white man. His brother-in-law, in fact. It was some years ago."

"Was he convicted?" Dave asked.

"It was ruled justifiable homicide. The Sisk family is very prominent in that part of the state."

"I'll have to talk to the Postmaster General," Dave said.

"You'll find him familiar with the case," MacKenzie promised. "So far, he's refused to consider the appointment."

"Well, I'll check it," Dave said. "And thanks for your help."

"You're quite welcome," Charlton MacKenzie said.

Dave called the President and explained the situation. Barney thought it pretty funny; his final comment was: "If you can get it past Hinkle, and Spingarn will sponsor the guy, it's okay with me."

So Dave called Oscar Hinkle, the Postmaster General, a one-time postman himself, who predictably protested that the appointment would be improper, immoral, and probably illegal. He didn't relent until Dave had invited him and Mrs. Hinkle to the President's next cruise on the Potomac, promised to support Hinkle's request for three new assistants, and hinted he might initiate a cut in the Post Office budget unless Hinkle okayed the deal.

Then Dave called Senator Spingarn's administrative assistant. A half-hour later the senator's committee authorized five million dollars for a program to treat alcoholics in the District of Columbia.

He paused at the threshold of the East Room, dazzled by the great ballroom's brilliant, white-and-gold grandeur. The red-coated Marine Band was playing a Sousa march and its beat lifted his spirits. The afternoon's guests were filling the room. There was a festive air as senators, generals, cabinet members, and other notables laughed and waved, circulating slowly beneath the three huge, glittering crystal chandeliers.

A speaker's platform, with the presidential seal on it, had been placed on the east side of the room midway between the life-size portraits of George and Martha Washington; opposite were a dozen television cameras, their crews, and three dozen reporters, who had come to hear the President's statement on the bombing in Caravelas.

Dave had stopped in the President's office on the way to the ballroom. General Walton, one of Barney's old war buddies, now to be Deputy Secretary of Defense, was there with him. So was Sharon Flatt, with a dictation pad on her knee, although no one was giving dictation. She gave Dave a wide, conspiratorial smile as he entered.

"Hello, General. Congratulations," Dave said. "Your remarks all set, Mr. President? Anything I can do?"

Barney puffed on his cigar. "Tubby, you see what happens when you hire a ghostwriter? They think you can't talk without 'em. Everything's fine, kid. Just trust old Barn."

"I trust you, Mr. President. Anything new on the bombing?"

"Yeah. Our glorious ally Colonel Molina has vowed revenge."

"If we send him a thousand men and ten million dollars."

"How'd you guess?" Barney said. "Go join the party. I'll be over in a minute."

As he left the President's office, Dave had passed the chief of protocol and a thin, attractive woman of forty—the Duchess of Cornwall, arriving for her courtesy call.

Now Dave leaned against the wall, enjoying the panorama of the East Room, glad to be an observer for a while. A dark-eyed, beak-nosed little man in a wrinkled white suit appeared beside him.

"Get a load of this, Davey. Twenty-to-one and this baby won it going away."

Dave glanced down and saw that the man was flashing a huge roll of ten-dollar bills.

"Put that damned money away, Mickey," he snapped. "This isn't a racetrack."

"Don't get sore, Davey. Hey, I've got a sure thing at twelve-to-one tomorrow. You want me to put down a ten-spot for you?"

Dave's eyes were sweeping the room. He didn't want to be seen talking to Mickey.

"No thanks, Mick. I'm not a gambler. See you later."

The little man moved away reluctantly. Mickey Daley was Eddie Gooch's friend, a press agent of some sort who of late had been hanging around Eddie's office, running errands for him. Dave resolved to speak to Eddie about his friend Mickey Daley.

He was studying the press corps when he felt a tug on his sleeve. He turned and found Cathy Quinn staring up at him.

"Hello," he said.

"Hello yourself."

She was a skinny little thing, but he liked the way she carried herself, shoulders thrown back and chin high.

"Nice place you've got here," she said.

"Your first time?"

She nodded. "I never got out of the West Wing before."

"Come over some afternoon," he told her. "We have a special tour for important people."

"Who decides if I'm important?"

"I do," he said. He smiled at her and she smiled back, a wide, cocky smile.

"Who's that one over there, with the red tie?" she asked.

"Congressman Wingard of Ohio. Don't turn your back on him."

"You're nicer than when I interviewed you."

"Wasn't I nice then?"

"You were a nice machine. I could hear you going click-click-click. But you're more like a person now."

"I don't have to worry about you now."

"Not any?"

He shook his head. "Not any."

Sid Frankel, the Secretary of Health, Education and Welfare, joined them.

"Dave, I don't believe I know this young lady."

"Secretary Frankel . . . Cathy Quinn."

"Quinn? Of course—you wrote that story on Dave."

Dave nodded; Sid didn't miss many tricks.

"Miss Quinn, if you'll write a story like that about me, I'll run for President."

"Then what happens to Dave?"

"You write the story and I'll take care of Dave." He winked and moved away.

"He's nice," Cathy said.

"He's the best man in the cabinet. Would you excuse me a second?"

Dave caught up with Secretary Frankel and they turned away from the room for a moment.

"Sid, Roy Hailey's back in the city, organizing over around Fourteenth Street. I wonder if you couldn't open a storefront office over there, put in some social workers, an ombudsman operation, to take the wind out of his sails."

Frankel nodded. "You'll back me up?"

"Sure."

Dave rejoined Cathy just as the Marine Band began *Hail to the Chief*. Barney marched in with General Walton on one side of him and the Duchess on the other. He introduced her to the Chief Justice, the Majority Leader, and other notables in the first row of chairs, before he returned her, blushing and delighted, to the chief of protocol. Brenda Newfield had followed her husband into the room and taken a seat on the speaker's stand, looking gorgeous and bored.

Barney began the ceremony, smiling out at the audience, speaking of his long friendship with General Walton, finally asking the Chief Justice to come forward and administer the oath of office. This was a different man from the Barney who had guffawed at Eddie Gooch's crude humor that morning, or the cold, watchful sphinx of the NSC meeting. Here he was graceful, charming, super-host, mesmerizing two hundred of America's most powerful men as effortlessly as he had charmed the visiting Duchess.

After the swearing-in, Tubby Walton spoke briefly, then the President returned to the microphones.

"Most of you know there was an incident in Caravelas this morning. Somebody set off a bomb outside our embassy, causing minor damage and injuring two employees. I've talked to the ambassador and he's added new guards so this won't happen again. I've instructed him to make a full investigation. Until we have the facts, we won't make any assumptions."

Dave was nodding as he listened. Barney was calm, matter-of-fact, perfect.

"We all know there's a guerrilla war going on down there, and I expect there's some people who'll say the guerrillas bombed our embassy so let's send in troops and get 'em. But the truth is we don't know who bombed the embassy and we're not going to overreact to a small incident. Weak nations can be trigger-happy, but great nations can't."

Dave wanted to cheer. Across the room, he could see Leon

Kerkelot smiling and, a few feet away, General Boswell, grim-faced.

"That's all I have to say now. Except that I'm proud that we have a man like General Walton to take this important job at the Pentagon, a man who's spent thirty years defending America, a man who knows what power is, and what it isn't. Thank you."

The audience stood and applauded as he left the room.

"Boy, he's really something," Cathy said.

"Yeah, he is," Dave agreed. It was one of those moments when it all seemed worthwhile.

The crowd was moving toward the Green Room, where a reception was to be held.

"You staying for this?" she asked.

"If people see me sipping punch, they'll say I haven't enough work to do. But you should stay."

"I guess I will. I see some people I want to talk to."

"Come by my office later for a drink."

"I'll do that," she said.

Back in his office, he returned a call from the Secretary of Agriculture, who wondered if the President would attend his daughter's wedding. Then he skimmed a letter from his mother. The landlord had fixed the front screen but he'd raised the rent ten dollars. Marsha had a part-time job but after she paid the baby-sitter she really didn't make much. Her car had broken down and cost a hundred and twenty dollars to fix, and she would have to postpone her visit to Washington, unless she got a lot of overtime that month. Dave wrote a check for one hundred and twenty dollars and sent it with a note saying he was working hard, Eleanor and Sally were fine, she was to come as planned, love, Dave. His mother was one of life's victims and he owed to her, among other things, his determination that he would never be a victim.

The President called and said he was flying up to Camp David for the night. He asked Dave to bring him any papers he wanted him to read overnight. Dave gathered up a half-dozen memos and took them to the President's office. Eddie Gooch and Sharon Flatt were with him. Outside, the President's helicopter was warming up on the grass.

"No use you coming," the President told Dave. "I'll be back tomorrow morning. Where's Leon?"

"He's already in the chopper," Eddie said.

"Okay, let's get moving."

Not until they reached the helicopter did Dave realize that Sharon was making the trip. He knew Brenda had a speech the next morning and wasn't going. Not that it was unusual for one of the secretaries to accompany the President, but Dave assumed this was a special case—fast work, even for Barney.

The helicopter roared, rippled the grass beneath it, and lifted easily into the sky. Reception guests waved from the windows of the Green Room. The last thing Dave saw as the helicopter shot off toward Maryland was Sharon Flatt's excited face at the window and the glint of the afternoon sun on her hair. He sighed and started back to his office. Was Sharon Flatt of Charleston, West Virginia, to be the Madame Pompadour of this regime? Who could say? Stranger things had happened.

Mrs. Gill ushered Cathy Quinn in twenty minutes later, as Dave was struggling to decipher an Interior Department report.

"I came for that drink," she said. "What're you reading?"

"Words," he told her. "Words, words, words. Scotch or sherry?"

"Scotch. On the rocks."

"How was the party?"

"I never saw so many big-shots at one time. I kept thinking, What if they dropped a bomb on this place? Who'd be left to run the government?"

"I know some Republicans who'd like to try."

His phone buzzed. It was the Secretary of Labor, and when Dave finished with him, Mrs. Gill buzzed again.

"No more calls, Ethyl."

"It's your wife."

"Okay, but no more after her."

He frowned slightly as he reached for the phone. So we're speaking again? he thought. He wondered what she wanted.

"Dave?"

"Yes?"

"Dave . . . I'm sorry about last night." Eleanor's voice was a whisper, sad and vulnerable, filled with pauses and tiny breaks. The Loving Wife Seeks Forgiveness. One of her greatest roles.

"Forget it."

"You're sweet. I want to see you."

"You will. What's on your mind?"

"I just had a call from Walt Tyson. You remember Walt? The director?"

He remembered Walt. A fat queer who drank too much and once told Dave he'd look lovely in drag.

"I remember Walt."

"He's in town making a picture about politics and he wants us to join him and some people for dinner tonight. He'd like to get some ideas from you."

"What kind of a picture?"

"Something about a President who's really a Communist. Can you come, Davey?" Now her voice was kittenish, the way she was when she wanted something and wasn't sure she could have it. He wasn't moved, not after her performance the night before. He'd wanted something then, and hadn't got it, and now she could do without what she wanted.

"I can't possibly get away for dinner. You go on if you want to. And tell Walt I don't know any Presidents who are Communists."

Eleanor, her voice less kittenish, agreed to go without him. He turned back to Cathy, curled up in the chair, her thin legs tucked under her, studying the books on his shelves, taking everything in.

"You wife's an actress, isn't she?" Cathy asked.

"She was once."

"She's pretty—I've seen her pictures."

"This isn't a very good place to talk," Dave said. "It's hard to stop the phone."

"Let's go for a walk," Cathy said. "Can you leave?"

"I shouldn't," he admitted. "But what the hell? Where to?"

"How about the Tidal Basin? Would you believe I've never seen the cherry blossoms?"

"I'll believe almost anything," he said, and called for his car. Five minutes later it deposited them a mile away at the great domed temple that is Thomas Jefferson's memorial.

5

He sent the driver on, and they walked around to the front of the Memorial and climbed its steps until they could see the statue of Jefferson inside. Turning, letting their eyes follow Jefferson's, they could see across the Tidal Basin, through the opening in the trees, back to the White House—a tiny white box, a doll's house in the distant dusk.

"You suppose all those people are still in the Green Room?" she asked.

"People tend to linger."

The Washington Monument rose off to their right, and past it they could see the dull red towers of the Smithsonian. Out on the Tidal Basin, two tourists churned along in rented paddle boats, and on the opposite bank a Negro fished with a cane pole. Below them, at the bottom of the steps, a red-and-yellow bus discharged three dozen teenagers, who came scrambling up toward the Memorial.

Dave and Cathy moved down the steps, off to the left, along the sidewalk that circled beneath the cherry blossoms, beside the water. Dave breathed the cool air deeply, glad the week was over, glad Barney was away, glad to be here with this girl.

"What are you smiling at?" she asked.

"I was thinking of something that happened today."

"Tell me."

"Off the record?"

"Everything's off the record now."

"Good. The thing was, I made a deal today where I got five million dollars for an alcoholism center and a senator's friend who once killed a man got a Post Office job."

She laughed and he laughed too.

"Do you make many deals like that?"

"All I can. As deals go, it wasn't bad."

"What would you call a bad deal?"

"Oh, if we'd made the fellow Postmaster General, I'd call that a bad deal. But he'll do all right as a regional director."

"Is that your secret of success? Making good deals?"

"My secret is I'm a damn good speechwriter—behind every great man there's a great speechwriter."

"I interviewed one of your old rivals who didn't think so. He said, 'Dave's a real sweetheart, just don't turn your back on him or you might find a knife in it.'"

"That sounds like Irv Bohn—I got his job."

"How'd you do that?"

"I outhustled him," Dave said. "What else did my critics say?"

"One young lady said you were an arrogant, hard-hearted son-of-a-bitch and she'd like to strangle you with her bare hands."

"That's little Susan what's-her-name from the campaign. The trouble was that she made me an offer one night and I didn't accept it. Isn't that a crazy way to make an enemy?"

"How many ways are there?"

"To make enemies? God knows. I keep finding new ones."

"But you like your job, don't you?"

"It's the best job in Washington. No, the second best. But the best available to me."

The sidewalk curved through the pink and white tunnel of the cherry trees. A young couple passed, pushing a baby carriage, and Cathy gave them her wide, crinkly smile. They passed an old Negro carrying a big fish. Dave asked what kind of fish it was and the Negro grinned and said something they didn't understand. The air was cool and clouds were blowing in from the west, low-flying rain clouds washed a pale gold by the setting sun.

"I liked your article on Senator Bartle," he said.

"He didn't. I may have been too hard on him."

"You couldn't be too hard on Bartle. He's a liar and a drunk and a molester of small boys. But he's a pretty good liberal."

She looked up at the sky. "Uh-oh."

"Uh-oh, what?"

"Uh-oh, I just felt a raindrop," she giggled.

"Come on, I'll get you a cab." They crossed the grass to the street. Rain began falling and they stood close together under a magnolia tree while he waved for a cab.

"Where are you going now?" she asked.

"Back to the office to work."

"Important work?" she asked.

"Not particularly."

"Why don't you come to my place and I'll fix you a hamburger? It's not far, just up on the Hill."

He looked down at her; her short brown hair was spangled with raindrops and she seemed very small and young there in the shadows.

"Sure," he said.

A cab stopped and they climbed into the back seat.

"822 D Street, Southeast," Cathy said.

"Take the Southwest Freeway," Dave added.

The driver, a young Negro, shook his head. "Quicker straight up Independence," he said.

"Take the Freeway anyway," Dave said. "I like the view." The driver shrugged.

They curved right, then twisted to the left, away from the river, and climbed twenty feet up into the dusk. From that height, looking left toward town, they could see the new government buildings around L'Enfant Plaza, huge modernistic boxes wherein tens of thousands of bureaucrats labored by day, buildings nearly deserted now but their lights ablaze as silent old women emptied countless wastebaskets and mopped endless corridors. On their right, as they sped along the freeway, was the Southwest redevelopment area, where in the 1950s an old slum had been destroyed and in the '60s a new slum created, with drab high-rise apartments for the rich, drab public-housing projects for the poor, and clusters of psuedo-townhouses scattered among them, a new world, charmless, treeless, hopeless. They passed the HEW building, a terrible place, a great gray prison that even to enter made Dave physically weak, a place of gray people in gray clothing doing gray jobs in gray offices, forever. They could see that vast marble mistake, the Rayburn

Building, and hovering above it, bathed in light, the white dome of the Capitol. Then they were into Southeast Washington, into the Capitol Hill restoration area, block upon block of Victorian row houses where affluent whites and poor blacks coexisted uneasily, the whites in brightly painted, expensively restored houses, the blacks crowded into crumbling, unrestored buildings. They descended from the freeway, passing the Washington *Star* building and, beyond it, row upon row of dull-red public-housing units. They turned left, up Sixth Street, moving past houses with clusters of Negroes sitting on the steps, past a corner grocery called the Little Cuckoo, past the 5th Precinct police station, past a tavern called Mr. Henry's, then right on Pennsylvania and left on Ninth until they stopped at Cathy's address. The fare was a dollar-fifty. Dave gave the driver two singles and told him to keep the change. The driver didn't waste any breath saying thanks.

"Well, this is it," she said, flipping on the light. It was a small, cluttered apartment, the first floor of an old townhouse.

"It's very nice," he said.

"It's a dump," she said cheerfully, "but it's convenient. There's some beer in the icebox."

"Can I get you one?"

"I don't like beer," she said. "Somebody left that here."

"Anybody I know?"

"You might know him." She mentioned the name of a young lawyer who worked for Ted Kennedy.

"He's a bright guy. You go with him?"

"Not any more."

"Why not?"

"Because he wants a wife and twenty kids and I want to make a name for myself."

Dave decided not to drink the spurned suitor's beer. Instead, he poured himself a Scotch and another for her. He made a phone call in the bedroom and when he returned they sat on the sofa.

"How'd you get where you are so young?" he asked her.

"I'm a darn good reporter," she said. "Also I had a break."

"What was that?"

"When I started with the *Globe*, the city editor thought it'd be a good joke to put a girl reporter on the police beat, the days the regular police reporter was off. I was the joke. Except pretty soon the cops were telling me things—little wide-eyed me—they never told the regular guy. And then those basketball scandals came along, and I broke the story and won some prizes. So I began to make a name for myself, and after a while I decided I'd come down to Washington, where the action is."

"Are you happy with National Newsfeatures?"

She shrugged. "It's getting me what I wanted," she said. "I could of gone with the *Post* or the *Times*, but they're too big. I'd have to spend five years proving I was good. I already knew I was good, and National was the best place to show it. The bureau chief is a drunk and the other two reporters are numbskulls, so I'm the one who gets the good assignments. And who's making a name for herself."

"And you want to be a political writer?"

"If I'm good enough," she said.

"The stuff of yours I've seen has been good."

"That's just feature writing. You're a good guy. Senator Bartle's a bad guy. Any idiot can do that. I want to understand politics, understand this town, understand this whole crazy country."

"You want a lot," he said. "There aren't ten writers in Washington who see the whole equation."

"Then there's room for one more," she laughed and jumped to her feet. "Come on, I'll burn the burgers now."

He leaned against the kitchen doorway, watching as she squeezed out the hamburger patties. Outside, there was a clatter of broken glass and the wail of a police siren. He looked around.

"It's just Friday night on Capitol Hill," she said. "If you want to go watch out the window you'll probably see a couple of muggings."

She grinned and tried to flip one of the hamburgers, but it tumbled back, the same side up, into the frying pan. She finally edged it over with a fork and a wooden spoon.

"I'm not much of a cook," she admitted.

"Nobody's perfect," he said.

"I was a darn good waitress once."

"When was that?"

"I worked a couple of summers in a hotel on the Cape. I was so skinny they were afraid I couldn't carry a tray full of food, so they put me in the coffee shop. God, I made a fortune. Nice old ladies would drink a dime cup of coffee and tip me a quarter. They thought I was starving, but I was just skinny." She smiled at the memory, lifting the hamburgers from the pan. "You ever do stuff like that?"

"Sure," he said. "Threw papers, pumped gas, set pins—the whole stinking thing."

She served the hamburgers on paper plates, with pickles and potato chips. He opened one of the ex-boy friend's beers and joined her at the small kitchen table.

"You have any brothers or sisters?" he asked her.

"An older sister," she said.

"Married?"

"She's being divorced."

"That's too bad," he said.

"No it's not. She married her high school sweetheart and he turned out to be the biggest bastard in the world."

"What'll she do?"

"I don't know. Get a job I guess. Sue's smart. She was always the favorite. She was smart and sweet and pretty—little Cathy was always the screw-up in the family."

"But now little Cathy's making a name for herself," he said.

"That's right," she said.

A fire engine wailed outside. He took a bite of the hamburger and washed it down with beer. "The hamburger's good," he said.

"Mine's too rare," she told him. "Listen, there's something I want to know. Everybody says President Newfield is off to such a great start. Are you really all that excited?"

"You're still interviewing me, aren't you?"

"Not for publication. Just for my education."

He smiled at her. "Okay, then I'll break all precedent and tell you the truth. But it'll sound like propaganda."

"That's okay."

The Scotch before dinner had made him feel good and the beer and food were making him feel even better. It was raining outside, with low rumbling thunder, and gusts of cool air blew in through the kitchen window.

"All right," he said. "I don't get many chances to brag. How are we doing? We're doing great, just great. The worst of the transition is behind us, and the President is coming into his own. We're starting to soar. My God, it's something to see. Barney Newfield is going to pick up this country and make it sing."

"What things?" she pressed. "What things are going so great?"

"Foreign affairs, to start. Other countries are finding out Barney is a man they can work with. Things are getting better with Russia and France, and maybe next with Cuba and China. And at home, we're doing good with Congress. The tax reform bill. The new drug laws. The new minimum wage. And the New Cities—my God, we're talking about building five or ten brand new cities, from the ground up, for a million people each. That's the one Barney thinks he'll be remembered for fifty years from now. And he will."

She was leaning forward, her eyes narrowed into her odd little squint. He was being studied but he didn't mind. "You *are* excited, aren't you?" she asked.

"You're damn right I am. If the New Cities bill passes, this year will be remembered with 1933 and 1965 as one of the great legislative years."

She remained unconvinced, her cool eyes fixed on his face. "But don't they all start out with those same big ideas?" she asked. "Didn't Kennedy's administration in 1961 and Johnson's in '65 and even Osgood's last year? And then don't things always get screwed up somehow?"

He laughed softly and shook his head. "Sure, you're right. No administration ever lives up to its dreams. Things go wrong. But you do the best you can, that's all."

"What did you think of President Osgood?" she asked.

Dave shrugged. "You have to give the old fellow credit. He said he'd settle the war in Vietnam and he did."

"What'd of happened if he hadn't settled it?" she asked.

"This country would be falling apart."

"Yeah. When I graduated from high school, I was offered three scholarships. I took the one that was farthest from Texas."

"But why'd you end up in Washington?" she asked.

"Cathy," he said slowly, "I got here for the same reason you did and ninety-nine percent of the people here did, regardless of race, creed, or political persuasion. I have an immoderate amount of what is politely called ambition. Or is sometimes described as having rats in the belly. Because I want to do good and to do well too. Because I'm a little crazy and a little idealistic and a little bit of an egomaniac—and that's the end of the interview. Okay?"

They stared at each other, he smiling a bit, she frowning, and before either spoke again the telephone rang.

"That may be for me," he said.

"You want me to answer it?"

"It's all right."

It was his secretary, Mrs. Gill. "The Secretary of Defense's office just called," she told him. "They say page twelve of your budget summary lists $3.75 billion for missile systems and it should be $3.85 billion."

Dave listened intently. He was a little drunk, it had been a hard day and a hard week and he did not begrudge himself being a little drunk, but there was a corner of his mind that was forever sober.

"My figure is right," he told her. "The other was a Budget Bureau mistake. Tell them to call Womack if they want an explanation."

He was grinning as he put down the phone. He could imagine those bastards at the Pentagon tearing their hair at ten o'clock on a Friday night, sure he had screwed them out of a hundred million dollars. Would that he could.

Cathy was standing beside the sofa. "You can't get away from it, can you?" she asked.

"I don't want to get away from it," he said, and finished his beer.

"What if the President called right now and asked what his bright young man is doing?"

"It'd never happen," he said. "The President is a very discreet man."

They laughed, and the moment seemed right, and he pulled her toward him, lowering his head, watching her tough, curious face until their mouths met. Her kiss was warm and wet but he could feel the muscles in her neck tighten, feel her head pulling back.

"What's wrong?" he asked her after a moment. He was fraternity-boy drunk, drunk enough to think himself irresistible.

"For starters, you're married."

"Not right this minute."

His arms were around her shoulders. Her hands rested lightly at his waist, but she kept her eyes down, away from his.

"It's not fair," she said bitterly. "It's damn rotten."

"What?"

"The way it is with men. You know what they say—eighty percent are idiots and the rest are married."

"Thanks for putting me in the twenty percent," he said, smiling down at her. He still thought charm could get what he wanted.

"Oh, you are," she said. "You're the kind who would be. The kind with a beautiful wife and a beautiful kid and a beautiful everything."

"Maybe things aren't as beautiful as they look," he said.

"So you go looking for a quick lay," she snapped.

"You haven't been so quick," he said. "Look, Cathy, what I'm suggesting is very simple. A little pleasure for both of us, and no complications. I think you're a very pleasant girl, if that means anything. But if you don't like the idea, fine, I'll leave now."

"That's swell for you," she said. "But what's in it for me?"

He jerked his shoulders impatiently. "You're a big girl, Cathy. You know what's in it for you."

"I can get that a lot of places."

"Okay," he said. "You do that. I'll see you around."

He stepped back, but she held his arm. "You know a lot," she said. "Will you teach me things?"

He laughed helplessly. "Sure," he said. "I'll teach you a thing or two."

In her bed, a minute later, her body was taut and tingling with surprises. He touched and tasted it, a slow, contented exploration, finding her soft here, hard there, sweet here, wet

there. He rolled a forefinger gently against her nipple until
sparks seemed to fly between them, a tiny orgy of flesh on
flesh. Even after she pulled him atop her with a cry, he moved
cautiously, studying her pace, coasting until she began her final
fierce response, and he knew it would be good and it was,
more than good. In the last seconds images flashed through
his mind—poems, songs, jokes, memories of other girls—and the
words of a long-forgotten rock-and-roll song echoed for an instant: "One thing 'bout her I can understan'/She wraps all around
me like a rubber band." He smiled as they relaxed and he could
feel her body warm beneath his.

"My God, you're good," she whispered. "I didn't want to make
it. I just wanted to go on and on."

The last line of a limerick danced through his mind—"Lady,
my name is Simpson, not Samson"—but he said, "So did I."

"Was I good?"

"Not bad for an old police reporter," he said.

"Be nice to me," she said and pressed against him. He
kissed her eyes and the hollows of her shoulders and her hard
little breasts and he felt an affection for her he had not expected
to feel. He knew her secret now, that she was not so tough
as she pretended, and he liked her more for it, felt for her the
instinctive warmth he always felt for those who were vulnerable.
Soon they made love again, not cautiously but greedily this
time—like amorous birds of prey, he thought—a long duel that
left them spent and silent in one another's arms. She slept, and he
lay quietly until midnight, when he slipped out of bed and
dressed.

"Don't go," she whispered.

"I have to," he said.

"Stay and I'll give you a wild breakfast."

"I'll bet you would." He leaned over the bed and kissed her
on the cheek, and as he did he thought: Little lady, you are a
promising writer, a passable cook, an amusing companion, and
a fantastic lay.

Then he hurried out to find a taxi to take him home.

Dave feigned modesty with others but he did not fool himself.
He was for the moment one of the most important men of his
age in America. He had power and he liked it, and he knew

too how fleeting it might be, so while it lasted he wanted to enjoy its amenities. He did not care much, as some of the others did, about the expensive cars or the exclusive restaurants, but he wanted the more exquisite luxury of being appreciated, being admired, being feared. That was the best thing: to be young and to be very good at what you did, and to have it known that you were good, to have success but not let it spoil your work.

And there was something more he wanted, something that might have been provided by his marriage but wasn't, an affection and admiration and privacy that would be a little more than sex, a little less than love. Perhaps now he had found that. As his taxi crossed the Potomac into Virginia, he thought for the second time that night of Marvell's great poem:

> *For, lady, you deserve this state*
> *Nor would I love at lower rate.*

He did not know what state Cathy aspired to—that was her concern—but he found much that was excellent about her, and he would not love at lower rate. He imagined she felt the same way, for he thought them much alike: proud, ambitious, greedy people, people who wanted all the prizes. He thought they might have an affair that was crisp and sensible and fun. That was what he wanted—the best, perfection. And why not? This was a time when all things seemed possible, when he was soaring.

The Vantage Ground

1

They met again the next afternoon on the embassy bombing and the President decided that Leon Kerkelot should fly to Caravelas for a firsthand report. But Leon had a long-scheduled meeting with the NATO ministers, and the President turned to Dave as his second choice. He was briefed that evening by officials from State and the CIA—and briefed, secretly, by his man at the CIA, Rod Sinclair—and he took off from Andrews Air Force Base that night. At dawn his jet was circling the airport at Johnstown, the capital of Caravelas.

The surf glistened in the morning sun as his plane descended. The beaches outside Johnstown were gray and rocky, and behind them the city ascended steep green hills. At the top of the hills, pastel villas were nestled among the trees. His plane landed in a corner of the airport restricted for military aircraft—U.S. and Caravelian. As he climbed down he was met by a husky U. S. Army colonel with a broad, pitted face.

"Mr. Hyer? I'm Bob Huffaker, the military attaché with the embassy. I'll be showing you around."

An enlisted man took Dave's suitcase and put it in a waiting Chevrolet. Dave and the colonel got in the back seat of the car and the enlisted man guided them onto the highway to Johnstown.

"I understand we have a mutual friend," Huffaker said, after closing the glass partition between the front and back seats.

"Oh?"

"Rod Sinclair."

"Yes, I know Sinclair."

"He's asked me to give you every assistance while you're here."

"Do you deal with Sinclair a great deal?"

The colonel shrugged good-naturedly. "This is a small country. But I try to keep him informed. A lot of bad information reaches the Director's office, from various sources . . ."

"Like the ambassador?"

"Various sources. So I try to see that Rod gets the straight poop, and I'll see that you get the straight poop while you're here."

"Good," Dave said. "Let's start with this bombing. Did Rivera do it?"

Colonel Huffaker grinned. "Mr. Hyer . . ."

"Let's make it Dave."

"Dave, one thing you can bet your ass on. If Rivera had bombed that embassy, there wouldn't be anything there now except a pile of dust. Believe me."

"Okay, then who did it?"

"Probably the government. Possibly some independent agent. I doubt if we'll ever know."

"What about those students they arrested?"

"Oh, hell, they'd just come from a wedding and they're rich men's sons to boot."

"What's all that?" Dave said, pointing out the window. They were passing a long row of multicolored shanties on the rocky land between the road and the beach. Dozens of naked children and a few dark-skinned, haggard women stood outside the shanties.

"The natives call it La Plaza. It's where the peasants from the countryside settle when they come to the big city. They make those shacks out of a few scraps of wood and hundreds of cans, beer cans from our garbage dumps mostly, that they flatten out."

"You'd think the government would do something, if only to spare the tourists."

Huffaker shrugged. "That's one way of seeing it. But I think Molina figures that if enough Americans see La Plaza, he might get more U.S. aid. He's a funny guy."

"He sounds hilarious," Dave said. "Okay, what's my schedule?"

"Lunch with the ambassador. Dinner with Molina. And tomorrow I'd like to take you out in the countryside, show you the terrain, some of the military situation."

"Okay. Tell me about the ambassador. Fred Ball? Is that his name?"

They had entered Johnstown now, passed a huge marketplace, and were moving up the hillside along nearly deserted streets. Dave heard church bells tolling in the distance.

"Fred's not a bad guy. You'll meet him."

"Come on, Bob. Talk. I need information."

"Okay. Fred, as you probably know, was a wire-service executive. For thirty years, he resisted ever having a personal opinion on a political issue. Fred doesn't want to think about politics. Just the 'facts,' whatever that means. So at age sixty, because he knew President Osgood, he got to be ambassador to a small country where the weather is nice and the people are good to him. Cocktail parties and dinners every night in those big villas you see up there. When his grandkids come to visit, they get to swim in the private pools and ride horses on the big estates. Fred Ball never had it so good."

Huffaker pulled out a Camel and lit it with an old Zippo.

"So along comes Alberto Rivera, trying to overthrow the government, and the government happens to be all these people who are wining and dining Fred Ball. Fred's no raving reactionary, but given his background, and the position he's in, you have to expect that if Molina tells him that Rivera's troops are barbecuing babies for breakfast, Fred's gonna believe it."

"And so inform Washington," Dave said.

"And so inform Washington," Huffaker agreed. "Here's the place you're staying. It's the best we could do on short notice."

"Looks fine," Dave said. They had stopped in front of a small, pale-green villa, set back amid a cluster of palms. "Where's the owner?"

"Vacationing in Europe." Huffaker grabbed Dave's suitcase, and told the driver to wait. "Come on. You've got time to shower and change."

They met Ball at noon at the embassy. It was a modest enough building, two stories, with a reception room, a dining room, and a study downstairs, plus the kitchen at the rear, and offices upstairs. Fred Ball, a small, natty man with a salt-and-pepper mustache, had a manner both hearty and nervous.

"Now this is where they put the dynamite, Dave," he said.

"Two sticks, we think. You see the hole it dug up. Ten inches deep."

The hole was up against the foundation of the embassy, beneath the shredded remains of some hedges.

"But where they made their mistake, Dave, was putting the charge right up against the foundation. The force of the explosion ricocheted right off of there—that foundation's six inches thick—and you can see over across the way where it broke five windows. Now come on in, we'll have a drink."

The afternoon was like that—many facts and little enlightenment. Ambassador Ball called into two young foreign-service officers, one to report on the investigation, and the other on the embassy's new security precautions. Both young men—they were about Dave's age—told the ambassador exactly what he wanted to hear. Dave thought one of them seemed bright, but he was trapped in the system. At the end of the year, Ambassador Ball would write a long, totally subjective evaluation of both young men, and their advancement would, to a large degree, depend on his report.

The meeting broke up about four.

"Well, Dave, you're seeing Colonel Molina tonight," the ambassador said.

"That's right, sir." If Ball was miffed at being left out of that meeting, he didn't show it.

"He's quite a fellow. A little touchy sometimes, but once he solves this guerrilla problem, Molina's going to be a leader on this continent. Now, what about tomorrow?"

"I plan to take Mr. Hyer out into the countryside," Bob Huffaker injected. "Let him get a feel for the military situation."

"Good, good," said the ambassador. "I'd join you, but my daughter and her twins are coming in late tonight and . . . you know how that is."

"I certainly do, Mr. Ambassador," Dave said, and shook the man's hand in formal farewell.

Dusk was settling over Johnstown as Colonel Huffaker guided their car over the long gravel road that led to the estate where Colonel Molina lived and worked. For much of the distance, the road paralleled a cliff, and far below they could see the distant lights of the city and the ripple of moonlight on the ocean. Then the road swerved in toward the villa, which was U-shaped and set back amid formal gardens.

"Quite a layout," Dave said.

"It was the colonial governor's home when the British ran the country," Huffaker said.

As they mounted the steps of the villa, Dave caught a glimpse of a door opening, then of something glistening above him. He looked up, and saw a small, almost dainty man who seemed to glitter from head to toe. His black hair shone in the porch light, as did the two rows of medals on his chest, his gold belt buckle, his highly polished riding boots. Even his smile glittered as he took Dave's hand.

"Welcome, sir," he said in a soft, feline voice. "I am Luis Molina, President of Caravelas. Please come in." He paused. "And welcome to you, Colonel Huffaker. Colonel Huffaker is a great friend of my government."

"I'm sure he is," Dave said.

He led them into a huge, paneled library. What appeared to be a Constable was hanging above the fireplace, and Dave glimpsed the complete, leather-bound works of Dickens, Wordsworth, and Sir Walter Scott on the shelves. Molina poured drinks from a bottle of Chivas Regal, and they seated themselves in over-stuffed chairs.

"I trust your President is well, Mr. Hyer?"

"Very well, Colonel."

"I drink to his health." Molina raised his glass and the others did the same. "Now, Mr. Hyer, tell me how I and my government can assist this unexpected, but most welcome visit."

Dave tasted the Scotch, and held it in his mouth for a moment before he answered.

"Primarily, Colonel, I'm here to confer with our embassy about the bombing incident. However, the President has asked me to send his warm regards to you, and to convey to him personally any message you may have."

"The bombing?" Molina said with a flutter of his hand. "What is there to investigate? I told your ambassador this would happen. Your ambassador is a kind man, but naïve. All that has hap-

pened is that Rivera's men have tried to blow up your embassy
but bungled. Is that not what you have concluded, Colonel Huffaker?"

"There can be little doubt of it," Huffaker said.

"You see?" Molina said to Dave. His gold wristwatch flashed
in the soft light from the chandelier. "I will surround your
embassy with soldiers tomorrow if you like, Mr. Hyer, but that
will not solve the problem. The problem is Rivera and I am
most hopeful, as you know, that President Newfield will send
us the support we need to eliminate him."

"You mean U.S. combat units?"

"Whatever is necessary."

"The President is hopeful that your army can end the rebellion
without our troops."

Molina frowned. "My men are brave soldiers, Mr. Hyer, but
they are poorly supplied, while the enemy is well supplied by
his Communist allies. My men have little combat experience,
while Rivera has Cuban officers, and perhaps Chinese. My men
are preoccupied with civic-action programs, to assist our
people, while Rivera's terrorize the countryside. No, the best
and quickest solution is military aid from the U.S. ally."

"Colonel Molina, what will you do if the U.S. does not extend
military aid?" Dave asked.

Molina's onyx-hued eyes flashed. "Then we will defeat Rivera
singlehanded," he snapped. His voice lowered again. "But I
am confident in President Newfield's wisdom and statesmanship.
Come, let us go to dinner."

The meal was excellent. The three men dined alone, around
a circular table with a huge silver candelabra in its center.
White-coated waiters poured dry Spanish wine and served a
spicy bouillabaisse. Dave, on pretext of picking up his napkin,
glanced beneath the table and confirmed that Molina's feet did
not reach the floor.

Molina told them about his years in the U.S. He had studied
for two years at The Citadel, in South Carolina, and later for
another year at the U. S. Army Officer's School at Fort Leavenworth.

"Didn't Rivera also spend a year at The Citadel?" Dave asked

"Yes, we were classmates."

"Friends?"

Molina shrugged; his face was pale in the candlelight. "I have known Bert, as we called him then, since childhood. But we were not close. Even as a boy he was a troublemaker. Now he has become—what do you say in the U.S.?—a traitor to his class."

"How was he difficult?"

"Argued with his professors. Fought with the other students. Disrespectful to his elders. A troublemaker."

"Yet it's a long way from being a difficult student to being a revolutionary, Colonel. How do you explain his transition?"

Molina clapped his tiny hands and a waiter brought espresso. "I think, Mr. Hyer, that the potential was always there. Then . . . who knows? He studied law in Madrid, and some say he fell in with the Communist underground there. Or perhaps it was after. We have evidence that he made secret trips to Cuba throughout the Sixties."

"He made an attempt to work within the political system here, did he not?" Dave asked.

Molina frowned at the question. "After my government took power, six years ago, we took steps to expand and perfect our democratic system. Elections were held for Parliament, and Bert was chosen to represent one district of Johnstown. But it soon became clear that he was parroting a Communist line, so the Parliament chose to expel him."

Molina lit a small cigar and Huffaker lit a cigarette. Dave waved away the box of cigars and sipped his coffee.

"He chose to continue his criticisms of my government as a private citizen," Molina went on, "and it was necessary to send him into exile. Only my personal intervention prevented even sterner measures."

"But now he's come back from exile," Dave said.

"Only temporarily," Molina said with a glittering smile. "Come, let's go back to the library for brandy."

Dave was tired and ready to go, but Molina wanted to talk about the social reforms he would carry out after Rivera was defeated. As Dave and Huffaker sipped their brandy, he paced before the fireplace excitedly, talking of schools, hospitals, land reforms, higher wages. It sounded like the ADA platform.

Dave didn't believe a word of it, but it was a spirited performance, and he listened for forty-five minutes until Molina
ran down and they could leave.

"How'd that guy get to be head of this government?" Dave
asked Huffaker as they drove back down the long gravel driveway.

"Don't underestimate him. Right now, he's balancing about
six factions in this country, Protestant and Catholic, military
and civilian, workers and landowners. There's nobody else who
could pull it off."

"What time do we start in the morning?" Dave asked.

"Could you be ready at six?"

"Bob, I was up all last night getting here. If all we've got to
do tomorrow is see the scenery, let's start a little later."

Huffaker laughed happily. "That's just our cover story," he
said, as he swung the car round a curve, and the city lights
burst into view below them. "Tomorrow we see Rivera."

2

Eleanor Hyer spent the evening at home. After dinner, she read to Sally for an hour, often interrupted by the child's polite but persistent questions: Why did the Little Prince slay the dragon? What were step-sisters? Why were they always wicked? Sally had Dave's literal, logical mind, a fact which did not entirely please Eleanor. At nine she put Sally to bed and mixed a gin-and-tonic. She consulted *TV Guide* and found nothing worth watching. She leafed through a woman's magazine for a few minutes. She took a Colette novel from the shelf and read a few pages, but the heroine's misfortunes paled beside her own. She put the book aside and fell into an uneasy reverie.

For a lonely and troubled young woman, Eleanor looked improbably lovely. Her hair was brushed a rich gold; her make-up artfully applied, her white pants and pale blue blouse fresh and crisp and flattering to her slender body. Eleanor believed in looking her best at all times. For some years she had operated on the principle that beauty, or at least her own beauty, was an end in itself. She had been a freckled tomboy, a climber of trees and a lover of horses, when in the spring of her fourteenth year she discovered she was growing into a leggy, soft-eyed, honey-haired American beauty, at once as conventional and as perfect as a rose. For a decade and a half now she had enjoyed her beauty, nurtured it, traded on it, laughed at it, been embarrassed by it, been spoiled by it, employed it tactically (her smile at close range, her breasts immodestly exposed, her eyes blinking as if with tears) and she knew as well as any woman how good it is to be beautiful.

Perhaps it was not all good; Dave said that beautiful women and rich men share a sophistication and a softness that comes from receiving too much for too little. Yet she found it good, good for the attention it brought, good also for the unpleasantry it spared you. Someone had said that a social success was a beautiful woman who behaved as if she were plain—that was Eleanor's style. If you were beautiful and also were pleasant to people, so much of life was yours for the asking; you were spared the conniving and bitchiness that other women had had to employ to achieve their ends.

Bitchiness had never been part of Eleanor's repertoire—not until these past few months. Now she had been more of a bitch than she would have believed possible. She had treated Dave badly, was still treating him badly, was doing it as a calculated repayment for the pain he was inflicting on her. She hated it, but it was his fault. He had driven her to it. He knew how to stop it. She shook her head bitterly, angry at Dave and missing him too, wanting him here with her, not off on another trip to wherever it was he had gone.

Eleanor had known little of anger or loneliness until these recent months. Since childhood, she had moved from success to success with only the necessary, transitory sorrows that accompany a love of life and men and excitement. Her father had been a successful advertising man, and her mother was a happy, vague woman who busied herself with antique collecting and the Leauge of Women Voters. Eleanor went to the best schools and made the best grades and had for her friends the nicest girls, yet she decided early that the life she saw spread out before her was not enough, too many girls were pretty and popular, she wanted something more. It was then she decided to be an actress.

As it happened, she had talent. She proved this in a summer playhouse, and in the one year of college she endured before she could persuade her parents to let her study in New York. Her luck was good. After a few months she landed a part in an off-Broadway musical, and after that a continuing role as a doctor's troubled teenage daughter in a television soap opera; then her first Shakespeare, off-off-Broadway; and her first movie role as an ill-fated Indian girl in a big-budget Western.

At twenty, Eleanor was making more money than she could spend, had earned some good reviews, was becoming respected in professional circles. She had reached the point where her career should have taken off, should have propelled her upward to good roles on Broadway or in the movies. But her career did not take off, and now, a decade later, she thought she knew why. First, there were limitations on her talent. She was, in appearance and by temperament, a lady. She had aristocratic beauty, intelligence, and poise. She lacked fire, passion, the fine edge of madness that carries an actress past artifice and into art. Walt, one of the directors, told her she lacked the killer instinct, that he would cast her as Ophelia but never as Lady Macbeth.

Eleanor knew the criticism was true enough. She had her share of passion, but a proper childhood had left her indelibly a lady, one whose passion was more comfortably spent in private than onstage. (Once she had turned down a chance to be Playboy's Playmate of the Month, explaining that she preferred to undress for one man at a time. Later, one of her lovers had been a young playwright, a gentle giant from Oregon who had expressed amazement that a "lady" should show such talent abed. "Ladies like to screw, too," she'd told him, a line he'd immortalized, or at least perpetuated, in his next play.) She lacked, too, the desperate gnawing ambition she saw in other actresses. Eleanor wanted stardom, but she wanted even more to live her own life her own way. She hated Hollywood—and Hollywood paid enough to demand of young women an enthusiasm and a humility that Eleanor refused to grant it. So she had the good life and she did not have stardom, a fate she accepted with regret but without bitterness. To Dave it was all quite simple. "You can't have it both ways," he'd told her once, as if that explained everything, as if he had not been driving himself as long as she'd known him to do just that.

Life in New York had been good, for a time. From the vantage point of almost thirty, she looked back in amazement at the life she'd lived in her early twenties. She had never denied herself men; men were the prize you won for talent and beauty, your choice of the most attractive men of your time. She had taken lovers in discreet, leisurely affairs that usually lasted about a year, which she found to be the limit that two self-centered people can live together without the constraints of marriage. There had been an actor, then the Oregon playwright, then (in part because the actor and the playwright had proved to be so undependable) a wealthy Wall Street lawyer and after him a well-known director. She could have married any of them, but she wasn't ready for marriage. She worked off-Broadway and on television, she traveled, she went to openings and to the posh parties afterward. She was not a star, but she was a success—yet she was also restless and wondering where she was heading. It was then, at twenty-four, that she'd begun her affair with Les, the agent.

The affair with Les had begun because the director had proved to be such a bastard. Les was not a bastard. He was an extremely successful, extremely sweet, middle-aged Jewish theatrical agent, and he was hopelessly hung-up about being an extremely successful, extremely sweet, middle-aged Jewish theatrical agent. But he was kind and generous at a time when she needed kindness and generosity, and he'd fallen in love with her and then she was playing the role of mother-confessor to a man three decades her senior. It was a juicy role but ultimately a tiring one. One of Les's problems was dwindling potency and he alternated between tearful renunciations of sex and the difficult evenings when he'd insist they smoke pot together to encourage the various acts that might rekindle his potency. She'd done all those things without pot, with men whose bodies were far more appealing than his, and in time she'd tired of his demands, his tears, his apologies, his promises, his hang-ups, even his generosity. One night she walked out, ignoring his pleas and threats. The next night, after a hysterical call, she rushed back to his apartment, and found him on the floor beside his Christmas tree, in a pool of blood. She managed to call the police before she went to pieces.

Les recovered from the nicks on his wrists in a few days; Eleanor was still recovering from her breakdown four months later when she met David Hyer in Nashville.

Her great-aunt, a spirited woman of seventy, owned the Nashville *Herald*, a prosperous and relatively enlightened Southern newspaper, and upon learning that her favorite niece was ill, insisted that Eleanor come for a long visit. Eleanor's great-aunt had reached an age at which bourbon, politics, and matchmaking were her chief joys, and as the owner of a newspaper she was in a position to indulge herself in all three.

Eleanor objected to the matchmaking at first, but soon she was enjoying the role of Southern belle as her aunt paraded the city's most eligible young men beneath her nose. For a week or two they were only a blur, a drawling, door-opening, chair-holding, name-dropping, small-talking blur of Southern manhood; then one evening she met one who seemed different. She was at a cocktail buffet, you-alling a half-dozen of her new admirers, watching their gazes dip furtively toward her plunging neckline, when she noticed a slender, dark-haired boy standing alone by a window, staring at her. A minute later, she made an excuse to speak to him.

"Aren't you enjoying the party?" she asked.

"Very much."

"Just standing there?"

"I'm admiring your performance."

"My what?"

"Scarlett O'Hara entertains at Tara."

"So I'm playing a role?"

"To perfection. But take it easy. You've got Sammy Second National and Danny the Doctor's Son so het up that they're liable to fight a duel."

"What do you mean?" she asked, knowing what he meant.

"Well, I take it from that whispering a minute ago that Sammy offered you a ride home, and from the way you blinked your big blue eyes that you encouraged his aspirations. But there's Danny, your nominal escort, over there at the bar, trying to screw up his courage to claim you. This can only lead to catastrophe, Miss Scarlett."

"What's your name?" she asked in a new tone of voice.

"Dave Hyer."

"If you're so superior to everybody, why are you here?"

"I'm in politics. If your aunt invites me to a party, I go."

"What do you do?"

"Work for Governor Newfield."

"Would you like to avert the duel by taking me home?"

The young man shook his head. "I don't want to take you

home," he said, and as something sank inside her, he added, "But I'd like to take you to Printers Alley for a drink."

They went to a place called the Carousel where Chet Atkins was playing guitar. They sipped stingers and talked about the theater. He asked good questions and he had read an amazing number of plays for a lawyer. He got a little high and on the drive back to her aunt's house he recited for her, long passages from *Cyrano* and *Hamlet* and *Long Day's Journey*. He was sweet and funny and at the door, when he'd begun an elaborate goodnight-Miss-Scarlett routine, she'd leaned forward to kiss him once lightly on the lips.

The next night he took her to Fisk University, where the film club was showing some Chaplin one-reelers (they were the only white people there) and after that she saw him almost every night. He took her out of the country club crowd and introduced her to Nashville in all its variety. She met politicians, young lawyers like Dave who held office or planned to soon. She met reporters from the *Herald*, and the intellectual crowd that centered about Vanderbilt, and the black militants at Fisk and A&I. Dave had friends in the local music world, songwriters and musicians, and some nights they'd end up in a bar listening to jazz or to country music. One Saturday night he took her backstage at the Grand Ole Opry.

The spring became the long Tennessee summer and Eleanor was happier than she had been in years. After a month she was sleeping with Dave; after two months she thought she loved him; after three months they were married—at the Governor's Mansion, with Barney Newfield as Best Man.

Eleanor's marriage shocked her friends in New York, as indeed it shocked Eleanor at times. She might have married any of a dozen well-known men in Manhattan, instead of a young, penniless Tennessee lawyer. But Eleanor had faith in her instincts, and they told her that Dave offered her a rare combination of qualities, a goodness that she wanted and a toughness that she needed, and in those first years of their marriage, before Washington, she had never regretted her decision. In those days, they had thought of themselves as lucky people. Other couples suffered endless calamities—balky children, falling stocks, kitchen fires, frustrating jobs—but things always broke right for Dave and Eleanor. Perhaps that was one reason she was so bitter now —because it had been so good before. She had not even missed acting. Once, in the first year of their marriage, she went to New York for a television role, but the work bored her and the week seemed endless. The next year Sally was born, and she had no wish to resume acting after that. She had all she wanted with her husband and her child.

It helped that Dave was physically attractive, handsome in a lean, boyish way—Eleanor knew men's faces, and his would age well; he would be more handsome at fifty than he was at twenty-five—and of course he was wonderful in bed, gloriously uncomplicated, strong, anxious to please her. And how he had pleased her. Those first weeks they would go to his little cottage on an estate outside of town and play records and drink wine and make love all night, stopping a while to talk or doze, then making love again and again until the dawn, until she had lost all sense of time and place, until her body seemed a string of firecrackers exploding joyously in the sweet Tennessee night.

He had known many women. He told her once that college almost always bored him and women almost never bored him so he had spent most of his college years enjoying women in all their variety. He liked to tell of the time he was about to mount a reluctant hillbilly lass when she halted him with the prostestation, "But, Dave, if'n we do, yew'll catch it too." He had told her too of his riotous twenty-first birthday celebration in a Monterey whorehouse, a night he spent wandering about the girls' quarters drunk and naked and proudly erect, and the girls had cheered and fought for his services and called him "el joven toro"—the young bull. After that Eleanor would sometimes call him Toro and he would frown and love it, for he was so proud of his sexuality, was such a little boy about it, really. And sometimes Eleanor would smile and envy those Mexican whores for having known her Davey, her wonderful young bull, when he was twenty-one.

He was twenty-six when they married. He had no money beyond his $10,000 salary but there was no doubt in his mind, or anyone else's, that he was a man with a future. He told her that he'd probably stay with Governor Newfield two or three more years, then he'd enter private practice to make money, a lot of money, and then he'd run for office, probably for Congress. Eleanor wanted him to leave Newfield and be on his own, for she was not charmed by the governor. He was attractive, certainly, and he could be amusing, but he had an arrogance, a very sexual arrogance, that reminded her of certain Hollywood stars she'd met and not liked.

Eleanor knew that part of her attraction to Dave was that she'd be a useful politician's wife—a "Jackie type," as they said —and also that her aunt owned the state's leading newspaper. But she did not mind Dave's ambitions, she wanted him to have ambition enough for both of them. He had the killer instinct she lacked, a capacity for hate and a willingness to drive himself to achieve his goals. She had seen him go two or three nights without sleep, writing some speech for Newfield, more times than she could remember, and she had seen his fury at the railroads and the corporations when he thought they were vio- lating the public interest.

She knew his vanities and passions without knowing all that lay behind them. She had asked him once to tell her about his childhood and he had said, "Why should I talk about my past? I've escaped it," but a moment later he told her that was not true, that he had escaped his past and not escaped it, as a man may murder his enemy and still be haunted by his ghost. So he had told her his story, in bits and pieces over the years, when the mood was upon him.

He had told her a little about his father, Eugene Hyer; she knew that he was a handsome, slight, retiring man, "an intel- lectual by Texas standards," Dave said, who at seventeen had gone off to Texas A&M to study architecture. He had told her one long night about his father's experience at A&M, which then was famous, or infamous, for its hazing of freshmen. A senior, a football star, had taken a dislike to Dave's father, and had paddled him nightly, and on Thanksgiving night, after A&M had lost a football game with the University of Texas, the foot- ball player had gotten crazy drunk and taken Dave's father into his room and locked the door and beaten him until other stu- dents, alarmed by the screams, broke down the door and carried Dave's father to the hospital. Dave told her that many years later, when he was fifteen or so, his father had passed out naked one night and as Dave was struggling to get him into bed he saw the scars on his buttocks and his legs and back from that beating. After the beating, Eugene Hyer dropped out of college and began drinking heavily and instead of becoming an architect became a commercial artist, a talented one, Dave said, but unable because of his drinking ever to hold a job very long. Eugene Hyer was thirty when he married Dave's mother, who was twenty and a student at SMU; the marriage had lasted only three years, until one day when Dave was two and his father beat him in a drunken rage and his mother left Eugene Hyer and divorced him.

When Dave was four, his mother had remarried, to a man named Jerry Watkins, an accountant in the office where she'd worked as a secretary since her divorce. "I asked her once why she married Jerry," Dave had told Eleanor once, "and she said, 'He was the first one who asked me.' Actually, Jerry wasn't a bad guy. He was a country boy who liked to hunt and fish and watch the wrestling matches on TV and to shoot the shit with the fellows in the neighborhood tavern. The trouble was, he'd blow all his money on beer and fishing equipment, and then drop bad checks all over town—that was Jerry's little weakness. Not hot checks, which is forgery, just bad checks, where you write the check on money you don't have, then claim it was just a mistake. There was a time when I was twelve or so when he was out of work for several months and he had bad checks bouncing all over Dallas. There'd be three or four calls every evening from some outraged grocer or bartender, and Jerry naturally wouldn't be home to take them, so Mother and I would try to calm them down, and after a while we got tired of being yelled at so we quit answering calls, and we'd just sit there all night and listen to the phone ring."

Dave's mother had divorced the stepfather just after he'd graduated from high school and won a college scholarship; she'd assumed then that she could earn enough to support herself and Dave's half-sister. Dave had once described that scene to Eleanor: "He was out of a job again and we were broke and there was no food in the house and old Jerry comes waltzing in with a case of beer he'd scrounged somewhere. Well, that did it. Mother told him off and I told him off and he just stood there and took it and finally he started crying and said, 'I'm doing the best I can, Grace, honest to God, I'm doing the best I can.' Suddenly the whole horrible truth struck me—that Jerry *was* doing the best he could, and it just wasn't good enough. So she finally divorced him and I don't know what happened to him after that and I don't care."

She knew that he had no love for his hometown. A friend of his had told her of the night after John Kennedy was killed, when Dave had furiously blamed "those rich murdering Dallas sons of bitches" and continued to blame the city's reactionaries even after Oswald's arrest. Eleanor had seen his bitterness and his anguish four years later when the news came that his half-sister's husband had been killed in Vietnam, but by then his hate was directed at more than just one city. Marsha had married Billy Reese, a skinny, towheaded boy who wanted to be a schoolteacher but decided to get the Army out of the way first, so he'd have the GI Bill to help him through college. Two weeks before the end of his year in Vietnam he'd been killed. The news had come at night and there'd been no flight to Dallas until the next morning. After he'd called Sharon and said what he could, Dave got drunk and beat his fist against the wall until it bled and cursed the generals and cursed Johnson and cursed the journalists and corporations and labor unions, cursed everyone who had made the war and supported the war, cursed everyone who he thought had helped kill his kid sister's husband. "She had a chance to be happy," he had cried, "one lousy chance for a little happiness, and they killed him."

After the funeral he'd never mentioned Billy's death again. By then he was deeply involved in Newfield's quest for the presidential nomination—for that was what they'd aimed for: a darkhorse nomination from a deadlocked convention, and even after Milton Osgood got the nomination, they viewed the vice-presidency as a steppingstone. "Milton Osgood may be the greatest statesman in America," Dave had said, "but he ain't the greatest physical specimen." But Eleanor knew the passions she'd seen the night of Billy's death were still there, simmering beneath the mask he showed the world.

She knew how Dave loved power, loved its excitement and

challenge and dangers, and she was never quite sure which he loved more, the power or the good he could do with it.

These were things Eleanor knew about her husband, things she loved him for, things that made her sometimes fear him, but now in these months since Newfield became President, these months that had been so exhilarating to him and so painful to her, she found herself thinking less about Dave and his problems and more about her own. The move to Washington had been a hard one for her. Nashville was a woman's town, and Eleanor had been a star attraction there; but Washington was a man's town, and now Dave was a very important man, the balance between them was shifting, she was supposed to raise Sally and be a good soldier. The vice-presidency had been bad enough, but now their life together had completely fallen apart. In those first chaotic weeks he would stay at his office, sleeping there, three or four nights in a row; she couldn't even get through to him on the phone. Sally would cry herself to sleep at night asking where he was. Even the nights he came home early—by eight or nine—and played with Sally and ate a late dinner with her, and she hoped they might talk, just talk for a while, the phone would always ring, he'd be on it for hours talking to someone about some speech or some crisis, and Eleanor would sit and listen, wanting to shout "What about me? Why can't you talk to me?" but not shouting, only sitting there hurt and helpless until anger and self-pity became a dull pain inside her. One night when he talked for an hour while their dinner grew cold, she left the house and walked the dark streets of their suburb aimlessly, fighting back tears, but soon she became frightened and returned quietly home—and he was still on the phone and had not even missed her.

She had tried to be the good soldier. She had tried and tried, thinking it would end soon, thinking he could not keep on at this pace, but it did not end, and it was she who could not stand the pace, night after night, week after week, of never seeing him, never having any time together. Three times he had promised her he would take a week off and they would go to the Caribbean, and all three times some crisis had forced him to cancel the trip—it would have been a joke, it they still had jokes between them.

Eleanor was hurt, she was lonely, she was angry, and she had found one way to give back some of the pain he was causing her. It was obvious enough. He wanted only one thing from her these days and she would deny him that. Not deny him entirely, for that would have been too final, would have made reconciliation impossible, would have lessened the pain by ending the uncertainty. No, she would yield to him now and then, but more often she would shake off his hand, protest that she was sick, or sleepy, put him off in any of a score of ways. What could he do? Force himself on her? He'd done that once, but it had been a victory for her. No, he could only protest, and there'd been angry scenes, many of them, but more and more he ignored her, worked late in his study until long after she was asleep. But she knew he was hurt. She knew Dave's vanities and she knew he raged inside when she rejected him. But she did not care—she would not care. Let him suffer as she was suffering. If he would not be a husband, why should she be a wife?

Damn him, damn him, damn him!

Eleanor began to cry. It was all so wrong, so unfair. She didn't want to be a bitch; all she asked was to be loved. She knew she was right—he *admitted* she was right—yet still he said he could not do otherwise. Eleanor wanted security, she wanted laughter, most of all she wanted love, a man's love, arms to hold her, lips to kiss and flatter her. She thought she deserved that.

The phone rang and Eleanor jumped up to answer it, thinking Dave might have returned early from his trip.

"Mrs. Hyer?"

"Yes?"

"This is Mike Bates. We met at dinner Friday."

After a moment she remembered. When she had dinner with Walt, her director friend, there had been several others in the party, among them a tall, deeply tanned man of about forty, a writer named Bates. She recalled that he'd made a few witty, cynical remarks at dinner, but otherwise maintained an aloof silence.

"Yes, you're writing the script," she said.

"Trying to. Listen, we've got a bitch of a problem. The girl playing the President's wife has run off with some Swede. We're in a jam, and Walt wondered if you would consider taking the part."

"Mike, I haven't acted in years."

"I've seen you act, Mrs. Hyer . . ."

"Eleanor."

"Eleanor. I've seen you act, and this part would be a piece of cake for you. And it really might be fun."

"I have a daughter to take care of," she protested.

"All the shooting would be here in Washington, and your part could be wrapped up in two weeks. And Walt can pay for a lot of babysitters."

The idea of the money appealed to her—to have some money of her own again, to have the independence it could bring.

"I'd have to talk to my husband," she said. She wondered if Dave would think they were trying to use her to exploit him somehow—Dave thought of things like that. "He's away for a few days."

"Great—talk to him. But let's have lunch first and I'll show you the script."

"All right."

"Tomorrow?"

"Tomorrow will be fine," Eleanor said.

3

"How strong is Rivera?" Dave asked, as the jeep moved slowly through the quiet streets of Johnstown, just after dawn.

Huffaker shifted gears expertly as they rounded a corner near the marketplace. He was wearing starched khakis with no insignia, and he carried a pistol in a holster on his belt. "Strong enough that the ROC army won't go in the mountains after him," he replied. "But not strong enough to take Johnstown. If he had fifty more men, he could. The government's that shaky."

"I thought he could recruit all the men he needed," Dave said.

"I mean fighting men," Huffaker said. "He's training an army up there. He's got twenty-five men he's taught to shoot, to ambush, to march twenty miles a day. They're tough customers, VC-tough. If he had fifty more like them, that'd be all she wrote."

"How many are Cuban?" Dave asked.

Huffaker glanced over at Dave, his rough face softened by the morning light. "Four or five," he said.

They passed the shanties at the edge of the city and soon the highway pointed due west toward the blue wall of the mountains. For the first few miles the highway passed small farms, with goats and chickens and pigs outside the shacks, then it began to slant upward into the lusher lands of the foothills, through banana plantations, the great American-owned plantations that brought Caravelas much of its income. Now and then, as the jeep whizzed along the highway at fifty miles an hour, another car or truck appeared; one stayed behind them for five miles before turning off.

"How do you know we're not being followed?" Dave asked.

"Trust me," said Huffaker, "trust me."

That summed it up—Dave settled back and asked no more
questions. He could trust Huffaker or not, see Rivera or not.
He had plenty of doubts about this rendezvous, but he did
not see how he could refuse. Part of his job was to gather
information for Barney, and a talk with Rivera might be a
goldmine.

The morning was hot and humid. By eight o'clock, when they
turned off the highway onto a dirt road that twisted up into
the mountains, Dave's khaki shirt was soaked with sweat. The
jeep jogged hard, mile after rugged mile, until dust from the
narrow road coated their faces. Palm trees arched over them
and thick foliage scraped against the sides of the jeep: once,
atop a palm tree, Dave saw a bright red and yellow bird,
some sort of parrot.

They were several thousand feet above sea level now and
when the road skirted the mountain's edge for a moment Dave
could see a long green valley and the shimmering line of the
river that ran through it, and at a bend in the river, the
thatched huts of a fishing village. Then the dirt road cut back
under the palms and became only a grassy trail bounding up the
mountainside. Dave's back was sore from the jolting ride and he
was thirsty.

Suddenly the jeep headed straight into the jungle. Dave
ducked, leaves and branches slapped against the windshield,
and they stopped in the shadows of a small cave. It was nine
o'clock.

"We'll walk the rest of the way," Huffaker said. He led Dave
out of the cave. A bearded man in fatigues was standing atop
a large rock, a rifle cradled in his arms. Huffaker called to him
in Spanish and the man nodded.

Huffaker plunged into the jungle and Dave followed. At first
he thought they were zigzagging aimlessly, then he realized an
almost invisible trail had been cut so a man who knew the way
could walk rapidly up the mountainside. After a quarter-mile
Dave was breathing hard, and they stopped at a mountain
stream. Huffaker cupped his hands and drank, and Dave did
the same. The water was clear and icy cold. Dave heard a
bird call nearby, a high-pitched coo-ah, coo-ah, and as he stood

up he saw a short, dark-skinned man in a beret disappear behind a tree.

"Another sentry?" he asked.

Huffaker nodded. "Ready to push on?"

"Sure," Dave said, wondering how much farther they would climb. But he did not ask, only followed Huffaker back into the jungle, up the invisible trail. Soon he was gasping again, his shirt was soaked in sweat, his arms covered with mosquito bites, and he could feel a blister starting on his heel. They scaled a twenty-foot cliff, then suddenly they were on level ground and Dave got his first look at Rivera's camp.

It was built into a narrow ledge halfway up the mountain. The foliage had been cleared but enough palm trees remained to conceal the camp from the air. The cleared-out space was perhaps fifty feet wide and thirty feet deep. At the rear, it ended in a rock wall where the mountain rose up sharply for a hundred feet. At the base of this wall of mountain, Dave saw the mouth of a cave, and a man with a rifle guarding it. To the right and left, a semicircle of dark green tents followed the edge of the jungle.

Huffaker pulled his Zippo from his pocket and lit a cigarette. "Wait here," he said, and walked toward the cave.

Dave saw the guard staring at him, so he turned and looked back at the valley. The river glistened in the morning sun, far below them, and he could see the distant thread of highway as it stretched east through the foothills back to the city and the sea.

He heard footsteps. Turning, he saw Huffaker emerge from the cave with a man he recognized as Rivera.

The guerrilla leader was a short, powerful man. He wore fatigues, heavy black boots, a red bandanna knotted around his neck, and a gun on his hip. His skin had been burned a deep brown by the sun and his black hair, thinning in front, was worn long so that it curled over his collar. He had a wide mouth, a large nose, deepset, suspicious eyes, and wore a full mustache. As Dave shook his hand he felt the vitality and he realized abruptly that Rivera reminded him of Barney—not in appearance, but in the electricity he gave off, the power, the certitude, the violence stirring beneath the surface.

"Welcome, Mr. Hyer," Rivera said in excellent English. His voice was both musical and precise, and irony flicked in and out of it like a lizard's tongue.

"I'm glad to meet you, Captain." For reasons Dave did not understand, Rivera's military rank was captain, and Huffaker had suggested he be addressed by that title.

"I hope your climb was not difficult," Rivera said.

"It was not easy," Dave replied. He spoke with the deliberate candor he would use throughout his talk with Rivera. He had learned early in his political career that it is easy to lie to fools but it is foolish to lie to one's equals.

"There are no mountains in your native Texas, I believe," Rivera said.

"No, my only experience in mountains was when I was in college, and worked two summers in the state of Idaho, near Canada."

"What sort of work?" Rivera asked. The three men were standing at the edge of the mountain, feeling the cool air blow in from the valley.

"A plant called the ribiscus produces a disease called blister rust that kills the white pine tree. Each summer the Forest Service hires students to kill the plant."

"Kill them how?" Rivera asked.

"In the mountains, we pulled them up by hand. In swampy areas, where they were extremely thick, we sprayed them with a chemical."

"And you enjoyed your summers in the mountains?"

Dave thought for a moment. He remembered icy swims in Priest Lake, a drunken weekend at the Priest River Logger's Celebration, a wild weekend in a motel with two nurses from Spokane. He remembered one of his tentmates who'd been killed by a falling tree during a forest fire. It all seemed very long ago.

"It was good for a summer or two," he said. "But like you, Captain, I considered the mountains only a stopover on my way to the city."

Rivera laughed and took Dave's arm. "Come, let's have some wine, then I'll show you my camp." He led the two Americans into the cave. Dave, the tallest of the three, had to duck his head for the first dozen feet, then the passage emerged into a large cavern. There was a long table with benches beside it, a fireplace in one corner, and sacks of food along the walls. The cavern was lit by kerosene lamps and two tunnels branched off at the rear of it. At the table a girl sat slicing dried meat. She had huge brown eyes and wore her hair in a knot behind her head. She was about twenty and wearing fatigues like the others. Dave wondered whose woman she was.

"Elda," said Rivera, "this is Señor Hyer, an American." The girl glanced up, then returned to cutting the meat.

"Elda, Señor Hyer is our guest. Bring us some wine."

The girl brought a bottle of wine and three clay cups, then returned to her work. Rivera poured.

"Your health," he said, lifting his cup.

"And yours," Dave said. It was a light white wine, dry and very cold. Dave felt better after he drank it, but he was still hungry, for he had eaten only two doughnuts for breakfast. The girl was making some sort of stew.

"Come, now we'll continue our tour," Rivera said when they finished the wine.

Outside, the guard was sitting on a rock reading a paperback book. Rivera snapped his fingers and he scrambled to attention. He was only a boy, not over eighteen, with a scraggly beard making little progress on his chin.

"This is Arturo," Rivera said. "He is a great fighter and also a great lover." He repeated the words "fighter" and "lover" in Spanish and the boy blushed, still standing stiffly at attention.

"We have Arturo to thank for that wine," Rivera continued.

"How is that?" Dave asked.

"A major in the junta army made him a present of it," Rivera said, and repeated the phrase in Spanish, and he and the boy laughed. Rivera cuffed the boy lightly on the cheek and they walked on.

"We were caught in an ambush," Rivera said, "and Arturo slipped around to the rear and killed three of them to relieve us."

They entered the jungle and followed a trail for fifty feet until they came to a place where a small stream had been dammed with rocks to make a pond. Three men were bathing naked in the pond. They looked odd, naked men with beards, pale bodies and sun-baked arms and faces, splashing about in the water beneath the thick palms. One had a long red scar on his upper leg. Rivera called to them, introducing Dave; the men waved and returned to their swim. Another man who had been sitting on the bank repairing a boot came over for an introduction.

"*Un Norteamericano?*" he asked Rivera.

"*Sí. Un amigo del Presidente de los Estados Unidos.*" The man shrugged and returned to his boot.

They toured the tents at the edge of the clearing, and Dave saw another dozen men. Four of the guerrillas were playing cards in one tent, and in another a man was repairing a radio transmitter.

Dave could see no pattern to the guerrillas. In age, they ranged from late teens to late thirties. Some looked like peasants; other, with their pipes and eyeglasses, might have been professors on a hunting trip. Some appeared good-natured enough; others had the cold-eyed look of professional killers. Dave wished he knew all their stories, knew what had brought them to these mountains.

This tour was something Dave understood. He was on display. Morale must be a great problem for Rivera and now he had the President's friend as proof of how close they were to victory. He had been on similar tours in the U.S. when some state chairman or county chairman's troops needed encouragement. It was part of the political game. Still, he did not like the display. There was too much chance that one of these men would desert or be captured and talk about the American he had seen. But that was a risk he had to run.

"Here," Rivera said, ducking into the last tent, "we'll see if our gypsy is at home." He emerged with a bright-eyed, olive-skinned man of thirty or so who wore a red bandanna like Rivera's knotted around his neck.

"This is Alonzo," Rivera said. "He is a superior cook and a superior musician, but a soldier of dubious merit. He is on kitchen duty for the rest of the month for having slept on guard duty." Alonzo caught the word "slept" and lowered his eyes. Then, when Rivera looked away, he winked at Dave.

"Show us your friend," Rivera said, and the gypsy re-entered the tent to emerge leading a monkey on a piece of cord. The monkey chattered shrilly.

"What is his name?" Dave asked. Rivera repeated the question and the gypsy replied in a torrent of Spanish.

"He says the monkey's name is Luis Molina," Rivera said, "and he is the true President of Caravelas and soon he will be installed in the presidential palace in the place of the impostor who is using his name."

Rivera waved the gypsy back into his tent and they started toward the cave. "You see how the revolution advances, Mr. Hyer," he said. "Six months ago we would have eaten that monkey. Today we start a zoo with him."

Dave recognized in Rivera the proud, expansive mood that often overcame Barney after a good day on the hustings.

"You had a food problem six months ago, Captain?"

"Six months ago we ate monkeys, parrots, two horses, and ten pounds of lard. You have tried lard soup, Mr. Hyer?"

"No," Dave said.

"Don't," Rivera advised. "Not even a capitalist should eat lard soup."

They passed Arturo, who was still reading his paperback—a Spanish edition of Hemingway's stories—and once inside the cave Dave could smell the stew cooking. His mouth watered.

"Now we will eat," Rivera said. He poured more wine and the girl, Elda, brought them bowls of stew and a basket of dark bread. She joined the three men and they ate silently, in the Latin manner.

"Another bowl?" Rivera asked when they finished.

"I'll have one," Bob Huffaker said. "That climb gives me an appetite."

Rivera filled their glasses again and the girl served them more of the stew.

"The stew is very good," Dave said to the girl. She stared at him coldly and did not reply.

"The lady does not care for me," he said to Rivera.

"She does not know you," Rivera said. "Tell us about you. You are from Texas, I understand, where everyone is rich with oil."

"Not everyone," Dave said.

"And you became a lawyer?"

"Like yourself, Captain."

"Why did you choose to be a lawyer?"

"My country is run by lawyers. Isn't that why you became one?"

Rivera shook his head. "No, my country is run by soldiers. After I was a lawyer I realized that and became a soldier. But more about you. You have worked for Mr. Newfield—how long?"

"Four years as governor. Nine months as Vice-President. Six months now during his presidency."

"But you were never in the military with him?" Rivera asked.

"No, that was before I knew him."

"He has men working for him now who served with him in the war, does he not?"

"Yes," Dave said. "Several."

Rivera nodded. "It is in battle that you learn if you can trust a man. There is nothing else like battle."

"Perhaps a hard-fought election is something like it," Dave said.

"No," said Rivera, "there is nothing like it."

"I wish you could meet President Newfield," Dave said. "You could be friends."

"Yes," the girl said suddenly, bitterly. "You can be fine friends if he does not send soldiers to kill us."

"Be silent, Elda," Rivera said.

But the girl sprang to her feet. "Why has he come here?" she cried. "Is he another spy? Another CIA agent? Another of the American butchers?" She broke into Spanish and threw her clay cup across the table, narrowly missing Dave, and rushed out of the cave. Rivera followed her.

"What's her problem?" Dave asked Huffaker.

"Her brother was captured and died under questioning."

"So why throw things at me? Her own countrymen killed him, didn't they?"

"Americans were present," Huffaker said.

Rivera returned. "Excuse me," he said. "The girl is upset.

Now, Mr. Hyer, you were telling us why you became a lawyer.
Was your father also a lawyer?"

"No."

"What did he do?" Rivera asked.

"He drank, mostly," Dave said.

Rivera gave a slight shrug. "A reasonable pastime."

"No," Dave said, "it was not reasonable. It was most un-
reasonable. But my father is not relevant to your revolution."

"Perhaps he is," Rivera said. "He has produced a most intelligent son, who now will return to the United States and give
its President good advice."

"I will tell the President what I think are his best interests."

"I understand you have already spoken on my behalf in the
highest councils of your government."

Dave was not pleased that Rivera knew about the NSC meeting but he was not surprised either. General Boswell had gone
back to the Pentagon and Drummond had gone back to the
CIA and they had talked to their people and the news would
spread. Presumably it had traveled from Rod Sinclair to Huffaker to Rivera.

"I told him I don't think it's in his interest to intervene here.
What happens to you is secondary."

"That is all we ask," Rivera said. "Your view is an enlightened
one."

"Many Americans share it."

"Not at a high level of government, it seems."

"Our government is changing," Dave said.

Rivera smiled but his gray eyes remained cool. "The question
is whether your government is changing fast enough to accom-
modate my plans."

Dave stared back at him. That was indeed the question.

Rivera offered the two Americans a cigar. Huffaker accepted,
lit Rivera's cigar, then his own. Rivera blew a smoke ring.

"You do not smoke?" he asked Dave.

"I did for several years, but I stopped."

"Why?"

"Cigarettes kill people."

"Many things kill people," Rivera said.

"Captain Rivera has another sort of smoking problem," Huffaker said, and Rivera laughed.

"What's that?"

"Marijuana grows wild in this area," Rivera said. "I returned one day to find half my men . . . what is your phrase, Colonel?"

"Turned on," Huffaker said. "Stoned."

"What did you do?" Dave asked.

"I ordered that the smoking of marijuana cease. Wine is permitted, but no marijuana or drugs."

"You enforce a strict morality," Dave said.

"The revolutionary is the highest level of the human species and he must adhere to the highest standards."

"You mentioned your plans," Dave said. "What are your plans, Captain?"

"To drive the present government from Caravelas and create a government of the people."

"And when can this be accomplished?"

"Soon. The junta sees the tide turning. The question is whether its leaders will flee or stay and fight."

"They've shown no signs of fleeing," Dave said.

"They're waiting to see what your government will do. They know they are lost without your intervention."

"And with it?"

"The revolution will triumph. If you intervene, it may take longer."

"What happens to Molina and his associates if you take power?"

Rivera puffed thoughtfully on his cigar. He was serious about the cigar, for it was a most excellent Cuban cigar. He rolled it horizontally across his mouth and he studied its ash carefully.

Finally he shrugged. "What happens to Molina is a small matter."

"He tells me you were schoolboys together."

"Yes," said Rivera. "I should have killed him then."

"And now you will correct your oversight?"

Rivera waved his hand impatiently. "Mr. Hyer, Molina has several million dollars—money your aid program sent to help my country—in European banks. If he lacks the good judgment to flee before I capture him, to kill him will be an act of mercy."

"I would advise against unnecessary bloodshed," Dave said.

"If it matters to your country, I could avoid unnecessary bloodshed," Rivera said. "It is something we can discuss."

Dave nodded. They were getting down to business now. It would hurt Barney if a leftist government took power here and began a "bloodbath" against its enemies.

Suddenly there was a scream, and a clamor of voices outside. Rivera jumped to his feet, his pistol in his hand, and was gone. Dave stood up, but Arturo, the young sentry, silently leveled his rifle at Dave's chest. Dave sat back down. Huffaker was still seated, puffing on his cigar. The shrieks continued outside, then Rivera reappeared and waved them out.

The gypsy's monkey was loose and the gypsy was halfway up a palm tree after him. The monkey had leaped down, thrown his arms around the gypsy's neck, and sunk his teeth into his ear. Now the gypsy was stalled halfway up the tree, and four or five of the guerrillas had gathered to cheer the monkey. Rivera called to them and one shimmied up the tree to knock the monkey off the gypsy's back.

"Perhaps you had better eat that monkey after all," Dave said.

"Perhaps we had better eat the gypsy," Rivera replied.

They walked back toward the cave.

"I believe we have serious matters to discuss, Captain," Dave said.

"Yes."

"Colonel Huffaker, would you excuse us?" Dave disliked pulling rank on Huffaker, but there were too many leaks in this business already. Huffaker nodded and sucked on the Cuban cigar.

"You wait here, Colonel," said Rivera. "I will take Mr. Hyer to a place where we can talk undisturbed."

He led Dave into the jungle, and up a steep, rocky trail. They climbed for five minutes before they emerged on a tiny ledge that overlooked the camp and the valley beyond. Rivera motioned for Dave to sit down, then he reached into a trickling mountain spring beside the ledge, and pulled forth a bottle of wine.

"I come here sometimes in the evenings to read and meditate," Rivera said.

Dave wondered if Rivera brought the girl Elda here with him. Rivera uncorked the bottle and took a swig. He handed it to Dave, who drank from it, then handed it back. Rivera relit his cigar.

"Now, Mr. Hyer," he said, "what can you do for me?"

"Perhaps nothing," Dave said. "As you know, my President must decide whether or not to intervene militarily against your revolution. There are many powerful forces urging him to do so. There are some of us who tell him it would be unwise. Perhaps the question is what you can do for us."

"All right, what can I do for you?"

"First, you should avoid any unnecessary actions that will arouse American opinion against you. At the moment, the vast majority of our people are unaware of you. Try to keep it that way, at least until you take power. Things like this embassy bombing build the pressures for intervention."

"The government bombed the embassy precisely for that reason. Why would I bomb your embassy?"

"All right, but there are other things. Atrocities. Violence against civilians. These things arouse our people."

"We commit no atrocities. The government burned the farms of peasants who supported us, then one of your newsmagazines said we burned them."

"But there has been terror by your men."

"Early in the revolution, selective terror was necessary to neutralize the peasantry. Now the need has passed and the terror is ended."

Rivera took another drink of the wine and passed the bottle to Dave.

"There is the very great question of U.S. investments, Captain. The fruit and mining companies with holdings here are politically powerful and are bitterly opposed to you. Perhaps you could take steps to neutralize them."

"How do you mean?"

"I doubt if you need my advice on politics, Captain. You have your political spokesmen. They could pass word to the U.S. corporations that you will deal fairly with them. Perhaps you can play the corporations off against each other. You'll find they're practical men, men who like to hedge their political bets. They may not like you, but if you look like a winner they'll talk to you."

Rivera puffed at his cigar but made no reply. Dave knew damn well Rivera would like to confiscate every dime's worth of American property in Caravelas. That was what he had to prevent. It was time to speak bluntly.

"This is extremely important, Captain. If President Newfield allows your movement to succeed, and your first official act is to nationalize U.S. investments here, the result could be very bad for President Newfield and very bad for you also."

Rivera gave him a hard look, but when he spoke his voice was soft and his words carefully chosen. "You may tell your President that if he does not intervene against me militarily, I will guarantee U.S. investments in Caravelas for the duration of his presidency."

Dave was impressed by the audacity of the offer—and he thought it unwise to linger on it, better to push on to other matters.

"I will tell him that, Captain. And I must raise one other important question. There is concern in our government that if you take power, Caravelas will become a base for revolution throughout the continent."

Rivera shook his head slowly and took a final drink from the wine bottle. He was sitting with his back against the mountain, his legs extended straight out to the edge of the cliff. He gazed out across the valley as he answered.

"The Continental Revolution will move forward regardless of what happens in Caravelas."

"It has been said that you dream of leading a continental army," Dave said.

"That is not true. I dream of bringing a better life to the people of my country, as your President dreams of bringing a better life to his countrymen. My concern is Caravelas. Other men will lead the revolutions in Guatemala, in Bolivia, in Brazil, and elsewhere."

"But you are now the most famous revolutionary on the continent," David said.

"No one man matters. Men do not give up their comfort, their children, their lives, because of a leader, only because of an irrevocable belief in a cause."

"And you believe the cause is irresistible, despite all the setbacks?"

"Yes, because the human spirit is irresistible. Because we live in an era of internationalism—you yourself share that spirit, or you would not be here—and the triumph of the worldwide revolution is inevitable."

"And it must come through violence?"

"That is the only way."

"You do not regret the violence?"

"Life is violent. Luis Molina practices the violence that represses; I practice the violence that releases. Each man must choose between us."

"And yet you say you do not intend to lead revolutions elsewhere?"

"To fight in Bolivia, in Laos, in Guatemala, in Vietnam—each would be an honor. But there are other men to lead the revolutions there. My duty is here. You may tell your President that once I have taken power, the domestic affairs of my country will be my concern. I will seek no hostility with your country. You have the means to assure yourselves that we are not, as you say, 'exporting revolution.'"

It was a crucial point, and Dave searched Rivera's face for some hint of his true intent. He saw only the cool, slightly mocking gaze of a most capable politician. Dave had seen that look often before on courthouse politicians in Tennessee, on suave bureaucrats in Washington. Yet he was aware of a new, chilling dimension to these negotiations. Other men settled their disputes at the ballot box or around a conference table, but Rivera was playing the politics of revolution. Dave kept in mind that, however, much he might sympathize with Rivera, he was a man who would, literally, cut his throat if that would suit his ends.

"If you mean what you say, Captain, it will be of great interest to my President."

"What I say, I mean," Rivera said. "If you wish to serve your President well, you will tell him not to oppose the Continental

Revolution. No power on earth, not even your Pentagon, can halt it."

"There will be two, three . . ." Dave began.

"Yes," Rivera said, raising his fist to the sky. "Two, three, many more. Many, many more."

On the plane back that night, Dave thought hard about what Rivera had said. The basic question was whether he could be trusted. Would he do as he had said? Would he leave U.S. investments alone? Would he stay out of neighboring countries? If so, perhaps Barney could take the risk of staying out of Caravelas.

Certainly he could be lying. He thought he was on the brink of victory and he would promise anything to keep the U.S. from intervening against him. Yet it was Dave's instinct to believe Rivera—and that was all you had in politics, your instincts, your feel for people and situations—to think Rivera was shrewd enough to seek accommodation with the U.S.

But was he right? Or was he letting his own views on Latin America color his judgment on Rivera? He tried to be objective, for it was his job to give good advice to Barney Newfield, not to do favors for Alberto Rivera. He felt strongly about Latin America. He believed that U.S. policy there, stripped of all the pretty phrases about Good Neighbors and Alliances for Progress, had for decades been a policy of exploitation. The American fruit companies and oil companies and mining companies made vast profits there—made them out of the sweat of the peasants and the wealth of the soil—and they took their profits back to the U.S., where they could buy influence in Congress and the press and could pressure the U. S. Government to support further exploitation. The government supported every tin-horn dictator who would suppress his own people, and if popular movements arose against the dictators we would send the money, the Marines, or the intelligence agents needed to eliminate them. We had engineered coups, rigged elections, supplied arms, trained armies, sponsored invasions, all in the sacred name of anti-communism, and in the sacred interests of capitalism.

Dave was not pro-Communist. He knew he enjoyed a political and intellectual freedom in America he could enjoy in no

Communist country, and he was far too selfish to reject a system that had treated him so extraordinarily well. Yet he was not convinced the American political and economic system could work in less developed nations, and he suspected that some sort of socialism might be better suited to their needs. It seemed to him self-apparent that the vast majority of Cubans were better off under Castro than they had been under Batista. Yet to voice that opinion in an America conditioned by a quarter-century of ceaseless anti-communism was political suicide.

Or was it? Or had Vietnam been the turning point? Had the people finally seen down what bloody paths the super-patriots would lead them? Had they come to understand the limits of American influence? Could not Barney Newfield be the man to guide the nation to a wiser, more restrained foreign policy? Dave thought so, and so did others, and they believed Caravelas would be the first, perhaps the crucial test.

So the issue came back to Rivera. To trust him was dangerous. It was far less of a risk to send in troops and crush him. But if that precedent was set, where would it end? If national policy was ever to be brought around, someone would have to take some risks. And Dave's judgment was that Rivera was an acceptable risk for Barney to take.

Dave wished his nation would press for social reform in Latin America but he did not believe that would happen. Rivera was right—revolution was the only way, and revolution would come in country after country. It sometimes seemed to Dave that the truly important events of his time, the ones that would be remembered a hundred or two hundred years in the future, were not taking place in Washington or London or Moscow, but in the jungles and mountainsides of Southeast Asia and the Congo and Caravelas, and that men like Castro and Mao and Rivera were the ones history would care about.

That was one reason he had agreed to this meeting with Rivera. He wanted to meet the man, and he was glad that he had. The accidents of politics and geography had made them adversaries, even enemies. Yet Dave believed they were men who shared the same passions, the same dreams. This was something Dave did not expect men like Charlton MacKenzie or Warren Cutliff to understand—he was not sure if Barney would understand it—but he and Rivera were of the same generation. They shared, as Rivera had said, a new spirit of internationalism that was sweeping the world. Dave recalled the day in the fall of 1967 when he had been in Washington on business and had joined the huge march on the Pentagon to protest Vietnam. There he had seen young Americans cursing the name of a President of the United States and bearing aloft photographs of Che Guevara, whom their government's agents had captured and killed only weeks before. He had attended that march only by accident and yet it had been a turning point in his political transmigration. He was by nature a loner, yet there among that vast army of the night, marching triumphantly across the Memorial Bridge toward the Pentagon, not knowing what dangers might lie ahead, half-hoping for the worst, he had felt a sense of belonging to something bigger and better than himself, had sensed in the anti-war movement the beginnings of a better America.

It was not a feeling easily communicated. The next Monday morning Dave had been in the White House talking to a most pleasant young man who had laughed and said, "Did you see the picture of those kids putting the flowers in the soldiers' gun barrels? My God, what are they trying to prove?" Dave knew what the kids had been trying to prove but he did not try to explain it to the pleasant young man, although he wondered if the young man perhaps understood it four months later when his boss quit politics.

Dave had been radicalized not by theories but by events. He had been radicalized by Vietnam and by the death of a boy he knew there and by the insanity of the generals and by the inability of the best people in America to stop the insanity for so very long. He had been radicalized by the bloodbath in Chicago. If the people who produced Vietnam and Chicago were liberals, then liberalism was no longer enough. He had been radicalized and yet he was past the point in life where he might change his style. He had spent a decade learning to work inside the American political system, and in recent years he had come to regard himself as a kind of spy within the enemy camp.

All this was part of Dave's feeling for Rivera. He viewed

the rebel leader with the respect the armchair liberal must always accord those reformers who put their lives on the line. He remembered in the movie *Viva Zapata* when the revolutionary Zapata was killed by the government soldiers his white horse escaped to the mountains, and the peasants told one another that as long as Zapata's horse ran free their dream of freedom lived. Dave thought all men needed some symbol of their dreams, some white horse to race through the lonely mountains of their souls, and he found Rivera assuming that symbolic role in his own thoughts. He knew the very real limits to what he could do to help the guerrilla leader, for his first and greatest obligation was to Barney Newfield, right or wrong. Still, Dave gave Rivera a low cheer in the privacy of his mind; he accorded him the respect he granted few men in the world; he tipped his spirit's hat to him and wished him well.

4

Barney Newfield had a dream, and as President he intended to make his dream come true.

He dreamed of building cities. Already he could see them in his imagination, could see their shining towers, their winding streets and freshly painted houses, their new schools and hospitals, their lush green parks filled with laughing children. The dream possessed him; he wanted to do it all himself, draw the plans, drive the bulldozers, lay the bricks. Of course, he could not, so he was forced—sullenly, suspiciously, jealously—to delegate to other men the job of making his dream come true. It happened that the man to whom he delegated the most authority was David Hyer.

Dave guessed that some day historians would speculate on why this particular President at this particular time had put the resources of the U. S. Government behind mankind's age-old dream of new, perfect cities. Dave imagined the historians would study population figures, statistics on substandard housing, the record of slum riots in the Sixties, the political and financial results of the Vietnam truce, and would conclude that by the 1970s a massive home-building program was inevitable, that the passage of the New Cities Act was therefore a classic instance of an idea whose time had come.

They would, of course, be dead wrong.

The New Cities came about because of Barney Newfield's dream, and his dream came from within, not from without. Barney was strong and stubborn enough to have resisted the political pressures had he thought them wrong, but because he thought them right he used and shaped them to conform to his inner vision.

As far as Dave could see, the origins of Barney's dream

were to be found in his youth in Tennessee in the 1930s. Barney's one political hero was Franklin Roosevelt, and the Roosevelt achievement that meant most to him—could on occasion move him to tears—was the Tennessee Valley Authority. As a boy he had seen what TVA's dams and power plants had meant to his family and friends. As governor of Tennessee he had praised it, studied it, defended it. Now, as President, he was determined to equal, even to surpass, the great monument FDR had built to himself among the twisting rivers of the Tennessee Valley.

Dave's understanding of Barney was partial at best. A flash of sentiment or drunkenness or candor might illumine a motive here, a passion there, yet the whole of the man's character remained shrouded in mystery and ambiguity. People who thought Dave "understood" Barney were wrong—he had simply ceased to show surprise at Barney's contradictions. Still, from what he did know, he thought that Barney had entered politics less from a love of power than from a love of self, from a fierce desire to prove Barney Newfield was not just a big brawling girl-crazy soldier, was beneath his rugged exterior a good, even a great man. He had been a soldier, then a prosecuting attorney, and it infuriated him that some people felt that in his first career he had been a professional killer and in the second he had specialized in sending people to jail. He had felt the scorn of the liberal ladies, and it had lashed him on, until in time he could boast, unchallenged, that he had done more for the schools and prisons and hospitals of Tennessee than any other governor in its history.

Dave had watched as Barney, during the governorship, began his monument-building. Soon his name was inscribed on a half-dozen high schools, two hospitals, a six-lane highway, the state's biggest man-made lake, even a new wing at the state prison. At the same time, Dave had watched Barney's interest in national politics grow, along with his realization that the memorials available to a governor were not equal to his ever-widening vision of himself, his talents and his destiny.

The nine months of the vice-presidency had been agonizing for Barney—to be so close to such incredible power and yet so far from controlling it. So he drank a lot, he was moody and withdrawn, yet he was watching and learning too. Then, one day in the fall of that first year, an incident rekindled Barney's dream and gave it a more tangible shape than it had ever possessed before.

It began when President Osgood's appointments secretary, Leo Horgan, a tough New York politician who missed no opportunity to put the Vice-President in his place, called and told Barney he was to tour a new housing project in the Bronx. Some bright PR man at the National Committee had dreamed up a before-and-after tour, with the Vice-President visiting not only the new housing project but a nearby tenement such as it had replaced. Thus, one crisp fall morning a sullen, hungover Vice-President was led by an eager black bureaucrat deep into the bowels of a dark, crumbling tenement where the smell of urine hung in the air like fog, where garbage rotted in damp corners, where finally as he reached down to touch a naked child in a doorway a rat rushed out of the darkness, brushed against his pants leg, and bit the screaming child on the ankle. At that, Barney broke away from his guide, stumbled into the apartment, and vomited into a stinking toilet that wouldn't flush when he had finished.

That night, back in Washington, still grim and shaken, he talked to Dave far into the night, with a bottle of Scotch open on the desk between them, talked angrily of the misery and inequity of the slums—he said, in short, things he had said before in countless speeches, but this time he meant them because they were as real to him as the rat that had brushed his leg that morning.

"The only thing to do is burn the bastards down and start over," he whispered furiously at 3 A.M., when the bottle was empty, the city quiet. "This country is full of open land, plenty of room for people to have some air and trees. All we have to do is build the houses. Hell, it wouldn't be much to build a couple of million houses. If you'd seen the Channel on June 6th, seen those ships in the sea and planes in the sky as far as a man could see—if you'd seen that, you'd know this damn country can do anything. Anything!"

Throughout their talk, Dave kept agreeing, kept asking questions, kept fighting to keep Barney's enthusiasm alive. But it was the blind leading the blind, for neither of them knew much about home-building, much less city-building. The next morning Dave set out to find someone who did. He called around town until he had the name of a man who reputedly knew more about the New Cities concept than anyone in Washington. His name was Elias Abbot, he was an assistant to the Federal Housing Administrator, and by noon he was on his way to Dave's office.

Dave was momentarily startled when this housing expert appeared. Elias Abbot was a short, gnomelike Negro of about Dave's age. His eyes were close together and deepset, his nose was wide and prominent, his lips were thick and twisted downward in what seemed a perpetual scowl. There was an aura of hostility and arrogance in his features, in the slow, skeptical way he entered the room and looked Dave up and down without speaking. The half-dozen people who had mentioned Abbot to Dave that morning had all used two words to describe him. The first was brilliant; the second, abrasive. Dave knew the first word was accurate—he had checked and found that Elias Abbot, a scholarship student from the Newark slums, had led his classes at Choate, Yale, and Harvard Law. Now Dave wondered, as he extended his hand to his visitor, if the abrasiveness would render the brilliance useless.

"What can I do for you?" the young Negro asked, after Dave had waved him into a chair.

"You can tell me about the idea of building new cities," Dave said.

A faint smile crossed Elias Abbot's face. "How far back do you want to start?"

"How far back does it go?"

Elias shrugged. "They were building new towns in Europe in the fourteenth century. In this country, in the nineteenth century, places like Gary, Indiana, were new towns, built for workingmen. In World War I the government built some towns for shipyard workers. In the thirties Roosevelt built the Greenbelt communities. Take your pick."

"Start with Roosevelt," Dave said. "That's far enough back."

Elias began to outline the various New City proposals that had sprung up in America and Europe in recent years, and

Dave listened intently, breaking in with an occasional question. He was gathering information and he was also evaluating Elias Abbot. Many incompetent Negroes had been elevated to high government jobs in recent years, and if this was one of them, Dave wouldn't bother Barney with him.

It took only a few minutes. Elias Abbot knew everything there was to know about urban renewal, land acquisition, prefabrication, the politics of home-building, about the hundred other issues involved in the New Cities concept. In Dave's experience, about one government expert in twenty really knew his stuff—and Elias was one, superlatively so.

Dave learned something else about Elias during that first talk. He had a way of sitting motionless in his chair, his short legs barely reaching the floor, his small eyes fixed on your face, never blinking, never looking away, just staring at you with a cool, arrogant expression on his homely face, one most people found unnerving. Dave, for the first few minutes, found himself unconsciously seeking excuses—a pencil to fiddle with, a button to twist—to avoid that scoffing, unblinking stare. Yet it took only minutes for respect, and the beginnings of affection, to spring up between them, feelings based on the enthusiasm both men felt for the idea of the government building new cities. But Dave would see in the future how many men never got past that cold stare, the one Barney called Elias's "evil-eye."

After an hour, Dave buzzed Barney.

"Yeah?" came the gruff, tired voice.

"Mr. Vice-President, I have a man here who can answer a lot of the questions we were talking about last night."

"Bring him in."

Elias's looks took Barney aback, too, but after a few minutes he was won by the force of the young Negro's ideas. In the next two hours Barney Newfield's dream was born. Dave and Elias saw it born, saw the shining towers rise before Barney's eyes, saw his tired face glow with excitement at a vision of streets and parks and laughing children. When finally their talk ended, Newfield believed with all the passion within him that America must build new cities. At last he had found a monument equal to his ambition and his self-esteem.

"Okay," he said to Elias at the start, "tell me how this country can build cities."

"There are several ways," Elias said in his cool, precise voice. "Different groups have put forward four 'New Cities' plans in the past few years."

"I want to know about the real thing," Barney said. "New Cities—new from the ground up. New houses, new schools, new factories, a half million, maybe a million people."

"That's the most ambitious of the four proposals," Elias said, his eyes fixed unblinkingly on the Vice-President. "And also the most controversial. Perhaps I should outline the three other proposals first."

"Okay," Barney said. "Start outlining."

"First, there's what is called the 'New Towns in Town' plan. This is what the big-city mayors want, massive urban renewal and high-rise apartment construction, in existing slums."

"God damn," Barney said, "with people squeezed in like sardines already, you'd think the mayors would get them out of there."

Elias shook his head. "These are Democratic mayors, and when you start talking about moving thousands of their safest Democratic votes out to rural areas, they get very possessive about their disadvantaged brethren."

"First things first," Dave said.

"And it cuts the other way," Elias continued. "When you start talking to conservative governors, in the South and Midwest, about bringing tens of thousands of new people into their states —most of them probably black, poor and Democrats—they start having second thoughts."

"They should," Barney said. "If you had a surplus of Democrats in one state and a shortage in another, that'd be a sweet way to even things up."

"But the mayors' main concern," Elias said, "is that if New Cities are built, all the federal funds will go to them, and they'll be cut off."

"So if you wrote a New Cities bill you'd have to make a deal with the mayors," Barney said.

"Right," Elias replied. "You'd have to buy them off with money for a New Towns in Town program."

"What's the second plan?" Barney asked.

"Satellite cities. In effect, a ring of new suburbs, ten or twenty miles outside our big cities."

"How big?" Dave said.

Elias shrugged. "Twenty, thirty, maybe forty thousand each. The point would be that the satellite cities would be connected to the central city by rapid transit, so workers could commute to jobs there."

"Who's pushing this one?" Barney asked.

"No particular political support," Elias said. "But it makes a lot of sense. You'd get people out of the ghettos, yet keep them close to their friends and their jobs, and you'd be spared the problem of creating new jobs in rural areas."

"Dave, mix us all a drink," Barney said. "You'll take one won't you, fellow?" Elias said he would and when they all had a Scotch and water, he continued.

"The third proposal is for Regional Growth Centers. The idea is that you'd take existing communities of, say, fifty thousand people, and put new jobs and housing there, so they might expand to one hundred thousand. Let's say you make Wheeling, West Virginia, a Regional Growth Center. Then a miner who otherwise would leave West Virginia for Cleveland or Chicago, and end up on welfare, can go to Wheeling instead and find a job and housing."

"I guess this is the one the Southerners like best," Barney said.

"Right," Elias answered. "The Southerners and some Midwestern Republicans, because they figure it'd build up their small towns."

"If the federal government goes into small towns with thousands of new jobs and housing units," Dave said, "it'll turn them upside down socially and politically."

"It depends on your degree of federal control," Elias said. "That'll be your big fight if this ever gets to Congress. With tight federal control you could overturn job and housing and school discrimination in these smaller towns. With local control, you perpetuate them."

Barney finished his drink and poured himself another. He had been drinking hard these past months. But this session was going well—Barney seemed as excited as he had been about anything in a long time. Still, Dave wondered where it was leading. Barney might get excited about New Cities, but he was still Vice-President, and his enthusiasms did not count for much in Milton Osgood's administration.

"Okay," Barney said, "now let's hear about the real thing."

Elias nodded. "If you could build ten New Cities, for a million people each, in the next decade, you'd be doing something substantial about urban problems."

"Build them where?" Barney said.

"Politics would be one factor," Elias said. "So would weather. You'd surely want one in California. Another perhaps in New Jersey, to draw from New York City. One in the South, one in the Southwest, one in the Midwest, and so on."

"And they could have a million population?" Dave asked.

"A million total," Elias said. "But you'd divide them into semi-autonomous communities of fifty thousand or so, each with its own school system, local police, local government and so on, with greenbelts and industrial parks in between."

"How do you get business and industry to locate there?" Barney asked.

"Tax incentives would be one way. Or you could make defense contracts conditional on plants being located in the New Cities. You could locate new universities there and attract aerospace industry spinoffs."

"How do you get the guy in Harlem to move out to the boondocks? Maybe he likes it where he is."

"I'd suggest, Mr. Vice-President," Elias said dryly, "that getting people to move out of Harlem won't be hard. The problem will be getting middle-class whites to move to the New City, so you'll have racial and economic balance."

"Okay, how do you do that?"

"By convincing him this isn't some radical program for black people, but a good deal for him. Your white worker has got to think he can get a better job in the New City, his kids can go to better schools, even if they're integrated, and he can get a house there for thirty thousand dollars that would cost thirty-five if he bought it from Levitt."

"The racial thing is going to be tricky," Dave said.

"Sure it is," Elias shot back. "Southerners will want the New

Cities all-white and black militants will want them all-black. NAACP types will want you to stress housing for the middle-class Negro, and SCLC types will want to stress housing for poor Negroes. Urban politicians won't want to lose the black voters and rural politicians won't want to gain them."

"It could be worked out," Barney said. "With those semi-autonomous towns, you could have some all-black and some all-white and some mixed. There's room for manuever."

"I think that's true," Elias said.

"The real problem," Barney went on, "is gonna be the pressure to slice the pie thinner. You talk about ten New Cities. That's ten states that get one and forty states that don't. So they start pissing and moaning. They say instead of ten cities of a million each there ought to be a hundred cities of one hundred thousand each. And pretty soon they've got you whittled down to nothing."

"Except that you've got—" Elias began.

"Yeah," Barney broke in impatiently, "you've got the Regional Growth Centers and the Satellite Cities and the New Towns in Town to give everybody a piece of pie."

Barney slapped his fist into his palm. "God damn it," he said, "there's a bill here that can pass. You could build those cities— all you've got to do is put together the right package and sell it the right way."

They sat for a moment in silence while Barney contemplated the new world he had discovered. Dave finished his second Scotch and watched the pale afternoon light slant in from Barney's floor-to-ceiling windows. He wondered if they'd been wasting their breath that afternoon.

"Elias, you never said how much all this would cost," Dave said.

The young Negro laughed. "How much have you got?"

"I haven't got a fucking dime," Barney said. "But I know a guy who's loaded."

But the guy wasn't interested. They wrote President Osgood a long memo the next day about the New Cities idea. Then they waited. They waited a week, when the memo finally came back with *Interesting—why don't you talk to Don Duffey?* scribbled across the top. Duffey was Secretary of Housing and Urban Development (HUD) and he was not one of the administration's deep thinkers. So Dave and Barney and Elias Abbot (who was coming in each evening now to talk about the New Cities) fumed and cursed and plotted—and then one bright Sunday morning in October it was a new ball game.

The news came about noon, as Dave, Barney, and Brenda were sitting on Barney's terrace with the Sunday Washington *Post* and New York *Times* spread out around them, reading and talking and drinking Bloody Marys. The air was crisp and cool and the smell of burning leaves drifted in from the next yard. Brenda was reading the *Post*'s comics, Barney was reading the *Post*'s editorials, and Dave was reading the *Times Book Review*.

Brenda looked up from the comic strips with a question. "What ever happened to Barry Backwater?" she asked.

Barney frowned and sank deeper in his deck chair. But Dave enjoyed Brenda's banter—Dave enjoyed Brenda, for she was a happy, guileless, uncomplicated girl, and gorgeous besides. She looked wonderful, with her strawberry blond hair piled atop her head and her skin burned honey gold by a summer of tennis and swimming. Dave admired Brenda even when he was sober and he was not entirely sober now after two of Barney's Bloody Marys. But his admiration of Brenda was purely platonic; as Eddie Gooch said, you don't screw with the sheriff's girl.

"Backwater's pretty quiet these days," he said.

"What about the Trickster?" Brenda said. "Where's he now?"

"He's dropped out of sight," Dave said. "Practicing law."

"He couldn't drop out of sight with that nose," Brenda giggled.

"He was damn near President," Barney growled. He didn't like to hear politicians ridiculed, even the opposition, for it reminded him of what his enemies might be saying of him. "Hand me the pitcher, Dave."

Dave was reaching for the pitcher, enjoying the October sun on his face, debating whether to have another drink, when the phone rang on the table beside Barney's chair. Dave poured himself a drink and paid no attention to Barney's brief conversation. But when he leaned forward to hand Barney the pitcher he saw the strange look on his face. Dave was still leaning forward, the pitcher of blood-red drinks outstretched before him, when Barney spoke.

"Osgood's dead," he said. "A heart attack."

"Jesus Christ," Brenda cried.

"Son of a bitch," Dave whispered.

"Let's get busy," Barney ordered. "Brenda, fix some coffee. Dave, take down what I say. First, fire that bastard Horgan. Second, call an NSC meeting for three o'clock. Invite the congressional leaders. Third, find out what Brenda and me ought to do about the funeral and make damn sure we do it right. And fourth, get some people working on a New Cities bill. Keep it quiet. And damn it, think big!"

5

In midafternoon Dave rushed down the hall with a letter that needed to be signed and sent to the Hill fast. But when he tried the door to the President's office, it was locked.

"What's up?" he asked Mrs. Purvis, the President's secretary.

"He's dictating," she said. "Can't be bothered."

Dave glanced over and saw that Sharon Flatt was not at her desk. He shrugged and gave the letter to Mrs. Purvis to get signed when she could. He had been through these periods before when Barney gave dictation behind locked doors. Lovely, lovely, lovely, he thought. Newfield Rides Again.

An hour later, with Mrs. Gill busy and his other girl out sick, he returned to the President's office and, seeing Sharon idle at her desk, asked her to type a letter for him.

"Gee, I'm really sort of tired, Dave," she said. He had always been Mr. Hyer before. "Maybe one of the other girls could do it." He let it drop, having decided earlier it was poor policy to offend the Playmate of the Month. And Sharon did indeed look tired.

That evening Dave paused outside the President's bedroom when he heard voices within.

"Damn you, you'd better get rid of her."

"I don't know what you're talking about."

"I'm talking about Sharon Hot-pants, that little twit in your office."

"The kid from West Virginia? What about her?"

"What about her? You took her to Camp David the last three weekends, that's what about her."

"She's a good secretary."

"Ha! I know what she's a good, and it's not a secretary."

"God damn it, Brenda, if all the women in my office were eighty, you'd think I was laying one of them."

"If all the women in your office were eighty, you *would* be laying one of them, you son of a bitch."

"Come on, Brenda, I've got work to do. Go plant a tree."

"You listen to me. You get rid of that little slut. Make her an ambassador or something. If you don't, I'll come down there and throw her out myself."

"You come around my office causing trouble and I'll throw your ass out the window."

"That'd make a cute story. 'President Throws First Lady's Ass Out Window!' That'd swing the housewife vote."

"I'm warning you, Brenda."

"I'm warning you, buster."

Brenda's footsteps click-clacked across the floor, then the door to her bedroom slammed sharply.

Dave backed away from the door and returned to his office. He had noted Sharon Flatt's ascension to favor in recent weeks—she must have appropriated Eddie Gooch's credit card, because she was wearing a new dress every day—but he hadn't the time to worry about it.

After five minutes he returned to the President's suite. He had been reporting to Barney most evenings about this time on the progress of the New Cities bill. He knocked lightly on the door and Barney called to him to come in. He found the President in his shirtsleeves, sitting in a chair beside the window, reading the new *Time*.

"How's it going?" he asked. "SAU?"

"More or less," Dave said. "I talked to the man from the big home-builders today, and he warned me that the small home-builders are incompetent. Then I talked to the man from the small home-builders, and he warned me that the big home-builders are crooked."

"I believe 'em both. What other statesmen you talked to?"

Dave poured himself a drink and sat down opposite the President. He often started these sessions with some of the lighter episodes—Barney enjoyed them and it helped get him in a good mood.

"Well, there was a famous architect in yesterday with a plan for floating cities."

"*Floating* cities?"

"Right. You'd build these floating cities in the harbors off New York and Boston and Seattle."

"Get kind of cold in the winter, wouldn't it?"

"That's the thing. In the winter you'd tow them South."

"Beautiful," Barney said.

"And there's a lady from the DAR who wants to talk to you about the moral standards in the New Cities."

"Tell her to talk to my wife—she's interested in moral standards."

Dave switched to serious business. "I'm seeing Senator Cathcart again tomorrow."

"He still holding his ground?"

"He won't give an inch. He's got this idea about building villages, hundreds of villages, and he won't listen to anybody."

"Well, you listen to him then. He's chairman of the committee, and he's a good old fellow, so we'll just keep talking friendly to him. We've got time yet."

"Another thing," Dave said. "Elias wants me to meet with Roy Hailey and Elijah King about black control in the New Cities."

"Hailey's the white one, isn't he? The one that had his picture on the cover of this?" He waved the magazine.

"Right. And Elijah King is head of the CBA—the California Black Alliance."

"What do you think?" Barney asked.

"I think I ought to see them and stall them and try to keep them quiet. Elijah King can blow up California anytime he feels like it, and Hailey's got a network of radicals in a dozen cities who'd like nothing better than to sound off against the New Cities."

"What about this all-black business?"

"The way I see it, if each New City will have six or eight semi-autonomous communities, why not let the blacks run a few of them? It'll keep them out of trouble."

"We may have to," Barney said, "but we damn sure can't talk about it until after the bill passes."

"I understand that, but a few hints to Hailey and King might keep them quiet."

"Okay, talk to them. But on your own. I don't know anything about it. And not here in the White House. And don't make any promises. Okay, what else you got?"

"There's a lot of pressure building for you to name a permanent head of the New Cities." It was a touchy point, for in truth the President did not want any other man even nominally in charge of his New Cities.

"You and Elias are still holding things together, aren't you?"

"Mainly Elias. But he's got a hundred people over there now, and you need a top-level administrator. What I hope you'll do is make somebody like Sid Frankel your director and make Elias his deputy."

"He's awful young," Barney said.

"He's awful good."

"Yeah? What's this about him having a run-in with some Oklahoma congressmen?"

"I hadn't heard about it."

"Check it out. I heard he pissed off a bunch of them. The best thing is to keep him off the Hill. That damned evil eye he gives people is just gonna cause trouble. Okay?"

"Sure."

"Now, about the director. Who'd be your choice after Frankel?"

"Steve Vale," Dave said.

"What about Duffey?"

"Duffey's not on my list."

"Well, he's on mine, and I'll tell you why. Sid Frankel's great for HEW because he's a born bureaucrat. But Sid's a nearsighted little Jew with a stutter and I've got to have somebody dynamic to run the New Cities. Besides, Sid's got a problem."

Barney frowned and pulled at his gold cuff-links, the rectangular ones, shaped like Tennessee, the staff had given him when he was re-elected as governor. Dave thought for an instant of Tennessee, of the soft rolling hills west of Nashville, a rich green now in the first burst of summer, and he wished for an instant he was not here arguing about Sid Frankel and Donald Duffey.

"What problem?" he asked.

"Sid thinks he's smarter than me."

"Mr. President, I've never heard Sid say anything . . ."

"Hell, he probably is smarter than me. But I'm still chief honcho, and Sid stays at HEW."

"What's your objection to Steve Vale?"

"He's too radical. That doesn't matter as long as he's at Labor, because they're not doing anything anyway. But I can't have a radical running the New Cities. It's a radical program, so I need a conservative to run it."

"Which means?"

"Which means Duffey. Old Duff-the-Stuff. He's my man."

"He's a fraud and a hypocrite and a lightweight."

"He's also the greatest salesman I ever saw. Duffey could sell a rubber machine to the Vatican."

"But he hasn't got any sense, Mr. President," Dave insisted.

"So what? Duffey's my cheerleader. He'll go out and sell the New Cities like he's been selling HUD."

"I don't like it. This is a serious program and Duffey isn't a serious man."

"Look, kid. Who do you think is going to run this program? I'll tell you—me. Old Barney. That's the good thing about Duffey—he won't get in my way. Sure he's a silly shit, but he'll handle the PR and I'll run things. And you'll help me run it. And, yes, we'll put Elias over there as his deputy. That make you happy?"

"It's your decision, Mr. President." But the more Dave thought about it, the more he was pleased—he *would* have more power over the New Cities this way.

"Anything else on your mind?" Barney asked.

There was something else on Dave's mind—the war in Caravelas. When Dave had reported to the President on Rivera's promises to leave U.S. investments alone and not to stir up revolution in other countries—if the U.S. did not intervene against him—Barney had been interested but skeptical. Rivera's promises seemed vague and far away; domestic pressures were more real.

The bombing of the U.S. embassy in Caravelas, and the news stories that the Pentagon was pressing for U.S. intervention there, had finally put that small, troubled country on the map. There had been newspaper editorials, a few speeches in Congress, a group of students picketing the White House with signs saying KEEP OUT OF CARAVELAS. About a thousand letters had come in, with slightly more opposing intervention than demanding it. But Dave feared the most important development on Caravelas came when four corporation presidents called separately on the President that week. Each of the four corporations had extensive holdings in Latin America. Dave checked and discovered that the appointments had been arranged by the Secretary of State, Charlton MacKenzie.

"Yes, there's something else on my mind," he said. "I wondered if you've thought any more about Caravelas."

Barney frowned, as if the subject was distasteful to him.

"I may have to send some men down there," he said.

"What do you mean?"

"Fifty or a hundred advisers, to train their stinking army for them."

"The Caravelian army can't be trained in time to do anything. But if you send advisers, and they get fired on, the Pentagon will be screaming for combat units. The advisers are just bait for the trap."

"I've got congressmen telling me they won't vote for the New Cities unless I stop Rivera."

"They're bluffing," Dave said.

"Prove it."

"I can't prove it, but I think we can pass the bill without being blackmailed."

"Look, all I mean to do is send the men down there, then pull them out as soon as this cools off."

"But will it be that easy to pull them out?"

"You got a better idea?"

"I think there are plenty of possibilities of dealing with Rivera. Maybe he'd agree to lie low until after the bill passes."

"I can't trust Rivera," Barney said.

"Well you can't trust a bunch of corporation presidents and reactionary congressmen to make your foreign policy either."

"I'm making my foreign policy," Barney snapped. "Not corporation presidents. And not you, either."

Dave had pushed too far, a mistake he rarely made. "Okay," he said. "But I feel strongly about this thing. The people who want you to intervene in Caravelas are thinking about their interests, not yours."

"Most people are," Barney said.

Dave left a moment later, with several matters on his mind. He was concerned that he had annoyed Barney on the Caravelas issue, and wondering if he would have to go easy for a while. At the same time, he was wondering if there was still a way to persuade Barney to stay out of Caravelas. Finally, he wondered if Brenda would really try to run Sharon Flatt out of Barney's office and, if so, if Barney would make good his threat to toss her ass out the window.

Elias Abbot was waiting in Dave's office, sprawled across the sofa, studying Department of Labor reports. They met most evenings to talk about the day's progress on the New Cities. Outsiders would never know the impact the young Negro had had on shaping the New Cities. The President gave the program two hours a day, Dave gave it four, but Elias was on the scene sixteen hours a day, seven days a week, and his thinking permeated the program, from architecture to zoning laws, from pre-school programs to plans for community government.

Dave did not begrudge Elias his power. He had learned that their thinking on the New Cities was as nearly alike as two men's could be. They saw the same goals as desirable, the same means as necessary, the same men as wise or foolish; it was a rare affinity and Dave intended to make the most of it.

"How goes it?" Elias greeted him. "SAU?"

"Yeah," Dave said. "Maybe a little more S than U."

Dave poured himself a stiff Scotch, as he generally did around this time each evening. The drink was less an intoxicant than a form of energy. After ten hours of work your nerves became taut, your thoughts began to slip, and a couple of drinks relaxed you, focused your mind, helped you push on an extra two or three hours. You paid for it with the headaches each morning and with the roll of fat around your middle, but you got what you wanted and you expected to pay for it.

"What's up?" Elias asked, sitting up, a gnomelike man in a rumpled shirt.

"Item one. Donald Duffey to be New Cities Director."

Elias's eyes widened. "You're kidding," he said. It was the first time Dave had ever seen him show surprise.

"I'm serious," Dave said. "The President wants a salesman."

"He'll get one," Elias replied. "But who runs the program?"

"That's item two," Dave said. "The President told me he'd make you Duffey's deputy."

A smile spread across Elias's face. "Well, now," he said, "that *is* a statesmanlike decision."

"It means we can keep on top of this thing," Dave told him. "It also means we've got to bend over backward to get along with Duffey."

"I'll throw rose petals at the silly bastard every morning," Elias said.

"Say, what's this I heard about you having a run-in with some Oklahoma congressmen?"

Elias frowned. "I couldn't promise them that we'd use that closed-down air base of theirs for a New City site, and they didn't like it. Matter of fact, I don't think they liked me either."

"I think it'd be best if you stayed off the Hill from now on," Dave said. "Let Duffey be the salesman and you mind the store."

Elias nodded, and a moment later there was a knock at the door and O. B. Perkins looked in.

"You got a minute, Dave?" he asked.

"For you, Mr. Press Secretary, two minutes," Dave said.

"I'll get back to the office," Elias said, rising to his feet.

"Nah, you ought to hear this," O.B. said, jerking his thumb in Elias's direction. "Listen, I've been up on the Hill this afternoon, and I've been hearing a lot of feedback about this idea of sending two-year-olds to nursery classes in the New Cities. Taking a two-year-old out of his home sounds like a commune or the Nazi youth or something to a lot of people."

"What age do our congressional friends suggest?" Dave asked.

"Hell, four of five, something reasonable. Not *two*, for Christ's sake."

"The thing is, Mr. Perkins," Elias said in his softest voice, "these congressmen are thinking about the kinds of homes they know. This program is designed for kids whose homes don't have any toys, any books, any conversation to speak of, kids who'll be far better off in nursery school than at home."

"Well, it sounds like the state's trying to raise the children," O.B. said.

"Some of us don't think that's a bad idea," Elias said, fixing the press secretary with his unblinking gaze. Dave frowned— there was no sense in baiting O.B.

"Well, some of us do, pal," O.B. snapped. "You want to pull off these fancy social experiments and some of us just want to get the bill passed."

"All right, O.B.," Dave said, "I appreciate your telling us about it."

"Think nothing of it," the press secretary drawled, and left the office.

"What was that all about?" Elias asked.

"He's going to tell the President about that two-year-old thing, and now I can't say I wasn't warned. Look, you'd better write me a memo telling why classes for two-year-olds are the best thing since bottled beer. I'll be needing it."

"I'll have it in the morning."

"And look, Elias, let's take it easy on O.B. We have enough enemies already."

"Sorry. I lost my head." Elias started to rise, then sat back down. "If it'll cheer you up," he said, "I've got some news for you."

"What's that?" Dave said.

Elias spread his hands wide and grinned. "Would you believe I'm getting married?"

"Getting married?" Dave echoed. He felt a tremor of apprehension. "I thought we had you working eighteen hours a day."

"You do," Elias said, "so I'm marrying somebody from my office."

"Who?"

"Sandy Cappitt. You met her the last time you were over."

Dave remembered Sandy; he'd stopped and talked to her for a few minutes. She was a small girl, not pretty but with a sharp intelligent face, and button-bright black eyes. She was an economist, with a Master's from Columbia. But what he remembered best about Sandy was that she had the biggest boobs he'd ever seen on such a tiny girl.

"Yeah, I remember Sandy," he said.

"I know what you remember," Elias said. "But she also happens to be a very intelligent girl."

"Then why's she marrying you?"

"She says it's my good looks," Elias said.

Dave laughed helplessly. It had been a long day and he hoped there would be no more surprises. "That's great, Elias. Just great. When's the big event?"

"Saturday," Elias said. "At the District Building."

Dave leaned forward over his desk. He suspected Elias knew what he was thinking.

"With things so busy right now," he said, "you couldn't put this off a couple of months, could you?"

"Sorry, Dave. It won't wait."

Dave nodded. "Well, Elias, I'm very happy for you. Can I come throw rice?"

Elias's mouth twisted into a wry smile. "Better not," he said. "Folks start throwing things, you don't know what might happen."

After Elias left, Dave sat staring out his window, not seeing the roses that trembled in the June dusk, trying to anticipate what trouble this happy news might bring. Finally he sighed deeply and focused again on the papers before him. SAU, he thought. Shit As Usual.

6

The first time I met Roy Hailey—

(Dave told Elias Abbot the night before their meeting with Hailey)

—was in September of '59, during Rush Week of my senior year at Warren, that little school I went to in Tennessee. Oh yeah, I was a frat rat, big frat man, secret grip and mumbo-jumbo, the whole thing. By then, by my senior year, I realized the system was absurd, but it was the system, and I was a big campus pol and I needed the fraternities—I'd put together quite a political machine, actually.

Anyway, it was Rush Week and two hundred pimply doctors' sons from Nashville and Birmingham were parading through the fraternity house in their Haspel coats and regimental ties, when in comes Roy, looking like the proverbial foreign object in the punchbowl.

Roy didn't exactly have straw in his hair, and he wasn't wearing overalls, but—well, you could see he wasn't far removed from it. He had this shaggy haircut, high over the ears and long down the front, and of course Roy's ugly as sin, and he had that lousy complexion, and he was wearing a shiny, twelve-dollar black suit, and a starched white shirt that must of been in the family a while, and he was skinny as a rail—Roy's put on weight since then.

Well, sometimes when real dumb ones, the closet cases, came through rush, the boys would have some fun with them, gather round and feed them a line—a little harmless sadism. So the boys closed in on Roy, but I went over and chased them off. I didn't like to see the fraternity make enemies. And I didn't like to see rich boys pick on poor boys, for that matter. I remember our conversation very well.

"I'm Dave Hyer," I said. "Are you interested in joining a fraternity?"

"No," he said. "Why should I be?"

Even then he had that cold stare, the one that goes right through you—blue fire, some writer called Roy's eyes. And, God damn, you could see the fire burning that day. It began to dawn on me that this boy was no hayseed.

"Well," I said, "why are you coming through rush then?"

"They said at the orientation that all freshmen go through fraternity rush."

"There's nothing mandatory about it," I told him. "They just assume that freshmen want to."

"What's the sense of fraternities?" Roy asked me. "What good do they do?"

"Well, it's a way to make friends," I told him.

"You can make friends in your dormitory," he said. "I don't see what these clubs do except grade people like cattle. Why can't you stand on your own without being an Alpha or a Beta or all that crud?"

Well, I didn't really disagree with him, but I gave him the line about they were an old tradition, part of the college life, and so on. Roy didn't buy it.

"I don't care about the past," he said. "Either it makes sense or it don't."

Incidentally, don't be taken in by Roy's grammatical lapses. He plays the country-boy bit to amuse himself. But he did have a strange way of pronouncing words—I didn't understand that until later.

"What do these things cost?" he asked. I think by then he'd sensed the weakness in my position—Roy has a genius for that —and so he went on the offensive. "Where does the money go?"

"You pay a hundred dollars to the national office when you're initiated," I told him. "And twenty dollars a month dues to the chapter for our operating expenses."

"What's the hundred for?" he asked. He had a gleam in his eye by then.

"I guess you'd say that's the price of belonging to this particular national fraternity," I said.

"In other words," Roy said triumphantly, "some Jew bastards in New York are robbing you idiots blind."

Actually, it was some Episcopalians in Atlanta, but Roy had grasped the principle of the thing.

Anyway, that was how I met Roy Hailey, and even then you could see his genius for getting right to the heart of the matter. In any situation, he saw the power equation, he saw who was doing what to whom, and you couldn't divert him with irrelevancies. He sure as hell wasn't like any college freshman I'd ever met before.

Needless to say, he didn't join our fraternity, or any fraternity, but we began to spend some time together that fall. I guess I was the only friend he had—Roy didn't go out of his way looking for friends. But he interested me, and lots of afternoons we'd take my old Plymouth and drive down to some honkeytonk and drink beer and play the jukebox. Roy introduced me to Hank Williams and Johnny Cash. Anyway, we'd go drink beer—or white lightning, sometimes—and I got to know more about him.

Roy was on a scholarship, of course. He was from a little town, a wide spot in the road, about forty miles from the Warren campus, and he'd made the best grades in the history of that school system. Don't ask me how. He told me the only books in his house were the Bible and the Montgomery Ward catalogue and he'd memorized them both by the time he was twelve. After that he'd hitchhike to Memphis on Saturdays and spend all day in the public library. That was why he couldn't pronounce words right. He knew hundreds of words he'd never heard spoken. He was embarrassed about it, and he'd almost never speak out in class, but professors said he wrote the most beautiful, logical, utterly radical papers they'd ever seen.

We'd drink beer and talk, and right there before my eyes, with Hank Williams wailing in the background, he started developing ideas that eventually blew up half the colleges in America. "Why do you have to take Latin and Biology and all that crap?" he'd say. "What the fuck has Beowulf got to do with anything? Why don't they teach what rich men do to poor men in this country? Why can't we decide what we want to study? Who's the college for, us or them?"

I thought he was crazy. In those days, you did what the dean said, or you had your ass tossed out. But it took Roy about two months at Warren College to decide that the whole system stank and ought to be changed. And, five or six years later, he did change it. Because it was Roy, more than anyone else, who planned the strategy at Berkeley, and later at Columbia and most of the other big ones. Roy and his disciples.

But in 1959, at Warren College, in Hilltop, Tennessee, believe me, that was thinking the unthinkable. I remember asking Roy how he thought he'd change the colleges.

"You organize," he said. "Like the unions did. Find the right issue to organize around, and you'd have 'em by the balls."

Of course, Roy didn't stay at Warren long enough to put his theories in practice. The only reason he went there in the first place was that his father was sick and he didn't want to be far from home. Warren wasn't his sort of school—Roy's the kind of kid who traditionally goes to the state university and on to law school and politics. I'll bet you George Wallace was a lot like Roy at seventeen. But he stayed through that first semester, and there was one lovely incident that fall I'll tell you about. It was at Homecoming, at the school president's annual open house for parents and alumni.

I was on hand, in my capacity as campus hotshot, and all the little ladies in flowered hats were guzzling the raspberry punch, when in the front door comes this old man in overalls. Well, it was Roy's father. They looked a lot alike, except the old man was stooped and wrinkled and he didn't have the fire in his eyes. Just an old tenant farmer who knew he didn't have long to live. He was proud as hell of having a boy in college, so there he was.

Roy wasn't there, of course, but I sent for him and then I went over and attached myself to the old man—he'd stood there in the door for a couple of minutes, literally hat in hand, looking at the people and them looking at him. There was nothing to do except take him through the reception line. I rather enjoyed it, watching the deans and the trustees do a double-take. And the old man was great—he had a natural dignity. This was a party for students' parents, and he was the parent of a student, and he was quite oblivious to the stir he was causing.

After we got through the receiving line, some students gathered around us and began hotboxing the old man. It was a bunch that hated Roy's ass—some Sigma Nus who'd ganged up and shaved his head one night, and the next night he'd broken every window in their fraternity house—and so they began asking his father questions, very polite of course, just like they'd ask anybody's father, "Tell us about your business, Mr. Hailey," and the old man was trying to answer them, not even seeing what they were doing, and about that time Roy showed up.

God, Elias, if you could have seen his face. There's been a lot written about how Roy Hailey hates America, but I've never seen hate like the way he looked at those Sigma Nus.

Hate and frustration. Because what he wanted to do was to tear those bastards apart with his bare hands, but he couldn't make a scene, for fear of embarrassing the old man. So he just stood there with this agony in his face—I was afraid he might explode, literally go crazy, start tearing the place apart. The worst part was, Roy was really embarrassed. At that point, he didn't have the cool to handle the situation. So he just stood there, speechless, until I was able to steer the old man out gracefully.

We got out on the porch and Roy was gasping like a man who's run a mile, his face still scarlet, and all the old man said was what a right nice bunch of boys they'd been.

I took them on to lunch, and Roy barely spoke the rest of the afternoon. I thought to myself, Sunny Southland, you have spawned your Nemesis. Or something equally prophetic. And you know, Elias, it was one month later that Roy dropped out of school to join the first sit-ins, then he helped organize the Freedom Rides, and the old Sunny South hasn't been the same since.

You sure you want to hear the rest of this? I'm not keeping you from the anxious arms of your bride? Okay, if you insist. Let's have another drink first. Well, the next few years we kept in touch. Roy spent most of his time in Mississippi and Alabama, registering voters and organizing boycotts and so on, and I was

in law school in Nashville, and he'd get up there once in a while.
We'd get together and talk, but we really didn't communicate
much anymore. He was already seeing things that most of us
didn't see until the late Sixties. I thought he was crazy when he
told me you could register voters and integrate the schools in
Mississippi. "All you've got to do is manipulate the federal
government," he said, like it was as easy as throwing a switch.

You've got to remember that this was '62 or so, and Roy was
quite a hero then. Not in the South, of course, but among
Eastern liberals. He met with Bobby Kennedy a couple of
times and they got along pretty well—he thought Bobby was
naïve at first, but toward the end, when he got to the Senate,
they were on the same wave length. But I don't think Roy
ever kidded himself. By then he knew he was a revolutionary
and he'd part company with the liberals soon enough. He used
them—us—as long as he could, but in the end we want to repair
the house and he wants to burn it down.

Remember, Elias, that Roy was developing all this time. You
no doubt recall, from your days as a Yalie, that Plato said there
were three levels of love. Well, I think Roy has been through
three levels of hate. When I first met him, he hated the people
who had held him and his kind down—the bankers, the railroads,
the big landowners and so on. Then, when he got down to
Mississippi, I think he began to hate injustice in America—
racial injustice, economic injustice. That's essentially a liberal
position—you and I could agree with it. But finally, sometime
in the mid-Sixties, he passed to the third level. Not hating injustice in America, but hating America. Thinking that America
is injustice, is built on injustice, can't be reformed, has to be
destroyed.

Of course, Roy's got plenty to hate about. The life of a sharecropper in west Tennessee is no joy. I visited Roy's place once,
a shack, and six or eight acres, and if his father worked twelve
hours a day he might break even. Bad soil for cotton, but damn
good for a revolutionary. Then, of course, there was Mississippi.
"Mississippi was my college," Roy told me once. "They taught
me my political science." He spent a couple of weeks in that
jail in Royster County where the sheriff liked to work people's
balls over with a billy club. One story is that Roy came out of

there sexually impotent. I don't know if it's true. Then he came north, went to Cleveland first, to organize in Hough, and of course he got caught up in the anti-war thing.

But I'm getting ahead of myself. I saw Roy a couple of times when Barney was governor of Tennessee. I sprang him out of jail once when they threw the book at him in Memphis for trying to organize garbage collectors—three years before Dr. King tried it.

God damn, they had Roy on everything from sedition to indecent exposure—some deputy saw him taking a leak behind a tree. But I had friends in the courthouse there, so I got him out. He came to Nashville to thank me—and borrowed fifty dollars he never paid back.

I saw him again in Cleveland in the spring of '65. I finished my business there early and took a cab out to Hough where Roy had his headquarters in a storefront office. I remember when I went in, he was trying to get some little Negro girl to take a spoonful of cough medicine.

"Behold the revolutionary at work," he said, and gave me that twisted grin of his. Only seeing Roy every year or two, I could see how he was changing. Putting on weight. By then he had that long scar over his eye—that was from Birmingham, I think. And his hair was starting to thin, even then. The startling thing was how his face had changed. It was more than maturing. There was a basic change, like a boxer's face gets changed, except the beating Roy took came more from within than from without. You saw it in the way the lips twisted and the way the eyes burned. The hate was there, all the time, like a light you can't turn off.

By then, by the middle of 1965, the lines were drawn—it was Roy Hailey against America, no time limit, no holds barred.

We talked for a couple of hours that afternoon, until I had to catch my plane. That was the afternoon he told me he was going to beat Johnson on Vietnam. Honest to God—it wasn't six months after the '64 election. At that point, Vietnam was the farthest thing from my mind. I was up to my ears in the governor's legislative program, and I only had the vaguest idea that we had a few thousand men in some little Asian country. But Roy had seen the issue already—that office of theirs was covered with anti-war posters, pictures of Vietnamese who'd been napalmed. Hell, at that point, I thought napalm was a tree. But Roy had found his issue—he was already grinding out anti-war manifestos and speaking on campuses. It wasn't long after that when he helped organize the first teach-ins and draftboard demonstrations.

His anti-war work was in addition to the slum organizing he and the SDS people were doing then. I remember asking Roy if it wasn't enough to try to end poverty without trying to stop the war, too.

"Couldn't you concentrate on one or the other?" I asked him—real smart, I was.

"No," Roy said. "They're part of the same thing. You've got to fight them together."

And of course he was right. I guess that's what I admire most about Roy—he was right from the first. He told the truth for three years when our government was telling lies. You know how I feel, Elias—virtue in this country in the 1960s consisted of how early and how hard you opposed that damned war. And Roy opposed it earlier and harder than anybody I know of. Those early demonstrations he organized in '65 and '66 paved the way for people like Lowenstein and McCarthy to do their bit in '67 and '68. People credit Al for starting the Dump Johnson movement in '67—hell, Roy Hailey started the Dump Johnson movement in the spring of 1965. And I don't think all the later things would have happened—could have happened—if he and his people hadn't taken the first steps.

What do I think about Roy today? Several things. First off, he's a problem I have to contend with. If Roy causes trouble here in Washington, it'll hurt the administration, and I want to prevent that—that's why we're seeing him tomorrow.

And there's one level on which I honestly like Roy—granting that he's become one of the least lovable figures in American public life. He's sort of the kid brother I never had—a crazy, mixed-up kid with guts and a genius for getting in trouble. Remember, I knew Roy before America had kicked him in the balls and broken nightsticks over his head and tried to send him to prison. Knew him and liked him. Of course, I don't kid myself that it's requited. Roy thinks people like you and me, people who try to work within the system, are the worst sort of chickenshits.

Finally, there's a level on which I see Roy as a doomed, a tragic figure. Because he has greatness in him—he's easily the most impressive leader to come out of the New Left—but Roy doesn't have any braking mechanism, he can't compromise, he's got to fight you to the death. He's tried to challenge America head-on, and that's like trying to stop a runaway truck by running straight into it. You've got to slip in from the side and get a hand on the steering wheel. But Roy's challenged America, and he can only lose. Either we'll send him to prison, or somebody will kill him. People like Roy don't die in their beds.

Oh yes, our esteemed Attorney General would like nothing better than to indict Roy for the Houston demonstrations—didn't I tell you? He's been sending over these alternative plans that run from indicting Roy and two others to indicting Roy and twenty others. For conspiracy, needless to say. Our esteemed Attorney General's mouth waters at the thought of sending Roy to prison. He keeps pushing for it, and I keep talking against it, and the President stays non-committal.

I honestly don't know what the President thinks about Roy. Of course, he instinctively dislikes any political figure he can't control—that's inherent in his position. But he knows Roy's got guts, and he admires that in anybody. But you see, Elias, the President is different from you and me—the very powerful are different from you and me, to coin a phrase—in that he doesn't think of Roy as a person. I do—I can't help it—because Roy's a contemporary, a friend of sorts. It's different for the President. He might *treat* someone as a person, flatter him, charm him and all that, but he doesn't really *think* of them as people. They're just factors in his equation. Cards in the computer. Ultimately, a President can't have feelings. Insofar as he does, he's that much less a President.

But, to answer your question, I don't know what the President will do about Roy, particularly if he gives us any more trouble. The point is, it won't turn on what Barney Newfield thinks of Roy Hailey. It'll turn on six or eight factors. The polls. What the blacks do this summer. What happens in Caravelas. My standing with the President, and the standing of our esteemed Attorney General. All in all, I'd have to say the fate of my revolutionary friend Roy Hailey is very much in doubt.

7

Elijah King's angry face was framed by a ferocious Afro, and he waved a switchblade knife as he spoke:

"You white mother-fucker, Ah don't trust you an' Ah don't trust that cowboy you work for. You gonna show us some *action*, else we gonna blow this mother-fucking country sky high!"

I'd like to show you some action, like a swift kick in the ass, Dave thought, but he said nothing.

It had been like that for an hour. The four young men—Dave and Elias, Roy Hailey and Elijah King, two whites, two blacks, neatly divided—had met at Dave's house to talk about black control in the New Cities. They were making little headway. Dave would not say how much black control, if any, the administration might grant, and the two militants would not say what they would do if their demands weren't met. Vague promises were countered by vague threats, as each side probed the other's intentions. It was a ritual Dave had endured before, with other militants, and he rather enjoyed it. He did not even mind the insults and name-calling. He had been insulted by some of the most vociferous black men of his time, and he accepted that as part of the ritual. You put up with their crap because these two men, slouched on the sofa in their denim jackets, sullen, scowling, smoking joints, had power and would use it. With a few phone calls, Hailey could activate white radicals in a dozen cities, and Elijah King could set blacks marching in California. They could inflame the political process, and before that happened it was better to seek some accommodation with them.

"No one is asking you to trust us," Dave told Elijah King. "I'm trying to tell you where we stand."

"Tell us where you stand?" the young black snorted. "All you've done is tell lies. You gonna build a city in California or not?"

As he spoke, Elijah King trimmed his fingernails with his knife, tossing the shavings onto the floor of Dave's study. His manicure, Dave thought, was their biggest accomplishment so far.

"I told you nothing was definite," Dave said. "I agree that California is a logical place for one of the first cities."

"Why don't we pretend there'll be one in California and work from there?" Roy Hailey said in a bored voice. Roy had been sitting quietly, puffing on his joint most of the evening. Dave suspected that his alliance with Elijah King was an uneasy one.

"Okay," Dave said. "Let's assume we'll build a New City in California."

"It must be under black control," Elijah King declared, rocking his knife slowly on his fingertips.

"That's impossible," Dave said.

"Then it will never be built," the young black declared.

"Let me finish, please," Dave said. "We're talking of cities for perhaps half a million people, but split into semi-autonomous communities of fifty thousand or so. Some of these smaller communities might be all-black."

"How autonomous?" Roy Hailey asked. His gaunt, hillbilly's face was burned red by the sun. His blond hair was thinning in front, but long in back, so that it curled over the collar of his denim jacket.

"Elias, will you answer that?" Dave said.

"Yeah, Tom, we ain't heard much from you," Elijah King said, and the two young blacks stared coldly at each other for a moment.

"We're talking about a high degree of autonomy," Elias said. "Each community will elect its own government, control its own schools, hire its own police force, et cetera."

"How many of these will there be?" Hailey asked.

"Five to ten making up each New City," Elias said.

"Half of them must be black," Elijah King declared, jabbing the knife in Dave's direction.

"Half of them might be black," Dave said, "if that many blacks want separatism. There must also be integrated communities."

"How about all-white ones?" Roy Hailey asked dryly.

Dave shrugged away the question. In truth, the administration had not settled the issue of endorsing white racism as well as black racism. On this, as on the whole tangled issue of race relations, Dave felt a terrible uncertainty. He increasingly saw that they in government did not know what was "right," and neither did the warring factions with which they dealt. The government, having spent the Sixties seeking integration, now seemed in the early Seventies to be willing to accept some forms of separatism. But was separatism a first step toward genuine integration, or a step backward toward endless segregation? Had integration in America gone as far as the prejudices of the white majority would allow? Dave didn't know and he didn't think anyone knew, but in his job he had to affect a certitude he did not feel.

"Then you're saying that half of the towns in the first New City in California will be under black control," Elijah King said.

"No, I'm not saying that," Dave told him. "Let's get that clear. I'm telling you that some of us in the administration think black community control is a good idea, if we can work it out."

"What's stopping you?" Roy Hailey asked.

"You know the answer to that, Roy. Congress. Until we get this bill passed, the less talk about black control, the better. If you start making demands, you'll just stir up opposition on the Hill."

"So you're telling us to keep quiet?" Hailey asked scornfully.

"It would help," Dave said.

"You think we're gonna trust you, whitey?" Elijah King demanded.

"I don't know what you're going to do," Dave said. "But I think you might see that our interests are the same in this."

"Listen, mister," Elijah King shouted, jabbing the air with his knife, "your interests and my interests ain't never been the same. And me an' my people ain't gonna keep quiet for you."

"Okay," Dave said, "but you may hurt your people more than you help them."

Elijah King jumped to his feet. "You white cocksucker, who are you to tell me about my people?" His arm whipped forward and the knife shot across the room and stuck in the wall a foot from Dave's head. Dave did not move. He was furious, but he would not give King the satisfaction of knowing it.

"Ah've had enough of this shit," the black militant shouted. "Let's go, Roy."

Roy Hailey remained seated. "You go on," he said. "I'm not through talking."

Elijah King marched out of the room. They heard the front door slam and the squeal of tires as he raced away. Then Dave relaxed.

"That's quite an exit he's got," Dave said.

"I think he likes you," Hailey said.

"Yeah, I like him too," Dave said. "Maybe I'll invite him to a cabinet meeting."

Dave pulled the knife out of the wall and tossed it to Hailey, who was lighting another joint. "Sure you won't try one?" he asked. "Bethesda Gold."

"No thanks," Dave said. "I'll just have another drink. That is, if you won't mind, Roy. If the alcohol fumes won't disturb you."

"Feel free," Hailey said, granting them his twisted grin.

"Okay, Roy," Dave said after they were settled again, "what do you really want out of the New Cities?"

"Not much," Hailey said. "I figure you'll do a pretty good job of running them."

"That's unexpected praise," Dave said.

Hailey blew out a long column of smoke and the sweetish smell of pot filled the small library. "I figure you'll give us all the black control you can, trying to buy some peace," Hailey said.

"That's what it comes to," Dave agreed.

"But it won't work," Hailey continued.

"Why not?"

"Let's say you put five million poor people in the New Cities," Hailey said. "You won't, 'cause you'll end up building them for the middle-class, but let's say you got five million poor in them. Wall to wall carpets and Muzak and pretty little parks —the whole scene. So what happens to the twenty million poor who are left back in Rat City? I'd say they'd be pretty pissed."

"I figured that out a long time ago," Dave said.

"So what do you do about it?"

"Between now and the year 2000, with the New Cities as a start, I'd say we build fifty to a hundred million new housing units in America, until public housing is as widespread as public schools."

"It'll never happen," Hailey insisted. "Not through legislation."

"How do you think it will happen?" Dave asked.

"Through revolution," Hailey said.

"There'll never be a revolution in this country, Roy."

"There won't? Ask your black friend there. Ask him about those fifty thousand black men who learned to kill in Vietnam. Ask him about those ten million black boys in the slums who've been hating whitey since they were old enough to walk. You think those people are going to join the Young Democrats? They're going to tear this fucking country apart."

"Your mistake is thinking we'll stop with this one program. Newfield is going to be President for six more years. This is only the start. There'll be school programs and job programs and health programs, and when his time is up he'll have a successor picked who can finish what we—what he started. Roy, this country began to move in the early Sixties, then we got off the track and we lost five years, but now we're back on the track. We're going to make this country sing. I wish you were on our side."

But Roy Hailey only smiled his crooked smile and took another deep drag.

After Hailey had gone, Dave and Elias settled back to finish their drinks.

"How'd we do?" Elias asked.

"Not bad," Dave said. "Despite our black friend's theatrics, I think they see that our interests are the same. Or almost the same."

"Hailey sees it," Elias said. "Hailey's smart. But don't be too sure about that damned Elijah King. God, sometimes I want to join the movement to keep fools like him from screwing things up."

Dave guessed Elias was still angry at Elijah King's calling him a Tom. That amused him—he'd never thought Elias thin-skinned.

"Well, you've got to give him one thing," Dave said. "He does hate whitey."

Elias laughed bitterly. "It doesn't take any talent to hate whitey," he said. "The question is how you use your hate."

"That's true," Dave said.

"I consider myself something of an expert on the subject," Elias went on, fixing Dave with the cold stare he remembered from their first meeting. "From age ten on, because I happened to be the smartest black boy in the state of New Jersey, I got scholarships to whitey's best schools. And you know what I majored in? Hating whitey."

Dave sipped his drink. This was the first time he'd seen Elias open up.

"If somebody wants to learn to hate whitey," Elias said, "they ought to try being the class nigger at Choate and Yale in the Fifties. You know what they hated most? That I was smarter than they were. Guys would try to transfer out of classes rather than have me make a better grade than theirs."

Elias stood up and paced the floor a minute, then stopped beside the window. Outside, chalky clouds drifted beneath a full moon.

"The hell of it is, all the time I was hating those bastards, I was learning to be like them, to dress like a white man and talk like one and think like one. Listen, they made me half a white man. Sometimes I want to be out there in the streets, but I don't fit there now, any more than you would. I've been trained to work inside the white man's system. So that's what I'll do. That bastard can call me a Tom, but I'm going to do something big for my people, something bigger than he could ever dream of. I'm going to help build those New Cities."

"The amazing thing," Dave said after a moment, "is how we all end up at the same point. You and I and King and Hailey sit here and yell at each other, but we're really on the same side. I agree with Roy on more issues than I do with our esteemed Attorney General, who wants to put Roy in jail. Personally, I think Roy Hailey is a hell of a lot more useful American than our esteemed Attorney General."

Dave jiggled the tiny slivers of ice left in his glass. "We start at different places," he continued, "but we end at the same place. You hating those rich bastards at Choate and Yale. Me growing up in Dallas, hating the oil men's sons. Roy, the sharecropper's son, hating the white South. And our friend Elijah King—what's his story?"

Elias shrugged. "His mother was a prostitute who died of an overdose of heroin. After that, orphanages, reform schools. A textbook case."

"So we all learned to hate, early in the game," Dave said, "to hate everything that's rotten in this society. And we're all crazy enough to think we can change things." Dave stood up and loosened his tie. "You remember what old Joe Kennedy is supposed to have said about Bobby? 'He hates the way I do.' That shook people up, but it shouldn't have. A man who doesn't hate anything isn't worth a damn. A man who won't hate, can't love."

"Is it safe to come in now?"

Eleanor smiled at them from the doorway. She was wearing a blue robe and her hair was tied back with a narrow white ribbon.

"Yeah, the rowdies have gone," Dave said, "come on in."

Eleanor gave Elias her hand and her brightest smile.

"I'm so thrilled for you and Sandy," she told him, in a soft, excited voice. "You're going to be so happy together."

Elias was moved by her warmth. His gnome's face broke into a grin as she held his hand in both of hers and beamed at him. If it was only a part she played, she played it exceedingly well.

"We appreciated those towels," Elias told her. Dave had not known she had sent them a wedding gift. But Eleanor always did the right thing, simply because it was the right thing. What an excellent woman my wife is, he thought. What a pity we don't get along.

"I'd better get home now," Elias said.

"Can you and Sandy come to dinner next Saturday?" Eleanor asked. "Is Saturday all right, Dave?"

"It's fine," he said. "I think the President's going to Camp David."

"We'd be glad to," Elias said.

"Are you all settled now?" Eleanor asked.

"Yes, we're settled fine, in a little house near DuPont Circle," Elias replied. He said his goodnights and hurried out the door.

"Come sit down for a minute," Dave told her.

"All right," she said. "How was your meeting?"

"A million laughs." He poured her a glass of sherry and sat down beside her on the sofa. He was not sure how things were between them this evening. They had quarreled the past Sunday, when he had canceled plans to take Sally to the zoo, and they had the usual bed fight that night, and for the next two nights he had ignored her, working until long after she was asleep. Now, with her beside him, Sunday's argument seemed far in the past, but he waited for some sign from her. An air of uncertainty hung between them, as it so often did these days. Past affection and present discontent struggled within them, leaving them unsure whether their mood was nearer anger or forgiveness.

"How are Elias and Sandy doing?" she asked.

"They had some trouble finding a house," he said.

"What kind of trouble?" Her girlish, social voice was put away now, and this was the other Eleanor, a cool, precise young woman whose mind, he thought, was not unlike his own.

"The first couple of houses they wanted, the owners wouldn't rent to them."

"How can they do that?"

"They just say it's already rented."

"Aren't there laws?"

"Elias hasn't got time to screw around with it," he told her. "The funny thing is, these are people who'd probably rent to a black couple. But a mixed couple bugs them."

"Did you see that item about their wedding in the *Post*'s society column?" she asked.

"Yes," he said. "*Time* used it too, in the Milestones column. The bastards."

"Will it cause problems?"

He shrugged. "I don't know. It could."

"Why in God's name did she get pregnant?" Eleanor asked impatiently. "Hasn't she heard about the Pill?"

"They've got to invent a pill to make women take the Pill," he said. "That's the next challenge."

"What kind of problems could the stories cause?" she asked.

"This kind," he said, and drew two clippings from his pocket. One, from a hate-sheet called *The Thunderbolt*, raged about pinko niggers marrying Jew girls from New York. The other, a more refined journal called *The American Constitutionalist*, warned about miscegenation and the decline of the West.

Eleanor handed the clippings back quickly. "Has Elias seen these?" she asked.

"I think so."

"How awful for him," she said.

"He can take it."

"What about her?" Eleanor asked. "Is she that tough?"

"I don't know," Dave admitted. "She'd better be."

Eleanor stood up and drew her robe more tightly around her. "I'm going to bed now," she said.

He glanced at her, uncertain whether her words were an invitation or a dismissal.

"Have a hard day?" he asked.

"Very hard," she said. "I'm tired."

"Yeah," he said. "Goodnight. I've got some more work to do."

8

The Beatles were on the hi-fi and all was right with the world. Dave was smiling as he and Eleanor entered the big cheerful room where Brenda was giving her party, the room on the back where Harry Truman had built the balcony overlooking the south lawn. Brenda gave them both a hug, and led them to the bar where Barney was ladling out his famous Singapore Slings. He looked grand in his white linen pants and maroon polo shirt, and he felt grand too. It was his fifty-first birthday and Mr. Gallup had given him his best present that morning.

"Hi, sweetheart," he called to Eleanor. "How 'bout a birthday kiss for the old timer?"

Eleanor laughed and stood on tiptoe to nuzzle his cheek. Barney hugged her a bit more fiercely than Dave thought necessary, but that was a risk you ran if you brought your wife to Barney's parties. Eleanor didn't seem to mind; she gave Barney a dazzling smile.

"Hey, baby-doll," Eddie Gooch called to Dave, "you seen this?"

He waved the clipping from the morning paper.

"No, what's that?" Dave said in mock innocence.

"Sez here that an unprecedented seventy-one percent of our esteemed fellow citizens think President Bernard A. Newfield is doing a slam-bang job," Eddie declared loudly.

"No kidding," Dave said. "He must have some great people working for him."

"That's a laugh," Barney said, and handed Dave a drink. "If it wasn't for you numbskulls I'd of got eighty-one percent. Say, sugar, I hear you're making a movie."

This last was to Eleanor, who batted her eyes in the affirmative.

"What part you playing?"

"I'm the President's wife," Eleanor said.

"God help you," said Brenda.

"How about me playing the President?" Barney asked. "I always wanted to be an actor."

"I'm sure you'd be marvelous, Mr. President," Eleanor said.

"Whose picture is this?" Barney asked.

"Irving Rosenthal is the producer," she said.

"This is one of Rosy's pictures?" Barney asked.

"He called this afternoon," Eddie Gooch said.

"Well God damn, Eddie, get him over here," Barney ordered. Rosy Rosenthal was Barney's Hollywood friend, a nervous, free-spending man with a genius for producing grade-B epics. He also produced grade-A starlets when his politician friends were in California.

Other people were arriving and Dave circled the room for the obligatory hello to his colleague's wives. He spoke first to O. B. Perkins' wife, Vivian. He always spoke to Vivian early in a party because if you waited too late she'd be drunk and possibly troublesome. Vivian was a pleasant enough girl, but O.B. had married her back in his police-beat days and she was out of her league now. She was uncomfortable at these parties. She would be nervous and edgy when she arrived, fearful of putting forth an opinion lest it be laughed at, and she would hang on the edges of other people's conversations, chain-smoking and downing one drink after another, until finally she was high—and loud and silly, and O.B. would say something about the baby-sitter and pack her into a car for home. So Dave chatted with Vivian for a few minutes, expressing great interest in her children, then when her drink was empty he maneuvered her to the punch-bowl and deposited her with Gooch. As he drifted away, he saw his wife chatting with Charlton MacKenzie and he gave her a smile. He and Eleanor had their problems but she was an absolutely first-rate girl, and she'd never let him down in public.

He greeted Leon Kerkelot's wife, Adria, a dark-eyed, sharp-featured woman of forty who had written a couple of avant-garde novels (Dave had started one of them but never finished it). Adria made no secret of her distaste for Washington, but she had always been pleasant to Dave and he enjoyed her.

She was bright and malicious, and they always sparred a bit at parties. Adria was the sort of woman he'd have contemplated an affair with if she hadn't been Leon's wife; failing that, he sparred with her at parties. It was much the same thing.

"Help me, David," Adria said, her dark eyes glistening. "I think I'll write a Washington novel and I need your advice."

"I thought you loathed Washington," he said.

"I do, dear, but that doesn't foreclose one little potboiler."

"What sort do you have in mind?" he asked.

"Oh, the usual thing. A what-if novel."

"A what?"

"What if a Negro became President? What if the generals tried a coup? What if the President went cuckoo? What if the President's plane got lost? The trouble is, David, that so many of the what-ifs have already been used up. Help me think of a new one."

"Well, how about a woman as President? Call it *The President Wore Skirts* or something."

"That's a little tame, dear. It might be better if he was a man who wore skirts."

"Or maybe a President who died," Dave suggested, "but his family found a double to imitate him for the rest of the term."

"A twin brother, perhaps," Adria mused.

"Or there's the idea from the Mark Twain story about the Siamese twins with opposite personalities—one a hell-raiser and one very pious. What if those Siamese twins got elected President? You could have one an ultra-liberal and one an ultra-conservative. Lot of symbolism there."

Adria flashed him a serpentine smile. "You have such good ideas, David. Give me another one."

"Okay, Adria, here's a hell of an idea. Why don't you write a novel about a big, rugged, idealistic soldier who gets to be President and wants to build new cities, wants a sensible policy toward China and Latin America, wants peace, and finds that half the Congress and half the big businessmen and half the newspapers in this country will fight him every inch of the way?"

Adria gave him a little pouting frown. "David, dear, nobody

would read a book like that. But your idea about the Siamese twins—that's a possibility!"

"Are you working on anything now?" he asked.

"A piece for *Esquire*," she said. "It's called, 'Is John Lennon Jesus?'"

"Is he?"

"I rather think so," Adria admitted. "There's a good deal of evidence."

"All that 'I am the walrus' stuff?" he asked.

"That, and the parables, and the disciples—they are the new religion, you know."

"Lennon does sort of look like Jesus," Dave said, and just then he felt someone pulling on his arm. He turned to find Flo Gooch, Eddie's wife, staring up at them open-mouthed. Flo was a sweet, birdlike little woman, and something of a nut on religion.

"David?" she began in her wavering voice. "What is this about a Communist being . . . being the Lord?"

"What Communist, Flo?" he asked, confused.

"The one you're talking about. Lenin. She said he was . . . Jesus."

"No, no, no, Flo. Not Lenin. John Lennon. The Beatle."

"The what?" Flo said. Now she was confused.

"John Lennon. He's one of the Beatles, and Adria is writing an article about him." He glanced at Adria, who was on the brink of laughter.

"But what's a Beatle got to do with Jesus?" Flo asked.

"Nothing, Flo," he assured her. "Nothing at all. It was just a silly joke. Forget it. Tell us what you're up to at church." Adria was delighted at the misunderstanding, but Dave was not. Keeping peace in their rather unlikely circle was one of his more difficult jobs.

Barney came up and began talking to Flo. One of Barney and Eddie's standard jokes concerned Flo's praying incessantly for their salvation. Flo may indeed have prayed for Barney's soul, but she was terrified of him in the flesh, and he never tired of teasing her. Tonight, Flo had come to the White House straight from her church, where she had been rehearsing her Sunday school class in a skit of some kind.

"Tell me about your production, Flo," Barney insisted.

"Well sir, it's a historical pageant, where the children act out patriotic things like the Boston Tea Party and the Gettysburg Address."

"You got me in there?"

Flo shook her head in dismay.

"I ain't patriotic enough, huh?"

"Oh, Mr. President, it's not that."

Barney laughed. "How big is this show?"

"Twelve boys and girls in all, sir."

"You integrated?" Barney demanded.

"Yes sir," Flo assured him.

Barney turned to his press secretary. "O.B., what say we bring these kids in next week to put on their show for the cabinet and the reporters?"

"Great idea," O.B. said.

"How 'bout it, Flo? Your troupe ready for the bigtime?"

Flo babbled with delight. Dave smiled at the complexity of Barney's simple-seeming gesture. He would thrill Flo and her youngsters; he would pull off (Dave did not doubt) a successful publicity stunt; and he would satisfy his own highly refined sense of the absurd by making his cabinet sit and watch a dozen eight-year-olds act out the Boston Tea Party.

Dave poured himself another Sling and was absorbing the loud vibrations of The Who (Brenda had the world's most with-it collection of rock records) when he saw Cathy Quinn arrive.

He'd seen her a half-dozen times in the past two months. He wasn't delighted to see her here tonight, but he smiled politely as Brenda brought her over for an introduction.

"Dave, you know Cathy Quinn, don't you?"

"Sure," he said. "How are you, Miss Quinn?" Cathy extended her hand and he gave her fingers a squeeze.

"Call me Cathy," she said.

"Cathy wrote that article on me a couple of months ago," he explained.

"Oh, sure," Brenda said. "Well, now she's writing one on me, so I figured she ought to come to one of our little wing-dings. You kids excuse me a minute."

Brenda hurried off and Dave leaned closer to Cathy. With her short, tousled hair, and her blue party dress, she looked about sixteen.

"You should have told me you were writing something on Brenda."

"I didn't want you to think I'm trying to use you."

"You're not going to use me. But I like to know what's going on around here."

"I didn't think of it that way," she admitted.

"What about this party? You can't write about this."

"The party's off the record. Your friend O.B. has already made sure of that."

"I want to talk to you before you write your article. Brenda's a very decent girl who's got some problems."

"Aren't we all?" she said, and then she looked up and smiled, because Barney was bearing down on them with a glass of punch for her.

"Drink this, little lady," he said. "It'll make a believer of you."

"In what?" Cathy said.

"In me."

"But I already am," she said with her tomboy's grin.

"Yeah? Well I wish you'd convert some of those wise-guy editorial writers at the *Post*." Barney was furious with the Washington *Post*, which one day that week had criticized his defense budget as too costly, his Israel policy as too vague, and his wife's skirts as too short. "If the Washington *Post* was on fire," he'd roared, "I wouldn't piss on it."

"I don't work for the *Post*, Mr. President," Cathy protested. "They just carry my articles sometimes."

"Okay," Barney said, but the distinction seemed academic to him—when he was angry with the press, it was all part of the same vast conspiracy. "You say you're writing something on Brenda now?"

Cathy said she was.

"I'll bet she never told you how I met her," Barney said. "I was on this overnight flight from Honolulu to L.A., and she was the stewardess, and she says, 'What'll it be, soldier, coffee, tea or me?' and . . ."

"Very funny," Brenda injected. "The truth is, this big jerk called me twenty times before I'd even go out with him. If I hadn't lost my mind and married him, I'd be married now to the number-one quarterback in the NFL."

"Yeah," Barney said, "you'd be married to some bonehead jock and living in a crackerbox in California."

"At least it'd have a pool out back," Brenda shot back. One of Brenda's several complaints about the White House was that it lacked an outdoor swimming pool, but Barney for political reasons refused to have one built.

"Where you from?" Barney asked Cathy. "You sound like Boston."

"I am Boston," she said, and he began quizzing her on Massachusetts politics. Dave listened for a moment, and he could see that Barney was attracted, as he had been, by Cathy's defiant, show-me manner. She was clearly not awed by the President; that was one of the nice things about Cathy, she wasn't awed by anything. Her father had been a drunken longshoreman who'd beaten her until she was twelve, when she split his skull open with a frying pan. After that he left her alone and Cathy embarked on a lifelong policy of taking no crap from anyone.

Dave saw his hostess alone by the punchbowl and he went to speak to her.

"Good party, Brenda."

"You think so, sweetheart? Stick around, it'll get better." Brenda tossed her head and her strawberry blond curls bounced merrily around her baby-doll face. She was wearing a simple, expensive green silk dress that displayed her magnificent figure to best advantage. When Brenda and Barney had met, she'd been a ripe twenty-five, he a lusty forty. After a tempestuous romance, she had succeeded where many had failed and become Mrs. Newfield. Barney, conventionally chagrined at having surrendered his freedom, sometimes declared, "You know why I married that woman? Because she's the best little lay between here and Hong Kong." No one doubted him.

Barney entered politics not long after they were married, and his fast-moving political career had caused problems for Brenda, who cared little for politics or politicians. Dave had set out from the first to cultivate Brenda, because she was his boss's wife, but he'd found that he genuinely liked her. She was a pert, good-natured girl, only four or five years his senior, and incapable of malice or pretension. Brenda didn't give a damn about being First Lady; all she asked of life was a good time and a husband who'd treat her right. Barney didn't always treat her right, but things had been quiet of late and Dave hoped they'd stay that way.

"Get you something to drink?" Dave asked her.

Brenda winked. "I'm on the wagon, sweetie. You've got to stay sober to keep up around this place."

"Hey, come on in, you kids," Brenda called over his shoulder. She whispered to Dave, "Mama's got a little surprise." Then she hurried to greet the late-comers, who proved to be Sharon Flatt—the new, improved Sharon, her flame-colored hair piled elegantly atop her head, her dress a $200 concoction from Garfinckle's—and a round-faced, apple-cheeked young man who was vaguely familiar to Dave.

Leon and Adria Kerkelot joined Dave as Brenda greeted the young couple.

"What a *robust* girl," Adria said. "Who is she, Dave?"

"Her name is Sharon Flatt. She's a typist in the President's office."

"Oh yes," Adria said. "I've heard of her. I understand she and the First Lady are quite good friends."

"Brenda's friendly with everyone," he said vaguely. He didn't know how much Adria knew about Sharon—he didn't know the whole story himself. But he knew that Brenda had not followed through on her threat to evict Sharon from the President's office; to the contrary, she'd become great friends with Sharon.

"Who is the young man, David?" Leon asked.

"I'm trying to remember," Dave said. He shut his eyes to place the young man's plump, pleasant face. It came to him after a moment.

"His name is Winnie Boatwright. He worked on the campaign and now he's a special assistant at Interior."

"Of the Philadelphia Boatwrights?" Adria asked.

Dave nodded. "Winnie is a very rich young man."

"And a very eligible bachelor," Adria added, "to be dating a typist."

"Well, she's not just anybody's typist," Dave said.

"What does he do at Interior?" asked Leon, who could not tolerate being in a room with anyone whose secrets were unknown to him.

"Publicity of some sort," Dave said.

"Is he bright?"

"Not terribly," Dave said. "But he's nice and industrious and he gives great parties at his house in Georgetown. His greatest asset is that he'll work for free. You'd be surprised the jobs you can get in Washington if you'll work for free. Winnie's doing penance for the fact that his grandfather was a robber baron."

"What will happen to him?" Adria asked.

"He'll eventually contribute enough money to the right campaign and become an ambassador," Dave said. "If not Secretary of State."

Brenda and the young couple were moving toward them.

"You're so darn sweet to have me," Winnie was saying. He was well dressed and there was something immensely likable about him.

"You're a doll to come," Brenda told him. "The party wouldn't of been any fun for Sharon without a fellow."

"Hello," Dave said.

"Hi, Dave," Sharon Flatt cried joyously.

"Winston Boatwright," Brenda said, "this is David Hyer, and Mr. and Mrs. Kerkelot."

"Call me Winnie," the young man said. "You wouldn't remember it, Mr. Hyer, but we met once before."

"Sure, during the campaign," Dave said. "And you're at Interior now."

"Winnie produced my Smokey-the-Bear tapes," Brenda said. "That's how we met."

"That was *such* fun," Winnie said enthusiastically.

"Hey, Birthday Boy, come over here and greet your guests," Brenda called.

The President was not smiling as he joined them.

"Hi, Mr. President," Sharon squealed.

"Hi," Barney said dourly.

"This is Winnie Boatwright, Sharon's date," Brenda said. "You work the poor girl so hard she never has a chance to meet fellows her own age."

"It's mighty big of you to help her out," Barney said.

"It's an honor to meet you, sir," Winnie said.

"Winnie's got the most fabulous house in Georgetown," Sharon announced. "With famous pictures all over the walls."

"You're interested in art, Mr. Boatwright?" Adria asked.

"Oh, I collect a bit," Winnie said modestly.

"Barney, how about getting these kids a drink?" Brenda said.

"Oh, let me get them," Winnie said, and dashed off to the punchbowl.

Dave was watching the President as he frowned at this new development. Then, moving to regain control of the situation, Barney turned off the hi-fi, and called out a familiar command:

"Okay, everybody, gather 'round. It's game time!"

At Barney's parties you played games. Sometimes they were well-known games like charades. More often they were elaborate new games of his own invention. In either event, they were always games that Barney organized, supervised, and won. There was no record of Barney ever losing one of his games.

Dave at first had hated this, hated jumping when Barney said frog, hated this intensely personal way he had of playing God, for that was what it was. Yet he had learned to grin and bear it, because playing Barney's games was part of the price you paid to inhabit Barney's world. They were, among other things, a way he tested people. If you weren't willing to play the fool at his parties—to stand on your head or whistle a tune or whatever—there was a good chance your devotion might be found wanting at other, more crucial moments.

Dave tried to see it from Barney's viewpoint. He surrounded himself with talented and ambitious men. He knew that some of them fancied themselves wiser than he, and that many of them were trying to use him for their own political or ideological ends. And so from time to time he would remind them—by a joke, a command, a snarl, a cold stare—who was boss. It did not take much. Given the strength of his personality and the grandeur of his office, Barney could reduce most men to Jello in seconds. The trick, for Dave and the other assistants, was to combine intellectual independence with social submissiveness. It was a delicate balancing act; Dave was not sure anyone could manage it indefinitely.

"Okay, we're gonna have us some theatrics," Barney announced in the exaggerated drawl he used at such moments. "Mrs. Gooch, the world famous impresario, had written a little epic which she'd generously agreed to recite for us. The rest of us will act out the parts. Okay, Flo, what's first?"

"The Boston Tea Party," Flo said. "We need an English soldier on a ship and some Indians to slip in and tie him up and throw the tea overboard."

Barney surveyed his cast. "MacKenzie, you're the English soldier. Stand up on that chair there—that's the deck of the ship."

The Secretary of State, unflappable, mounted the chair.

"Now, we need some Injins. Eddie—make like an Injin."

Eddie Gooch, a veteran performer, began a wild whooping war dance around the chair.

"Beautiful, Eddie, beautiful. Okay, you other guys join in. And Flo, you start reciting."

As Flo squeaked out her third-grade version of history, the men whooped and hopped around the chair like madmen. MacKenzie smiled benignly down at them, awaiting his fate. Barney let out a few whoops himself and then started the women—"lady Injins," he explained—dancing around the chair too. At the proper moment the whooping Injins snatched MacKenzie from the chair, tossed him atop a sofa, bound his arms and legs with Barney's $20 silk ties, and, still whooping, cast the hated crates of tea (shoeboxes from Brenda's closet) off the balcony into the night.

Barney roared his approval, and filled everyone's glass, and they all rested for a moment. Everyone was flushed and laughing—even Dave admitted that these stunts were fun, in an insane way, once you accepted that Barney was God. Cathy was grinning, and even the dark-eyed Adria Kerkelot was smiling—or was that the smile of the novelist-in-progress?

"Flo, you got Pocahontas and old John Smith in there?" Barney asked.

Flo admitted she did not.

"Oh, honey, with all these fine Injins, we got to have Pocahontas."

And so a beaming Eleanor Hyer was Pocahontas to O.B.'s John Smith. Then Winnie Boatwright was Custer and the rest of them pounded him mercilessly with pillows. More drinks followed, and more skits, and everyone joined in, except Brenda, who staged-whispered, "I don't have to play your damn games; I'm your wife." When they finally finished a warm glow had settled over their party. In the stunts and the laughter, men as different as Leon Kerkelot and Eddie Gooch, women as different as their wives, could share a common ground—that was the special magic that Barney cast over those who inhabited his world.

A buffet dinner was served, and they sat around in small clusters on the floor, eating and talking. Cathy was listening to Sharon Flatt catalogue the wonders of West Virginia, and Eleanor Hyer and Winnie Boatwright were discussing art. Eddie Gooch was telling war stories to Charlton MacKenzie, and Leon Kerkelot was listening intently as Flo Gooch gave her views on China. When coffee was served, O.B. said something about the baby-sitter and started Vivian on her way home. Ten minutes later, when O.B. returned to the party, he was carrying a sheet from the AP wire. He handed it to Barney, who read it and nodded. O.B. then handed it to MacKenzie, who read it and passed it without comment to Leon, who handed it on to Dave. The bulletin was brief:

PENTAGON OFFICIALS ANNOUNCED TONIGHT THAT PRESIDENT NEWFIELD HAS APPROVED THE SENDING OF A ONE-HUNDRED MAN COUNTERINSURGENCY TEAM TO INSTRUCT THE REPUBLIC OF CARAVELAS'S ARMED FORCES IN ANTI-GUERRILLA PROCEDURES. THE MOVE WAS TERMED NECESSARY TO DEFEAT THE GUERRILLA UPRISING THERE. PENTAGON SOURCES SAID IT WAS NOT ANTICIPATED THAT THE U.S. FORCES WOULD BE USED IN COMBAT.

Dave handed the paper back to Leon mechanically. God damn him, he thought. God damn him.

"Did you know about this?" Leon whispered.

Dave shook his head. He saw Barney across the room slicing

himself a piece of birthday cake. His instinct was to go talk to him, to plead with him, but he knew it was too late.

"It's MacKenzie and those corporation presidents," Leon said.

"No," Dave told him. "It's that damned seventy-one percent. He thinks he can get away with anything now."

He went onto the balcony and stared into the night. He had a terrible feeling that they—Barney, himself, all of them—had stepped into the dark, that no one could know where the journey might end. He still had the impulse to go to Barney, to talk to him, to reason with him, but a warning voice told him, no, to keep quiet, that this was not the time, that tomorrow or the next day there would be a chance to see what could be done to correct, to modify, to counteract this step. The Pentagon had won this battle but the war was not over.

He kept quiet, too, because after dinner, after drinking one glass of brandy, he had realized that he was not sober, that he was very close to being drunk. He resolved to say as little as possible for the rest of the night. He went back inside and listened while Leon told a long story about being stuck in an elevator with William Buckley and Mae West. Dave was thinking of Rivera in the mountains of Caravelas and the scene around him now seemed distant and unreal.

Suddenly there was a loud shout from the doorway:

"Everybody stick 'em up!"

He jerked his head in astonishment and saw a white object shoot toward him, felt it pop painfully against his ear and bounce away.

"Gotcha," Barney cried. He fired his plastic airgun again and another ping-pong ball shot across the room and struck Eddie.

"Secret weapon from the Pentagon," he said, striding into the room. "Gonna zonk the Commies with 'em. Okay, everybody up for the war game."

The party had come to life again. Barney had donned the grimy old fatigue cap he liked to wear during games. He handed each guest an airgun loaded with a half-dozen ping-pong balls. Then he explained the rules. There would be two armies. He would head one, consisting of himself and all the women, called the Patriots. The other army would consist of all the other men and would be called the Commie Rats. (Brenda, at this point, excused herself, Sharon, and Winnie from the war game, and led the young couple out onto the balcony.) The entire second floor would be the battleground, Barney explained, with all but a few lights extinguished. The Patriots would start in the dining room on the west end of the floor; the Commie Rats from the Rose Room on the east. If you were struck by a ping-pong ball fired by the enemy, you were dead. The war ended when one or the other army was wiped out.

Dave listened to the instructions and nodded slowly. It seemed an eminently reasonable game. He studied his weapon. Although plastic, it had a good heft to it. Barney poured them all another drink before they started, then the war began. The Commie Rats huddled in the semi-darkness of the Rose Room getting their orders from MacKenzie, who'd been an infantry officer during the war.

"Leon and I will advance along the main corridor," he was saying. "Eddie, you and Dave cut through the Lincoln Room and try to outflank them. O.B., you wait here and move up fast when you hear us firing.

"All right men, let's move out. Good luck."

They moved off into the darkness. Dave broke away from Eddie as soon as he could—Eddie was too clumsy; he'd be a sitting duck. Dave kept low, staying close to the walls, and he'd reached the Treaty Room when he heard the first sounds of battle: the sudden *whoosh* of the airguns, the cries of the wounded, the ominous plunk-plunk-plunk of the ping-pong balls bouncing on the wooden floor of the hallway. From the shouts, Dave could tell that MacKenzie had picked off Eleanor and Adria but had lost Leon.

A shadow wavered in the doorway; Dan fired his gun and was gratified to hear Flo Gooch, hit on her bony rump, yelp loudly. Then, just outside the door, Barney sprang from ambush and cut down Eddie and O.B. That left only Barney and Cathy of the Patriots and Dave and MacKenzie of the Rats. Dave decided to have another drink. He slipped through the darkness to the punchbowl, but as he filled his glass a ping-pong ball whizzed past his head. He turned and fired at a dark shape ten feet away—and Cathy expired with a curse. He hurried to the hallway, hoping he and MacKenzie could gang up on Barney, the last of the Patriots.

He found MacKenzie and Barney shooting it out in the dining room. Barney was behind an Oriental screen, firing at Mac-Kenzie, who was crouched beside a large mahogany sideboard. The lawyer tried to make a run for it but Barney cut him down with one quick blast.

Dave took aim from the doorway but Barney saw him, sent one shot speeding past his ear, and came charging toward him. Dave turned and fled down the hallway. Another shot zipped past his head and Dave ducked into the first doorway he came to—the library. He crouched behind the sofa, eying the door. There was only one door—he would have to make his stand here.

"Okay, boy, say your prayers, 'cause I'm coming in." Barney's voice was an arrogant snarl from the shadows outside the open door.

Dave was ready. There was a faint light in the hall, enough to silhouette Barney in the doorway when he entered. Dave checked his gun—three shots left. He could handle Barney this time—let him come!

"Better get ready, you Commie Rat," Barney whispered. Dave pointed his weapon at the doorway. He expected a sudden charge and he waited confidently.

Then he saw the bill of Barney's fatigue cap and the curve of his head silhouetted in the doorway—Barney was trying to locate him. As Dave zeroed in, head and cap disappeared, then returned a moment later. Dave had the moving shadow in his sights. He could hear Barney breathing. This was it.

Zap! Zap! Zap! He squeezed off three shots, saw two of them strike the silhouette, then leaped to his feet with a shout of victory.

Suddenly the lights went on. The "head" in the doorway came flying toward him—a football, with the fatigue cap atop it, that Barney had waved in the shadows to draw his fire. The oldest trick in the book—and he had fallen for it. His humiliation was complete as Barney bounded in and blasted him point-blank.

"Sucker," Barney roared.

"You win, boss," Dave sighed, and sank into the soft cushions of the sofa.

The rest of the party was a blur.

It was eleven. Rosy Rosenthal had arrived, along with the writer of the film script, a tall fellow named Mike Bates.

Barney had a proposition for the producer.

"I saw in the paper that when they made one of McQueen's pictures in San Francisco, they paid the city for using it as their set."

"That's accurate, Mr. President," Rosy said, licking his lips nervously.

"What're you doing for this picture of yours, Rosy—building some phony-looking set to look like the White House?"

Rosy nodded unhappily.

"How'd you like to use the real thing?"

Rosy's mouth fell open. "You mean . . ."

"Sure, shoot the damn picture in here. How long would you need?"

Rosy turned to Mike Bates, his writer, who said, "No more than a week if we schedule it tight." Bates was fortyish, tall and deeply tanned, with dark circles beneath his eyes.

"A week, huh?" Barney pondered. "Okay, Rosy, suppose we charge you ten thousand?"

"Ten thousand would be most reasonable, Mr. President," the producer said. "Perhaps we might even . . ."

"I mean ten thousand an hour, Rosy," Barney added, and Rosy's face fell again.

"An hour . . . ?" he sputtered.

"Come on, Rosy, that's only three, four hundred thousand and you get a million in publicity. Hell, I ought to make it twenty thousand. But for you, Rosy, a cut rate."

"What happens to the money?" Brenda asked.

Barney shrugged. "You pick it. Crippled kids. Cancer research. Something like that. Call me tomorrow, Rosy."

Later, Rosy cornered Dave on the sofa for a fatherly chat. "You are a young man on the rise," he kept saying. "You must plan for the future. Consider films. Travel. Adventure. Beautiful women. The joy of creation. We must have a long talk."

Dave kept saying he was a lawyer, he didn't know anything about movies, and finally he escaped. Later he heard Rosy telling Cathy she should write for the movies and Cathy saying she liked writing for newspapers.

Midnight. Dave saw Eleanor talking to Mike Bates, the writer, and he was about to join them when he heard a scream from out on the balcony. He went out and saw that Barney had forced Eddie Gooch out over the edge, so that he was hanging from the railing by his fingertips, his feet dangling toward the flowerbeds twenty feet below. Barney watched him calmly, and glanced at his watch from time to time.

"Boss, pull me back, pull me back," Eddie wailed.

"He's tougher than you'd think," Barney remarked when he saw Dave. "He's been hanging there for five minutes." Dave went back inside—this was none of his affair. A minute later a white-faced Eddie stumbled in and collapsed in a chair.

"You okay?" Dave asked.

"Think you're pretty hot stuff, don't you?" Eddie whispered bitterly.

"Take it easy, Eddie."

"You take it easy, bright boy. You better watch it."

"Say what you mean."

"You'll find out what I mean, bright boy. You'll find out."

Dave shrugged and walked away. He knew Eddie resented him but this was the first time he'd let it show.

Then Barney was telling him to fire an Assistant Secretary of Commerce who'd somehow offended an important senator. "Fire the silly bastard, you hear? Fire him first thing Monday morning." Dave nodded but he planned to wait a few days and see if Barney didn't forget about it.

Then he had lost all track of time and everyone left at the party was linked arm in arm around the piano. Leon was playing and they were all laughing and swaying and singing:

"Happy Birth-day, Mis-ter President,
Happy Birth-day to you!"

9

"Hope you don't mind me barging in like this," Elton Carr said, settling his big frame in the chair beside Dave's desk.

"You're always welcome, Elton. I'm sorry the President is away."

"Don't matter," Carr said, waving his fat, unlit cigar. "I'll call him next week. How you been?"

"Not bad," Dave said. "Working hard."

"What on?"

"A lot on this New Cities bill."

"That's a big 'un," Carr said. "Makes me hark back to the TVA fight. When you look for a vote?"

"In a month, I think," Dave said. "How are things in Tennessee?"

Elton Carr, a big rumpled man, lit his cigar before he answered. Forty years before he had worked his way through Cumberland Law School selling Bibles; now he was the richest lawyer in Tennessee, and the kingpin of the state's Democratic party. Eight years earlier, he had been the first professional politician to sense Barney Newfield's potential.

"Things been a little rough, Dave," Carr admitted. "The boys at the *Herald* just had to back young Ed Kemble for governor, and they got their fingers burned like I knew they would. A newspaper can do a lot, but it can't elect somebody folks don't like."

"You did all right in the Senate race, though," Dave said.

"We did indeed," Carr admitted. "It was right satisfactory."

"I heard you predicted he'd win by ninety-three thousand votes, and he won by ninety-two-five."

"I was just a tad optimistic," Carr said, and they laughed.

Dave had an editor from *Life* waiting to see him, but he would have to wait.

"Well, I guess you're wondering what's on my mind," Carr said.

"It's a pleasure to visit with you," Dave said. You didn't rush Elton Carr. He had come to talk politics, and his style was a circuitous one.

"You know Clay Whitelaw's been sick, don't you?" Carr asked.

"I'd heard that."

"He's getting worse. They say he won't last out the year."

"That's too bad," Dave said. "You think he'll resign?"

Carr shook his head. "He's represented that district sixteen years now, and the only way you'll get Clay out is feet first. He's stubborn as a mule. Besides, he probably figures if he dies in office, his wife can be elected to succeed him."

"You think she'd run?"

Carr sighed. "I don't know, Dave. Somebody'll have to talk to her. We need some forward-looking young man to speak for us in Congress, not Millie Whitelaw."

"Who're the leading contenders? They're lined up, aren't they?"

"For half a mile," Carr said. "Larry Houston been doing a right smart job in the City Council, and Alf Herndon might decide to run on the law-and-order thing. But there's another candidate some of us are interested in."

"Who's that?"

"You, Dave."

Dave paused before replying. He wouldn't insult Elton's intelligence by pretending he was surprised, but it would not do to appear too blasé either.

"You know I'm flattered, Elton, and grateful. But I don't see how I could consider it. I've got a job to do here."

"You'd have to clear it with Barney," the older man said—Dave assumed he'd already cleared the offer with Barney before he made it. "But I don't think he'd stand in your way. You've got your own future to think of."

"I've been away from Nashville for two years," Dave said. "And I'd only lived there eight years before that. People may want a hometown boy."

Carr waved his cigar impatiently. "The city's growing, changing. New people coming in. They don't give a tinker's damn where you were born. You came to town when you were—what? —twenty-one?"

"Yes, when I started in law school."

"So you know half the lawyers in town from Vanderbilt," Carr said. "Then you were Public Defender and you got some attention out of that."

Dave nodded. "Eight thousand a year and all the publicity I could eat."

"The publicity didn't hurt you. And now you've got yourself some Washington experience. Folks'll think, 'Here's a boy can go up there and pull strings for us.'

"I'm saying, Dave, that I can give you some help, and I think the fellows at the AF of L would like to help you, and you know the *Herald* will back you . . ."

"I didn't marry the publisher's niece for nothing," Dave said.

"Eleanor would be a big help to you no matter whose niece she was," Carr said. "But the connection won't hurt any. Dave, the question is what you want to do. You've got to tell us, so we can be looking ahead."

Dave nodded. He had been thinking about this since he had first heard of Whitelaw's illness, and he knew he had no desire to serve in the House. The Senate would have been different, but no one was offering him a shot at the Senate, not yet. To be a first-term congressman left him cold—he was better off where he was.

"You know I'm interested in running for office someday," Dave said. "But I can run two years from now, or four or six, whereas I'll never have another chance to do what I'm doing now. I think I'd better stay where I am, Elton."

Carr chewed on his cigar a moment. "I figured you'd see it that way," he said, "but you've got to give me a nickel for trying."

"I appreciate it," Dave said. "I really do."

Carr rose to leave, but he stopped at the doorway.

"Dave, tell me something," he said. "What's got into Barney about this Caravelas place? What's he doing sending our boys down there?"

"He thinks he's got to prop up that government."

Carr's face flushed. "Who gives a hoot in hell who runs that pipsqueak country?" he demanded. "Has he forgot about Lyndon already?"

"It's strange, Elton. You get in that office over there and you start feeling pressures you didn't feel before. The generals. The corporations. Foreign opinion. What history will say about you."

"Bull!" Carr said. "Some of our boys are going to get shot at, and they'll shoot back, and then where will we be? Where does it stop? This isn't the Barney I know."

"Talk to him, Elton. Get other people to talk to him. It all helps."

"By God, it better," Carr said. "He's got to get taxes down and do something about the cities if he wants to get re-elected."

"Talk to him," Dave repeated, and they shook hands and the old lawyer left.

He left the *Life* editor wait a few more minutes while he thought about this offer and what refusing it might mean. He did not doubt that he could be elected to Congress—Elton Carr was not known for backing losers—but he did doubt most seriously that Congress was what he wanted. It seemed to him that all his life he had been trying to decide what he wanted—for he had always assumed he could get whatever he settled upon. Up to a point you could have it both ways, have it all. In college he had been both scholar and campus politician, and when he graduated he had toyed with the idea of a teaching career before electing to attend law school—for he believed he might make an imprint on the world, and a law degree seemed the best first step. As a law student at Vanderbilt, he had moved easily among Nashville's rich, yet when he graduated he turned down offers from the city's best law firms, and, instead, ran for the newly established office of Public Defender. Idealism? Yes—and politics too, for he knew the low-salaried job would repay him with a fortune in publicity. And it had, but after two years he had tired of the grime and the heartache of representing the indigent. He was thinking of running for the state senate—thinking, too, of accepting an offer with a leading law firm—when the new governor called him one day and said he needed a young lawyer to help with his legislative program.

Newfield's offer seemed an opportunity to have it both ways

—to serve good ends, and also to have power and prestige. He thought himself tough-minded, no wild-eyed idealist, yet he liked to think there was a certain idealism within him, a concern with ends as well as with means. He was not indifferent to the amenities his talent could bring him, but he hoped to have it both ways—to do good and to do well too. Yet the higher he rose in public life, the more he sensed a painful dilemma: it is not hard to be a powerful man in America, and it is not impossible to be a good man, but it is almost impossible to be both.

He mentioned Elton Carr's proposal to the President the next night.

"Hell, maybe you ought to," Barney said. "You might make a pretty fair congressman, as congressmen go."

"I'd like to think I can do more good here," Dave said, knowing it sounded pious.

"You mean you can have more power here," Barney shot back.

"It's not really power. It's delegated authority."

"Sure it's power. You're a big man in this town. That's what all the papers say." Barney was enjoying the conversation more than Dave was. "Okay, kid. You know I need you here. But if you ever want to go run for anything, do it. A man's got to look out for his own interests."

"Maybe later," Dave said. "I've got time."

"Being a first-term congressman may not look like much," Barney said. "But remember, all of those guys can do one thing that you can't, or Leon or MacKenzie or anybody in my administration."

"What's that?" Dave said.

"They can tell the President to kiss their ass anytime they want to."

Dave laughed. "I don't want to tell you that."

"You will someday."

"When I do, I'll go run for Congress," Dave said, and they left it at that.

10

"Dave I need you to take another little trip for me."

"Where to?"

"Mexico City. We got some pissant problem with the Mexicans. They want Texas back or something."

"God damn, Mr. President, let 'em have it."

"No, I may need it sometime. Anyway, they're mad as hell at the striped-pants boys, so you gotta go down and smooth it over for me. Okay?"

"Whatever you say. But I've got a lot of New Cities work piled up here."

"Oh, hell, you need a break. Maybe you can latch on to a little señorita down there."

He was briefed by the State Department the next morning—it was a dispute over oil rights near the border—and he arrived in Mexico City the following Monday. He lunched with the American ambassador, then dined with the Minister of the Interior that night. There were more meetings the next day and the problem was amicably solved—it hadn't been much of a problem, until State got into it—and that evening Dave had dinner with the President of Mexico. He was a short, mustachioed man who drank a lot and laughed a lot and wanted to know the significance of President Newfield's sending military advisers to Caravelas. Dave wanted to know that too, so he said as little as possible and, pleading exhaustion made his departure shortly after midnight. When he entered his hotel suite, he found an unexpected guest sitting on his sofa reading a magazine.

"Well, Colonel, what now?"

"Rivera's in town," Bob Huffaker said, "and he wants to talk to you."

Dave slipped off his dinner jacket and sat down.

"Slow down, Bob," he said. "Why is he in Mexico City?"

"To see a doctor," Huffaker said. "And to buy arms."

"Then the stories about him being wounded were true."

"Yeah," Huffaker said. "Things have got pretty hot down there."

"Because of our advisers?"

"Because of our helicopters, mainly. They can run Rivera ragged."

"Why does he want to see me?"

Huffaker shrugged. "Ask him."

"Okay, where is he?"

"At an estate outside town. I can drive you there in half an hour."

Dave picked up the phone and ordered coffee. The interminable wines and brandies of the dinner had left him a little high. He washed his face and slipped into slacks and a sport coat.

The coffee came and Dave poured them both a cup.

"Let me ask you something," he said to Huffaker. "Why do you carry on this liaison with Rivera? There must be tremendous risk."

Huffaker smiled. "Maybe I'm an idealist and I think Rivera is the savior of his country," he said.

"Maybe."

"Or maybe I'm just ambitious. Remember, if Rivera wins, I'm the boy who can deal with him."

"Or maybe it's both," Dave said.

"Maybe it is," Huffaker said. "Don't mean to rush you, but it's getting late."

"Okay," Dave said, "I'm ready."

They stood up. "One bit of cloak and dagger," Huffaker said. "I'll go out now and you wait five minutes before you follow. Turn right at the front and I'll be in a black Chevrolet one block down."

Seven minutes later they were moving through the streets of Mexico City. They passed first through a noisy, neon-bright slum, then through quiet suburbs and into the hills outside the city. The night was clear and the sky filled with stars. They rounded curve after curve, always moving higher into the hills, until at last the road narrowed, followed a high brick wall for almost a mile, then stopped before an elaborate iron gate. Past the gate, the road plunged into a cascade of trees. Huffaker honked twice and the gate swung open. They drove another half-mile through the dark tunnel of the trees, then suddenly the stars burst overhead again and they stopped before a white stucco mansion.

The two Americans got out of the car and climbed the steps to a wide veranda. Four or five men, talking and smoking in the shadows, made no objection as they entered the house. Dave had a glimpse of marble floors and crystal chandeliers before Huffaker led him up a wide staircase. Huffaker knocked on a door at the top of the stairs. Rivera's voice called impatiently, "Come in, come in."

Rivera was sitting in a red leather chair and the girl, Elda, was standing beside him, her large brown eyes fixed on the two Americans. Rivera rose to greet them, leaning on a cane. He was wearing cream-colored pants and an expensive, reddish-orange silk shirt. He was thinner than when Dave had seen him in the mountains.

"We meet again, Mr. Hyer," he said as they shook hands.

"You're living in higher style this time, Captain," Dave said.

"It is only temporary," Rivera said. "Soon I will return to the mountains."

The girl Elda spoke sharply in Spanish. She was elegant in her long, green-flowered dress; she looked as if she belonged here in this mansion, not back in a cave in the mountains.

"Excuse me a moment, gentlemen," he said, and taking the girl's arm, led her out of the room.

"She doesn't want him to go back," Huffaker said. "She says he'll be killed if he goes back."

"What does he say?"

"He says for her not to worry."

"Who is she?" Dave asked.

"She and her brother, the one who was killed, are from an old family in Madrid. They slipped into Caravelas to join the revolution right at the start."

"She may be right," Dave said.

"He knows that."

Rivera returned alone and asked if they would have brandy. They asked for coffee and Rivera called out in Spanish. A moment later a bearded man in fatigues brought in two steaming mugs of Mexican coffee.

"How does the war progress, Captain?" Dave asked.

"It has grown more difficult," Rivera said. "But the eventual outcome remains the same."

"I hope so, Captain," Dave said. "Now what can I do for you?"

"You told your President of our last conversation?" Rivera asked.

"Yes."

"And he was not interested in my proposals?"

"He was interested," Dave said, "but in the end he felt he must do as he did."

"And send your advisers and your helicopters to prop up the junta," Rivera said.

"There were those who wanted him to do more than that," Dave said.

"He will have to do much more than that if he seeks to destroy my movement," Rivera said coldly.

"The President is not greatly concerned about destroying your movement," Dave said. "But he is concerned about other matters that could be affected by your movement."

"Such as your legislation for the New Cities," Rivera said.

"Yes. We expect a vote on it soon and it may be very close."

"And your Congressional elections in November," Rivera added.

Dave nodded, sipping at the hot coffee. "Yes, that is another consideration."

"What about after that?"

"After what?"

"After the elections," Rivera said. "Will conditions have changed? Or will you have new reasons to oppose me?"

"What are you getting at, Captain?" Dave asked.

Rivera lifted his injured left leg slowly and crossed it over his right. "I am willing to propose," he said, "that for the remainder of this year my men and I suspend offensive operations. In return, U.S. personnel and helicopters shall not be used against us. You may declare a victory for yourselves, for whatever good it may do in your elections. Then, after the elections, you withdraw your forces from Caravelas. Have the boys home for Christmas."

Rivera paused. "And then what?" Dave asked.

"And then, on the first day of January, while your newspaper offices are half-empty and your people are watching their football games, I will execute a bloodless coup in Caravelas. Colonel Molina will be ousted—imprisoned but not killed—and I will take power. The next day, before opposition has arisen in your country, I will send a friendly message to your government, stating that my government will be non-Communist and seeks good relations with the U.S."

Dave was taken aback. "This coup," he said, "how do you know it would succeed?"

Rivera stared at him without replying.

"I think it's all right to explain that," Bob Huffaker injected. "Captain Rivera has learned that a very high officer of the junta army will support him, one whose assistance would virtually assure the success of the coup."

"If there were no Americans around to get caught in the middle," Dave said.

"That's right," Huffaker said.

"You've heard my proposal, Mr. Hyer," Rivera said. "What is your reply?"

"Captain, what I think doesn't matter. It's what the President thinks."

"What do you think his response will be?"

Dave shut his eyes, groping for an answer. He was trying to think with the President's mind, trying to put himself inside that cooler, more complex intellect. If he took Barney another offer from Rivera, and it was refused, there would be no more communications. He tried to imagine Barney, his eyes narrowed, his mouth twisted into a scowl, driving the hardest possible bargain.

"I don't know," he said. "I don't know. There's always one question he'll ask—can he trust you?"

"He runs little risk," Rivera said dryly. "I am the one who suspends military operations. And if I do not keep my bargain, you always have a military alternative."

"That's true," Dave said, staring at the guerrilla leader, still trying to see him with Barney's eyes. He drank the last of his coffee and put the mug on the floor. Rivera had picked up his cane and was holding it across the chair before him.

"There's one other problem, Captain, that will be difficult to explain," Dave said.

"What is that?" Rivera asked.

"You, Captain. Let me try to make myself clear. In the past few months, your name has become increasingly well-known in the United States. With the publicity about your revolution, the reports of your battles, the rumors that you were dead or wounded, you've become a symbolic figure. To the young, you've become a symbol of revolution, another Castro or Che. But to many older people, you've become a symbol of something else, of communism gaining a foothold in Latin America. No matter what you say or do, those people will continue to oppose you."

Rivera spread his hands wide. "What do you suggest, Mr. Hyer? How can the leopard change his spots?"

"He can't, Captain, that's the problem."

"Then what do you suggest?" Rivera said impatiently.

Dave hesitated, his mind still trying to mesh with that distant mind he would have to satisfy.

"I think, Captain, that even if the coup came off perfectly, and you issued your friendly statement, your name would create built-in hostility in the United States."

Rivera started to speak but Dave went on: "I think that the answer may be that after you have won the revolution someone else, someone who isn't controversial, may have to head the government. Someone like that doctor who Molina's had under house arrest—what's his name, Bob?"

"Hernández-Ortega," Huffaker said.

"That's right," Dave said. "If I recall correctly, he's liberal but non-Communist, and has a good record."

"He could have come with us to the mountains," Rivera said scornfully. "He chose not to."

"All right," Dave said. "But I'm suggesting that perhaps there are those who fight in the mountains and those who can perform a ceremonial role afterward. I'm not saying you'd be on the outside. Maybe you'd be Minister of the Interior. Probably you'd be the real power in the country. But I'm saying it'd be a hell of a lot easier for President Newfield if some nice non-Communist doctor was the next President of Caravelas instead of you."

"You ask too much," Rivera said.

"I don't ask anything," Dave said. "I'm just trying to find a solution that will persuade my President to give you what you need to win your struggle. What do you say, Captain? Will you agree to my plan, if the President will accept it?"

Rivera stared at him for thirty seconds before he answered. "Yes," he said finally. "Yes, I will agree to it if that is what is required."

"Good," Dave said.

"But how do we know President Newfield will agree to it?" Rivera asked.

"We don't," Dave admitted. "But I'll talk to him. I'll do what I can."

11

"Look at that crazy bastard," the President whispered to Dave. "He's my secret weapon!"

With crashing cymbals and thundering drums, Donald Duffey rounded the corner of Fifteenth Street and led his parade up Pennsylvania Avenue. Duffey stepped high to the rousing music, pumping a drum major's silver baton, waving to the crowds along the avenue, shouting encouragement to those who marched abreast of him in the parade's front rank—a governor and a mayor, a soul singer, an astronaut, the nation's top disc jockey, a seven-foot basketball star, a husband-and-wife acting team from Hollywood.

As Duffey drew nearer to the White House reviewing stand, more and more of the parade rounded the corner by the Treasury and marched into view—ten rows of short-skirted, pert-bottomed baton-twirlers from Mississippi, a small army of black Boy Scouts from the Bronx, the University of Texas marching band. Stretched out behind them on Pennsylvania Avenue, almost to the Capitol, were scores of other bands, floats, twirlers, and delegations, three thousand or more civic-minded Americans, all come to march in Duffey's parade.

"I don't believe it," Dave said to himself. "I just don't believe it."

Then, as Duffey jabbed his baton toward the bright July sky, the bands began a deafening *Hail to the Chief*—a rousing tune, one that made even Dave tingle with pleasure and pride—the President grinned, the crowd cheered, and Dave settled back helplessly to enjoy the show.

When Duffey reached the reviewing stand, the parade halted, and the President, the thousands along the avenue, and the millions more watching on television, were treated to a concert, tumbling, baton-twirling, lariat-spinning, and finally a speech by Duffey.

"Mr. President," Duffey roared into the silver nest of microphones, his green eyes blinking against the sun, "Mr. President, today is New Cities Day, a day of national pride and unity, and on behalf of all America, I want to say, Thank you, Mr. President. Thank you for sharing your great dream with us. Thank you for pointing the way to a better, brighter future for all of us. Thank you for . . ."

Dave tuned out Duffey's oration after a few moments, yet his eyes stayed fixed on the barrel-chested speaker, and he found himself regarding Duffey, as he always did, with a mixture of fascination and horror. Duffey was one of this administration's success stories. He was a bartender's son who had been a college football star, married well, and built Indiana's biggest Ford dealership. It was as a Ford dealer that Duffey had first exhibited his flair for publicity. Other dealers may have offered lower prices or better service, but only Duffey offered fireworks displays, parades, string bands, dancing girls, carnivals, raffles, patriotism ("Don Duffey's Fabulous Fourth Ford Festival"), an endless stream of gimmicks that dazzled the car-buying public and soon enriched Duffey.

His fame might have remained regional, had not Duffey's wife happened to be Mrs. Milton Osgood's favorite niece, and his talents been employed in the presidential campaign. Duffey specialized in parades and rallies, and there were hardened political pros who called him a genius. After the election was won, the First Lady-elect and her niece demanded of the President-elect a cabinet seat for Duffey. Osgood protested, but the women prevailed, and Duffey became Secretary of Housing and Urban Development, the post in which it was hoped he might do the least harm.

Duffey quickly saw that HUD was a hodge-podge of fiercely independent dukedoms, essentially ungovernable, so he let the bureaucrats alone, and devoted his energies to selling himself to America. Within months, he became the Cecil B. De Mille of government. Duffey led a torchlight parade in Harlem and launched a Slug-the-Bug campaign in Watts. He rode a balloon into the sky (to inspect new housing sites) and a submarine beneath the seas (something about ocean-bottom development). He was photographed with an endless procession of beauty queens, movie stars, and athletes. He was a regular on the *Today Show* and the *Tonight Show* and he sang *God Bless America* on the *Ed Sullivan Show* with Diana Ross and the Supremes. He commissioned a "Mister Clean-Up" comic strip and sold it to a hundred newspapers. He came within a whisker of persuading Elvis Presley to sing in Yankee Stadium on behalf of National Love Thy Neighbor Week.

In short, no gimmick was too brazen, no stunt too self-serving for Donald Duffey to perform if it promised publicity, and as a result he was soon the fastest-rising star in American politics.

Even Duffey's critics conceded that he was a genius of sorts, and his talents were never more apparent than when the President gave him the job of selling the New Cities. First off, Duffey persuaded Andrew Wyeth, Andy Warhol and three other artists to portray their conceptions of the New Cities, and he got *Life's* promise to carry a color spread of the five paintings. He named Mickey Mantle, Johnny Unitas, and Floyd Patterson as New Cities Sports Advisers in a televised ceremony. He persuaded Andy Williams to devote a television special to the New Cities theme. The publicity poured in, and when Duffey came up with the idea of a national New Cities Week, complete with parades and speeches in a dozen old cities, no one could find any reason why it should *not* be done. Therefore . . .

"And so, Mr. President," he was concluding, "as America looks forward to another Glorious Fourth, my thoughts turn back to that first Fourth when Jefferson and Adams and Franklin and all the other Founders signed that noble document, almost two hundred years ago, and I know in my heart that if they were with us today they would applaud this latest chapter in the American Dream, and I know that Jefferson, that great architect, is looking down on your New Cities and wishing that he was here to help us build them. So I say, thank you again, Mr. President, for your vision and your inspiration."

What an ass-kisser, Dave thought, but the President was

beaming. The bands began playing *It's a Grand Old Flag* and the parade started moving again, as Duffey and his celebrities scrambled up into the President's box. Dave was standing with his wife and daughter at the back of the box, watching the spectacle through a sheet of bulletproof glass.

"It's a fabulous parade," Eleanor said. "But what's it all about?"

"Nobody knows," Dave told her. "Duffey just decided to have a parade."

"Does he really know that Jefferson is looking down on us?" she asked.

"I don't know," Dave said. "That's Duffey's secret."

Duffey, meanwhile, was bounding about the box, shaking hands and waving to people.

"Look at those little sweethearts, Mr. President," Duffey said as two hundred short-skirted drum majorettes pranced by. "There's the real America."

"It's like a candy store," the President muttered.

"No more candy for you, Big Daddy," Brenda said. She was sitting next to the President, wearing round sunglasses and a high-necked white dress. She looked around, then called to someone in the next box.

"Hey you sweethearts, come on over and socialize."

Sharon Flatt and Winnie Boatwright grinned and entered the President's box.

"Hey, Barney, look who's here," Brenda announced.

"Haven't you got any work to do?" Barney asked Sharon.

"Come on, Scrooge, it's your parade," Brenda said.

"It's a magnificent parade, Mr. President," Winnie Boatwright said. He looked very elegant in a blue blazer and white pants.

"Glad you like it," Barney muttered.

"Hey, Mazie, come meet these kids," Brenda called to a society reporter who was hovering as near as the Secret Service would allow. Dave smiled as Mazie scurried forth. It was a good bet that the twosome of Boatwright heir and presidential typist would rate a paragraph in Mazie's column the next day.

"There's a good thirty million watching on TV," Donald

Duffey told the President. "We picked up an extra five million or so because the Mets game comes on next."

"How long is this thing, Duff?" the President asked.

"The last float is just now passing the National Gallery," Duffey said proudly. Circles of sweat were showing beneath the arms of his white linen suit. "This is bigger than my Fifth Avenue parade in the campaign. And wait till you see the finale—twenty elephants from Ringling Brothers."

"Hey, Ellie, bring my little sweetheart over here," the President called. Eleanor smiled radiantly and took the empty chair beside the President, who put Sally on his lap. The child jerked at his tie, and the President gave her a kiss, which a dozen photographers recorded. Duffey frowned at losing the President's attention, and ran his fingers impatiently through his thick reddish-blond hair.

"What's that out there?" the President asked Sally.

"Prade," the child said. "Big prade."

"Biggest prade you'll ever see," Barney said.

"Biggest parade she'll see until January 20, two years from now," Duffey injected, and the President grinned.

"What's that big thing there, sugar?" he asked the child, indicating a float from Oklahoma.

"Don't know," Sally admitted.

"That's an oil well, sweetheart. See the oil gushing out the top?"

Duffey brought the husband-and-wife team from Hollywood over to meet the President. The husband, considered one of the movies' great sex-symbols, was a slight, rather bewildered fellow, most unprepossessing alongside Barney Newfield. His wife, a tall, intelligent-looking brunette, seemed more formidable.

"How ya feeling, fellow?" Barney asked the actor.

"Boy, could I use a drink," the actor admitted. "We must of marched ten miles."

"Come over to the house when this is over," Barney said, "and we'll have one."

"Mr. President," the actress said, "I have a plan for a Children's Theater I hope you'll consider for the New Cities."

"Why, sure, honey," Barney said. "Tell me about it. Dave, listen to this."

"The idea," the actress said, "is to form a classical acting company to tour the New Cities and present Shakespeare and . . ."

Iowa's famed Seventy-six Trombones passed at this moment, temporarily silencing the actress.

". . . if you had an average audience of one thousand youngsters," she continued when the Seventy-six had marched on by, "that would mean you could reach two hundred thousand children a year with the classics . . ."

"My God, would you look at that?" Barney said, as a float from California came into view: It featured two bears dancing to the tune of *I Left My Heart in San Francisco*.

". . . and in effect you'd be building a future audience for the classics . . ."

"I think it's a hell of an idea," Barney shouted over the din of the parade. "Why don't you get together with Dave here and . . ."

"Mr. President," said another man Duffey had brought up, "I'd like to second what Miss Martindale has said. I'm Len Devine of WGR—World's Greatest Radio—and I have a plan for fighting juvenile delinquency that . . ."

"Duffey," the President cried.

"I want all you folks out to my house tonight for a real meaningful dialogue on all this stuff," Duffey said.

"I have something to say about Caravelas," the actress persisted. "A great many of us think the U.S. intervention there is a terrible mistake, Mr. President."

"Gosh, I don't know about that," the disc jockey said.

"Hey, give us a smile, Marge!" a photographer called, but the actress wasn't smiling.

"Why can't we keep hands off Latin America?" she demanded.

"Say, let's talk about the New Cities," Duffey urged.

"This country has responsibilities in Latin America," Barney said with an edge to his voice.

"This country has responsibilities to decency and sanity," the actress shot back.

"Sister, you make your pictures and I'll make my foreign policy," Barney said angrily.

"Why you big . . ." the actress began, but her husband grabbed her arm. "Come on, Marge," he said. "Cool it."

"Hey, Rafe, how's the weather up there?" Duffey called to the seven-foot basketball star, who was standing nearby chewing gum.

"Well if we came three thousand miles to this circus, I don't see why we can't talk to him," Marge told her husband.

"Oh bull, Marge," the actor said.

"Let me take you over for a drink," Dave told the couple.

"Boy, can I use one," the actor said.

"I'll make my foreign policy—what kind of crap is that?" the actress demanded. "It's my foreign policy too."

"It's this heat," Dave told her. "He gets irritable in the heat. He appreciates you coming and helping with the New Cities."

They stopped on the front porch of the White House, where they could see the parade stretched out for three blocks like a multicolored ribbon. The bands were playing *Yankee Doodle Dandy*.

"You're supposed to be a bright guy," the actress said. "Do you think we ought to be sending soldiers down there?"

"I've got my doubts about it," Dave said. "But it's not an easy or simple decision. There are a lot of conflicting pressures."

"Why can't this stinking government just do what's right for a change?" the actress demanded.

"Miss Martindale," Dave said, "I happened to see your last picture and it was a real dog. What was an actress of your talent doing in a fourth-rate farce like that?"

She looked at him angrily. "You can't always do what you want to do in the movie business," she said.

"Well, you can't in the foreign policy business either," Dave told her.

"Hey, how about that drink?" her husband asked.

When he returned to the President's box he found Cathy Quinn, a big PRESS badge pinned to her lapel, talking to his wife. The President was still holding Sally on his lap, although now the disc jockey and the basketball player had been replaced by a governor and an astronaut. The parade still surged by.

Eleanor smiled at him. "I was just telling Cathy what a wonderful article that was she wrote about Brenda."

"I liked her," Cathy said, brushing her hair out of her eyes. "She's real."

"Where is Brenda?" Eleanor asked.

"She took Sharon and Winnie inside for a drink," Dave said. "You covering the parade, Cathy?"

"I'm thinking about doing a feature on Duffey," she said.

"That ought to be fascinating," Eleanor said.

"You girls want to come by my office for a drink?" Dave asked.

"I've got to get Sally home," Eleanor said. "She's tired. Mr. President, can I have my daughter back?"

Barney turned around in his chair. "No, I'm gonna keep her. Dave, you get rid of that nutty actress? Ellie baby, after today, you're the only actress I talk to."

Dave glanced for a moment at his wife and his mistress. Eleanor was crisp and lovely in a red silk suit. Cathy's slip was showing and her hair might have been cut with a bowl. He was wondering how he could get away to spend an evening with her.

"When you start shooting that movie?" the President asked.

"A week from now," Eleanor told him.

"I'll be keeping an eye on you," Barney said.

"It's your house," Eleanor said, and lifted Sally from his lap. "Goodbye, Mr. President. Goodbye, Cathy. Dave, will you be home for dinner?"

"I don't know," he told her. "I'll call you."

Eleanor left with Sally half-asleep in her arms.

"I'll take that drink if you'll tell me about Duffey," Cathy told him.

"Okay," Dave said. "See those elephants down there? That means the parade's about over. Come on."

"What do you really think about Duffey?" Cathy demanded, after he had poured their drinks.

"What do you think about him?" Dave countered.

"I think he's the biggest phony in Washington."

Dave shrugged. "Sure he is. But that's not all."

"What do you mean?"

"Go talk to the Indiana politicians. They're begging him to come back and run for governor or senator."

"You think he will?"

"He's already running for something else."

"You mean Vice-President next time?"

"That's right," Dave told her.

"The President wouldn't do that, would he?"

"I don't think he would. But he wouldn't discourage Duffey either. He's working his ass off on the New Cities."

"But what's it mean, all these TV shows and nutty parades and committees and speeches?"

"I'll tell you what it means. It means that in one month's time about two-thirds of the adults in America have heard or read something about the New Cities. And this week's poll says sixty-five percent of them think the New Cities are a good idea. Duffey's got people talking about the New Cities all over America. They read something in the paper, or they see something on television, and they talk to their neighbors, or maybe they write a letter to the editor, or write their Congressman, and all this somehow adds up to a national climate of opinion. There are fifty or sixty Congressmen really undecided about this bill, and they'll sense this national mood, and that may be how the bill passes."

"And you'd give credit to Duffey?"

"Even the best product needs a salesman. Duffey's selling this thing ten times better than Sid Frankel or Steve Vale could. Just as they could run the program ten times better than Duffey could."

"But what has this parade got to do with anything?" Cathy demanded.

"Don't knock it. Everybody loves a parade. Hugh Johnson was leading parades for NRA back in the New Deal."

"Who?"

"General Hugh Johnson. Read your Freidel."

"There ought to be a way to run a government without phonies like Duffey," Cathy insisted.

"If you find it, let me know," Dave said. "And anyway, if you're going to write about Duffey, you'd better consider his talents, too."

"Are you going to defend that guy?" she asked indigently.

"Look, Cathy, I'm not denying that Duffey is a fraud. I'm saying that you ought to look beyond the obvious and ask the real question—does it take some fakery to succeed in American politics today? And you might consider, too, whether the New Cities—*homes* for five or ten million Americans— aren't worth our tolerating Duffey's bullshit for a few months."

Cathy twisted her small face into a frown. She's like a child, Dave thought—you can actually see her learning.

"What do you think will happen to Duffey?" she asked.

"Plenty could. He's forty-five years old, he's fantastic on television, and he's bound to be a governor or a senator in a few years. I'd say that Duffey, who was selling Fords three years ago, today is one of the six or eight men who's going to matter in the Democratic party in the next fifteen years."

"You mean like for President?" she asked incredulously.

"Reagan almost got nominated, didn't he?" Dave asked. He got up and poured himself a second drink. "Now let's talk about this weekend," he said.

There was one small by-product of Secretary Duffey's publicity campaign that Dave did not mention to Cathy. The week before, Elias Abbot sent over to Dave a boxful of letters that had come in from poor people all over the country—an unemployed miner in West Virginia, an aged widow in Harlem, a crippled Mexican-American in the Rio Grande Valley, a tenant farmer's wife in Alabama. All these people had heard so much about the New Cities that in their innocence and ignorance they thought the New Cities had somewhere already been built, and they were asking, in these painfully written letters, where they might apply for admittance to this bright new world.

There were at least a hundred of the letters in a cardboard box. After he had looked at a few, Dave took them in to the

President. Barney read one of them, then he had his phone calls cut off and he sat for three hours reading them all, one after another, never speaking, and when he had finished the letters he put them back in the box and put the box on the floor beside his desk and the box stayed there beside him for a long time.

12

Leon Kerkelot frowned as he sipped the lukewarm tomato soup from the White House mess, frowned and continued to contemplate the young man sitting on the other side of his desk.

"Think of all those people over at San Souci, eating a decent meal," Dave said.

"And wishing they were in the White House, eating a horrid meal," Leon replied. "Eat your food, David, it'll be worse cold."

Leon liked David Hyer, liked him and also found him useful —if there had not been a David Hyer, et cetera. He had a remarkably quick mind, excellent instincts, and a good deal of subtlety for an American. It was hard to imagine anyone else doing a better job as buffer between Newfield and the world— as Newfield's intellectual valet, someone had put it. He and David had sensed from the first that they were natural allies, and over the months the younger man's understanding of the President's moods had spared Leon many unpleasantries—for the President, rubbed wrong, could be exceedingly unpleasant.

Yet Leon did not expect perfection in this world, and for all his admiration of David Hyer, he did not think him without flaw. He was, Leon thought, a shade impetuous—a small shading to be sure, almost invisible, one measured in millimeters, yet the imbalance was there. To move effectively at the highest level of government one must maintain a precarious balance between the demands of idealism and of realism, between the lofty thoughts that defined one's goals and the grubby means that attained them. Few men attempt to walk the tightrope very long; it was easier to be a theorist on the one hand, or an operative on the other. But only the handful of men who played both games—who had ideals and who fought for them—really mattered in government. Leon and Dave had been discussing this one night and Dave had quoted from a poem that Andrew Marvell wrote about Cromwell:

> "*So much one man can do*
> *That does both act and know.*"

Of course, they who did "both act and know" had the highest casualty rate, for they were constantly exposed, stretched too thin, a target for those with opposing ideas, or no ideas at all. Leon thought there were only four of them at the top of this administration who were playing the dangerous game—himself, David, Sid Frankel at HEW, and Charlton MacKenzie at State. To an extent, in foreign affairs, Leon and David had been allies against MacKenzie's hawkish inclinations, but Mac-Kenzie seemed stronger of late, more confident with the President, and the equation seemed to be shifting, so that MacKenzie and David Hyer were antagonists—most friendly, most proper, most cordial, but antagonists, nonetheless—and Leon was more in the middle, between them, unallied, watching, waiting. Leon, of course, did not think that he had begun to move more cautiously, that he had left David to fight the good fight alone, but rather that the younger man had become a shade rash on this Caravelas issue.

"Aren't there any more details you can give me?" Dave asked.

"Only what I told you this morning," Leon said. "The truck ran over a land mine, the mine exploded, and four of our men were killed."

"And there's no way to establish whose mine it was?"

"No. There's only the assumption, by our intelligence people . . ."

"Who are not always the soul of disinterest."

". . . the assumption that, while the Caravelian government might have faked a bombing of our embassy, it's not likely to have planted a mine outside our Special Forces camp."

"It's not impossible," Dave said grimly.

"It's unlikely," Leon said. He removed his silver-rimmed eyeglasses and wiped them with his napkin. His eyes seemed pale and unfocused without the glasses. "It seems to me that Rivera is demonstrating that we can't send our men there with impunity."

"As we might have known he would."

"He might have chosen to lie low, or to negotiate with us," Leon said.

"We haven't given him much encouragement in that direction," Dave said. "Leon, what have you said to the President about this thing?"

"I told him I think we should move cautiously."

"Is that all?"

"What more would you like me to tell him?"

"A lot, Leon. The Joint Chiefs will be all over him to send our troops into the mountains after Rivera. You're the foreign policy expert. I'd like to see you argue the other side. I'm feeling damn lonely."

Leon pushed back his plate and lit an English cigarette with a thin silver lighter. "David, you know, and the President knows, that I'd prefer that we stay out of Caravelas. I don't see that it would help for me to say it ten times a day."

"Sometimes you have to say things ten times a day to make Barney Newfield listen to you."

"Or stop listening to you," Leon said.

"So you won't help me?" Dave asked.

"No, David. I'll give my opinion, but I won't risk my position to help Rivera."

"Damn it, it's not for Rivera. It's for our own interests."

"That, of course, is the debatable point," Leon said.

"It's China, isn't it?" Dave asked in a weary voice. "It's that damned plot of yours to turn us around on China."

"My damned plot, David, is moving along quite nicely. The President has agreed to an ambassadorship for Coates, and that will remove another obstacle. I think we are nearing the point at which a new policy is possible."

"And you're afraid that if Rivera takes over in Caravelas there'll be enough of a reaction to upset your China scheme?"

"In effect, yes. I've never pretended to you that China wasn't at the top of my agenda. Or, for that matter, that Germany and Israel and several other matters weren't well above Caravelas on it."

"I think you're wrong in thinking Caravelas doesn't matter, Leon. I'll grant that we can crush Rivera easily enough. But once that precedent is set, we'll be committed to crushing a dozen Riveras, and we'll be bogged down all over that damned continent, and then see what happens to your China plan."

"David Hyer's domino theory," Leon said.

"Call it what you like. The point is we've got a chance for this government to do something right for a change and I wish you'd help."

"I don't disagree with your morality, David. But I fear that a small victory in Caravelas might cost me a large victory elsewhere."

"China," Dave said with a sigh.

"Yes, China. In Caravelas, we are discussing whether two or three hundred men die. In our dealings with China, we may be discussing whether two or three hundred *million* men die in nuclear war. China is the key to peace for the rest of this century, and as much as we can predict of the next. For a quarter-century we have had an idiotic policy toward the world's largest nation, that nation is on the brink of becoming a nuclear power, and I am on the brink of injecting some sanity into our policy."

Leon paused and shook his head. The afternoon sun glinted on his eyeglasses. It was past two.

"I'm sorry, David, but I can't endanger the greatest contribution I can make to world peace, not for the sake of one romantic guerrilla leader in the mountains of a minor Latin American nation."

Dave nodded wearily. "Okay, Leon, I appreciate your candor. We just see this thing differently and there's nothing to be done about it."

"I'm afraid that's the case," Leon said.

"It goes back to your youth, doesn't it?" Dave asked. "I don't mean to pry, but the more I see of people in politics—you on China, me on Caravelas, the President on the New Cities—the more I think we get our values set early, and after that there's no changing our minds."

Leon Kerkelot tapped out his cigarette before he answered. Dave was the first of his colleagues in government to mention his youth to him. It was known, it was mentioned in articles, but it was not asked about. He had spent three years, from age eleven to fourteen, in a Nazi concentration camp in Poland, somehow surviving while everyone else in his family perished. Dave, for one, could not imagine that experience; he did not want to imagine it, it seemed to him something best left unimagined, yet he knew that now, three decades later, the experience still shaped Leon's view of international politics. Leon had seen the worst, he had seen Hell, and he was left with no illusions about the nobility of man. If one highly civilized nation would murder six million Jews, it did not seem to him improbable that another highly civilized nation might start a nuclear war. So Leon Kerkelot had chosen to focus his abilities on the great issues—the isolation of China, the division of Germany, the proliferation of nuclear arms—the ones that seemed most likely to give the human animal an excuse to incinerate his planet. There was no room in his equation for marginal problems like the fate of Alberto Rivera.

"Perhaps you're right, David," Leon said. "Certainly my experience was one that left me with a firm sense of priorities. An exceedingly firm sense of priorities."

Charlton MacKenzie felt both curiosity and concern as he waited for Dave Hyer to arrive for dinner that evening. MacKenzie respected Dave's abilities and he hoped they might be allies. He believed the President needed both of them—he needed younger men for action, and he needed older men for advice. The trouble was (and MacKenzie had observed this process in five administrations now) that the younger men, given access to a President, were not content to implement policy, but sought to make policy. In time their ambitions would outstrip their judgment and they would come to grief. MacKenzie thought he had seen this happening to Dave Hyer on the Caravelas issue, and he regarded this meeting as a last chance to caution Dave before he did irreparable harm to his standing with the President.

MacKenzie did not doubt his own position on Caravelas, nor was he concerned that he might lose the debate over the rebellion there. He possessed the absolute certitude of a man who has known a lifetime of achievement—as campus politician, as tennis champion, as war hero, as thirty-year-old congressional candidate, as Washington lawyer. He did not expect his luck to change now that he was Secretary of State. His certitude enabled MacKenzie to regard Dave Hyer not as a rival to be eliminated, but as a potential ally to be courted. He considered Dave a talented and useful young man. He understood the political process and (this Caravelas thing aside) he had a sure sense of what the President's interests were. More than most men his age, Dave understood the nature of the presidency—that a President may sometimes do what is right, but he must always do what is necessary.

MacKenzie, after having known Dave less than a year, and having often been in disagreement with him, had paid him a considerable compliment—he had speculated that when they both left government, Dave might be the young lawyer he needed to become his partner and the eventual heir to his law practice. It was a compliment worth between a quarter and a half million dollars a year, for MacKenzie's was a very special, very personal, very rewarding branch of the law. Indeed, when MacKenzie's critics declared that he was hardly a lawyer at all, he privately agreed with them. He couldn't remember when he last entered a courtroom. He had made his fortune because for two decades, in certain areas of government policy (oil, mining, the airlines) he had possessed more information, or had certain access to it, than any other lawyer in Washington, the various Attorneys General not excepted.

He got his information from many sources: from scores of friends in Congress, from ambitious government lawyers who dreamed of joining his law firm (dreams MacKenzie did not discourage); from lobbyists, newspapermen, other lawyers with scraps of rumor and information to exchange. One phone call, the right phone call to the right regulatory agency official at the right moment, might be worth a million dollars to one of Mac-Kenzie's clients—but it might have taken MacKenzie twenty years to be able to make that call. That was why his retainers started at six figures.

MacKenzie knew that his enemies saw him as a master manipulator, an influence-peddler on a cosmic scale, as the corporations' key strategist in their battles against the public interests, and he accepted the criticisms without bitterness for he thought the critics unsophisticated men. He viewed himself in quite a different light. He saw himself as a negotiator, a legal statesman, mediating between government and business. He knew how often his skill had prevented costly clashes between the two powers. If his brand of law was little understood, he nonetheless regarded it as a kind of public service.

MacKenzie saw his new job, as Secretary of State, as not vastly dissimilar from his previous one. He had a new client now, but he would employ the same talents he had always employed—information, judgment, patience, experience, persuasion, a sense of the possible. Yet government was different—more complex, more challenging, more exhilarating. As a lawyer, he had been a lone wolf; in government he needed allies, yet first-rate men were as rare there as elsewhere. So MacKenzie hoped it might yet be possible to make an ally of Dave Hyer. It would be a shame to lose him.

Dave arrived at MacKenzie's house at eight, vaguely apprehensive about the evening ahead. MacKenzie wanted to talk about Caravelas, and Dave would state his views again, but he had no real hope of converting the older man. Dave thought MacKenzie's mind would eventually be changed, but not by ideas or theories, only by hard experience. Yet Dave felt a growing sense of urgency. Barney had been interested in Rivera's offer to suspend operations until after the U.S. elections, but this landmine incident, killing four Americans, would increase the pressures for military action.

Dave wondered how candid he could be with MacKenzie. The problem was that no matter how much he disagreed with MacKenzie politically, he could not dislike him personally. In all their dealings, the Secretary had been gentlemanly, courteous, patient, seemingly straightforward—that of course was MacKenzie's style, to combine maximum power with maximum charm, and it had made him a multimillionaire. As he rang MacKenzie's doorbell, Dave reflected that the Secretary was probably at heart a very decent person—if politics ever obliged him to cut Dave's throat, he would do so only with the deepest regret.

MacKenzie lived in a vast Italian villa in Northwest Washington that had been built in the 1920s for a quarter of a million dollars and now was worth five times that. He and Dave had drinks on a stone terrace at the back of the house, looking down on formal gardens, divided by neat hedges and dotted with statuary, that descended for two hundred yards until MacKenzie's property merged with Rock Creek Park. They watched the brilliant arc of the July sun slip behind the hills above the park. Below, on the road beside the creek, distant headlights cut through the dusk.

"It's a magnificent view," Dave said.

MacKenzie smiled. He was wearing a dark blue suit and a silver tie, and he looked a decade younger than his fifty-two years. "Yes," he said, "I've always considered it the second finest view in Washington."

Dave thought of that other view, the one they both knew so well now, across that lovely, surprisingly private park, to the two great monuments to the south.

"The other fellow's only got a four-year lease," he said, "and this one's all yours."

"That's true," MacKenzie said. "Did the President get his statement issued?"

"About an hour ago. That's why I'm late."

"Were you pleased with the final language?"

"Yes," Dave said. "I didn't think we should overreact to this one incident, but I thought the tough warning about future incidents was appropriate. Were you pleased?"

MacKenzie nodded. "As I told the President, a great nation needn't react to one land mine. There are larger issues to consider—and to act upon."

It was those larger issues they intended to address, but neither man wished to start yet, so they strolled through MacKenzie's gardens.

"Who's that gentleman?" Dave asked.

"Mozart," MacKenzie said. "And that's Verdi over there. This house was built by a woman named Fryer, the widow of a lumber baron, a lover of the opera. In the Twenties and Thirties she would have her favorites performed up on the terrace, and her guests would sit here in the gardens and listen. I'm told that Franklin Roosevelt was once a guest here."

They rounded a corner and encountered another brooding marble visage.

"That's Bach, I believe," MacKenzie said. "You must bring your wife the next time you come, Dave. I discovered at Mrs. Newfield's party that she and I share an interest in antique furniture."

"I'm sure she'd love to see your house."

"A lovely and charming young woman," MacKenzie said.

They ate at nine on the terrace with two white candles flickering between them and two white-coated waiters bringing food and wine from the villa.

"The soup is delicious," Dave said. "It tastes like some I've had at Rive Gauche."

"It's quite possible," MacKenzie said. "I lured my chef away from them."

"Doesn't he miss it?"

"I suspect he does," MacKenzie admitted. "But he wants to open a restaurant of his own, and I've agreed to help him after he's been with me for a specified period."

Dave smiled—he imagined a grieving Frenchman in the bowels of MacKenzie's villa as an indentured servant—but said nothing.

"I must confess, Dave," the older man said, "that I'm a wicked man. I've made a good deal of money and I'm determined to enjoy it."

"Why not?" Dave said, and enjoyed a sip of MacKenzie's excellent wine. Why not indeed?

Dave asked about MacKenzie's sons—one was in medical school, the other in the Peace Corps—and it was not until midway through the meal that they reached the evening's real topic.

"Let's speak frankly about Caravelas," MacKenzie said. "If we can't agree, let's understand one another's point of view."

"My view on Caravelas is fairly simple, Mr. Secretary," Dave said. "The country is run by military dictatorship, and there's a popular revolution in progress which, unless we intervene, will surely win. I think we ought to let nature take its course. This may be the decade when we come to grips with Latin America, and I think Caravelas may set a precedent, one way or the other."

"And you'd prefer a policy of non-intervention?" MacKenzie asked.

"I think the forces of revolution are eventually going to succeed in Latin America, and it's futile and self-defeating for us to keep opposing them."

"But isn't it a fact that for more than a century the forces of revolution have been rather weak in Latin America and the forces of reaction rather strong?"

"With two or three exceptions, yes. But largely because we've given arms and military support to the wrong side."

"And why do you think, Dave, that we've followed this policy?"

"It's complicated, but essentially because our corporations make fantastic profits in Latin America, and they use their money and influence to persuade Congress to support a policy of gunboat diplomacy."

"The corporations also employ high-priced lawyers to advance their interests in Washington," MacKenzie said lightly.

"I've never doubted that your positions now are based on what you think is best for the country." The statement was necessary, if not entirely true.

"I appreciate that, Dave. I'm aware that my critics picture me as a tool of Wall Street and all that. It's amusing, really, because the truth is that on most political issues I'm well to the left of my friends in the corporate world. After all, it's rather well known that I'm a Democrat."

"It is indeed," Dave admitted.

"Actually, if anyone checked the record, they'd find that during my brief career in Congress I was considered rather liberal. My ADA rating was slightly higher than Jack Kennedy's, as I recall. And I believe my politics have been consistent ever since. When I was called upon to offer advice to Presidents Kennedy, Johnson, and Osgood, I advocated liberal domestic programs. I believe you know that I've spoken to President Newfield on behalf of the New Cities, and the minimum-wage bill, and other reforms."

"I know you have," Dave said. "I've appreciated it."

"I stress this, not to toot my own horn, Dave, but to make the point that I don't believe you and I embody the 'liberal' versus the 'conservative' viewpoints on Latin America. I think rather,

that we are two liberal Democrats who differ on whether intervention in Caravelas would be good or bad for America."

"There's also the question of what's good or bad for Caravelas," Dave said.

"I believe that's a secondary issue. Dave, I'm not going to
pretend that the Molina government is anything but corrupt and
repressive. It is. If I had a choice, I'd gladly see it replaced by
a liberal, non-Communist government. But we don't have that
choice. The choice is between Molina's government or Rivera's
communism. If Rivera takes power, he'll seize U.S. property, stir
up trouble in other countries, and otherwise spit in our eye."

"Our diplomacy might be a factor in how he behaved," Dave
said. He was tempted to tell MacKenzie of the deal Rivera
had offered, but instinct warned him not to.

"Let's assume for the moment that I'm right," MacKenzie said,
"and a few months from now we have a noisy, anti-American,
Communist government in Caravelas. To me, the question is how
this would affect the political balance here at home."

"What would you foresee?" Dave asked.

"I would expect the voices of the right—and I don't say 'the
Republicans' because some of the loudest voices would be
within our own party—to begin the cries of 'soft on communism,' and 'another Cuba,' and 'who lost Caravelas?' And the
attacks would be effective, because in fact we would have lost
Caravelas, and it would be another Cuba . . ."

"Which wouldn't have a dime's worth of impact on American
security," Dave injected.

"I'm not arguing that. I'm asking how millions of Americans
would respond to the soft-on-communism charge. And I'm saying
it would hurt. We'd be on the defensive. The political coalition
the President has put together in recent months—largely on the
basis of his own strength of character, his own credibility—would
begin to crumble. Politicians who never really wanted to support
him would have an excuse not to. And quite soon, all those
fine bills the President has been shooting through Congress—
with first-rate help from you, Dave—won't be getting through
so easily, perhaps not getting through at all." MacKenzie sipped
his wine. "That's what I fear, and I don't think it's worth losing,
or even running a risk of losing, for the benefit of one dashing

revolutionary in the mountains of an unimportant Latin American nation."

One of the waiters cleared away the remaining dishes and poured espresso for them. A full moon floated above the park and bathed the terrace in light. Dave dropped a slice of lemon peel into his espresso and stirred it slowly.

"I'll grant that could happen, but I don't believe it has to happen," Dave said. "I think Vietnam educated the public, and I think the President can talk sense to them, tell them it's time for us to let other countries settle their own affairs. I think most of the media would support us . . ."

"Don't count too much on the media," MacKenzie cautioned. "They'll go whichever way the wind is blowing."

"All right, but I think the wind will be blowing with us."

"I think you're more of an optimist than I—although perhaps not more than I was at your age. You see, your political experience is rooted in the early Sixties, a time of hope and progress, but mine goes back to the late Forties, to the McCarthy era. I know how bad it can be in this country, and I fear those forces are gathering strength again."

"And you think Caravelas could cause that much of a reaction?"

"I think it could be the excuse, the trigger," MacKenzie said. "Dave, I fancy myself a student of American politics, and I increasingly think of it as moving in cycles. There are tremendous forces at war within our constitutional framework—the greatest material wealth and the greatest idealistic vision the world has ever known—greed and hope, man's best and his worst, his dream and his reality—and I see now one, now the other gaining the upper hand. I'll grant you that the political balance has moved to the left, but it's a hard and irregular journey. Right now, I fear that we're near the end of an era of progress. I fear that because of the black militants and the white radicals, the pendulum is about to swing sharply to the right. I think the President has personally, singlehandedly, rather heroically, held it back since he entered office. Perhaps he can calm the nation and start us moving to the left again. But let's don't make it harder for him. Let's give on some of the lesser issues so we can win on the ones that matter."

At first Dave had suspected MacKenzie of cynicism, of rationalizing his self-interest; now he saw that MacKenzie believed what he was saying just as firmly as he himself did, and he knew they were irreconcilable.

"You understand, Mr. Secretary, that I think the results will be just as bad if we do intervene as you think they'll be if we don't. I think that once that precedent is set, we'll be fighting a dozen revolutions, and eventually we'll lose there just as we lost in Southeast Asia, with results on the domestic front just as bad."

"Would you join me in some brandy, Dave?" MacKenzie asked.

"Sure."

"Frank, brandy, please," MacKenzie called to one of the men serving them.

"Let me offer another thought," MacKenzie said. "As a practical matter, Dave, I think we Democrats are obliged, whether we like it or not, to take a firm line on foreign policy. I don't say it's rational, but because we're liberal on social issues, we become vulnerable to the 'soft-on-communism' charge. The result is that we have to seem tough abroad so we can be progressive at home."

"And the Republicans can be less tough abroad?" Dave asked.

"Exactly. Because no one questions the vigor of their anti-communism. That's why Eisenhower could settle Korea on terms that would have gotten Adlai impeached. And that's why Jack Kennedy—after he was bullied by Khrushchev—tried to prove his toughness by taking a hard line in Vietnam. And Lyndon took a *harder* line in Vietnam to protect his great social reforms at home."

"I'd have to say," Dave injected, "that Johnson's toughness abroad didn't do him much good at home."

"That's true," MacKenzie said. "Unfortunately, Lyndon chose the wrong country to be tough in."

Dave's brandy burned gently on his tongue. "Mr. Secretary," he said finally, "what you've said is based on years of political experience which I haven't had. It may be that I'm a naïve young man, although I don't think that's the case. But nonetheless I believe there's a rough justice at work in the world. I think that if a great nation like ours behaves decently and morally, in the long run it will profit by it, and if it behaves immorally, it'll suffer.

"In this case, I think it's unspeakably wrong for us to support the junta and oppose Rivera, and that if the President does that, he'll pay the price politically. That's what I'll tell him as long as he'll listen to me. And I'm afraid that leaves us with no alternative except to agree to disagree."

MacKenzie nodded slowly. They could hear the chirp of crickets, and for an instant Washington seemed far away.

"I'll agree to that," MacKenzie said. "We can disagree without personal animosity. Ultimately, the President will decide between our views, and I think we're both willing to abide by his decision."

"We don't have much choice, short of a coup," Dave said. MacKenzie laughed and poured them more brandy. Dave was ready to go, but it was pleasant here and he thought he'd finish his brandy first.

"There's one other point I'd like to raise," MacKenzie said, "and I hope I can do so without seeming presumptuous. You've managed your affairs quite well thus far without my advice."

"Good advice is always welcome."

"You have a remarkable future ahead of you, Dave. At the age of—what? thirty? thirty-one?—you're having a priceless exposure to the way things work in America. If all goes well, when you leave the White House you'll do extremely well in law. Or in politics."

"Or both," Dave said.

"Or both," MacKenzie agreed. "But the point I want to make is that you're operating in a very sensitive position. Many eyes are on you. I hate to use such a crude expression, but you're building . . ." He hesitated, as if the correct word eluded him.

"An image?" Dave suggested.

"Exactly. And should you develop a reputation for being too rash, too . . ." MacKenzie paused.

"Too radical?"

"Yes. If you develop that reputation, justifiably or not, it's going to limit your future effectiveness."

Dave knew the argument and he did not want to pursue it.

"Mr. Secretary," he said, "I know exactly what you mean. But

there's a good reason why I can't pull in my horns on Caravelas
or on anything else. I learned early in the game that you can't
fool Barney Newfield. He keeps me around for one reason—because he thinks my honest opinions might be useful to him. If
I start trimming my sails, thinking about my interests instead of
his, I'll cease to be of any value to him."

"I understand that," MacKenzie said. "But your value can also
be diminished if you make too many enemies, or lose too many
fights."

"That's a risk I have to run," Dave said.

Eleanor was awake when he got home. She was in bed, sitting
up against a big blue pillow, reading a Henry James novel.
Their tastes in literature were poles apart. Hers ran to James,
Proust, Nabokov, his to Hemingway, O'Hara, Fitzgerald. It was
exceedingly rare for them both to enjoy the same novel.

"How was dinner?"

"Good food, interesting talk." He hung up his coat and tossed
his tie on the closet doorknob.

"What was the talk about?"

"The revolution in Caravelas," he said. "MacKenzie and I
thought we'd see if we could reach any agreement."

"Did you?"

"No," he admitted.

"What's he like?" she asked.

"Very charming, very persuasive, very formidable."

"But he didn't persuade you about that revolution?"

"As you know, dear wife, I'm a hard man to persuade."

Eleanor smiled. She was wearing a short green nightgown.
Her legs were long and lovely. An elderly drama critic had once
written that Eleanor had "the grooviest legs on Broadway" and
for a time that had been a joke between them. They no longer
used the joke, but her legs were still admirable. She seemed in
one of her better moods.

"My friend MacKenzie seemed to be hinting, very softly, that
if I was a good boy I could come to be a rich lawyer with him
someday."

"What did you tell him?"

"I told him that being a good boy wasn't my game."

"You could make a lot of money practicing law, couldn't you?"

"One hell of a lot," he said.

"And not work half as hard as you do now," she said. "Maybe even have a little time for your family."

"I'm going to do that eventually, Ellie."

"But when?"

"After the election."

"Which election? The next one? Or the one after that?"

"I won't last till the one after that," he said, trying to make a joke of it.

"I may not last till the next one," she said. She put her book on the table and turned out her light. He picked up his pajamas and went to the bathroom. When he returned, she was lying on her side, facing the wall.

"MacKenzie wants you to come see his house," he told her.

"That would be nice," she said automatically. He could feel her pulling away from him, but he was not ready to let go.

"How's Sally?" he asked as he slipped into bed.

"She asked about you today," Eleanor said, and pulled the sheet tight around her shoulders.

He put out the light and turned toward her, raised on one elbow, knowing already what would happen. He moved his hand beneath the sheet and placed it on her breast. Beneath the thin gown, the nipple was hard. She did not move.

"Let's make love, Ellie."

"I'm tired."

They lay very still—he could feel her breast rise and fall with her breathing—and the room was quiet as a tomb. He smiled grimly into the darkness—to claim to be tired was the least imaginative of her excuses. On her more creative nights she was sick, sore, sleepy, sunburned; she had a toothache, a backache, a tummyache, a headache.

"You weren't too tired to read until midnight," he said.

"I'm tired now," she insisted. "Let's go to sleep."

His hand stayed at her breast for a moment more, while he searched for the right phrase to soften her or shame her or hurt her. But they had been through this too many times and he knew there was nothing to say. He had hurt her, so she would hurt him by this, the sharpest weapon at her disposal. He was angry and frustrated, and it did not help to know that, finally, she was right. All this went through his mind in a second or two, as he heard her soft breathing and the low whirr of the air conditioning, then he took his hand from her and turned over, careful not to touch her, and tried to go to sleep. It had not been a terribly successful day.

13

Three young blacks paraded across the park toward Pennsylvania Avenue, loose-jointed, narrow-hipped youths in tight, bright-hued pants, one swinging a transistor radio the size of a small suitcase, boys of sixteen or so moving with long, loping strides, shouting and bumping shoulders as they ambled toward the strip of bars and barbecue joints down Eighth Street. The smallest of them, a taffy-skinned boy in purple pants and a glistening black shirt, hoisted a bottle of green soda-pop skyward, sucked it dry, and flipped it over his shoulder to shatter on the brick walkway. Five winos clustered around a park bench looked up, and one muttered something after the youths. "Kiss mah ass, you white muddah-fuggah," the boy in the purple pants shouted back at them, his words audible even above the roar of the transistor radio, and the three danced on across the park, while the winos resettled themselves on the bench, wizened, grimy men, muttering grimly.

Dave watched from a sofa beside Cathy's front window, which overlooked the park and Pennsylvania Avenue, a half-dozen blocks east of the Capitol. He had been sitting there for an hour, drinking and savoring the luxury of a Saturday free—the President was away and Eleanor had taken Sally to visit her parents.

From the distance came the sound of six sharp explosions, like gunfire. Across in the park, two of the winos shuffled off toward a nearby liquor store. Cathy came out of the kitchen and handed him a fresh beer. Beneath the window, a half-dozen girls strolled by, giggling in shrill voices, clad in tight jeans and sleeveless blouses, clusters of pink plastic hair curlers clasped to their heads, slender girls moving slowly through the heat of early evening, nervously awaiting whatever thrill or mystery might arrive with the summer night.

"Enjoying the show?" Cathy asked.

"I really do. You sit in the White House and all you can see is trees and tulips and men in blue suits. You forget there's a real world out there."

"Kiss mah muddah-fugging ass, you black bitch," one of the girls shouted at another, and they locked in a brief shoving match before drifting on down the sidewalk.

"Well, that's the real world," Cathy said. "It's so real it's driving me batty."

"I remember the first time I ever heard anybody say mother-fucker," he said. "It wasn't one of our black brothers, either. It was the summer I was thirteen and I had a job as a locker boy in a city pool in East Dallas, the blue-collar part of town. The kids over there fought all the time, and the official way to start a fight was to call somebody a mother-fucker. It's funny, I thought then that only the most vulgar people on earth would talk like that, and now you pick up the *New York Review* or *Esquire* and all the deep-thinkers are using it."

"How was the locker-boy business?"

"It had its moments," he said. "One of my colleagues found a way to climb up into the attic above the women's locker room and drill peepholes. Unfortunately, on the Fourth of July, the ceiling collapsed under him and he tumbled down into the middle of the women's shower room, causing considerable turmoil.

"But aside from that, it was a pretty lousy job. We worked eight hours a day, seven days a week, with an hour's bus ride each way, and the city of Dallas, in its wisdom, paid us seven-fifty a week."

"You should have struck," she said. Cathy lit a cigarette and twisted sideways on the sofa, studying him with her narrow little squint. She was wearing jeans and a man's blue shirt.

"I wasn't that smart," he said. "Instead, one morning, another kid and I went to see the city's Recreation Director, a big-bellied, cigar-smoking old fool and asked very politely if maybe for sixty hours a week we shouldn't get ten dollars instead of seven-fifty. Well, he chewed on his cigar butt and mumbled about the ingratitude of youth, and when we went to work that afternoon we'd been laid off. That was my introduction to labor-management relations."

He laughed and put his feet up on the windowsill. "I remember thinking I'd get that old bastard if it took the rest of my life."

"Did you?" she asked.

"No. He had the good sense to die before I took power."

Across in the park, a tiny white-haired woman passed by with a huge black-and-brown German shepherd on a chain, and three wide-eyed teenagers scurried out of her path.

"Speaking of labor," Cathy said, "what do you think of me doing an article on Steve Vale?"

"You should," he told her. "He's a fine old man, and he's a great Secretary of Labor. Steve Vale's been fighting the good fight since the New Deal."

"That's the trouble," she said. "He's so noble I'm afraid it'd turn out blah."

"Check into the way he cut down Don Duffey when HUD tried to move into manpower training," he said. "Vale's tough too."

Both of them jumped as a new fusillade of fireworks exploded near the house. Two small boys raced down the street and one of the winos waved a bony fist at them.

"It's like a war," he said.

"It is a war," Cathy said. "A war of nerves. And they're winning."

"I know a fellow at Justice who bought a house near here," he said. "He and his wife wanted their kids to live in an integrated neighborhood so they'd grow up without any prejudice. What happened was, when their kids went out to play, black kids would beat them up and steal their toys. After six months his kids were terrified at the sight of a black person. So they sold the house and moved to Chevy Chase."

"It's rough," she said. "You walk down that street and you feel the hate floating in the air like smog."

He nodded. "The question is whether all America is going to be like that."

"What do you think?"

"I don't know," he said. "I think we could go either way."

"You see those stores over there on the corner?" she asked.

"Well, the night after Dr. King was killed you could sit here in this window and watch your neighbors bust those windows and haul off the goodies. The two guys upstairs told me about it."

"They're queer aren't they?"

"Yeah, there's a lot of queers on Capitol Hill. They don't have kids so they don't care about the schools. Those two guys told me they spent the night of the riots sitting up there armed with frying pans in case anybody broke down their door. They said the next morning, when the soldiers finally showed up, they spent all day making cookies for them."

Dave laughed and watched a young white man trying to persuade his poodle to pee against a park bench. Green D.C. Transit buses groaned and roared along Pennsylvania Avenue, depositing middle-aged black people who walked slowly across the park toward the public-housing projects around Thirteenth Street.

"Where's the President?" Cathy asked.

"He went to Camp David for the night."

"He take Sharon Flatt with him?"

"You know about Sharon?" Dave asked.

"Everybody knows about Sharon," she said.

"Well, you're a little behind on the story. He took his wife with him. Sharon's spending the weekend at Newport with her millionaire beau, Winnie Boatwright."

"That girl's really got something," Cathy said.

"Mainly she's got Brenda matchmaking for her. Winnie likes to come to the White House and he gets invited as long as he keeps dating Sharon."

"God, I wish they'd let me write that one," she said.

"Nobody'd believe it if you did."

In the park, a black wino, a huge fellow in faded army fatigues, tried to join the cluster of white winos, but their circle closed against him and he shuffled off.

"Talking about the two queers upstairs reminds me of another thrilling tale from my youth," Dave said. "Want to hear it?"

"Why not?" Cathy said.

"The story begins," he said, "with the fact that the summer I was twenty I ran around with some jet jockeys who were stationed at the base outside Dallas. They were a pretty wild bunch—you have to be a little crazy to fly jets—and the wildest of them was this baby-faced terror from Houston named Sherry Turner. Sherry weighed about one-thirty, but he was absolutely fearless. The others said he was the best pilot alive, nerves of steel and all that. Although he did have one problem. Sherry was a rather pugnacious atheist and sometimes, just as his squadron was going into a nosedive or something, he'd yell some terrible, anti-God remark into the intercom, which tended to unnerve some of his fellow pilots.

"Anyway, Sherry was never really happy when he wasn't flying, so he spent his free time in the local bars and I drank with him a good deal. Sherry liked me because I'd read a lot of books and in his more cogent moments he had intellectual aspirations. But he wasn't cogent much. When he was drunk, Sherry liked to bite women on the ass. We'd be in a bar and the waitress would be bending over to serve the next table and we'd catch him—this glassy-eyed, baby-faced madman—leaning slowly toward her rear end with his teeth bared like a barracuda. We'd grab him and get him out of there, except sometimes we wouldn't grab him in time and there were some memorable scenes when he sank his teeth into some poor girl's tail."

There was a knock at the door and Cathy answered it. A policeman asked if she'd contribute to the Boys' Club. She gave him a dollar and he handed her a receipt and went away.

"They come around in uniform asking for money," she said. "It's a damned outrage. But go ahead with your story. Your friend was biting people on the ass."

"Only women," Dave said. "There was nothing queer about Sherry. Anyway, that was one pastime, but his favorite was driving his car on the railroad tracks. He had this souped-up Olds 88 and he . . ."

"Driving it *where?*"

"You drive up onto the tracks at a crossing and you let some of the air out of your tires, so they fit down over the rails. Then you can put a brick on the gas pedal and fly down the tracks at a hundred or so, drinking beer and having a hell of a time. The best was when you roared through those little stations in West Texas, honking the horn and yelling, and the old boys sitting there would think it was the end of the world."

"You actually did this?" she asked.

"Only once," he said. "I wasn't as crazy as my friends. The trouble was, sometimes you'd be zooming along the tracks and you'd look up and see a train coming."

"Then what'd you do?"

"You got the hell off the tracks," he said. "But one time Sherry saw a train coming and he was up on a trestle with no way to get off. So he stopped and threw it in reverse and then he was racing along backward at eighty miles an hour, about fifty feet in front of the Dixie Belle Express."

"What happened?"

"Oh, the engineer finally slowed down and Sherry got away."

"Where do the queers come into this story?" Cathy asked.

"Oh yeah, the queers. Well, Sherry knew most of the high-type queers around Dallas and Fort Worth, and he'd hang out at the gay bars sometimes. He liked to beat up the sort of guys who like to beat up queers. Needless to say, the queers idolized him. One night we drove out to a ballroom outside of town where the local queer aristocracy was having its annual drag ball. We looked in the window and there were three or four hundred of them, all in satin gowns and jewels, dancing and drinking and having a grand old time. They'd even flown in an all-queer Dixieland band from New Orleans.

"Well, Sherry wanted to crash the party, but they wouldn't let us in. The guy at the door—he must have weighed three hundred—said, 'Sherry, you little *doll*, I couldn't guarantee your *safety* in there.'

"So we went back to the car and drank a while and Sherry brooded about this snub, and finally he had an inspiration. There were a couple of hundred cars parked there, mostly Cadillacs, and Sherry went down the line letting the air out of one tire on each car. Then we parked down the road and waited. Well, the party broke up about four and all these drunk queers staggered out into the moonlight, and I then witnessed a truly unforgettable scene. Three hundred Texas queers, in long gowns and high heels and wigs, stumbling around that parking lot, screaming and crying, some of them in hysterics, trying to get their cars up on jacks and the flats off and the spare tires on. Cars were falling off jacks and the gowns were ripping and fights were breaking out—and at dawn the Texas Rangers arrived, summoned by an unbelieving passerby, and the last thing we saw was three Texas Rangers chasing a dozen begowned homosexuals across a cornfield toward Dallas.

"Anyway, that's my queer story."

Cathy shook her head in disbelief. "You look like such a serious type," she said.

"I am a serious type," he said. "But I raised hell once. Texas does that to you. It's hard to explain, but it's so big, and there's so much money, that it makes people crazy. Everything is done in extremes. The trouble is, it's dangerous to live like that. Half the guys I knew in those days are dead now. A couple in car wrecks. One guy in a bar fight. One guy from trying to live on pills for a year."

"Which one was Sherry?" she asked.

"Oh, Sherry's fine. Sherry got religion. He was flying his jet one day, stoned, and yelled something at God and God answered. They had a long talk and Sherry resigned his commission and entered the Baptist Seminary in Fort Worth. He's a preacher somewhere in East Texas now."

The street lights came on outside. A small boy was noisily kicking a beer can down the street. Two of the winos were arguing over a bottle of Thunderbird. Cathy got up from the sofa and stood before him. Her jeans rode low on her round little hips and her small breasts poked jauntily against her shirt.

"You want another beer?"

"There's something I want more."

"What's that?" she asked. "To let the air out of some queer's tires?"

"No, to take a big bite out of your bony little ass."

"Promises, promises."

He grabbed for her and she jumped away. He hooked his fingers in the top of her jeans and they wrestled to the floor. She laughed and jabbed him in the ribs, but after a minute they were not playing.

"You want to go to the bedroom?" she asked.

"Here is okay." He slipped off her jeans and her shirt, and tasted her hard little nipples.

"Don't," she said. "They're sore."

"Why?"

"My period is about to start."

"Oh," he said, noting the date, wondering if she'd be back in action by the next weekend.

"Scratch my back," she said.

He ran his fingers lightly along her spine.

"There?"

"Umm. Yes."

"There?"

"That's not my back. Wise guy."

"It's my favorite part of your back. There. And there."

"Oh, you son of a bitch," she said. "Oh, yes, yes, there. Oh, yes."

The Green Oaks Motel, on the outskirts of Philadelphia, is not far from the turnpike that links Washington and New York. Eleanor arrived there in midafternoon that day, checked into her room, and took Sally out to the pool for a swim. The sun felt good and she did not mind the stares from the men at poolside. She splashed with Sally for an hour, then returned to her room and poured herself a glass of sherry.

Eleanor had stayed at the Green Oaks once on a trip with Dave, several years earlier. Eleanor was not easily pleased by American motels; sometimes she'd make Dave stop at four or five until she found one sufficiently clean and unpretentious to meet her standards. But she'd found the Green Oaks satisfactory, and remembered it, and thought it would do as well as any for the purpose of this trip.

She put on a blue silk dress. At seven she and Sally walked across the parking lot to the dining room. Eleanor had two martinis before dinner but she barely touched her steak.

"Mama, when will we see Grandaddy?" Sally asked, when they returned to the room.

"Tomorrow, dear. We'll stay here tonight."

She read to Sally and when the phone rang she turned her back away from the child to answer it.

"Hello?"

"You know what W. C. Fields had on his tombstone?" a man asked.

"No."

"I'd rather be here than in Philadelphia."

"Oh Mike," Eleanor laughed. "Well, you're in Philadelphia, like it or not."

"I'd only do it for you," Mike Bates said. "How soon can you come?"

"At least an hour," she said. "What's your room number?"

"One-twelve," he said. "My car's right in front."

"I'll come when I can," she said, and put down the phone.

"Who was that?" Sally asked. "Was it Daddy?"

"No, dear," Eleanor said. "Let's read another story."

She read for an hour, until the child began to rub her eyes with weariness, but Eleanor's thoughts were elsewhere. She knew the first time she met Mike Bates that he would make a pass at her; and he did, the second time they talked, perhaps less a pass than a standing invitation, issued casually but confidently. It was not accepted casually. Eleanor thought about it for weeks. The decision had little to do with Dave—*he* wouldn't notice if she moved a lover into the guest bedroom. It had to do rather with herself and the kind of woman she wanted to be. She yearned now to be the proper lady she had been raised to be, to lead the sort of easy life that affairs complicated, perhaps made impossible. She thought she had put that other life behind her when she married Dave. But in the past year he had destroyed the life she wanted. She had spent a year feeling lonely and helpless and she hated it and now she had decided that if he would not end the loneliness she would end it herself in her own way. It was not that she wanted a lover but that she wanted *something*, some passion, some affection, some excitement in her life. Finding the right man was not so simple as it would once have been. Not many men made passes at her these days. Dave's friends were not that type, at least not with her. But Mike Bates was, decidedly. She knew his sort from New York, although she did not know much about him personally. She had heard Walt say he was "a problem type," whatever that meant, but she no longer expected to find men without problems. She was not seeking a husband, only a lover. Mike was attractive—tall and graceful, with a sharp, arrogant, handsome face—and he was talented too. She had read his books that week, a novel and two collections of stories, and she was impressed with his craftsmanship, even though there was something disturbingly harsh, almost cruel, in his characterizations. But that was for the critics to worry about; Mike was attractive, available and experienced, and she thought he might serve her purpose well.

When Sally was asleep, Eleanor slipped out the door, leaned against it for a moment, seeing the stars high in the summer sky, then walked the hundred feet to Mike Bates's room. He opened the door quickly.

"Come in," he said, gesturing with a half-filled glass.

"Thank you," Eleanor said, returning his smile.

"You're looking lovely."

"Thank you again."

"A drink?"

"No, I'm fine," she said.

"You are indeed," he said. "But I think I'll have one. Sit down. How was your drive up?"

"Uneventful. We got in this afternoon and went for a swim."

"I wish I'd been here for that," he said, and sat down on the edge of the bed. He was wearing loafers, gray linen trousers and a white polo shirt. "This isn't a bad place," he said.

"It's unpretentious. Perhaps I will have a drink."

"Scotch all right?"

"Yes, with lots of water. Did you finish the script?"

"Yeah, it's finished. They can start shooting the damn thing next week."

"You aren't pleased with it?"

"It's a lot of crap," he said. "Brilliant crap, thanks to my contribution, but still crap."

"How did my part turn out?" she asked.

"Your part is not bad," he said. "Your part I gave special attention. Rewrote entirely, in fact, so the President's wife, instead of being a daffy blonde is a very sophisticated lady—kind of a Lady Macbeth in Jax pants."

Eleanor smiled. "I had a director once who told me I'd never be able to play Lady Macbeth."

"The Jax pants will help," he said. "You ever get that straightened out about your pay?"

"Not really. Walt offered to pay me twenty thousand, but my husband thinks that's too much."

"How much does he think is right?"

"He really wants me to work for nothing."

"He doesn't like money?"

"He likes money, but he's afraid of how it might look. He might have to make some decision about the movie industry sometime."

"Well, he's crazy," Mike Bates said. "There's only one thing a beautiful woman ought to do for free, the rest she ought to charge for."

"He's not crazy," she said. "Just careful."

"He's not so careful about some things."

"He's careful about his work," she said. "But let's not talk about Dave."

"Why not? I think he's interesting."

"He is interesting," she said. "But let's not talk about him."

Mike Bates stood up and poured himself another drink. "Sorry," he said. "An occupational hazard. What would you like to talk about?"

"I read your books this week," she said.

"Better late than never. Did you approve?"

"You write very well."

"I do write well," he said. "But slowly. Oh, how slowly. Thus do irresistible economic forces, including a thousand a month in child support, drive me to hackwork in Hollywood."

"You've written fine screenplays."

"I've written clever screenplays. I wrote one fine screenplay and no one would produce it."

"What was that?"

"An adaptation of my novel. They said it was too literary."

"I didn't think it was too literary," she said. "I thought it was fine."

"But what?" he said.

"But nothing," she said. "I liked it."

"I hear that note of reserve in your voice," he said. "You liked it, but what?"

"If I had any criticism," she said, "it would be that you make

your people awfully unattractive. I don't think people are all
that bad."

"I do," he said. "I think people are a lot more unattractive
than I make them. But I've seen things you haven't seen. I
fought my way across Korea one time and I saw some things
that haven't intruded on your young life."

"I'm sure you did," she said. She realized that he was a little
drunk, and she did not want to argue with him.

"The girl wasn't unattractive," he said. "The girl at the end
of the book."

"That's true," she said. "I forgot about her."

"And you're attractive," he said. "I can put you in a novel
if I want an attractive character."

"There are a lot of women like me," she said.

"Not as beautiful as you."

"Was the girl at the end of the book your wife? Your former
wife?"

"I think I'll turn out the light," he said.

When the light was out he pulled her against him. She returned his kiss and when his hands fumbled at her dress she
unhooked it. In bed, he probed her body with his hands and
mouth. "Don't be rough," she whispered, but he was rough, and
for a moment she resisted the pain and then as the night
closed in on her she knew the pain was what she wanted.

"Did you like that?" he asked when it was over. He had lit
a cigarette and poured another drink and he was sitting on the
edge of the bed.

"Yes," she said. It was true. She did not like him; but she had
liked *it*. She felt weak and she wanted him again.

"How much?" he asked.

"Don't be vain, Mike. It was fine."

"Can you stay all night?"

"No."

"Can you stay another hour?"

"If you'll stop talking."

"I like to talk. Let's talk about that husband of yours. How
come he lets you wander off on a Saturday afternoon? He got
something going of his own?"

"I told you I don't want to talk about him."

"What would you deign to talk about?"

"Oh God, Mike. Your books. Let's talk about your books."

"We've already done that. You think I make people too unpleasant. Did you go to Miss Porter's? You've got that exquisite sentimentality one expects from Miss Porter's girls."

"No I didn't go to Miss Porter's. And I didn't come here to be insulted."

"No, you came here to be laid and you got that, so now you want to tell me what I can talk about and what I can write about."

"You're drunk," she said.

"I'm drunk and you're another fucked-up housewife and I'd rather be here than in Philadelphia, sister."

"I'll go now." She got out of bed and began searching for her clothes. She didn't want to turn on the light.

He snubbed out his cigarette and she heard the squeak of the bedsprings and felt his hand close around her wrist.

"Don't be in a hurry. I might like a little more of you."

"Let me go," she said.

He laughed. "Or what? You'll call the cops?"

She tried to push him away but he caught her hand and slapped her hard across the jaw. He pushed her back onto the bed and put his knee between her legs, hurting her. She struggled but he slapped her again. She thought her lip was cut, and then her outstretched hand touched a heavy glass ashtray and she swung it against his head with all her strength. He went limp and she did not have to hit him again. She threw on her dress and she heard him moan as she hurried from the room.

Minutes later, she and Sally were back in the car, headed north along the turnpike. If she could stay awake, she would be at her parents' house for breakfast. She was tense for a while, but she found classical music on the radio and in an hour she was calm again. Ten years earlier she would have been crying; now she was past tears, and after a time she even managed a bitter smile. Her first venture into extramarital sex had not been a masterpiece of good planning, she thought. She would have to be more careful in the future.

14

The walls of Senator Tillman Cathcart's dim, cluttered office were covered with photographs of politicians who had been his friends and allies in forty years in Washington. Dave recognized many of the faces, Rayburn and Truman, Johnson and Roosevelt, Russell and Byrd, and there were other faces from before his time, men whose names he could only guess. The pictures had reminded Dave, as he met with Senator Cathcart through the spring and summer, of the vast distance between them in age and experience, of the patent absurdity of his being here negotiating with this man old enough to be his grandfather.

Yet he was in the senator's office again, this Thursday morning in early August, facing the frail, faintly ironic old Populist across his huge mahogany desk, trying to find some phrase or formula that might break the impasse between Senator Cathcart and the administration on the New Cities bill.

Tillman Cathcart, like Barney Newfield, had a dream of a better America, but a very different dream. In his mind's eye, he did not see shining towers; he saw, instead, the tranquil, tree-lined villages he had known as a youth in the Missouri of the early 1900s. To Senator Cathcart, the modern city was an abomination, a cesspool of crime and ignorance, and the nation's only hope lay in a return to the older, simpler way of life. When the New Cities bill reached his Committee on Housing, he countered with a bill to build hundreds of "new villages," each for five to ten thousand people, in rural areas from coast to coast. In effect, the senator wanted to decentralize America.

The administration responded that the "new villages," however admirable in theory, were not practical—it would be like returning to the little red schoolhouse in education. The senator smiled and nodded and waited, and the New Cities bill stayed bottled up in his committee.

"I've been talking with your staff again, Senator," Dave was saying to the old man, "and I keep thinking that your idea of villages of ten thousand or so is really not so different from our idea of the semi-autonomous communities of forty thousand. We want each community to have the same qualities you want, and we think it'll be even stronger if each community is part of a larger urban center."

Dave knew his argument was tenuous but it was the best argument he had. The President had not yet authorized concessions.

"Mr. Hyer," the old man whispered, "I don't think your ideas and my ideas are close together at all. Not at all. You're a busy young man and I'm afraid I'm wastin' your time bringin' you up here. You don't like my villages and I don't like your bill without them."

"We respect your idea, Senator . . ." Dave began, but Cathcart cut him off.

"Son, you tell the President that I don't expect his bill will ever get out of my committee."

Barney took the news grimly. Time was running out on this session of Congress. For an hour he quizzed Dave about the bill, then he picked up the phone and invited Tillman Cathcart to visit him the next afternoon.

The senator arrived at five and stayed until past nine. Dave never knew all that went on that evening. The President called him into his office at six and he found the two men sitting on the sofa with tumblers of bourbon in their hands. The President asked Dave a question about the federal power of eminent domain. Dave answered and left.

Two hours later, rising from his desk, Dave looked out his window and saw the two of them, the President and the senator, walking in the last soft light of evening. They had passed through the Rose Garden, past the magnolia trees John Kennedy planted, and were moving along the circular path that curves by the tennis court and the cascading fountain before making its long slow arc back to the mansion. It was almost dusk and the shadows were gathering beneath the trees. Barney was in his shirt sleeves, and he walked with his arms folded across his chest, his head twisted sideways to catch the senator's every word. He listened and nodded, then he spoke, suddenly extending his arms wide as though he was not addressing one old man but an invisible multitude somewhere there among the shadows.

They passed the fountain and reached the huge elm that towered over the path's most distant point. They stopped there and faced each other, talked a moment, then sat down in the thick grass beneath the tree. Barney sat Indian style, legs crossed before him, his big hands slapping the air excitedly as he talked. The senator stretched out lengthwise, resting on one elbow, and with his free hand he plucked a blade of grass and put it in the corner of his mouth.

Senator Cathcart had never been a person to Dave—he was a problem, a factor in an equation—but now as he watched the old man silhouetted in the dusk, he imagined the Tillman Cathcart of fifty years ago, the lean, shrewd Missouri farm boy who liked his corn liquor and his country girls, who knew the pleasures of evening air and soft grass, who even today might be lonely, might yearn for the companionship and understanding he was this minute receiving from Barney Newfield.

Darkness came, and the two could no longer be seen, but Dave stayed at his window until they appeared again, walking arm in arm into the circle of light flowing from the mansion. The senator's car waited there, and his chauffeur jumped out to open the door, but Barney waved him away and opened the door himself. They faced each other for a final moment and shook hands, and as they did Barney threw his left arm around the old man's shoulders and drew him close. Then the senator eased himself into the car, Barney gently shut its door, and the car moved off into the night. When it was out of sight, Barney walked through the Rose Garden back to his office.

Dave, watching from the window, shook his head in wonder. He did not know what had happened out there in the night, but he sensed that it was something rare, something that would not be captured in the history books, nor be understood by the people who call politics a science, and cannot see it is a kind of magic.

Five minutes later, Barney buzzed. Dave found him pacing the office nervously, a glass in his hand, his face flushed. He gestured for Dave to pour a drink.

"I guess you're wondering what that was all about," the President said.

Dave nodded.

The President laughed a hoarse, uneasy laugh. Dave could see him unwinding, like a gambler who had risked everything on the turn of one card. When the President spoke again, his voice was soft, almost sad.

"We talked a long time," he said. "We talked about when we were boys, him in Missouri and me back in Tennessee, and how damned miserable it was, people working like mules and living like dogs. We laughed about it, maybe we cried a little too. I told him, Tillman, for God's sake, you and me oughtn't to be fighting, you and me are a couple of country boys who want to make America better. I said, Tillman, I wish you had this job, but I've got it, and everybody and his dog is fighting me, and I can't do this job unless I get some help. And he said, Barney, I want to help you."

The President sank into his chair and a smile broke across his face.

"And then we made the damnedest deal you ever heard of. Get out your pencil, we've got work to do!"

In two hectic hours the next morning, five young men rewrote the New Cities bill into its final form. The work took place around the conference table in Dave's office. He and Elias were there for the administration, along with three lawyers from the Hill: one from Senator Cathcart's staff, one representing the Majority Leader, and one baby-faced Alabaman who spoke for the Southern bloc.

For two hours these five men debated, arguing that this word was too vague or that phrase too specific, pushing as far as they could without knocking the whole package apart. When they were finished, when the Alabaman had made his mandatory speeches and Dave had made his necessary concessions, the New Cities bill was finally settled. Dave had made one major concession on behalf of the administration—rather, he had ratified the agreement the President and Senator Cathcart had reached the night before. Now, ten percent of the New Cities money could be spent to build "small towns and villages" of up to ten thousand inhabitants. So Senator Cathcart got his beloved villages. Yet Dave and the President doubted that many states would wish to get into the village-building business. The final bill also, to pacify the big-city mayors, provided that up to twenty-five percent of the money would go for inner-city housing—the New Towns in Town.

But the morning's most important concession came in a telephone conversation between the President and a senior Southern senator, in which he agreed that in no New City in the South would Negroes comprise more than twenty percent of the total population. It was a hard concession to make, but the alternative was to lose Southern support, and thus lose the bill. It was not the first secret agreement on the racial question: Dave had already made his quasi-promise to Elijah King and Roy Hailey of black control in the California New City.

For all the compromises, the bill was a victory for the President. It gave him most of what he had asked for, it would be the largest housing program in history, and his dream of the shining towers was still intact. When Dave and Elias emerged from the drafting session, Barney was jubilant. He pounded them on the back, sent for champagne, and quickly began calling congressional leaders for a promise of speedy action in both Houses. He got the promises, and then the three of them sat down and got a little drunk.

The congressional leaders kept their promises. The New Cities bill was reported out of Senator Cathcart's committee on Monday afternoon and passed by the Senate on Tuesday. A House vote was set for Wednesday noon, and that morning Barney invited Dave, O. B. Perkins, and four members of the cabinet to his office to await the vote. Charlton MacKenzie was one, for he was increasingly an all-around adviser to the President. Donald Duffey was there too, his skin burned a deep red by a summer of parades and rallies, his face glowing with pride in his new job. The two other cabinet members were the two men Dave had hoped might run the New Cities instead of Duffey: Sid Frankel, the tough little Secretary of Health, Education and Welfare, and Steve Vale, the old liberal who headed the Labor Department.

Dave spent the morning on the phone, talking with Brian O'Neal of the Congressional Relations staff, who was standing by in the Speaker's office. The President laughed and joked with his guests, yet they all sensed an undercurrent of tension, for victory was by no means certain. Ten congressmen were uncommitted; if they broke as expected, the bill would pass by five votes.

At noon, Dave took a call from O'Neal. He cradled the phone against his ear, listening for the expected good news, struck suddenly by news that was not good at all. The President saw his face change.

"What is it?" he demanded.

Dave saw the others turning toward him and he felt his chest tighten. Outside, he glimpsed the cloudless sky and the elm trees rustling gently in the wind.

"Something serious had come up," he said, speaking slowly, trying to think ahead, to get his own position clear. "The six members of the Oklahoma delegation are saying they'll change their votes—that they'll vote against the bill—unless you drop Elias from the program. They say he's too young for the job, and that he's insulted them. The Speaker says they're still mad about that air base you closed in Ardmore. This is their revenge."

Barney grabbed the phone and fired questions at O'Neal, then at the Speaker, but there was little to add. No one thought the Oklahomans were bluffing; their support of the New Cities bill had always been tenuous.

Dave watched intently as the first flush of anger crossed Barney's face, followed quickly by a troubled frown. The President, too, was making his calculations.

It was, for Dave, one of those rare moments when he felt himself face to face with reality, with things as they are, when he felt he could see the entire Washington equation with cold clarity. Dave knew the Oklahoma congressmen and he had no illusions about them. Some were venal old men, one or two were simply ignorant, and at least one was decent enough but was weak politically and would go along with the others rather than risk retaliation back home. There had been more of the hate literature on Elias, circulated by the Birchers and the Wallace people. Elias was a natural for them: a Harvard-educated Negro with a white Jewish wife, deeply involved in a "radical" social program. Dave wondered how many others in Congress, not just the Oklahomans, must hate Elias for being what he was—a Negro who was too young, too bright, too confident, who had married a white woman, had risen too high in the white man's world. Now they sought their moment of power, of revenge.

Dave had read the memoirs in which aged politicians burbled of their love affairs with Washington. Dave did not love Washington. The city sometimes seemed to him a necessary evil, a place where a rich, selfish nation sent its hates and frustrations to be eliminated as quietly as possible. It was a kind of sewage plant; that was a fair analogy. Your job in Washington was to keep the nation's hate and greed moving inside the legislative pipes, to see that they didn't burst out of the pipes into anarchy or revolution. It has always been a city with a negative purpose, not to help the weak but to protect the strong, a city where at best the right things were done for the wrong reasons. There was necessary work to be done in Washington, but Dave saw no need to romanticize it. If you worked in a sewage plant it didn't help to pretend it was a candy store.

Or so it seemed to him at that moment as he watched the exquisite machinery of American politics moving to disembowel his closest friend.

Barney slammed down the phone. "I've got to give them an answer fast. The Speaker says if they switch, we lose by two or three votes. Is that how you figure it, Dave?"

"That's our best estimate."

"There's no other votes I can swing?"

"They aren't there to be swung," Dave said.

"What if we got the vote postponed?" Sid Frankel asked.

The President shook his head. "I asked about that. The Speaker says the trouble would just spread. I've got to settle this now, one way or the other. Okay, I want to know what each of you guys thinks. Duffey?"

Donald Duffey's ruddy face was ashen—he saw his new empire crumbling. His words came in anguished bursts. "This could kill our image," he said. "A big race hassle, stirring all those black extremists up, would ruin us. We've got to make it look like Elias is getting a promotion. An ambassadorship, maybe. Are there any colored ambassadors?"

The President pointed to the next man in the circle, Sid Frankel.

"It's a hard decision," Frankel said. "Clearly the bill is of paramount importance. But an administration has to protect its people, and protect its own integrity and credibility. I'd ask again, despite what the Speaker says, if there couldn't be a postponement, and either the Oklahomans can be bought off, or some other votes can be found. If not, then make the sacrifice."

The President nodded to O. B. Perkins.

"We've got to get this bill passed," the press secretary said. "This guy Elias Abbot may be smart, but he's rude and arrogant and he's been asking for this all along. The only thing now, like Secretary Duffey says, is to ease him out real gentle."

The President turned next to Steve Vale, the old New Dealer whose career had been capped by this appointment. Vale was seventy, a gaunt man with a corncob pipe clenched between his teeth.

"Mr. President," Vale said, "you're being forced to make, on the spur of the moment, as hard a decision as you may ever face. We all know how much the bill means to you and how you've fought for it. Now you're asked to choose between that bill and a young man who's served you as well and faithfully as anyone in this room."

Keep it short, Dave thought; Barney doesn't like speeches.

"It would be easy to throw this young man to the wolves," Steve Vale continued, cupping his pipe in a freckled hand. "And let's not deceive ourselves that there's anything but racial bigotry involved here. But if we do that, what will happen to our credibility with the blacks and with the liberals, the people who are your natural constituency? And what good will it do us to pass the finest legislation in the world if we must do it with the sacrifice of this fine young man on our consciences?"

As Vale paused, Dave let his eyes sweep around the oval office. Such a lovely room, he thought, to have had so much shit spilled in it all these years.

"No, Mr. President," Vale continued, "I say make your stand. Show the bigots they can't intimidate your administration. You still may win the House vote. If not, you can take your case to the people this fall, knowing you've done the decent, moral thing."

The President sat slumped in his chair, his face dark and brooding, his expression fixed. When Vale finished, the President flicked his forefinger at Dave, and Dave could feel the eyes of the other men on him. He sucked in his breath, and for a moment he thought this was the most important decision he had ever made. Then he realized that was not true, that in truth he faced no decision at all, that the decision had already been made, somewhere in the past, by a thousand other decisions that had made him what he was.

"No one here cares more for Elias than I do," he said evenly. "But this bill is more important than any individual. I'd say the same if it was my head they wanted. The vote is too close to take any chances. And I think the Speaker is right about the trouble spreading if we postpone the vote."

He stopped, feeling his heart pounding in his chest like a caged animal.

"Chuck?" the President said, nodding to his Secretary of State.

"I agree with Dave," MacKenzie said. "We have no real choice."

"Okay," Barney said suddenly, pulling himself up straight in his chair, his hand reaching for the telephone. "I'll call the Speaker. Dave, you talk to Elias. Cool him out. If he quits in a huff, we lose both ways. Tell him he can have any job he wants."

"Don't you think you ought to talk to him?" Dave asked.

"Maybe later," the President said. "But you talk to him first. You're his pal."

When Dave got back to his own office, he found Elias waiting for him. He had been up all night preparing for today's vote and there was a stubble of beard on his face.

"Have they voted yet?" Elias asked.

"Not yet," Dave said. "Sit down."

"Hey, what's the matter?" Elias said. "This is our big day."

Dave felt numb. "Look, Elias," he said, trying to pick his words with care, "something bad has happened. It concerns you. I want to tell you exactly what happened."

He saw Elias's smile fade, his eyes narrow, and another look settled over his face, the look Dave recalled from their first meeting. Dave had to force himself to meet Elias's eyes.

"Fifteen minutes ago, the President got a call from the Speaker," Dave said. "The Oklahoma delegation said they'd switch their votes unless the President dropped you from the program."

He paused, and Elias continued to stare at him.

"The President asked each of us for his advice," Dave said. "Steve Vale urged him to make a fight of it. The rest, me included, said we couldn't risk the bill."

"What did the President say?" Elias asked.

"He agreed that we couldn't risk it," Dave answered. "I can give you your choice of any other job you want."

Elias's gaze was so filled with contempt that Dave looked away. "The dirty white sons of bitches," Elias said.

Dave wondered if he meant the Oklahomans or all of them.

"It was the hardest thing I ever had to do," he said. "But I think the New Cities are more important than any one person, whether it's you or me or whoever."

"Fortunately, it wasn't you," Elias said.

"I'd have said the same," Dave said.

Elias stood up and paced the floor a moment. When he stopped, leaning against Dave's bookshelves, his voice was even again.

"You were right," he said. "What you told the President was right. You couldn't risk the bill."

"Thanks," Dave said softly.

"I'm the one who made the mistake," Elias said.

"You haven't made any mistakes," Dave said.

"Yes I have, a big mistake, a long time ago. The mistake of thinking I could be white. I went to their schools and I spoke their language and I thought I could live in their world. That was my mistake. Now the system's caught up with me, and I'm a nigger again."

"It's not the system," Dave protested. "This was a fluke, a terrible fluke where six bastards had us in a corner."

"It's no fluke," Elias said. "When a half-dozen Oklahoma congressmen can punch the button and the President pops up and says, 'So long, black boy'—it's the system."

"The President's not happy about this, Elias."

"I don't see him here hugging and kissing me."

"He wants to see you as soon as the vote is out of the way. He asked me to talk to you about jobs. Steve Vale needs an Assistant Secretary for Manpower, and I could open something up at HEW."

"Suppose I say fuck this administration?" Elias asked. "Suppose I walk out there and tell the reporters that Big Barney Newfield has sold a black boy down the river for a half-dozen seg votes? How would that grab you?"

"It wouldn't help any," Dave said. "I hope you'll think twice about it."

Elias laughed bitterly. "Don't worry, I'll play the game. Call that a favor to you, not to Big Barney. Or call it a favor to the New Cities."

"Okay," Dave said. "I appreciate it. There's still plenty for you to do in this administration."

"No there's not," Elias said. "Let's cut the crap, Dave. I'll hang on for a couple of months, but I'm finished in government. Our Oklahoma friends cut off my balls today. It won't matter now what job I have, I won't talk the same and people won't listen the same."

Dave did not reply. Elias was right. At their level, tangible differences between men's talents meant less than intangibles, prestige and contacts, and to be dropped by the President was a blow from which Elias, in the closed world of Washington politics, could never fully recover.

The phone rang. The New Cities bill had passed by six votes, one more than they'd expected. Dave put down the phone and told Elias.

"Who was the extra vote?" he asked.

"Forbes of Georgia."

Elias smiled without mirth. "That fool Forbes," he said. "He was probably so drunk he forgot how they told him to vote." He stood up and they walked toward the door.

"Elias," Dave said, "you deserve more credit than anybody. We both know that, and the President knows it too."

Elias stared at him without expression. "Yeah," he said, "that makes me feel real fine."

Throughout the afternoon, calls and telegrams of congratulation poured in on the President. He sat with his phone propped against his shoulder, beaming, allowing each caller a minute or two, then pressing the button to allow the next one his moment. Dave was in and out of the office all afternoon with messages. The afternoon's Washington *Star* bannered the news—CONGRESS OKAYS NEW CITIES. That evening Dave and O. B. Perkins and Charlton MacKenzie joined the President to watch the evening news shows. All three networks led with long reports on the bill's passage, and Eric Sevareid added a brief, graceful commentary, calling the New Cities "the latest, perhaps the greatest step in mankind's age-old quest for Utopia."

After that, MacKenzie raised his glass and said, "Gentlemen, a toast to our President and his magnificent victory." Dave lifted his glass and as he did he thought of the past ten months: Barney's visit to the slums and the rat and the screaming child; their discovery of Elias the next day; Osgood's death and the Task Force; Barney's walk on the White House lawn with Senator Cathcart; now, finally, the reality of victory, the realization that these incredible cities would be built and that millions of people would live better lives because of them. Dave held his glass high and found as he did that he was fighting back tears. He fought back, too, the prideful thought that the victory was in some small part his own.

At nine that night, Dave paused on the sidewalk outside a house in Georgetown, not wanting to go in. Yet he did go in, for the party was for the New Cities staff, to celebrate the bill's passage, and he had to attend as a gesture of support for Elias.

The house belonged to Winnie Boatwright, who greeted Dave at the door, a plump Gatsby in a Madras jacket, an unaccustomed look of pain on his boyish face.

"Oh, Dave," he said, "it's so awful. Somebody's got to do something."

Sharon Flatt was at his side. Their courtship had blossomed that summer, with many a timely nudge from Brenda Newfield.

"The bill passed, Winnie," Dave said automatically. "That's the main thing."

He got a drink and walked through the large townhouse, nodding at several people but not stopping. These were the people Elias had pulled together, lawyers, sociologists, writers, young politicians, economists, urban planners, admen down from New York, the usual strange assortment of hustlers and idealists who were drawn to any new government undertaking. They were Elias's people. He had recruited them, protected them, worked them like dogs—and now in their moment of victory they had lost him. Winnie's stereo filled the house with lively music but the mood of the party was funereal. Men stood in little knots staring into their gin-and-tonics. Some of the girls had been crying.

He found Elias in the kitchen, with Sandy beside him, surrounded by a dozen young people from his staff. Elias was cool and dapper in a white suit and blue shirt; Sandy's sharp face was pale above her bright green maternity dress. Elias greeted him warmly; the others mumbled or looked away. Dave stood beside Elias—that was what he had come here to do—and he could feel the hostility of the others leveled at him like guns. Elias kept the talk going, and Dave sipped at his drink, wishing he could toss down three or four. But he couldn't, not here, so he nursed his drink for half an hour, ignored by everyone except Elias. He had been these people's hero, their friend in the White House, and now that something had gone wrong, they would not blame the President, from whom they'd expected little; they would blame their contemporary, from whom they'd expected too much.

Cathy arrived at the party about ten escorted by a young government lawyer. Her wide grin faded when she saw Dave and when they had a moment alone, she whispered:

"If you want to come by, I'll be home by eleven."

"Okay," he said.

He left the party at eleven. Elias came with him to the front steps.

"Looks like I'm public enemy number one," Dave said.

"These people don't understand," Elias said. "They're just kids."

"Call me tomorrow, will you?"

"Sure. Goodnight, Dave."

Dave turned to start down the steps, then Sandy rushed out the front door and seized his arm.

"You bastard," she cried. "You gutless bastard. You just sat there and . . ."

Elias grabbed his sobbing wife and led her back inside.

Cathy opened the door without speaking. She had changed into jeans and a striped sweater. He brushed past her and poured himself the stiff drink he'd wanted all evening.

"You want anything?" he asked, without looking around.

"No thanks."

"I guess you've heard about my great triumph today."

"You don't have to talk about it," she said.

He put on some of her records, old things, Sinatra and Ella and Belafonte, and he stretched out on the floor, listening to the music and drinking. Cathy sat on the sofa reading the *New Republic*. Soon he was drunk, gladly drunk, drunker than he'd been for a long time, drunk and drifting deep within himself, relaxing, savoring the vast privacy of drunkenness. Yet he was never quite alone.

"You never got to know Elias, did you?" he asked her finally, when the records stopped.

"No," she said. "I wish I had."

"I never knew a guy I liked better," he told her. "That

guy is me with a black skin. We love the same things and we hate the same things. God, what we went through together these last months."

"You'll still be friends," she said.

"No we won't," Dave told her. "Not after this. We'll remind each other of something we want to forget."

"You'd just as well forget it," she said, but Dave wasn't listening.

"I might have turned Barney around if I'd tried. He might have made a fight of it if I'd pushed him."

"Then you'd have lost the vote, wouldn't you?" She had put down her magazine and was staring at him intently.

"Nobody knows," he said. "They might have been bluffing. We gave up without a fight. Steve Vale wanted to fight. But I voted against it, voted against Elias."

"There's no use blaming yourself," she said impatiently. "You know you advised your boss right and he did the right thing. You know that as well as I do."

"Okay," he said. "Okay, you're a bright tough girl and you're right. It's damned easy to be right about other people's troubles. But let me tell you something, it's not easy to sit there and see your friend get his throat cut. Believe me, it's not easy. I don't know how much more of this I can take."

"If you can't take the heat . . ." she began.

"Get out of the kitchen. Sure, that's a great line. But that's not how it is. Nobody ever gets out of the kitchen voluntarily. All that power is a magnet, pulling you back into the fire."

"Is that it, just the power?" she asked.

He was sitting cross-legged on the floor now, jiggling the empty glass between his knees.

"You love the power. It's like a woman you want to stay in bed with forever. But that's not all, not for the best people. There's all you can do with the power, if you're smart and tough and lucky. You get kicked in the teeth every day, but sometimes there'll be those moments when you've done everything right, when everything breaks your way, and then you're soaring, you've won your game, whether or not anyone else knows it or understands it or even gives a damn."

"Wasn't today one of those times for you?" she asked. "Weren't you proud when they passed that bill, despite Elias, despite everything?"

He nodded his head slowly. "Yes. Oh hell yes, I was proud. Despite everything."

Kings and Principal Persons

1

"See that ridge?" Bob Huffaker shouted above the noise of the helicopter. "The one with the three palm trees? Our patrol saw some movement there."

Dave frowned in the direction indicated. He saw the three palms but no movement. Looking down, a half mile beneath them, he could see the line of government troops moving beside the river. The river was in the middle of a long valley and the ridge was off to their left.

It was past three; a tropical sun, huge and fiercely hot, was dropping toward the western mountains. They had been up in the helicopter since eight that morning, except when they descended to the thick Caravelian jungle while Huffaker talked with the ROC Rangers and their American advisers. The time in the jungle was real, too real, but the time in the helicopter, with the roar of its engines and the white-hot glare of the sun, soaring over mountains and valleys, rivers and roads, soaring safe and Godlike while the soldiers cut their way through the jungle below—the helicopter was like a dream.

It had begun forty-eight hours before, when reports began pouring in from Caravelas. Rivera was dead. Rivera was surrounded. Rivera was about to defeat the ROC army. "We don't know what the fuck is happening," Barney had roared. "The embassy says one thing, the CIA says the opposite, then the Pentagon says something else. Look, I want you to fly down there and let me know what's going on. Okay?"

So now he hovered above the jungle, looking for movement on a rocky ridge, still not sure what was going on. Rivera's band was thought to be somewhere near this valley; if so, it might indeed be trapped, for the ROC Rangers had formed a huge circle for miles around. It was the ROC army's big push against Rivera, made after Barney had refused to accept the deal that Rivera had offered through Dave, refused in part because the Senate Minority Leader had made statements about "deals in Latin America"; perhaps he was bluffing, perhaps he knew something, but it worked and Barney had left the U.S. advisers in Caravelas and told them to get Rivera if they could. Now, in the helicopter, Dave felt a terrible sense of helplessness as he dangled above the action, not knowing what was happening, not knowing how he could affect it, just *there*, a spectator, furious and impotent.

He saw the tiny figures on the riverbank form a circle. A puff of smoke rose from their circle and a moment later a pillar of dirt and foliage rose a hundred yards below the ridge. A second mortar shell exploded nearer the ridge, and after that the blasts skipped neatly along its spine.

"They're good shots," Dave said.

Huffaker shook his head. "They're wasting ammunition," he said. "If the guerrillas were on that ridge, they're long gone now."

"Where? Down the other side?"

"No, we've got men over there. From that ridge, if that's where Rivera is, that patrol down below us, along the river, looks the weakest link in our chain. If he wants to make a break for it, he'll either try to slip past them, or else engage them."

Dave glanced at the tiny figures along the riverbank, and as he did a silver geyser rose in the river and the soldiers scattered.

"Look there." Huffaker pointed again toward the ridge, and below it Dave saw a flash of light among the rocks, and an instant later another explosion beside the river.

"Drop down closer, Chuck," Huffaker called to their pilot, a warrant officer, but there was nothing more to see. The government troops moved into the jungle and if there were sounds Dave could not hear them for the noise of the helicopter.

"What's happening?" he shouted to Huffaker.

"Rivera's trying to fight his way out. See those flashes?"

Dave could see some sort of disturbance in the foliage— a flash here, a puff of smoke there, soldiers running beside the river—but he couldn't tell what was happening, much less who was winning.

"Can he make it?" Dave shouted.

"He doesn't have a chance," Huffaker said coldly. "Look."

Dave looked, and low on the horizon, far down the valley, he saw four dots. The dots were approaching very fast and soon they became U.S. helicopters, the new Lockheed Apaches, $2,000,000 each, the very finest in combat helicopters, the fruit of the Vietnam experience, whizzing along low among the afternoon shadows that filled the valley. There was something very final about their approach. Dave felt a strange sensation of *déjà vu*. After a moment he knew what it was. The helicopters had reminded him of a scene from a thousand Western movies of his boyhood, the scene in the last reel when the cavalry comes galloping over the hill. Except here the cavalry was on the wrong side.

The helicopters landed all around the place where Rivera and his men were thought to be, unloaded several dozen ROC Rangers from their bellies, then began long, graceful arcs above the area, their cannon blazing, their rockets methodically ripping the jungle to shreds.

"What's happening?" Dave asked again.

"Rivera's surrounded. After we've softened that area up a while, the Rangers will move in."

"Can't you do anything?"

"I did all I could. Rivera made his mistake when he walked into this trap."

The gunships blasted the dozen-acre thicket until it seemed to Dave that no one there could possibly survive. When finally the helicopters withdrew, dozens of fires raged and the ROC Rangers began their advance.

"Take her down, Chuck," Huffaker called to the pilot. "I think it's all over."

But it was not. In the jungle, between two boulders that flanked a tiny stream, Rivera huddled with the girl Elda and the gypsy, Alonzo. The others were gone. Fires burned all around them: Alonzo, his bright red bandanna still knotted around his neck, was dying. His right leg had been mangled and they could not stop the bleeding.

There is no pain, Captain, Alonzo said. It is nothing. It is like a dream.

Brave soldier, said Rivera. You are the bravest of the soldiers, Alonzo.

He could hear machine guns in the distance.

I bless you, my Captain, the gypsy whispered. I bless you and the good days in the mountains.

Do not bless me, Rivera thought. Bless the revolution. Do not die for me; die for our cause, which will live.

He cradled the gypsy's head in his lap, waiting.

We must go, the girl said. There is a cave farther down this stream where we can stay until dark.

In a moment, Rivera said. He will be dead in another moment. Rivera had reinjured his knee and he did not think he could walk as far as the cave. He knew the soldiers were coming now. He thought most about the girl. After another minute Alonzo died and Rivera folded his arms across his chest.

Now, she said, now we must go. Her huge brown eyes blazed; she had not believed this could happen. He stood up, leaning his hand on the boulder for support, but when he tried to walk his knee buckled. He checked his pistol, then the rifle. He heard machine guns closer this time.

Put your arm around my shoulders, she said. I will help you.

There is no time, he told her. They are close now. We will await them here.

A sudden blast of gunfire sprayed fragments of rock down on them. They dropped down in the crevice between the boulders, and Rivera seized the rifle. He peered around the corner of the rock until there was another blast and he returned the fire. He heard more firing from behind and he knew they were surrounded. He turned to fire at those behind them and as he did a bullet struck his neck. He ducked back down behind the rocks and the girl tried to stop the bleeding.

There was more firing, closer, and when he rose to return it they fired at him from front and rear. There was an hour of daylight left; he saw no escape from this. The wound in his neck was not serious but he felt himself growing weaker.

What shall we do? the girl asked.

He put his arm around her. Nothing, he said. There is nothing to do except to keep fighting.

The girl trembled. She did not fear death but she feared the soldiers. She seized Rivera's arm.

You promised, she said. You promised that if this happened . . .

Wait, he said, there is still time. But there was another burst of the machine guns and he knew there was no time.

You must do it, the girl cried, pressing herself against him.

Above them, he could see smoke from the burning jungle rising against a flame-colored sky. He heard shouting, a man's voice calling for them to surrender.

You promised, the girl cried again, and he knew he must keep his promise. He kissed her, she buried her face against his chest, he put his pistol against her temple and kept his promise to her.

It was all a dream now. He stood up, wanting death but wanting it his own way, firing furiously at the places where his enemies were hidden, laughing as he waited for the end. But the machine-gun blasts did not come, and he did not see the hand grenade, only felt the explosion that lifted him toward the blood-colored sky, only thought once of the revolution before the sky surrounded him and there was silence.

"Take him to the base at Leticia," Huffaker shouted into the radio. "Do you understand? Take him there and see that he is cared for."

"Si, si," a man's high-pitched voice replied and Huffaker switched off the radio. In the momentary silence Dave could hear the dusk calls of jungle birds. The helicopter had landed in a small clearing near the river. Dave and the pilot waited in silence while Huffaker lit a cigarette with his Zippo.

"Chuck, head for the Leticia base," he ordered.

A thousand feet up they could see the sun's last glow over the western ridges, and the still flickering fires down in the jungle.

"They've taken Rivera alive," Huffaker said. "Tore up pretty bad but looks like he'll pull through. I told them to take him to Leticia. There's a doctor there."

"Is that where we're going?" Dave asked.

"Yeah," Huffaker said. "Now here's the deal. A Captain Ortiz has him now—that's him I was talking to—and he'll do what I tell him. But when Molina gets here I won't be able to handle him."

"He'll want to kill Rivera?" Dave said.

"The sooner the better. And Rivera's his prisoner, not ours. So you'd better start thinking fast if you want to keep him alive."

"How long until we get there?"

"Ten, twelve minutes."

"How long till they get Rivera there?"

"About the same. And our friend Colonel Molina won't be far behind."

Captain Ortiz, the field commander, met them at the airstrip. He was fat and florid—he reminded Dave of Eddie Gooch.

"Welcome, good friends," he cried. "We have met the enemy and he is ours."

Yeah, you're a fucking Napoleon, Dave thought.

One of the Apaches had already landed.

"Is Rivera here?" Huffaker asked.

"Yes," Ortiz said in a shrill, fat man's voice. "I have had him taken inside. The doctor is with him."

"Let's go in then," Dave said.

The base was not large. There was a two-story, brick building with military offices, a hangar for a dozen small planes, a motor pool and some weatherbeaten frame barracks. The three of them marched to the brick building, passing wounded ROC Rangers stretched out on the grass.

"I may need to call Washington," Dave told Huffaker.

"You can call from my office here."

"Is it secure?"

"Is the Pope a Catholic?"

There were two doors inside the office building. One said PRIVATE and the other said U. S. MILITARY COMMAND. Captain Ortiz knocked on the one that said PRIVATE and the doctor, an old man with a mustache, opened it. He looked at them blankly, then returned to the man stretched out on a leather sofa. The room was a small conference room, with a battered table, six straight-back chairs and a row of filing cabinets.

Rivera's eyes were closed and he was very pale. His shirt had been torn away. There were bandages on his neck, chest and arms. The doctor was working on a jagged wound at his waist. He dabbed away most of the blood and applied a bandage.

"How is he?" Dave asked. The doctor shrugged. Just then, Rivera opened his eyes. The doctor spoke but he gave no sign of recognition. His eyes shut again.

The doctor spoke to Ortiz in Spanish. "There is nothing more to be done now," Ortiz said. "The doctor requests that we wait outside."

"I want to see him a moment," Dave said. Huffaker nodded, and after the others left, Dave was alone with the wounded guerrilla leader.

"Can you hear me?" he asked. Rivera's eyes remained closed. Then Dave thought: This is silly; I'm wasting time. But just as he turned away from the sofa the door opened and Colonel Luis Molina stepped into the room. His eyes glistened as he studied his unconscious enemy on the sofa.

A smile spread across Luis Molina's small face, until the corners of his thin mouth curved upward into tiny dimples. The gold bars on his shoulders glistened in the bright light of the corridor as he called to the three soldiers standing by the front door.

"Colonel Huffaker has requested that the prisoner be treated with care," Captain Ortiz said, as the soldiers hurried over.

"Colonel Huffaker has nothing to say about this prisoner," Molina snapped.

"Colonel Molina," Dave injected, "I must urge that Rivera be treated with care and held for trial."

"Trial?" said Molina, as if the word was new to him. "Trial, Mr. Hyer? Sir, this is a military matter. I think trials are not greatly relevant."

"I suggest that you think of world opinion, Colonel," Dave said.

"And I suggest that you leave this matter to me," Molina said and spoke in Spanish to the soldiers.

"Colonel, on behalf of President Newfield, I tell you that this prisoner is not to be harmed."

"That suggestion will interest me only if it comes from President Newfield himself," Molina said.

They stared at each other coldly. Dave had made his bluff and Molina had called it. Now he had to produce. If he could.

"Colonel Huffaker," Dave said. "You told me I could call Washington from here."

"That's right," Huffaker said, impassive again. "Come with me."

Huffaker unlocked the door marked U. S. MILITARY COMMAND and when the fluorescent light blinked on they were in a small office with a desk and file cabinets and, beyond it, an even smaller room filled with communications equipment. Huffaker picked up the telephone and began barking commands.

"You shouldn't have any problem," he said. "I'll wait outside."

Dave took the phone and sat down at the desk, listening to clicks and static from the receiver. After a moment, he heard Barney's voice.

"Dave? What the hell is going on?"

The connection was perfect; Barney might have been in the next room.

"There's been a battle," he said. "Rivera's a prisoner."

"Hurt?"

"Yes. Shot up pretty bad. Unconscious. We're at a military base now. Colonel Molina's here and he's about to have Rivera shot."

Barney hesitated, and Dave could picture him at his desk, feet propped up, a drink in his hand, that bored, scornful look on his face. He heard Barney sigh and he imagined the shrug that went with it.

"Well," Barney said finally, "that's that."

"Mr. President," Dave said, "Molina is just outside the room I'm in. I urge you to tell him Rivera isn't to be killed, that at least he's to have a trial." Dave hesitated. "I suggested that, but he won't listen to me."

"I can't get involved in their squabbles down there."

"Mr. President, if you weren't already involved, Rivera would never have been captured."

"That's different."

"If Rivera is killed, progressives in the U.S. and all over Latin America will blame you."

"Yeah? Well let me tell you something else. We go up for the New Cities money next week and I want that whole ten billion. I want it so bad I'd give my right arm for it. And you know who decides? Five old men who already think I'm a Bolshevik and who'd have apoplexy if I lifted a finger for your friend Rivera."

"It would be the Caravelian government that would arrange the trial," Dave said.

"Do I sound dumb tonight, Dave? Are you saying that I'd get credit from the leftwing but wouldn't get blame from the rightwing? Let me tell you something else. There's gonna be a little election a couple of years from now, and I figure to be in it, and some Republican will tear me a new asshole if I've been running around bailing Communist guerrillas out of trouble."

It was time to stop arguing, but Dave was not willing to stop. He understood all the political problems, but politics seemed distant now and he could think only of the man in the next room, who he thought as good a man as Barney Newfield, and who now needed his help much more.

"Mr. President," he pressed, "I think you're underestimating the reaction. This would hurt you among the people you count on most—the liberals, the students. The people who want to see Rivera dead aren't going to vote for you no matter what you do."

"Okay, kid, you've made your point," Barney said impatiently. "Now pack your bag and get on home."

Dave shut his eyes. "Mr. President," he said finally. "If you let them kill Rivera I'll have no choice but to resign."

"The hell you would."

"That's how I feel about this."

"I don't like threats, kid."

"It's not a threat. It's just something I'd have to do."

"I ought to throw your ass out."

"Okay."

"You really care that much about this character?" Barney asked incredulously.

"Mr. President, I've only seen about ten people in politics I admire, and five or six of them have been murdered. I'd like to see this one saved."

He heard angry voices outside in the corridor as he waited for Barney's decision. Dave was very tired. He didn't much care what Barney decided, if he'd just get it over with.

"Okay, kid," the President said. "You win this round. Put our friend Molina on the phone."

While Molina talked to the President, Dave tried to think ahead. If Rivera was not killed immediately, he might be safe. Once news of his capture spread, worldwide pressures, political and diplomatic, would arise in his behalf. Two or three days from now, it would not be so easy to kill him. Dave knew that, and Molina knew it too, and he was furious as he emerged from the office.

"You have advised your President poorly," he said, eyes flashing.

"I think not, Colonel."

"There are those who will wonder as to your motives," Molina said.

"There always are," Dave said. "Colonel Huffaker, I'm ready to go if you are."

"You seem very anxious to help the Communist cause, Mr. Hyer," Molina hissed.

Dave looked at Molina. He found it impossible to think of him as a "military dictator." He was an arrogant little man who might have been a well-connected pimp in Mexico City or the headwaiter in a second-rate New York restaurant.

"Listen, you little bastard . . ." Dave began, then he caught himself. "Come on, Bob, let's get out of here."

He slept most of the flight back to Washington, slept dreamlessly as the Air Force jet cut through the dark sky at seven hundred miles an hour. He awoke before dawn, stiff and still sleepy, and sipped black coffee until the plane began its approach to Washington. They were landing at National and they came in low along the Potomac; ahead he could see Memorial Bridge and off to his right the gentle hillside of Arlington Cemetery and, halfway up the slope, the flicker of a flame. He stared out at the pinpoint of light and his thoughts went back a decade to the time when he was just out of college, just entering politics, and his nation had been at the dawn of a new era, and he thought how simple it all had seemed. Then everything had gone wrong and now two who might have mattered were down on that hillside and they who were left, who once had imagined great victories, now struggled for even the smallest ones. Dave raised two fingers of his left hand in the V sign and pressed them against the cabin window, toward that tiny light below. Then he turned away from the window and huddled in his seat, awaiting the landing.

2

From the moment Billy Doyle entered his office, Dave knew something was troubling him, for Doyle was not a man who could hide his emotions. Concern was written across his gentle, homely face, and he barely managed a smile when Dave rose to greet him.

Billy Doyle was the most beloved journalist in America. In a tough business, he was kind; in a cynical era, he was hopeful; in a complex society, he was a doggedly common-sense observer. All these qualities were reflected in his syndicated column, and they had won him the affection of millions of readers, as well as the respect of the politicians with whom he dealt daily. There was something special about Billy Doyle—an element of trust, of faith—that was rarely seen at the higher levels of his profession.

Dave had first met Doyle when he'd come to Tennessee to cover Barney's first campaign for governor, and they'd been on friendly terms ever since. Doyle admired the Populist strain in Barney Newfield's character, and he'd written warmly of his presidency. Dave wanted to keep it that way, so he focused carefully on Doyle's frowning countenance.

"Sit down, Billy. How about some coffee?"

"I'd like that, David."

"Drink it black, don't you?"

"That's right. Got the habit during the war, up on the front lines, where you couldn't get the niceties. How's your wife and your little girl?"

"They're fine, thanks. How is everything with you?"

"David, to tell you the plain truth, something's troubling me, and I'd like to get right to it."

"Go ahead."

"Maybe the best way is just to let you read a column I've written. I don't often do that, but it concerns you, and you're someone I think a lot of."

"I appreciate it," Dave said, thinking, What the hell?

The columnist handed Dave several sheets of carbon paper, and he leaned back in his chair to read them. By the time he finished the first paragraph, his face had settled into a frown. By the time he finished the last sheet, he was thinking very fast what he should say to this man.

"I don't suppose I should ask where you got this story," he said.

Billy Doyle shook his head. "I can't tell you that, David. But I'd like to hear your side of it."

Dave sipped his coffee. "Billy, part of this story is true and most of it is not. I don't see how I can comment at all, for the record, because it involves my confidential work for the President, in a sensitive area. I'm sure you understand that."

"I do, but I hope you can give me some kind of guidance."

"I think I'd better go down it point by point. But I can't have any of this attributed to me."

"I understand."

"Okay. In the first place, yes, I did take the trip to Caravelas and I was present when Rivera was captured. The President sent me down to find out what was happening. And, yes, the issue of how Rivera would be treated did come up and I did speak to President Newfield about it."

"Why was that, David?"

"Because they were about to shoot him and I didn't think that was in President Newfield's interest."

"Why not?"

"Because this country would be blamed, both here and in Latin America, and it would alienate the very progressive forces we should be working with."

"Another point that isn't clear to me," Doyle said, "is why you were sent down there to begin with. Foreign affairs isn't your area."

"My area is whatever the President wants me to do. It happened that Leon wasn't available to go, and the President didn't want to send someone from State or Defense because he never knows what special ax they'll have to grind."

"Almost everyone has some ax to grind," Doyle commented.

"Getting back to your column," Dave said, "it simply isn't true that I threatened or cursed Colonel Molina. I told him my opinion, he differed with me, and I suggested he get the President's view."

"Or you get it for him?"

"There wasn't time for formal channels. The soldiers were standing there ready to shoot Rivera."

"David, why are you so worried about what happens to this Communist terrorist?"

"I don't know that he's either of those things. He's a nationalist leader who's been driven into exile and who is leading what many people consider a popular revolutionary movement."

His phone buzzed. Mrs. Gill said the Secretary of Labor was on the line. "I'll call him back," he told her. "Now, Billy, there's one untruth in here that disturbs me more than all the others. I did not, repeat not, tell the President I'd quit unless he did what I wanted about Rivera. I don't threaten the President. We don't have that sort of a relationship. He's the boss."

He had never found it hard to lie if the stakes were high enough. And they were high. There had been enough friction with the President because of his threat to quit. If word of it got into the papers, that might be the last straw.

The question was how Billy Doyle had gotten the story. Dave had told no one about their exchange. It was possible that the President had told Doyle, or had him told, but if that was true, it didn't matter what Dave said because he was finished. It was more likely, Dave thought, that the President had let it slip to someone—O.B., MacKenzie, Eddie Gooch—who had leaked it to undercut Dave. And there was a third possibility, still unformed in Dave's mind: perhaps they two had not been alone on that line.

"It's a strange story for someone to make up," Doyle said.

"My experience in politics is that people who tell lies generally tell whoppers," Dave said. "Billy, I'm in your debt for telling me about this. All I can say is someone is trying to mislead you to get at me. This business about me threatening to quit is made out of the whole cloth."

He was trying to play the role of a candid, troubled, injured young man. You couldn't buy off Billy Doyle in the usual don't-print-that-and-I'll-give-you-this manner you could deal with most of the columnists. What you could do was play on his emotions—his patriotism, his generosity, his sentimentality—for Billy Doyle was an emotional man. The great passions of his professional life had been the New Deal, the loyalist cause in Spain, the war against Hitler, the two Stevenson campaigns, the Kennedy presidency—and finally, the war in Vietnam. Because of Vietnam, he had fallen out with longtime friends who could not see the parallel between appeasement of Hitler in the late Thirties and appeasement of Hanoi in the late Sixties. On college campuses, where once he had been something of a hero, he was jeered and heckled until he stopped his lecture tours. He had accepted the Osgood administration's settlement of the war as necessary, but his bitterness against those who had opposed the war, who denounced the American political structure which he so revered, had grown. His columns were filled with condemnations of "campus anarchists" and "black racists." His bitterness had multiplied when, a few weeks earlier, a young New Left journalist had written a scathing, highly personal attack on him in *The New York Review of Books*. Billy Doyle was a kindly man, but he was outraged by this generation of shaggy-haired, foul-mouthed radicals; he had no sympathy for them or for anyone who defended them. He liked David Hyer, but of late he had heard some disturbing things about him, and he intended to find out if they were true.

"David, it outrages me, to see the wide-eyed young people, hardly dry behind the ears, treating these Communist cutthroats like heroes. Don't they know that if Rivera took power down there the first thing he'd do is shoot down his enemies without a trial? Is that what they call democracy?"

"I think that many of today's young people, Billy, view men like Rivera—however misguided they may be—with the same enthusiasm and idealism that your generation felt for the loyalist cause in Spain."

"It's not the same, not the same at all. We were fighting fascism, but now it's this New Left that uses the bully-boy, Fascist techniques. My God, when I see those unwashed hooligans shouting down an elected official or a college president

. . . What are we coming to, David? What is America coming to?"

Dave nodded sympathetically. He did not intend to argue with a man who had in his pocket a newspaper column that might end his career. The need was not to enlighten Billy Doyle but to humor him.

"They're bitter times, Billy," he said, "and God knows we need men like you to help hold things together. The President was really moved by that column you wrote on the New Cities—he said that probably did more to pass the bill than all his speeches put together."

"It's a great program," the columnist said, a smile lighting his face. "It's worthy of FDR."

The time had come to wrap this up. "Billy," he said, "I don't know who gave you this information, but I've told you my version of it, and I guess it's my word against theirs. I'd be happy for you to talk to the President about this resignation thing." The bluff seemed a safe one. "Beyond that, as my grand-mother used to say, I just hope you'll give the matter prayer-ful consideration."

Doyle grinned sheepishly and Dave thought, Jesus Christ, I ought to get an Oscar.

"I'm going to think hard about it," Doyle said. "You've been honest with me, I know that. And I'll be honest and say that your word means more to me than the person who told me about this resignation threat."

Dave heaved an inner sigh and walked with Doyle to the door. He held out his hand to the columnist.

"You've been damn good about this, Billy."

"I try to be a fair man, David," the older man said. "Give my best to your family."

When Doyle was gone, Dave made two quick phone calls. The first was to a man at the CIA whom he told to check with Huffaker in Caravelas to see if there was any chance that the phone there had been bugged. Then he called Cathy at her office and asked her to come see him.

She arrived a half-hour later, thin and jaunty in a red dress, her hair freshly cut in a pixie style.

"Hi, slim. Where's your bowl?"

"My what?" she asked, frowning at him.

"Your bowl. For that haircut."

She jabbed him in the ribs with a bony fist. "Wise guy. This happens to be the thirty-dollar special from Mister Pierre."

"Old Lucky Pierre, huh? Sit down, slim, and give me some information. You know Billy Doyle?"

"Sure. His office is just down from ours. He pats me on the arm in the elevator and tells me what a fine little lady I am."

"Just on the arm?"

"He's not the fanny-patting type."

"Pity," Dave said. "Look, somebody has been giving Billy a cock-and-bull story about me telling the President I'd quit if he didn't save Rivera."

"Cock-and-bull?"

"Slim, you stay off my back. You're the only reporter in this town I can trust."

"I'm the only one you're sleeping with, I think."

"That was my plan all along. Listen, I want to know if you can find out where Billy got his information."

"I might could," she said. "What's in it for me?"

"How about my company next Saturday afternoon?"

"Oh, God, what more could a girl ask? But I was thinking more about some advance word on what Justice is up to on those Weathermen cases."

He scribbled a name on a slip of paper. "Call this fellow and say I asked him to fill you in. Now, is there anything else you want? My right arm?"

"Not yet," she said. "I'll call you this evening."

"Good God, Mr. President, you can't mean it!"

"I do mean it, Mr. Secretary."

"But, sir, six hundred million Chinese will die."

"It can't be helped."

"We can learn to live with them, sir. We can all try harder. There must be a road to peace."

"The Commies don't want peace. They want war, and I'm just the man to oblige them. Bring me the button!"

"I can't do it, sir. I refuse."

"Then you must be one of them. Take him away!"

"Wait! Perhaps he'll listen to me, his wife. Oh, Walter, I know you don't love me any more. All you love is power, power, power. But think, if you can, of the innocents who will perish in this mad plan. Can you condemn them all to a fiery death?"

"Florence, I must destroy China to save her. History will understand. Bring me the button!"

"Cut! Cut! Cut! Mel, baby, what is your problem?"

"My problem is this piece of shit you call a script," the "President" said, picking at his nose. "Jesus Christ, do I need a drink."

"I tell you, Mel, it is a *spoof*, a *spoof*, a *spoof*. It is *supposed* to be a piece of shit and *you* are supposed to *play* it as such."

"And I tell you that as a *spoof* it is a piece of shit and I don't know what the hell I'm doing in it."

"How 'bout you, Ellie baby, you know what you're doing here?" Barney Newfield called from the back of the room, which happened to be his office.

Eleanor Hyer, who was playing the President's wife, flashed her most wonderful smile. "Why of course, Mr. President," she said. "I'm just earning an honest dollar."

"Why don't all you thespians come have a little refreshment with me," Barney Newfield said. "Unless Mr. Director has any objections."

"No, no, Mr. President, sir, that'd be lovely," said Walt Tyson, who was directing the movie.

Dave was leaning against the wall watching. He had not really believed they would film part of this movie in the White House, but Barney was willing and the producer, Rosy Rosenthal, was eager, and since the money was going to charity there had been only a minimal outcry from the press. Mostly, the episode had been viewed as just another of Newfield's idiosyncrasies.

The President's office was crowded, with the actors up front in the circle of light, and many others behind the lights—cameramen, script girls, the producer, the director, the director's narrow-hipped young assistant, Barney and Brenda and all the White House secretaries, four or five privileged reporters—twenty-five or thirty people in all.

Dave had watched the filming with a dour amusement. He

did not find sketches about pre-emptive strikes against China humorous because he knew men at the Pentagon who dreamed each night of pre-emptive strikes against China.

The one lively spot in this otherwise incomprehensible film was his wife as the troubled First Lady. Eleanor was bright, she was funny, she was lovely. With the roll of an eye, the wave of a hand, the flicker of an eyebrow, she poured life into the inane script. Dave suspected that was why Mel Bravo, the matinee idol who was playing the President, had been so difficult—Eleanor was stealing scene after scene from him. Tough, pal, Dave thought; she's been stealing scenes from me for years.

They had hardly spoken for weeks, for he had been busy with his work and she with her rehearsals, and as usually happened they got along better the less they saw of one another. Now, watching her in the spotlights, with all eyes on her, he saw her afresh, remembered how lovely she was. The crowd moved to the Cabinet Room for drinks and sandwiches. Eleanor glowed with beauty and laughter, until even Barney was dimmed by her brilliance. Seeing that, Barney joined her, and the two of them became the center of the room.

Dave grabbed a sandwich and said hello to two or three people. Rosy Rosenthal was there, wet-lipped and worried, not understanding this film he had put two million dollars into, wondering if it would attract the "youth market." Dave told him it was a socially significant drama, and went to speak to Mel Bravo, whom he hadn't seen since he and his wife had marched in Duffey's parade.

"Jesus, pal, that your wife? Boy, she's something." Mel was drinking a glass of straight Scotch. He had taken off his elevator shoes, and in his socks he stood about five-five.

"How's your wife?" Dave asked, remembering the fiery Marge.

"Oh, Jesus, have you guys got *her* ticked off," Mel said, taking a swallow of the Scotch. "I dunno who this guy Rivera is, but she's signing petitions for him day and night. Jeez!"

Bravo returned to the bar and Dave said hello to Mike Bates, the scriptwriter.

"Are the actors putting what you want into the script?" Dave asked.

"They never do," Bates said. "That's why they're actors."

"I thought Eleanor was rather good."

"Your wife is a very clever woman," the writer said.

Sharon Flatt joined them and asked Bates if he was a Democrat.

"I don't have any politics," the writer said. Dave looked at him and realized there was something about him he didn't like.

"Everyone has politics," Dave said. "They just don't know it. Look at Sharon, here. She was a good West Virginia Democrat until she got herself a rich beau. Now I don't know about her."

Sharon Flatt, whose wonderful chest was concealed beneath a fluffy dress from Lord & Taylor, wagged an angry finger at him. "I am a Democrat, David Hyer, and I always will be, even if I do marry Winnie."

"How's chances?" Dave asked her.

"Golly, I don't know," she admitted. "Winnie's been talking to his mother. He wouldn't do anything unless his mother said so."

"Don't you worry, sweetheart, I've been talking to Winnie's mother too, telling her what a fine girl you are." Brenda Newfield had joined them, her strawberry blond hair piled high upon her head. "Now let's us have a little talk."

Brenda drew Sharon aside. Winnie Boatwright's bachelor days were numbered, Dave thought.

"How do I determine my latent political tendencies, Mr. Hyer," Mike Bates asked in an unpleasant voice.

"Who were you for in Chicago?" Dave asked. "The cops or the kids?"

The writer shrugged. "Neither, really. I saw them both as material."

"How about Vietnam? Did it engage you?"

"Ignorant armies that clash by night," Bates quoted. "We were somewhat more brutal, but only because of a superior technology. The other side would have napalmed us, if they could have."

"You ever voted?" Dave asked.

"No."

"Don't," Dave said. "I think you're a Republican."

Dave caught the President's eye and after a moment was able to take him aside.

"Billy Doyle came to see me this morning," he said. "He heard somewhere that I called you from Caravelas and threatened to quit unless you intervened for Rivera."

"So?" Barney said, with the coolness he had used several times recently.

"So if you told somebody, that's your business, but I didn't."

"Well, I didn't either," Barney said. "Does that make me a liar?"

"No, but it makes it look like there was somebody else on the party line."

"Check that out," Barney said and walked away.

Dave nodded and returned to his office.

Dave's man at the CIA called in midafternoon.

"Our friend in the South says, yes, that office may have been bugged."

"The phone?" Dave asked.

"No, only the office, so they'd have only your end of the conversation."

"Tell our friend in the South he damn well ought to be more careful," Dave said, and slammed down the phone.

Cathy called at six.

"You know who Jules LaFontaine is?"

"A PR man in New York?"

"Right. One of his clients is the government of Caravelas. And he was down here two days ago for lunch with Billy Doyle. That afternoon Billy wrote that column about you."

"How'd you get this?" he asked.

"Would you believe I traded my hot young body for it?"

"Sure."

"Well, I didn't, you bastard. I know Billy's secretary and I just loosened her tongue with three martinis. That's four-fifty you owe me, plus tip."

"You're magnificent, slim."

"Don't mention it."

He buzzed Mrs. Gill.

"Ethyl, would you pick up a bottle of perfume and send it to Cathy Quinn?"

"What kind?"

He thought a moment. "Caléche." That was Eleanor's favorite, so he knew it was good.

"How much?" Mrs. Gill asked. "An ounce? A half ounce?"

"Oh, hell, I don't know. Twenty dollars' worth. Now get me Jerry Drucker at the Bureau."

The talk with Drucker was mainly a fishing expedition. "Jerry, I want to know about the politics of a PR man named Jules LaFontaine. Particularly any rightwing ties. Did he ever do any work for Franco? Or Batista?"

"Right," the agent said. "Anything else?"

"Yeah," Dave said. "See if the son of a bitch has been paying his taxes."

Billy Doyle called about seven.

"David, I've rewritten this column and I wanted to read it to you before I send it off. Have you got a minute?"

"Sure, fire away."

The new column was a rambling essay about the threat of communism in Latin America and the parallel threat of "hooliganism calling itself politics" at home. "It has not previously been revealed," he wrote midway in the column, "but David Hyer, President Newfield's able, energetic aide, was on a fact-finding mission to Caravelas recently when Alberto Rivera, the guerrilla terrorist, was captured by the government forces. Soldiers on the scene wanted to give Rivera the same swift justice that he would certainly have meted out to them, but young Hyer insisted that the revolutionary be held for trial. Perhaps he was right. Perhaps democracy demands a higher standard. And yet when one sees unwashed young Americans burning their country's flag and howling their support of these Communist terrorists . . ."

The column rambled on, but said nothing about Dave's call to the President.

"It's a fine column," Dave said when he'd finished. "And it's more than fair, Billy."

That was the truth. He thanked Doyle effusively—perhaps he should send old Billy some perfume—and then he hurried to the President's office.

The film crew was packing up for the day. Eleanor was talking to the director and the producer.

"Come on, Mary Movie Star, I'll take you to dinner at Rive Gauche," he told her.

"What have I done to deserve this?" Eleanor asked in mock-dismay.

"You're beautiful," he told her. "And besides, I've had a pretty good day."

3

"Well it all looks pretty simple to me, Mr. Hyer," said J. Wesley Smallwood. "They're a bunch of Communist-inspired agitators, some of them not so inspired, either, and they're coming here looking for trouble and we've got to have the *men* and the *ordinance* to handle them."

It was once said of a certain United States senator that he possessed all the attributes of a dog except loyalty. Dave Hyer often thought of that remark when he contemplated J. Wesley Smallwood, the Attorney General of the United States.

J. Wesley Smallwood bore an uncanny resemblance to a hound. He had a long, dolorous hound's face, complete with floppy ears, sad brown eyes, large teeth, and quivering jowls. He had, too, a certain canine cunning, an instinct for pursuit, for covering his tracks, for sniffing out his enemies, for staying close to the pack. He lacked, however, a hound's agreeable nature, and this last fact helped account for his meteoric rise in national politics.

"How many people do you expect to turn out for this demonstration?" Dave asked, not wanting to debate the "Communist-inspired" issue.

"Our intelligence estimates range from twenty-five to fifty thousand," the Attorney General replied, his nose turning in a slow arc from Dave to Charlton MacKenzie to O. B. Perkins and finally to the President.

"And for a maximum of fifty thousand demonstrators you say you'll need three thousand plainclothesmen, five thousand police, and a reserve of fifteen thousand National Guardsmen and Marines?" Dave asked incredulously.

"Mr. Hyer, as one who has had a great deal of *practical experience* in these matters, I think my recommendation is, if anything, conservative. We are not only dealing with these forty or fifty thousand hard-core agitators, we are speaking of a potential outburst involving two or three times that many persons in the city's colored districts."

He had indeed had practical experience. J. Wesley Smallwood had been Attorney General of Kentucky when a small band of pacifists had bought fifty acres of hillside and established a commune. Before Smallwood was finished with them, half the commune-dwellers were in the state prison on charges ranging from sodomy to sedition. Smallwood emerged as a national hero. After reportedly declining an opportunity to be George Wallace's running-mate, Smallwood became a "law and order" Attorney General for Milton Osgood. He maintained that status under Barney Newfield who, although resentful of Smallwood's popularity, sensed his administration's need for the Kentuckian's hard-line rhetoric.

"It wasn't my information that the black districts were involved in this demonstration," Dave said.

"Not directly," Smallwood replied. "But the potential is there if one spark sets it off. It happened before."

"When was that?"

"In April of 1968," the Attorney General said, with an air of triumph.

"Those riots occurred because Dr. King was murdered," Dave said. "That isn't likely to happen again."

"Obviously," Smallwood said. "But it proved the revolutionary potential in this city, and no one can doubt that this Hailey is prepared to exploit it."

"Mr. Attorney General, Hailey is leading a 'Free Rivera' march on the White House which will attract ninety-nine percent white middle-class participants. I'd say the only way the local blacks could get involved is if we station so many troops around the city that we stir up trouble."

"Dave, what have you got against troops?" O. B. Perkins asked.

"It's a question of overreacting. If we bring in fifteen thousand troops to deal with twenty-five or thirty thousand peaceful marchers, first, we look silly, second, we look like a police state, third, we run the risk of stirring up the blacks, and, fourth, we look like we're trying to intimidate people out of marching."

"We really needn't send them engraved invitations," Charlton MacKenzie said.

"No, but we need to respect their right to assemble and not make an armed confrontation out of it." Dave was concerned that MacKenzie was taking the hard-line on this. Smallwood was a fool, but MacKenzie wasn't, and the President listened to him.

"We also have to think of the citizens of Washington," MacKenzie said, "and their right to be secure in their homes."

"I agree, Mr. Secretary, and I wish some representative of the D.C. government was here to speak for its people and its police force."

That was aimed at the Attorney General, who'd kept a long arm's length away from the District's black mayor.

"I think we can satisfy both needs here," MacKenzie said. "If we have an adequate number of troops, we can guarantee order, but by restraint in their use, we need not impede the right to assemble."

Very statesmanlike, Dave thought.

"The thing we have to keep in our minds, Mr. President," said Attorney General Smallwood, "is that we are dealing with a hard-core of radical revolutionaries. There is a Communist influence in this, have no doubt about it. These people will be armed, they're looking for trouble, and I've got to think of the safety and the security of the President himself!"

"You think they'd come in here after me, Wes?" the President asked.

"I can't predict what those radicals would do," Smallwood said, "but I've got to be prepared for the worst, and I can't let a lot of talk about the First Amendment stand between me and my duties."

"Mr. President," Dave said, "this is the kind of confrontation your administration will be judged by years from now, the same way you and I remember that Hoover sent the troops against the Bonus Marchers, but Roosevelt welcomed them and listened to them and won their hearts."

The President hesitated—the judgment of history was never far from his mind.

"Yeah, we need to think about this troop thing," he said. "Right now, Wes, tell me about this guy Hailey."

"Mr. President," the Attorney General said angrily, "the man is a Marxist-Leninist revolutionary who for a decade has sought to overthrow the U. S. Government."

"Mr. Attorney General," Dave interrupted, "in 1961 and 1962, Hailey was trying to integrate lunchcounters and register black voters in Alabama and Mississippi. I wouldn't equate that with trying to overthrow the government, since the government was trying to do the same thing. In the late Sixties, he opposed the war in Vietnam, rather effectively, but that's not the same as trying to overthrow the government. The present issue, in Hailey's eyes, concerns the U.S. role in the internal affairs of a Latin American nation. Hailey disagrees with what we're doing, but that doesn't make him a Communist revolutionary. Some people think Hailey will be running for Congress in a few years."

"He'll be running from Leavenworth if I have any say about it," Smallwood declared. "We have a grand jury ready to indict him now for the conspiracy in Houston."

"What conspiracy?" Dave said. "He was in town for a lecture and a riot broke out ten miles away. Is that a conspiracy?"

"This man's whole life is a conspiracy," Smallwood declared. "And we're going to prove it on this march. Pardon if I brag a little, Mr. President, but this man Hailey can't go to the toilet these days without us filming it in living color."

"So when do you bring your charges?" the President said.

"After this march," Smallwood said. "We'll have a tight case after this march."

"We don't want to let November get too close," O. B. Perkins said.

"Oh, no, the grand jury is ready to move when I say the word," the Attorney General promised.

"Mr. President, is this administration determined to indict Roy Hailey so we can have an extravaganza trial before the elections?" Dave asked.

"This man lives by manipulating the media," MacKenzie said. "We're simply turning the tables on him."

"There's always the question," Dave said, "of whether prosecuting Hailey will win more votes or lose more."

"Oh, I don't think there's any question about that," MacKenzie said. "The polls all make clear that the public supports firm measures against radical demonstrators."

"Particularly after he's been blamed for a bloody battle at the very gates of the White House," Smallwood said.

"Bloody?" Dave asked. "Who said it would be bloody?"

"You can't tell what might happen," O. B. Perkins said quickly. Too quickly.

"Mr. President, I don't know what's going on," Dave said, "but I know the Bureau has dozens of agents inside the radical groups, and I know some of them would like nothing more than to fire a gun or do something to give the police an excuse to crack heads. But we can't have that happening outside the White House, and I hope the Attorney General will assure us it won't happen."

"Just what are you suggesting, Mr. Hyer?" Smallwood demanded.

"I'm suggesting, Mr. Attorney General, that you have very grave responsibilities at the Justice Department and I hope and assume that you'll meet them."

"Mr. Hyer," Smallwood replied, his hound's face quivering with rage, "I've been meeting the responsibilities of public life for twenty years, and I might add that I've met them without any wishy-washy, mealy-mouthed worrying about the rights of Communist agitators."

This madman is the Attorney General of the United States, Dave thought helplessly. And we are stuck with him.

"I'm sure you'll continue your fine record, Mr. Attorney General," he said gently.

4

It was a bad time to be going to Texas but there was no good time to go to Texas and the trip was a favor to a congressman who needed all the help he could get. Dave arrived in Houston in the morning and spoke to a group of liberals. After lunch, he hurried to the airport, where an Air Force plane was waiting to fly him to Dallas. Thirty minutes later he deplaned, and found his mother and sister waiting for him at the terminal gate.

Dave kissed his mother, and kissed Marsha, his sister, his half-sister, really. Marsha was thin and sad-eyed and was holding her little boy. The child had been named for Dave, who had never been able to muster much interest in him.

"He's really growing," Dave said.

"Oh, he's a regular weed," his mother said in the mock-sarcastic tone she affected, the one that grated so on his nerves. "Where's your bag?"

"I didn't bring one," he told her. "I'm going back tonight."

"Oh," she said sharply. "We hoped you'd stay over."

He shook his head. "I've got to be back in the morning."

"Our celebrity," his mother said with a mock-sigh, rolling her wide eyes skyward. She was a short, buxom woman with a girlish face. Tight black curls bounced at her neck, and her pants suit revealed a trim figure. She projected a vivacity quite lacking in her daughter, Marsha, who stood beside her, an uncertain smile on her thin face. Dave and Marsha had almost nothing in common except that they had survived the same insane childhood and he loved her in a wistful, helpless way.

"How're Eleanor and Sally?" Marsha asked.

"They're fine," Dave said. "Sally's learning to read."

"Read?" Marsha repeated. "She's only three."

"She'll be just like her father," his mother said. "Little Davey was reading the funnies when *he* was three. His grandmother taught him the three Rs while I was out trying to earn a living."

They left the terminal and the Texas heat swept over them. "We're over there," his mother said. "In the C section."

"You still have the Ford?"

"What else?" she said. "Nine more payments and it's mine. There we are."

"What happened to your fender?" he asked.

"Oh, somebody hit me one night when it was parked on the street."

"You ought to get it fixed."

"You're so right, my dear boy, but the insurance is fifty dollar deductible and I don't have fifty dollars. Do you still drive, now that you have your own chauffeur?"

"I think I can manage, Mother."

"Let's go home and celebrate," she said. "The Prodigal Son has returned."

Dave glanced at his watch as he started the car. "You've got the afternoon off?" Dave asked his mother.

His mother laughed. "Yes, I told Mr. Cohen I was going to play hooky. One of the other girls can fill in for me."

"How about you, Marsha?" he asked. "Are you still working?"

"Just part-time at Rogers Brothers," his sister said. She and her child were in the back seat, the boy digging into her purse.

"Doing what?"

"Oh, saleswork. At the cosmetics counter, mainly."

"By the time she pays a sitter, there's hardly anything left for her," his mother said.

"How about the money you got from the government?" Dave said. "What are you doing with that?"

"It's put away," Marsha said. "It's for Davey's college."

"Why don't you take some courses at SMU?" he asked.

"Oh, Dave, I'm too old for college."

"Marsha, you're only twenty-three."

"I've got a baby, Dave. I wouldn't feel right with all those other girls."

Screw those other girls, he thought. But he didn't want to argue with her. They had argued about Vietnam the last time he was home, for the funeral, and it had been painful and pointless. ("Won't you let me believe he died for *something?*" she had cried. "Won't you even let me have that?")

"What she ought to do is take some shorthand and typing," his mother said.

"Oh, don't start that again," Marsha said.

"How's *your* job, Mother?" he asked, to change the subject.

"Oh, the usual. Overworked and underpaid. But I've been getting a lot of overtime. We've got this big contract from General Electronics . . ."

She talked about her job as secretary to the president of an electronics firm and his thoughts turned to the city ahead, its jagged skyline sparkling in the sun, this rich, proud city that had shaped him. A strange sensation crept over him, for he thought of Texas as a vast prison from which he had somehow escaped, and whenever he returned he had an eerie feeling that they might lock its gates behind him.

The highway in from the airport was a gaudy hodge-podge of motels, trailer courts, junk yards, taverns, churches, root-beer stands, used-car lots, a drive-in movie. His eye fell upon a faded pink stucco motel, a dreary place with a dozen small cabins, and a neon sign in front that said ROSEBUD MOTEL—VACANCY. He smiled, for it was at the Rosebud, on a beer-and-gin Saturday night fifteen years before, that for seven dollars (five for the girl, two for the nigger porter) he had been relieved of his virginity by a hefty, gum-chewing whore who'd barely moved her big milk-white body in the minute or two it took to drain his eager loins. In later years, he read many fine books by fine writers in which sensitive young men fled in horror from their first whore, but that was not Dave's experience. He hopped right on, and if the encounter was less thrilling than he had been led to expect, he nonetheless sensed there were better things ahead. He and his best friend, Jack Ripton, Jack the Ripper, were often at the Rosebud that year, until they knew the best times to go (early in the week and late in the month), knew all the girls' special talents (Sondra's sweet sodomy, Eddylou's beatific blowjobs, Vy's long, lingering trips around the world). Some nights, filled with beer and lust, destined for a whore's embrace, they would park first in some secluded spot, stand beside the

Ripper's Hudson, and quite calmly beat off, the better (shrewd devils) to get their money's worth when they reached the Rose-bud.

Jesus, he thought, Jesus, Jesus, Jesus.

The city glistened ahead; two skyscrapers had shot up since his last visit.

"Turn right up here," his mother said. "That's the new bypass around town."

Minutes later, they were in King's Park, the part of Dallas he had grown up in, a fabulously rich neighborhood even by Texas standards. They passed the King's Park Civic Auditorium and as his mother talked on about her job he thought of an evening when he was thirteen and he had gone to that auditorium with his father to see his first Shakespeare, a road-show production of *Romeo and Juliet*. That was long after the divorce. Eugene had moved to Houston but when he visited Dallas he often took Dave to a play or a symphony. The problem was that, more often than not, his father would be drunk before the evening was over. The night of *Romeo and Juliet* his father had a few drinks on the way to the theater, from the ever-present gin bottle, and several more at the first intermission and by the second intermission he had passed out in his seat. Dave tried to get him out to the car but Eugene kept falling down, and in the crowded lobby people stared and whispered and tut-tutted and Dave was frightened and humiliated but he remembered too that he had thought "Fuck all of you—this is my father and he's a better man than any of you." When finally he got his father to the car he had thought that after that night nothing could ever hurt him again. He was wrong about that, of course.

They moved along King's Boulevard, past expensive shops and the city's only good French restaurant, through traffic thick with Cadillacs, until they came to a fork. He turned right, up Antelope Drive, a wide, tree-shaded road that twisted between a golf course and a long row of mansions.

"I think our chauffeur is lost," his mother said.

"I thought we'd drive around," he said. "A sentimental journey."

"I didn't know you were so sentimental about Dallas," his mother said.

"That's George Hightower's house," he said, pointing to a huge stone house far back from the road. "Remember my friend George?"

"Of course," his mother said. "George's mother and I were in school together."

"Yeah, and my senior year I should have been editor of the paper but they gave it to George A. Hightower III instead. What ever happened to that bastard?"

"He went to medical school and the last I saw he was a doctor in the poverty program."

"He's probably doing it to beat the draft," Dave said.

They passed the Antelope River Country Club, a rambling white building with a pool and tennis courts beside it and a golf course stretching out behind it, along the river. It was there that the rich girls' sororities had given their formal dances, dances to which he had never rated an invitation. But what he remembered most was a scorching Saturday afternoon the summer he was sixteen, the summer he had driven a delivery truck for a local bakery, and he had been sent to deliver a carton of hamburger buns to the snack bar beside the country club pool. When he drove into the parking lot he could see at poolside the kids he knew in school, the rich kids who already he hated, and he did not want to walk past them in his khaki uniform with *Sunshine Bread* on the back, carrying his carton of hamburger buns. He sat in the truck, trying to decide what to do. It was a hundred and five and he felt dizzy and he shut his eyes and for an instant he saw himself and his father in the theater lobby and the people pointing and laughing and he knew he could not walk past the swimming pool, past those scornful rich eyes and yet neither could he return to the plant without making the delivery. Finally, he drove along King's Boulevard until (with the ingenuity for which I later became famous, he thought) he found a Negro who was happy to carry the carton in for a dollar.

"We'd better go home," Marsha said. "Davey hasn't had his nap."

"Okay," he said, and turned down Ivy Lane toward his mother's apartment. The streets were named alphabetically, starting on the north with Antelope Drive, then Brentwood Place and Crestline Road, and as you descended in the alphabet you moved from the mansions near the country club to the large, comfortable upper-middle-class homes in the middle range, and finally to the frame, two-bedroom bungalows from Vickery Street on down to Zebulon Road, beside the tracks. Dave remembered when he had known all these streets, knew the social shadings between them, knew which of his classmates lived where, knew the agonies of living on Wilshire Place, very near the tracks, on the wrong end of one of America's richest neighborhoods.

"I'll bet you remember that bus stop," his mother said, pointing to a faded bench beside a drugstore. "Do you remember the morning we had the blizzard? That was the first Christmas you worked for the post office. Marsha, this poor child stood there freezing for two hours before we found out the bus had turned over."

Dave nodded. "I remember that," he said. "And I remember the mornings the bus didn't turn over."

"I'd never let him go out without a hot breakfast," his mother said. "The winter he had the paper route, we'd get up at four and fold all the papers before he started out."

"We should have burned the damned things," Dave said. "Imagine me peddling that rightwing sheet."

They passed King's Park High School, its three parking lots filled with its students' shiny new Mustangs and Corvettes; it had not changed since Dave's day, except that back then the rich kids had driven Ford Victorias and Olds 88s. It was said that the only old cars at King's Park High School belonged to the teachers. That was how he remembered his high school, as a place where you were precisely ranked by the kind of car you drove and the street you lived on and who your father was and the sorority or fraternity you were invited to join. He had ranked low in all these things and he had hated the school then and he hated it now and the only lesson he had learned there was that if you hate enough you can do anything.

"So this is the famous Dave? By golly, fellow, I told Grace I didn't believe she had a son in Washington, I thought it was just something she made up. I'm Phil Briley and I guess your mother's already told you what a loudmouth I am!"

Phil had a round, red, contented face. Dave shook his hand. "I think she told me you're the neighbor who fixes her car for her."

"Oh, I try to give Grace a hand whenever I can. She's the only one around here with any class. Hey, this here, following close behind me, is my bitter half—I mean better half—the delicate Delouise, also known as Big D."

"Call me Del," said a blond woman, extending a beefy hand. "Brother, I'm glad to meet you, 'cause I've got a message or two to send back to the White House."

"Now, Del, you just met the fellow, don't scare him off. Dave, my little lady here thinks Senator Goldwater is too leftwing."

"Well I grew up without a pot to pee in," Del said, "and I done pretty well, and now all these niggers think we owe 'em the world on a platter."

"Del and Phil, you go get yourselves a drink," his mother said. "I've got somebody else my famous son has got to meet." She added in a whisper to Dave: "Del's sort of conservative, but the time I had pnuemonia she was over here every morning to make my breakfast."

"What does he do?" Dave asked.

"Sells trucks," his mother said. "Makes good money at it."

His mother was wearing a white silk dress with silver sequins. He had wanted to spend a quiet evening with her and Marsha but she had insisted on having "a few friends" to meet him and now her tiny living room was crowded.

A young couple came up, the fellow short and crew-cut and holding his head self-consciously above a blue cravat. The girl was plump and pretty. When she gave him her hand he held it a moment longer than he should have, and saw her dark eyes flicker uncertainly.

"Dave, this is Bill and Beth," his mother said. "Bill's interested in politics."

"You work for the party here?" Dave asked with interest.

The young man shook his close-cropped head. "I never went that far," he said. "But I read a lot about politics."

"Yeah, it's an interesting subject," Dave said.

Beth was wearing a white dress that pulled nicely against her breasts. "We have a daughter just the age of your little girl," she said. "Our little girl calls Grace her Granny."

Dave smiled and said nothing.

"Grace talks about you all the time," Beth said. "I can hardly believe we're really meeting you. We've read all the clippings and articles."

"All that's silly. I'm just somebody's assistant."

He had finished one Scotch and wanted another. They'd not gotten around to dinner, but his mother had promised sandwiches later. Bill and Beth drifted away and he got himself and his mother a drink, putting two jiggers of Scotch in his and one in hers.

He was introduced to a tall, sad-faced man whose name he didn't catch. The man said how he'd been wanting to meet Dave. Dave discovered that the man's great interest was fishing, and they talked about fishing. The man was pleasant enough and Dave kept him going until he injected:

"I guess you've wondered about your mother and me."

Dave didn't understand, so he nodded gravely.

"She's a wonderful woman," the man said. "I can't tell you what our relationship has meant to me."

Dave nodded again.

"But I'll be honest, Dave, as long as my wife lives, even if she stays in that damned hospital another twenty years, I just can't divorce her. I couldn't face my sons if I did it. So there I am, married and not married. Lord I don't know what I'd do without your mother."

Now Dave understood. This was Mac, the "beau" she sometimes mentioned in her letters.

His mother came and took Mac's arm.

"You fellows getting acquainted?" she asked. She was high but so was everyone else.

"Mac's been telling me about fishing," he said.

"And some other things," Mac added.

"I want the two men in my life to get along," she said.

Dave nodded and as soon as he could he went to the kitchen for another drink.

Then Del, the beefy blonde, had him trapped in a corner.

"You and Mother work together, don't you?" he asked.

"Lordy, yes. Me and Grace run that silly place. Those Jews that own it spend all day on the golf course—their own Jew golf course, naturally—but me and her keep things straight. She's one fine woman."

"Yes, she is," he said.

"Listen, I got some things to ask you," she said. "About the government. I guess you know what we say about Washington around here, don't you? We say it's like a Hershey bar—ninety percent chocolate and ten percent nuts."

"I guess I'm one of the nuts," Dave said.

"I don't know. Your mother's sure got a good head on her shoulders. But by God people down here don't know what the government's doing. My husband works hard for all he's got and he gets taxed forty percent to build new cities—cities!—for people who've already burned down the ones they've got!"

"The New Cities are for everybody," he said. "You and Phil could go live in one."

"Ha! Fat chance of me living with those black apes."

"Fat chance of them living with you," her husband said. "Let the poor man be."

"I've got something else to ask," Del declared. "Is it true, what I heard on Paul Harvey, that you were down there in South America and told them not to kill that Communist—what's his name?"

"Rivera," her husband said. "Like the Buick."

"Yeah, Rivera," Del said. "Is that true?"

"Yes, it's true," Dave said.

"Well, *why?*" Del demanded.

"I don't like to see men shot in cold blood," he said.

"As if *he'd* never shot anybody," Del responded.

"And also because I think he'd make a better leader of that country than the man who's running it now," he added, because he was sick of this woman.

"Sweet Jesus," Del said, "you talk like a damned pinko."

"I'm a Democrat," he said evenly. "A rather liberal Democrat. Maybe that's pink around here."

"Listen now," Del said excitedly, brushing a strand of hair back from her brow, "I say that if somebody had shot that damned Ho Chi Minh back when he was getting started, forty thousand American boys'd be alive today, including your own brother-in-law, and still you stand there with your teeth in your mouth and tell me that damned Rivera . . ."

"Come on, Del, we got to get home," her husband insisted and managed to pull her away.

Marsha came up to Dave. He had watched her all evening and he had not seen her smile. He wondered if there was any way to make her smile.

"I'm sorry, Dave," she whispered. "I told her you wouldn't want to see these people."

"It's all right. If it makes her happy, it's all right."

Beth and Bill came by to say goodnight. Bill had removed his cravat and he looked happier. Beth gave him her soft, plump hand and a shy smile, and he thought again that she would be nice in bed.

"We wanted to tell you something, Dave," she said, lowering her voice. "Not everybody's so conservative around here. We think President Newfield is wonderful. We're proud of what he's doing."

"Thank you," he said. "Thank you, Beth."

As they left, a well-dresssed, middle-aged man came in, and his mother brought him over. The man was bald and husky and had a big grin.

"This is my boss, Mr. Cohen," his mother said.

"Hiya, Dave," the man said. "Boy, have I heard all about you!"

"I've heard a lot about you too," Dave said.

"Yeah, I'm the old slavedriver. Boy, it's good to finally meet you."

Dave wanted to dislike Sid Cohen but the man had an infectious charm. He wondered where Cohen's wife was—probably she didn't mingle with the help. They talked a few minutes and Dave's mother urged Cohen to have a drink.

"No thanks, Grace, I don't even have time for a drink," he insisted. "Just wanted to shake this boy's hand, or I knew I'd never hear the end of it. Now I've got to get right back home. Come on out and see my new car, Dave, get some fresh air."

Dave followed the man outside. A new Pontiac convertible was in the driveway.

"It's a good-looking car."

"For five thousand smackeroos it ought to be," Sid Cohen said. He turned around and lit a cigar. "Listen, Dave, you mind if I say something personal?"

"Go ahead."

"You ought to come see your mother more often," Cohen said, leaning against his Pontiac. "That woman thinks you hung the moon, and by God it hurts her never seeing you. Last Christmas she was so damned sad it made me to cry."

Last Christmas I wrote the New Cities bill, Dave thought.

"I know, Mr. Cohen," he said. "It's hard to get away from my work."

"Listen, Dave, I'm not the buttinsky type, believe me, but I really admire your mother. I wish you'd think about her more. Okay, end of sermon."

They shook hands and Sid Cohen jumped into his shiny Pontiac and raced off.

The people left in the apartment were laughing and drinking and he did not want to laugh and drink with them. He called Marsha outside and they walked along the sidewalk until the sounds of the party faded behind them and he could hear a train whistling on the T & P tracks, a half-mile away.

"How'd you like Mac?" Marsha asked.

"He seemed all right," Dave said. "How do you like him?"

"Oh, Mac's nice," she said. "But, Dave, I don't think it's right, the way they go places together. Overnight. It doesn't look right."

"Who cares how it looks?" he asked. "Look, Marsha, don't you remember all those years she never had a new dress? Don't begrudge her a little happiness now."

Marsha nodded uncertainly, her face pale in the moonlight.

"I really wish you'd think about college," he told her.

"You know I was never good in school," she said. "You were the brain in the family."

"You could do it if you tried."

"No, Dave, I couldn't. I'm not like you. I'm just an ordinary person."

"Marsha, didn't we grow up in the same place and go through all the same crap? There's nothing special about me."

"Yes there is," she insisted. "You were always different. There's something different inside you."

"All right, if you won't go to college, do what mother says and take a secretarial course. Get your typing halfway decent and I'll get you a job in Washington."

"What would I do in Washington?" she asked. "Who do I know there?"

"Do you want to spend the rest of your life selling cosmetics at Rogers Brothers? Marsha, life is tough. You've got to fight for yourself."

They stopped at the corner, two cars raced by, an empty beer can clattered on the street, and she turned to face him. Her tears sparkled in the moonlight.

"Dave, don't you think I know it's tough? Don't you think I learned that when they sent Billy home in a box? But I can't fight back the way you did. I'm just one of those ordinary people like Mother who has to take things the way they come. Don't you think I'd like to be like you? But I *can't*, Dave, I've tried and I can't. You'll just have to let me live my life the best way I can, because that's all I can do."

He put his arms around her and felt the trembling of her thin shoulders. After a while they walked back to the apartment. A blue Plymouth was parked at the curb. Dave spoke to the Air Force captain driving it, who said he was twenty minutes early. Dave went inside and said goodbye to the remaining guests, then he and his mother walked outside onto the lawn.

"Sorry it was so short," he said.

"I'm glad you could come at all," his mother said. "I hope all my boisterous friends didn't get on your nerves."

"They were fine," he said.

"I know some of them are a little hard to take, like Del," she said. "But they're good people."

"What about Marsha?" he asked. "Does she have any dates?"

"Not really. Maybe she'll meet somebody in church. She's been going a lot since Billy died."

"I guess it helps," he said.

His mother laughed. "Well, it's caused some other problems," she said.

"What do you mean?"

"Oh, Dave, you know that Mac and I take trips together sometimes, go fishing or for a football game. Now Marsha thinks I'm immoral. Dirty old granny."

"She's just a kid," he said. "She doesn't understand anything."

His mother shook her head. "I don't know what's right, Dave," she said. "Maybe I shouldn't go places with Mac. But honey, I'm having more fun than I've had in thirty years, since I first knew your father."

"Have your fun," he told her. "All you can."

"How about you and Eleanor?" she asked. "I worry about that girl, with you gone all the time. You better treat her right."

"I try to," he said. "Are you coming up this fall?"

"I'd like to."

"I'll handle the plane fare," he told her. "Just work out the time with Ellie."

"I miss seeing Sally," his mother said. "I hardly know her. Oh, Dave, sometimes I wish I could come up and spend the rest of my life with little Sally."

"Maybe you can someday," he said. It was time to leave. He kissed his mother and held her close, thinking for a moment how incredibly brave she was, then he was in the Plymouth, speeding toward the airport, staring out at the luminous Texas moonlight, leaving it all behind him once again.

5

"Would you do me a small favor?" she asked in her sharp lady-reporter's voice.

"Sure, slim, name it."

"I heard Brenda was going to California in September. Know anything about that?"

"No, but I can check."

"Would you? I was thinking about going out when school opens and writing a piece on the student radicals, and maybe I'll go when she does."

"You two are pretty palsy, aren't you?" he asked.

"I really like her. More than I ought to like somebody in politics. You remember that piece I wrote on her?"

"Sure."

"Well, immodest me, but that piece really set the tone for everything since—the *Newsweek* cover and the *Times* magazine piece. And, brother, have you seen Brenda's Gallup?"

He had noted that journalists liked to make extravagant claims for the influence of their writings; it had begun when Mailer claimed to have elected Kennedy.

"Yeah, you really helped her a lot," he said. "I'll check that trip and call you."

A few minutes later, on the way to see the President, he stopped in Eddie Gooch's office. It was only a cubbyhole, but it was the office physically closest to the President's, a fact that meant a great deal to Eddie. Eddie was not in his office, but his friend Mickey Daley was sitting at his desk using the phone. Daley's liquid brown eyes darted up as Dave entered.

"Well, if Mr. Hammond isn't in," he said gruffly into the phone, "just tell him to call me. Michael Daley at the White House. Extension one-oh-four."

He hung up the phone and grinned at Dave.

"How are you, Davey, boy?"

"Okay, Mickey. What are you up to?" He asked the question pleasantly but he wished he *did* know what Daley was up to.

"Oh, just making a couple of calls, waiting for Eddie. Anything I can do for you?"

Dave shook his head. He noted that Eddie had six pictures of himself and the President on his walls, some sort of a record. He himself had only three.

"Well, hey, tell me what you want," Daley insisted. "I'll find out and call you."

Dave sighed. "I wanted to know if Brenda's going to California next month."

"Hey, that's easy," Daley said, and dug into a pile of papers on the desk. "Here's the dope right here."

He handed Dave the file on Brenda's trip. There was a memo from the National Committee on the politics of the trip—congressional districts that should not be visited, issues that should be avoided with the press. There was a two-page list of requested interviews and TV appearances from the Press Office. The Secretary of the Interior had sent over a list of parks and wildlife preserves she might visit, and the HEW Secretary has sent a similar list of education and welfare projects. Poor Brenda, he thought, all she wants to do is see her mother and get some sun.

He handed the papers back to Mickey Daley and walked to the President's office. The door was ajar and the President called to him to come in. Eddie Gooch was with the President, his round face dark and lined.

"How's Flo, Eddie?" he asked.

"No better," Eddie said bitterly.

Flo, the bony and pious Flo, had been stricken with a nervous disorder that left her paralyzed. They had put her in the NIH Hospital, where she had the best possible attention, but she had shown no improvement. Dave knew that Eddie had been spending every night with her, sleeping on a sofa in the hospital room. The strain had begun to show on him.

"I know her religion's a big help to her in this," Barney said.

Eddie managed a faint grin. "Sure, boss, she's got a regular revival going there, doctors and nurses prayin' with her all round the clock."

His grin faded and he slapped his fist into his palm in a sudden gesture of frustration.

"God damn the luck," he cried.

Dave looked away. There was something terribly vulnerable about Eddie in his distress.

"Well, I better get back to the treadmill," Eddie said, and got up slowly. As he left, he touched Dave on the shoulder. "Thanks for those flowers," he said. Dave nodded. He knew nothing about any flowers—he guessed Eleanor had sent them.

"He looks bad," Dave said, when Eddie had gone.

"It's a strain on him," Barney said. "I'm gonna have to make him take some time off. He's got money problems too."

"Medical expenses?"

"The doctors are free," the President said. "But he's got to pay for the medicine and he's had to hire a woman to look after their kid."

"What do you think may happen?" Dave asked. He did not say, "Will Eddie have to leave?" but the President understood the question. Eddie could easily double his White House salary by joining some corporation or PR firm. Dave would not have regretted his departure. He was sorry about Eddie's troubles, but he had never thought Eddie contributed to the administration's well-being.

"Eddie won't leave me," the President said. "He's a soldier. Now, what's on your mind?"

"Two things," Dave said. "First, Rivera's trial. The argument now is when it ought to be."

"And you've got a theory," Barney said dourly.

"That's what you're paying me for."

"What's the other thing?" Barney asked.

"This demonstration next week," Dave said. "All the reports I get are that the Attorney General is determined to turn it into Pickett's charge."

The President sighed wearily. "Yeah, that's what I hear too." He punched a button on his desk and an instant later Leon Kerelot's voice gave a brisk: "Yes sir?"

"Leon, come over here a minute, let's talk about this Rivera thing," the President said. Dave was annoyed but there was nothing to do about it. The President knew he wanted to discuss it alone and he chose not to oblige him. "Better get our foreign-affairs expert in on this," Barney added.

"What's the story on Dave's friend Rivera?" the President asked when Leon arrived.

"He's in the prison at Huasco," Leon said crisply, his eyes unblinking behind his silver-rimmed glasses. "He's well treated. He's to be tried by a three-man military court . . ."

"Headed by the celebrated Captain Kangaroo," Dave said.

". . . appointed by the celebrated Colonel Molina," Leon continued. "The only question now is when the trial should be."

"Who wants what?" Barney asked.

"The junta wants the earliest trial possible," Leon said. "We have persuaded them to wait, however, until you decide what your interests are."

"What are they?" Barney asked. It amused him to try to ruffle Leon's smooth feathers, but he rarely succeeded.

"I think everyone knows, Mr. President, that the junta wants Rivera dead. And that the longer the trial is delayed, the more domestic and international pressures will build for clemency."

"Clemency being life in prison," Dave said.

"Yes," Leon replied. "Or, to be precise, prison so long as the Molina regime stays in power."

"Or until they cut his throat some dark night," Dave said.

"Many things could happen," Leon said, lifting one eyebrow slightly.

They could indeed. Dave knew (and he wondered if Leon knew) of a plan to blast Rivera out of the Huasco prison. It involved an attack by two dozen of Rivera's followers, cooperation within the prison from a secretly pro-Rivera officer, and some additional assistance by one Colonel Huffaker. Dave's contact at the CIA had sought his support as a kind of insurance policy if the plan backfired, but Dave was fearful of any personal involvement.

"The question is what's in your interest, Mr. President," Dave said.

"What's your theory?" Barney asked.

"I say wait. As long as he's quote 'awaiting trial' unquote the monkey is off your back. But if they try him fast, before the November elections, you lose either way. If they shoot him, the pro-Rivera people are mad; if they don't, the hard-liners are mad. So stall, let things cool down."

"There is some question," Leon said coolly, "as to the degree of control we have over the timing of the trial."

"The hell there is," Barney declared. "You tell that little pimp Molina that I'm calling the shots in this game."

"Just as you say," Leon said softly.

"Look," the President said, frowning now, hunched forward over his desk, "Dave's right, we got to stall this trial. Not for any noble humanitarian reasons. That bastard Rivera's nothing but a problem to me—I should of let them shoot that son of a bitch when they caught him. But now I've got to keep my options open, and that means keeping him alive."

"It might ease the pain for Colonel Molina," Leon said, "if you could grant a few requests he has been making this last week."

"What's he want now?" the President asked.

"Helicopters," Leon said.

"What for?" Barney asked. "We stopped his revolution for him, didn't we?"

"Not entirely," Leon said.

"We captured Rivera for him," Dave said, with only a hint of satisfaction in his voice. "But the guerrillas are still in the mountains, more than before."

When Leon had gone, they talked about the "Free Rivera" march that Roy Hailey was leading on the White House. "Thirty or forty thousand marchers isn't a great many," Dave said. "But if the Attorney General keeps talking about calling in the troops he'll double the turn-out."

"He thinks he'll scare them off," Barney said.

"He's full of shit," Dave said.

"So what do you say?"

"Get him out of it. Let the D.C. mayor handle it. He's a good man and he's handled a dozen marches like this."

"Your friend Hailey wasn't behind those."

"Mr. President, Hailey's one genius is for exploiting his opponents' mistakes. And J. Wesley Smallwood is our biggest mistake to date. The people I talk to say Hailey might have got ten thousand people out for this march—Rivera's not that big an issue—but Smallwood's tough talk has already got us up to maybe forty thousand and if he keeps talking about Communist anarchy and calling in the troops he'll get a hundred thousand kids here."

"You don't think Hailey wants violence?"

"Sure he wants violence. But it's us that have to give it to him, and that's what the Attorney General is going to do if you don't stop him."

"So what do you want me to do?"

"Talk to the D.C. mayor. I'll get him in tomorrow. Let him explain the whole thing—the permits, the route of march, the police needed—and you see if he doesn't make more sense than Smallwood."

"Okay, bring him in," the President said.

"I really think that's wise," Dave said.

Barney nodded wearily. "Dave," he said, "don't you think I know Smallwood's a wild man? I have to listen to the bastard more than you do. But we've got him and we're stuck with him."

"What about the idea of him running for governor?"

"He's not interested. The governor of Kentucky never got half the attention he's getting as Mr. Law and Order."

"You've got to get rid of him," Dave said.

"No I don't. If I dump him, or he quits in a huff, you better believe the other side'd pick him up fast."

"That's where he belongs," Dave said.

"No, our side is where he belongs, 'cause he keeps a lot of working people under our tent. So we just got to work with J. Wesley Smallwood, handle him gentle, keep our heads, and maybe we'll make a good man out of him yet."

"I doubt it," Dave said.

"So do I," the President admitted.

"You don't believe me, Mr. Hyer," the wild-eyed young man was saying, in Dave's office an hour later. "You're not interested in my information."

"I don't know whether or not to believe you," Dave admitted, "but I'm interested or you wouldn't be here."

"You're very shrewd," the young man said, in another of his shifts. "You can't trust just anyone. I understand that. But my story holds up. Ask me anything. Cross-examine, counselor."

He grinned and sat up straight in the chair. He had long hair, a wisp of mustache, gray darting eyes, and almost no chin. For thirty minutes, he had alternated between arrogance, suspicion, and self-pity.

"You say you've been reporting to the Bureau for how long?" Dave asked.

"On and off for three years."

"And you're paid what?"

"It depends how much I tell them. I got five hundred dollars one time."

"For what?"

"I told them where the Panthers had hid some guns."

"That was in Houston?"

"Right."

"Who's your contact at the Bureau?"

"Fowler. Agent James Y. Fowler. A tall man, about forty-five, with a scar on his cheek."

"Where do you meet him?"

"At the Little Tavern in Southeast, near where I live, about every two weeks."

"And now you've infiltrated the Free Rivera Committee?"

"Joined, Mr. Hyer. I'm part of the staff. I very much want to see Rivera free. He's a great man."

"But you're still reporting to the Bureau?"

"I've explained that," the young man said indignantly. "I don't think you understand me at all. I wouldn't have come here if I hadn't thought you were intelligent."

"Explain it again," Dave said.

"It's the Bureau I'm fooling," the young man said. "I give them a few tidbits, to keep my credibility, but I'm on the other side, Mr. Hyer. Your side. The Free Rivera Committee doesn't know it, but I'm one of the most important men they've got. I'm going to do a lot for them."

"Like you did for the Panthers in Houston?"

"That was different," he said angrily. "They were going too far."

"And now you think the Bureau is going too far?"

"That's it exactly," he said. "It's all right to split a few skulls, but they're after blood this time. I want no part of it."

"Tell me again how you learned about this plan."

"I met Fowler at the Little Tavern and we went for a walk. He began asking me about guns. He said didn't I think some of the radicals might go armed in this march, some of the crazies. I said I thought the leaders would check them pretty close. He said didn't I think it would come to that, that if the police got rougher and rougher, the radicals would have to fight fire with fire, so finally it'd come to shoot-outs and guerrilla war. I told him that went against the whole non-violent philosophy and he said non-violence was dead, and we argued about that a while. Fowler's pretty intelligent. Finally, he asked me how I'd feel about carrying a gun if I thought there was going to be trouble."

"And you said?"

"I said, What did he think?"

"And he said?"

"For me to think about it, and we'd talk some more."

Dave paused and studied the young man. He was either an authentic nut or a hell of an actor.

"So you figure Fowler was trying to plant the idea that you should carry a gun on the march?" Dave asked.

"Exactly!" the young man said. "And, listen, some of those crazies the Bureau's got working for it, it won't take much suggestion."

"So you've come to me," Dave said, half to himself.

"Yes," the young man agreed.

"You say you know Roy Hailey," Dave said sharply. "Why don't you tell him about this?"

The young man smiled, as if amused at Dave's naïveté.

"If I did, one of three things would happen, Mr. Hyer," he said, and began to pace the floor nervously. "One, Hailey might call off the march, and give the Bureau a cheap victory. Or, two, Hailey might expose the plan, but who'd believe him? Roy Hailey Says FBI Plans Massacre. Like, what else is new?

Or, the third thing that could happen, is Hailey would just smile and say, Groovey, and lead his troops into the massacre."

"You don't think much of Hailey, do you?"

"Oh, he's a leader, I give him that," the young man said earnestly. "But he's ruthless. He wants violence just as much as the Bureau does. There are extremists on both sides, Mr. Hyer, and it's reasonable men like you and me who must stop them."

"Just what do you think I can do?" Dave asked.

"Why, stop the killing," the young man said.

"How?" Dave said. "By prohibiting the march, which would be unconstitutional? Or by searching thousands of marchers for guns, which is impractical? Or by disarming the police, which is impossible? Do you think there's a way to stop people from killing each other if they're hellbent on it?"

"There's got to be," the young man said.

"Yeah, you'd think so, wouldn't you?" Dave replied.

When the young man was gone, Dave made two phone calls. One confirmed that there was an agent named James Y. Fowler, and the second that the young man did have a low-level, volunteer job at the FRC (Free Rivera Committee) headquarters. He had expected that. The question was whether the young man was telling the truth, or was a Bureau plant or even an FRC plant. Each possibility suggested different courses of action and different dangers. If Dave passed on the story, it would strengthen the Attorney General's case for a massive show of force, or even for prohibiting the march. Or, if he didn't pass on the story, and the young man was a Bureau plant, and there was violence, Dave could be blamed. Or . . . doors led to doors led to doors . . .

6

The door opened and she met him with her most wondrous smile. Her hands were behind her back.

"What would you like most in the world?"

"Oh, God," he said helplessly, "don't ask me that."

"How about this?" she said, and handed him a gin-and-tonic.

"That's it, that's what I wanted."

"Let's go out back," she said.

Sally joined them, a small flaxen-haired angel in a white pinafore, and Dave put on some Beatles albums. The sun was sinking into the woods beside their house, and over the loud speaker came *Abbey Road*.

He sipped the icy drink and stroked Sally's hair and he felt relaxed, turned on, the way he once had felt so often. After a while, *Sgt. Pepper* came on, and Eleanor and Sally danced together, the child hopping and shuffling gaily, Eleanor twitching her lovely bottom in a more expert, more meaningful style. She was wearing white pants and a peach-colored blouse, and the last rays of the sun were tangled in her hair.

He mixed two more drinks while Eleanor coaxed Sally to bed. He kissed Sally goodnight and kissed Eleanor as she tucked in the child. Eleanor put on some Mozart and they sat on the terrace until the stars were out.

"I'm glad you could join me," she said. She had called him that afternoon, rather formally, to ask if he could be home for dinner.

"So am I," he told her. "It was a quiet day at the plant."

"Don't you have that march coming up?"

"Yeah, next weekend. But tonight Barney has the dinner for the Canadian Prime Minister, so he spent most of the day on that."

"What's going to happen?" she asked. "A girl I know wants to march, but she's heard talk about violence."

"I don't know," he said. "There are nuts on both sides."

"Should I tell her not to go?"

"Don't tell her *I* said not to go," he said.

"Oh, Dave, I won't embarrass you," she said in annoyance.

"Okay, just tell her you heard there might be trouble."

She went in to start dinner and he mixed himself a third G & T. He had a sense that there was something he should remember, something he ought to know, but it did not come into focus.

They ate by candlelight, two thick filets and a tossed salad and a bottle of good Burgundy, a 1962 Chambolle-Musigay. "I don't mean to look a gift filet in the mouth," he said, "but what's the occasion?"

"Can't you think of anything?"

"TGIF?" he suggested.

"It's Saturday," she said.

"Oh. Proust's birthday?" Even as he made the joke he felt a sinking sensation.

"You're getting warm."

"Oh good God in Heaven," he cried. "It's your birthday. And I blew it."

"Not just any birthday," she said. "My thirtieth. So I gave myself a party."

"Ellie's thirtieth," he said, "and I forgot."

"Oh, don't be so downcast," she said, laughing. "If you'd remembered you'd just have sent Mrs. Gill out to get me some perfume."

"Have some more wine," he said, filling her glass. "Ellie thirty," he mused. And then, almost meaning it, hoping it didn't sound too strained, "You've never been lovelier."

"Or you more charming," she smiled.

"I haven't been charming for a long time," he said. "I haven't had time for it. But, not to digress, you *are* lovely."

"Thank you," she said. "Do you want espresso?"

He shook his head. "Cognac."

"I'll get it," she said, and brought the bottle on a silver

tray with two tiny crystal glasses. He poured the cognac and raised his glass. "Should I say Many Happy Returns?" he asked.

"No, no returns, no more birthdays after this one," she said, her face glowing like ivory in the candlelight.

"Cheers, then."

"Cheers," she repeated and they clinked their glasses.

After a moment, she said, "There's something I'd like to talk about."

He had expected that, and he didn't mind; he was high and happy and ready to talk or argue or negotiate or whatever was required. Their relationship had become political, which is to say it was never quite spontaneous, so he never fully relaxed with her—a simple chat with Eleanor had become a chess game, in which each comment had to be plotted two or three moves ahead.

"Sure," he said, "let's talk." The cognac burned nicely on his tongue.

"I got an unexpected present today . . ." she began.

"Any present today was unexpected, wasn't it?" he injected.

"Just about. But this one was a call from Walt. He wants me to make another movie."

Dave nodded. "Okay, what's the story?"

His tone had changed and so did hers—they were back to The Problem.

"The story," she said, "is that it's a good part in a good picture, and I'll make fifty thousand dollars for two months' work."

"Where?" he asked.

"Hollywood."

"Which two months?"

"November and December, if they stay on schedule."

"What do you propose to do with Sally?"

"Take her with me, of course."

"What does she do while you're making the movie?"

"Dave," she said, with a touch of irritation, "I'd hire a very good nurse to look after her."

"That's a hell of a life for the child."

"*This* is a hell of a life for the child," Eleanor answered.

"Ah, we approach the heart of the matter."

"That's right," Eleanor said. "It is the heart of the matter. If Sally and I never see you here, why shouldn't we be where I can enjoy myself? *And* make some money, which wouldn't hurt us any."

He refilled their glasses and spoke deliberately.

"Eleanor, it isn't accurate to say you never see me. You see me as much as is consistent with my doing my job."

"Which, in the past six months, has averaged about one hour a day, most of which you and I haven't been speaking."

"Your various bursts of chastity haven't helped," he said.

"We're not talking about that."

"What are we talking about then?" he asked. "Your movie? Or my job?"

"My making the film really isn't so outrageous, you know," she told him. "We could fly back here every week or two, and you could visit us out there."

"I don't like it," he said. "It's not right."

"What's not right? For your wife to enjoy herself instead of sitting in a suburb all day waiting for you to waltz home at midnight and honor her with a quick lay?"

"For my wife and child to be three thousand miles away."

"Are you afraid I'd stoop to sin in Babylon?"

He shrugged. "If you want to get laid, you'll get laid as easily in McLean as in Hollywood," he said. "But it doesn't look right."

"You're so impossibly bourgeois," she cried. "Who gives a damn how it *looks?*"

"Okay, let's assume you make this movie," he said. "That really isn't the issue, is it?"

"Are you saying I can?"

"No, I'm saying that if you do, we'll still be having this same argument three or four months from now. So what is the real issue?"

"The same as it's always been—your job. This life that I hate."

"Well, what do you want me to say?"

"Is there any change? Is the end in sight?"

Was there any change? He wished he knew. He only knew that his relationship with Barney Newfield was as fragile and as complex as a spider's web, and . . . but he could not explain that to her.

"I don't know," he said. "Things will ease up after the elections. Maybe we could take a long vacation."

"No," she said, "because then you'll begin thinking about the next election. It's tomorrow and tomorrow and tomorrow, Dave, and the end of the rainbow keeps drifting farther away."

"So you'll take Sally and go to Hollywood. That'll show me, won't it?"

"I'm not trying to show you anything. I've given up on that. You don't give a damn what I do. I'm doing it for me. I love acting and I'll only have my looks for a few more years and I want to do it while I can."

"I'm fed up with this competition, Ellie. You're fighting me every step of the way and I don't want to fight. I've got other battles."

"You shouldn't mind the competition," she said. "You know you'll win. At thirty, I may hold my own, but at forty I'll be out of the race. But I'm going to enjoy these next few years, with you or without you. Can't you understand that I've got ambition too? I didn't play dolls when I was a little girl, Dave, I dressed up in strange costumes and talked to the wind. I never wanted to be a cheerleader—I wanted to be Juliet, to have people cheering me. And they did, Dave, when you were in law school I was making my debut on Broadway and people stood up and cheered and they threw flowers and gave me prizes. I loved it, the same way you love the power you have. And now it's all gone and I'm buried alive and I don't have to be."

"Okay, you should have married Tennessee Williams," he said. "But you married me and you knew I was in politics and now you've got to play the game."

"No, I don't have to, Dave."

"Which means?"

"Which means I'm going to make this movie and more after that."

"And I can go to hell?"

"And you can think about me a little. The trouble with you,

Dave, is that you never think of anyone but yourself. Sometimes I think you aren't capable of love."

"'That's very kind of you," he said. And after a moment, "You know, I loved you once."

"No, you loved going places with a beautiful actress on your arm. It's the same now—you think you're such a humanitarian, such a big liberal, but all you really care about is the picture of yourself playing God."

"Good old Ellie, full of constructive criticism. Look, I never claimed to be modest. I want to have the best and to be the best. That's how I am and I'm not going to change. The trouble is, my dear, you're as vain as I am, and you're getting left out."

"Which suits you fine, doesn't it?" she asked bitterly.

"Look, when we were married, and you were Mary Movie Star, I played second banana. Now I'm in the spotlight, and you might be graceful about it."

"In other words, stay home and darn your socks."

"In other words, realize that I'm under tremendous pressure, and I've got to give all I've got. If things go right, I win big. If things go wrong—and they can go wrong—I lose big and you lose too. Either way, I haven't got time for these theatrics on the home front."

"There won't be any more theatrics. I'm giving you until Christmas to tell me your plans—if you're leaving or if you're staying through the next election."

"And if I stay?"

"I leave."

"Is there someone else?" he asked.

"No, damn you," she shouted. "There's just me. Me. Eleanor. Can't you understand that?"

"And you'd leave?"

"Before I'd stay entombed here for two more years, yes."

"You don't care about me?"

"I've loved you. I could love you again, and be happy with you again, if things were right. But I can make it without you, too. I'm thirty, Dave, and I've spent all day thinking about it. It's like the crest of a hill where suddenly you see all those years spread out before you, a long, long road ahead of you."

"What about Sally?" he asked. "Isn't there her future to think of too?"

"Don't try to throw Sally at me," she said. "You're thinking about your job and I'm thinking about my happiness, and neither of us is worrying much about Sally."

"You're tough, aren't you?" he asked, half in admiration, half in anger.

"I can be. I can be as tough as you."

"I'm not tough," he said. "Who ever said I was tough?"

"Think about it, Dave," she said gently. "Until Christmas. Then show me an end to this. That's not asking too much."

"I will. I'll think about it."

He rose and blew out the candles, one by one. As he passed her chair, he saw her staring at him in the near-darkness.

"Ellie?" he said softly.

"Yes?"

"Happy birthday, anyway."

7

The Gooch Affair broke one morning in early September. Dave's first word of it came in a call from Jerry Drucker.

"Some bad news," Drucker said.

"Let's have it."

"You know this man Mickey Daley, a friend of Eddie Gooch?"

"I know who he is."

"Well, he's been around town a long time, been a press agent and a bookie and ran a strip-joint once, small-time stuff. But in the last couple of months he's made some big money."

"How?"

"In the stock market. Over the summer, he's bought stock in four electronics firms, always just before the company is awarded a big defense contract. Then its stock shoots up and Daley makes a fast profit."

"How much has he made?"

"About $20,000 so far. But he's only deposited $10,000 in his bank account, which could mean he's splitting with someone."

"Any proof of that?"

"No, but we know Daley is a friend of Gooch, and Gooch is the White House liaison with the Pentagon, which means he has advance dope on new contracts."

"What about Gooch's bank account?"

"Nothing there. If he's getting the money he's hiding it under his pillow."

"So you can't prove collusion between them?"

"Probably not, unless one of them admits it. But, look, we're not trying to *prove* anything. This is just a word to the wise. Remember, if we can find this out, so can others."

"Okay, Jerry, thanks. Call me if anything new breaks."

There was no use talking to Eddie; he would have to take

this straight to the President. He called Mrs. Purvis and was told that the President was meeting with some Central American ambassadors and wouldn't be free for fifteen minutes. Dave was mulling over the situation, wondering if they could keep it quiet, when O. B. Perkins rushed into his office and slapped a wire-service story down on his desk. Dave read it grimly:

HOUSE REPUBLICAN LEADER H. PHILIP RANSON TODAY CHARGED THAT WHITE HOUSE APPOINTMENTS SECRETARY EDWARD GOOCH HAS GIVEN CLASSIFIED GOVERNMENT INFORMATION ON DEFENSE CON-TRACTS TO WASHINGTON PUBLIC-RELATIONS MAN MICKEY DALEY, ENABLING DALEY TO MAKE SOME $20,000 IN STOCK MARKET SPEC-ULATION. REPRESENTATIVE RANSON CALLED FOR A FULL CONGRES-SIONAL INVESTIGATION OF GOOCH'S AND DALEY'S AFFAIRS.

Dave jabbed the button that sounded the buzzer on the President's desk.

"I've got to see you right away," he said when Barney answered.

"Okay, come on."

Barney was shooing the ambassadors out of his office like a flock of chickens—wide-eyed, clucking, feathers ruffled—as Dave and O.B. entered.

Dave handed the President the wire-service copy and explained about the call from the Bureau.

"How'd the Republicans get this so fast?" Barney asked.

"I'd guess that some of the Old Guard at the Bureau tipped them off," Dave said.

"So help me God, I'm going to clean house over there," Barney declared. "Okay, get Eddie in here."

Eddie Gooch's face reminded Dave of an uninflated football, full of sags and deep wrinkles and hollows; but when he was with the President—his Chief, his Pal, his Boss—his face puffed up round and happy. Thus, he beamed as he entered the President's office, but a moment later, after Barney had handed him the wire-service story, his football face slowly deflated again and was gray and shapeless.

"I swear to God, Boss, I don't know nothing about it. Oh, that damn Daley. Honest, Boss, I don't know nothing." His voice broke; he was near tears.

"All right, Eddie, shut up," Barney barked. "O.B.! The papers will be calling you. Tell them this. One, he admits he knows Daley. Two, he denies giving him any classified information. Three, he'll cooperate with any congressional investigation. Four, I've ordered a full FBI investigation—Dave, you see to that."

Eddie moved his lips but no sound came. The one thing the President had omitted was any personal endorsement of Eddie. Dave thought that was fine. This was the sort of idiotic incident that could wreck the legislative program, could lose the congressional elections. Dave had no doubt that Eddie was guilty as hell and he only hoped that by dropping him they could avoid serious damage.

"Eddie," Barney said coldly, "you go home and don't talk to anybody. And if you ever speak to that little pimp Daley again I'll nail your balls to the wall." Eddie made a gurgling sound and stumbled from the room.

The afternoon's papers broke the story and events moved quickly after that. Congressional hearings were set for the next Monday and Tuesday—a hoped-for one-two punch, with Daley on Monday and Gooch on Tuesday. Tuesday's hearing would end just before the President's previously scheduled news conference—short of canceling the news conference, there was no way to duck this one.

Daley was a terrible witness. He had some divorce-court lawyer who'd advised him to plead the Fifth Amendment, but Dave got wind of this and ordered Daley to answer the questions. Which he did, more or less:

Yes, he'd been playing the stock market.

No, he'd never done so before.

Yes, he'd had some remarkable luck with defense-related stocks.

No, he'd had no inside information.

Yes, he was a friend of Edward Gooch, the presidential aide.

No, he'd never discussed his investments with Gooch.

Yes, Gooch had gotten him a White House pass.

No, it'd never occurred to him to trade on his White House contacts.

Yes, he'd made $20,000 on the stocks.

No, he hadn't given anyone the missing $10,000—he'd lost it at the racetrack.

And so it went. His testimony stank, but the interrogators couldn't prove that his profits had resulted from Gooch's information.

Dave accompanied Eddie when he testified the next day. Eddie read a statement that Dave had written, one that stressed his military record, his long service to the President, and his innocence of any wrongdoing. He pictured Mickey Daley as just one of his hundreds of acquaintances.

"And you can't imagine why this Daley has had such amazing luck in the stock market?" Congressman Ranson demanded.

"No, sir, I can't," Eddie replied.

"And you don't think it looks suspicious that he invested in companies receiving Defense Department contracts, and he was your friend, and you had advance knowledge of these contracts?"

"I can't help how it looks. I didn't give him any information."

"Well, who did?"

"I don't know if anyone did, Congressman. But I know that a lot of other people knew about those contracts before they were announced."

"So you think we're here on a wild goose chase?" Ranson demanded.

"Call it what you like, Congressman. But I will say this. I'm proud to serve our great President, and I know there's people in politics who will do anything to stop his great work, and that includes attacking me if they think the mud will rub off on him."

"Is that what you think we're doing here?" Ranson asked.

Dave rapped his pencil against the ashtray—a prearranged signal for Eddie to slow down.

"Congressman, it's your duty to investigate possible wrongdoing, and I'm glad to cooperate with you."

Eddie was damn good. He had pulled himself together and there were times when Dave almost thought he was telling the truth.

Congressman Ranson, a sanctimonious old bastard who Dave knew had earned $28,000 last year as a silent partner in a law firm back in Ohio, ended the hearing with a tirade aimed straight at the afternoon papers:

"The evidence may be only circumstantial, Mr. Gooch, but it leaves no doubt in my mind that you conspired with your friend Daley to enrich yourselves by violation of public trust. If the President has any regard for the opinions of decent, law-abiding Americans, he will dispense with your services immediately. Your presence in high office is a blot on the national honor. The hearing is adjourned."

The President was waiting in his office with MacKenzie and O.B. when Dave and Eddie got back to the White House.

"Boss," Eddie whimpered as they entered, "I'll quit if you want me to."

"Go to your office," the President told him, "and stay there till I call you."

When he had gone, the President addressed the other men:

"Okay, I've got to decide what to do and announce it at this press conference. Either I back Eddie all the way, or I let him go. Dave, what do you say?"

"Mr. President, I don't like to talk against Eddie. But as long as he stays, we have a weak spot for the opposition to attack. I don't say he's guilty—I'll take his word—but it's a strong circumstantial case. Your associates have got to be above suspicion. So I think Eddie has to go, no matter how painful it is, to protect your administration."

"How would you handle it?" the President asked.

"I suppose you could announce at this news conference that he's offered his resignation and you've reluctantly accepted it. You could stress your continued confidence in him."

"Then what would he do?"

"What do you mean?" Dave asked.

"What would Eddie do, after he resigned?"

Dave was puzzled. "I don't know. I hadn't thought that far ahead."

The President nodded, his face inscrutable. He pointed to the Secretary of State. "Okay, Chuck, give us some of that million-dollar advice of yours."

MacKenzie shook his head in frustration. "If I'd only known that Eddie needed money . . . Mr. President, I know how

many people are making financial sacrifices to serve this administration, and anyone with a difficult situation should let me
know . . ." He paused. "But that won't solve the problem at
hand. My concern, Mr. President, is that Eddie's resignation
might be construed as an admission of guilt," he said.

"But damn it," Dave broke in, "it's the very *evidence of the
case* that makes him look guilty, not whether or not the President lets him go."

"Oh, I disagree, Dave. Most people aren't as familiar with
the case as you and I. They see a report on television that one
politician has charged another politician with shady dealings
and they don't pay much attention. It's not much money, as
these things go. But if the President *fires* the accused—then
they'll think there's been a scandal."

Dave did not reply. He was half convinced MacKenzie was
right. Who could say what was "right" in a mess like this?
There was no right, only a lesser evil. His very uncertainty
disturbed him. In large part, he was where he was because he
did not agonize over decisions—he made them with a hard,
sure certitude, with no emotion and no regrets. But something
had changed, or was changing, and answers no longer came so
easily.

The President turned to O. B. Perkins. "Okay, what's my
image-maker say?"

"I don't want to get in between these two distinguished
jurists," O.B. drawled. "But I agree with Secretary MacKenzie
when he says it'll look like an admission of guilt if you let him
go. It don't make a hell of a lot of difference as far as the
press is concerned. If somebody wants to clobber you on this,
they'll do it even if you took Eddie out and shot him."

"How's the line-up look?" Barney asked.

"Jack Anderson has already clobbered us on this once and
he'll do it again. Evans-Novak will probably sound off in a day
or two. One good thing—I just fed Billy Doyle a column on
Ranson's law practice. As far as editorials go, I think we can
cool out the *Post*, but maybe not the *Times*. I'm gonna talk to
some people as soon as this news conference is over. On the
magazines, I'd say *Newsweek*'ll go easy, but *Time*'ll probably
hit us hard."

"What about the tube?" Barney asked.

"That's up to you," O.B. said. "The evening news shows had a couple of briefs on this thing, but I talked to some of them about the libel laws, so they've been pretty careful. You've got a chance this afternoon to come on like Gangbusters, make a strong defense of Eddie, and if you do, that'll pretty much wipe the slate clean, that'll be all most people will remember about the thing."

"What about what Dave said—that Eddie would be a weak spot for the other side to fire at?"

"Well, now," O.B. drawled, "I wouldn't want to question Davey's political sagacity, but I kinda wish they would take after Eddie, and lay off of inflation and crime and some of the things that might really hurt us."

"So what do you say?" Barney pressed.

O.B. shrugged. "I don't see that they proved anything on Eddie. Just a lot of accusations. A couple of columnists will write columns about it—twenty-four-hour wonders, that's all— then it'll blow over. I'll say this—if Eddie stays, we ought to keep him out of sight for a while."

Barney stood up abruptly. "If Eddie stays, his new office is under the boiler room," he said. "Come on—let's go meet the press."

He led them to the East Room. Eddie Gooch joined them on the way. The ballroom was jammed with reporters, photographers, and television crews.

Barney marched straight to the microphones, and the others watched from one side. Eddie was still uncertain of his fate and his face was ashen in the glare of the television lights.

The first question was about the congressman's demand that Eddie be fired. The President looked beyond the reporters into the television cameras. He was speaking to the nation now.

"My answer is this," Barney said. "I'm standing by my friend. For the last month Eddie Gooch has worked twelve hours a day for me and then spent every night with a little wife who's flat on her back in a hospital bed. I'm not throwing Eddie to the wolves because of some baseless charges made for political reasons by the minority party.

"They're not after Eddie Gooch, they're after me and our

programs. They don't care about him. They care about the better
wages we're trying to get for the workingman and the better
schools for your children and the better hospitals for sick people.
This is just one more battle in the war between the people who
want progress and the people who're trying to protect their
special interests.

"Let me tell you something else. Eddie Gooch saved my life
when we were fighting together in Italy. He saved my life,
and that's something you don't forget. So they can make their
charges till the cows come home but I'm not deserting my
friend. And I don't think the people of this country would want
a President who did."

Dave watched Eddie as the President defended him. He had
pulled himself to attention, chin high, eyes straight ahead, his
face changing from gray to a glowing pink, his gut sucked in
and his chest thrown out, and for a moment you could see that
Eddie Gooch might once have been quite a man. He stood like
that until the half-hour ended and they could escape back to
the President's office. There, Eddie buried his face in his old
friend's shoulder.

"Boss, boss," he whispered, "my good old boss, my old buddy."

Barney smiled and put his arm around Eddie. MacKenzie
shook Eddie's hand, and O.B. and Dave did the same.

"Okay, Eddie," Barney said, "you take a couple of weeks
vacation and don't talk to anybody. I'll see you when you get
back."

Eddie departed, red-eyed, but standing ramrod straight.

"Well, gentlemen, how about a drink?" Barney asked. "Dave,
you pouring?"

"Mr. President," MacKenzie said, "you were magnificent."

The President's phone rang, and in quick succession he took
calls of congratulation from the Majority Leader, the president
of the AFL-CIO, and Billy Doyle. Then he cut off the calls.

"Mr. President," Dave said, "I never knew Eddie had saved
your life. Could you tell us about it?"

Barney swirled his ice cubes around in his Scotch.

"You think that tub of lard could save *my* life?" he asked,
and laughed at the notion. "Here's what happened. Me and
him stumbled onto the villa outside of Pisa where there was

this countess and her daughter. The old girl was about forty and hot to trot and the daughter was sweet sixteen. Well, we broke out some wine and I was stalling, trying to get Eddie drunk so I could have a whack at both of 'em, when some son of a bitch lobs a mortar shell on the roof.

"When I woke up the women were gone, half the roof was on my lap, and my ankle was broke. So Eddie comes crawling toward me, saying how he'll save me, and he takes one look at the blood—my blood—and he passes out. So I have to dig myself out, and make me a crutch out of a bed slat, and hobble a mile back to the road dragging him behind me like a sack of potatoes."

Barney smiled as he recalled the scene, but after a moment he was serious again:

"But you remember this. Eddie was there with me and he did his best. He would have saved me if he could. He was my friend then and he's my friend now. So we've all got to hang together around here, got to be more careful, got to help each other out."

They sat in silence for a minute. Dave was troubled that the President's decision had gone against him, troubled by his own uncertainty, troubled most of all by a sense that somehow he had been hurt more by this episode than Eddie had.

8

"So you won't tell me where you got this story?" Roy Hailey asked again, his hillbilly eyes narrow with suspicion.

"It doesn't matter where I got it," Dave insisted. "The point is that I've heard that the Bureau will have armed agents provocateurs in the march who'll try to provoke gunfire from police."

Hailey shrugged. "Okay," he said. "It's happened before."

"Well, I don't want it to happen tomorrow in front of the White House," Dave insisted.

"Talk to the FBI, then," Hailey said. "They're your boys, not mine."

But they were not Dave's boys. He could barely communicate with the Bureau, much less control it. That was why, the night before the Free Rivera march, he was here with Hailey.

He had decided it was too dangerous for him to sit on the wild-eyed youth's story, true or not, so he'd sent a memo on it to the President with a copy to the Attorney General. The Attorney General predictably had sided with the Bureau, insisted there were no agents provocateurs, and said the incident only proved the marchers intended violence. Stories about expected violence kept leaking to the press from the Justice Department. The situation was tense—within the government, among the police and the marchers, even in the small furnished room where Dave and Roy Hailey sat across a kitchen table, drinking beer and talking.

"I can't do anything about the Bureau," Dave admitted. "They're like a separate government."

"So you want me to bail you out?" Hailey said. He was wearing khakis and a white T-shirt. His thinning blond hair was

combed straight back and his face had been burned lobster-red
by a summer in the streets.

"I want you to help us both by avoiding violence."

"You keep assuming our interests are the same," Hailey said.

"Do you want to see violence?" Dave asked.

"No, but I accept that it's inevitable if progress is to come."

"That's very noble, but we're talking about a lot of innocents
who'll get caught in the middle."

"No innocents are coming tomorrow," Hailey said. "Your Attorney General has rattled his sabre enough to guarantee that."

"Roy, if there's bloodshed, and you haven't done everything
you can to prevent it, you'll share the responsibility."

"Don't lecture me about responsibility," Hailey snapped. "I've
paid my dues for ten years, while you liberals were fucking
up America."

"We're talking about tomorrow morning," Dave said. "I want
to know what you'll do to keep weapons out of your marchers'
hands."

"We have marshals," Hailey said. "I'll do what I think is
necessary."

"If there's violence tomorrow, the Attorney General would
like nothing better than to indict you for it."

"I expect to be indicted no matter what happens."

"He'll have a better case if there's bloodshed."

Hailey shook his head. "The only question is whether America
will destroy me for exercising the right of free speech and free
assembly. We'll go to court on that eventually, no matter about
tomorrow."

"Roy, we'll have a line of police around the White House.
I know the court has given you authority to march on the
sidewalk by the White House, but let me make a suggestion.
Stay across the street. Keep Pennsylvania Avenue and the other
streets as a buffer between you and the police. That'll make it a
hell of a lot harder for the kind of pushing and name-calling
that could lead to trouble."

"I've got a better idea," Hailey said. "You pull the pigs back
inside the White House fence. That way there can't be any
contact."

"We can't do that."

"Well, I'm not staying across the street, either. The permit says a march to the White House and that's where we're going. Round and round, and see if the walls tumble down."

"God damn you," Dave said, "you want trouble as bad as the right-wingers do!"

"Let's talk serious, David. Who wants violence? Who's got ten thousand troops around town? Who's got the agents provocateurs? Is it me? Or is it you, you in the government, you in the ruling class, you who're scared of the people? You're going for your guns because you're weak, not because you're strong, because your system is rotten, because its own children have turned against it."

"You've never minded violence, if it suited your ends."

"We haven't used violence, we've exposed it. We've made you liberals go behind your phony rhetoric and show that you rule by repression and force. We know you can bloody our heads or shoot us down, but we pick the issues—positive issues, like Rivera—and each time you use force against us, you only create more of us."

"Damn it, I'm not using force against you. I'm trying to keep force from *being* used against you."

"But you can't," Hailey said. "You're helpless. You think you're a great enlightened force within the government, but you're irrelevant. The people who are running this country are the MacKenzies and the Smallwoods. They've brought in the troops and they'll pull the triggers and they'll write the indictments against us. And you're one of them."

"I'm not one of them, Roy."

"Well, you're damn sure not one of us."

"You see this conspiracy that just isn't there. Smallwood is a clown, a fluke."

"He's not a fluke. He's Attorney General because the ruling class wants repression and he's a symbol of it."

"We inherited him," Dave protested.

"And your great enlightened Barney Newfield hasn't got the guts or the strength to get rid of him," Hailey insisted. "Because J. Wesley Smallwood is just the kind of mad-dog Attorney

General the ruling class wants, one who'll put all dissenters in jail and the Constitution be damned."

"Roy, this administration is going to do big things. The New Cities . . ."

"Aren't built yet," Hailey injected. "And may never be. And won't be for the poor if they are."

"You don't know that."

"I do know it," Hailey insisted. "The ruling class won't allow fundamental change, only rhetoric. All those phony speeches you write. The MacKenzies and the Smallwoods and the Pentagon will never let you make real change, so to shift attention from your lies and failures, you try to make an issue of disorder at home. You're scared, because you're trying to preserve inequality in a country—a world—that cries out for equality."

"We are doing all that we can," Dave said. "You can talk about revolution, but we have to deal with the realities, with Congress, with public opinion, with ignorance and greed and hate."

"But you can't deal with them," Hailey said. "You become part of them. Your position is worse than ours. We may get our heads bloodied, or be imprisoned, or killed, but we'll win. We're the future, and you people are already dying."

"You really believe there'll be revolution, don't you?"

"The same way you believe there'll be reform. People are waking up. The lines are drawn. The ruling class sees that we're a challenge to them—and the oppressed Americans are seeing who their true enemies are. You've been conditioned to think revolution is impossible . . ."

"It is," Dave declared. "In this country it is."

"Do you remember 1960, David? Back then, would you have thought Vietnam was possible, or Watts, or the Panthers, or Chicago, or the radicalization of the students? Think about those things—think about the massacre there may be tomorrow, that you can't stop—and tell me there can't be revolution."

"Listen, I've seen the Pentagon's plans for putting down insurrection. Believe me, you can't do it."

"Did you ever see their plan for putting down the Viet Cong?"

Dave shut his eyes. "Roy, all I can see is repression."

"Sure," Hailey said. "And I'll be the first to go. But repression will only speed the revolution."

"You believe in it, don't you?"

"Have I ever been wrong?" Hailey said with his tight grin.

"No," Dave admitted. "Not yet."

9

Saturday morning was cool and cloudy. The marchers began gathering about 10 A.M. at a park on Fourteenth Street, a dozen blocks from the White House. Hailey might have launched the march from the Mall, but by starting it in the heart of the black ghetto, he expected to attract thousands of blacks who would come as curiosity-seekers and stay as demonstrators. To that end, black militants were delivering angry speeches to the crowd, relating Rivera's cause to the black revolution, and between speeches a rock band kept the crowd on edge.

Dave arrived at eleven. He was wearing dark glasses, a sport coat and no tie, hoping that he might move in the crowd without being recognized. He had persuaded the President he could do more good on the scene than he would awaiting reports back in the White House. In truth, he didn't know what he could do, but he hoped somehow to help avert violence.

At eleven, as the sun began to break through, twenty thousand marchers had gathered. A festive air filled the park. Black children ran about laughing and shouting, and teenagers gyrated to the music. Young white couples, many with small children, stretched out on the grass, talking and smoking. About eleven-thirty, Elijah King, Dave's black friend from California, made an angry speech that concluded with a new chant.

"Tax the rich," he shouted.

"Help the poor," the crowd roared in reply.

"Tax the rich!"

"Help the poor!"

You sons of bitches, Dave thought, that's what we're trying to do.

He leaned against a tree and studied the security arrangements. About two hundred District police, most of them black, surrounded the park. Hundreds more lined the route of march to the White House. A dozen fire trucks were on alert in case of arson, and plainclothesmen manned nearby rooftops to scan for snipers. Dave was pleased; the District police were well-trained and they were keeping back, out of the way. But he knew too that two thousand armed GIs were posted in buildings along the route of march and eight thousand more were poised at nearby bases.

At noon, Roy Hailey got up on the bandstand to make the final speech.

"Rivera is as much a part of the black man's fight for freedom as Malcolm X was or Bobby Seale is," he said. "Rivera is fighting the oppression of American capitalism in his country just as we are fighting it here. Rivera has been captured and threatened with death by the American government, just as black men and white men who challenge oppression in America are imprisoned and killed.

"We march today not for an unknown warrior in a distant land, but for a brother whose cause is our cause, whose blood is our blood, whose dream is our dream. We march for a man whose cause will triumph, as ours will, because it is just, because it rises from the hearts of the people, black and brown and white, who are rising up all over the world to strike down their oppressors."

There were scattered, revival-meeting shouts of "Tell it, brother!" and "Right on!" and beneath that a new hum of excitement was spreading through the park. Dave sensed it with the others. It was the thrill of the unknown. The march was about to begin: no one knew what lay ahead. But they were fifty thousand strong now, they were stirred, they were ready.

"Who owns the streets?" Hailey shouted.

"The people," they roared back.

"Who owns the White House?"

"The people!"

"Who owns America?"

"*THE PEOPLE!*"

"Power to the people," Hailey called.

"*POWER TO THE PEOPLE,*" the thousands roared, and

Hailey jumped down from the bandstand. The people were on their feet and the marshals began to move out the first ranks of the marchers. As it left the park and turned down Fourteenth Street, the march was forty feet across. Dave stayed off to the side and a little ahead of the march, so he could see both Hailey and the police.

"*Free Rivera!*" the marchers shouted. "*Power to the People!*" Yet it was a good-natured crowd, and when marchers flashed the V-sign to the police, the police grinned back and some returned the salute. Many of the marchers carried pictures of Rivera held aloft on flimsy wooden frames. Dave thought of Birnam Wood moving toward Dunsinane.

A shot rang out and a black policeman fell to the street clutching his leg. Dave looked up at a nearby building from which the shot seemed to have come, but he saw nothing, and when he looked back down he saw dozens of policemen with their guns drawn and the marchers halted in confusion.

"Don't go any farther," a police captain shouted. He was standing in the middle of the street, thirty feet ahead of the marchers.

Roy Hailey raised a clenched fist. He took two steps forward, then a loud burst of gunfire cut him down. There were more shots and another policeman was down and then the marchers began to fall to the street or to run and the police began throwing tear gas. Suddenly, the march had become a scene of wild and bloody chaos. Teenagers fanned out around the park throwing rocks at police and shopwindows. The park was dotted with clouds of tear gas. Women screamed and police sirens wailed in reply. The first fire was in a pawnshop across from the park, and as the angry blacks spread out into the ghetto, other fires followed, dozens of them. Dave huddled behind a parked car until the shooting stopped, then he picked his way through the tear gas to the spot where Hailey had fallen. He passed two other men lying in the street. One was a black leader, moaning as a woman dabbed at his bleeding face with a handkerchief. The other was the wild-eyed young man, but his eyes were closed now and Dave did not think they would ever open again. Nor did he think he would ever know whose side the strange young man had been serving.

Hailey was pale but conscious, wounded in the right leg. Two men had pulled him to an upright position. A tall man with a scar on his cheek was going through Hailey's coat pockets, and when he tried to resist, the tall man slapped him across the side of the face.

"What are you doing?" Dave shouted at the man.

The man stood up, fastened cold eyes on Dave, and in one quick motion drove his knee into Dave's groin, then chopped him across the neck as he went down. After a minute, Dave rose to his hands and knees and vomited. He saw the two men dragging Hailey into a car. He stumbled to a police car, flashed his White House card at its driver, and sat in the back seat while he caught his breath. He heard on the police radio that soldiers were on their way. All around him he could see marchers huddling to the ground for safety, and police dragging others to paddy wagons. There was nothing more for him to do here, so he told the policeman to drive him to the White House, although it was the last place he wanted to be.

When Dave entered the President's office the four men there looked at him sharply. Attorney General Smallwood was on the phone, O. B. Perkins was standing beside him, and Charlton MacKenzie was sitting across from the President. A television news program was showing tapes and live coverage of the afternoon's violence, of police clubs flailing at marchers, of stores and automobiles ablaze.

"Patrolman Hager is critical," Smallwood said, the phone still cradled against his ear. "Two other officers are being treated. Two demonstrators are reported dead and about three hundred arrested."

"Well, you see what your noble friend Roy Hailey has done for us," the President said bitterly.

Dave's neck still ached from the karate chop. He did not feel diplomatic.

"It wasn't the first riot in America and it won't be the last," he said.

"Well you're pretty damned philosophical," Barney snapped. "It was the first riot since I've been President and the first one in D.C."

"We should have locked that son of a bitch Hailey up this time yesterday," O. B. Perkins said.

"What for, O.B.?" Dave asked.

"I don't give a damn what for," the press secretary said. "Because he's a revolutionary and anyone with half a brain could see he wanted violence."

"The President of the United States can't go locking up his political opponents like some banana-republic dictator," Dave said.

"The President of the United States is not going to be dumped on by that bastard again," Barney declared. "I'll promise you that."

"That'll hardly be likely, Mr. President," Smallwood said. "I intend to put Roy Hailey so far under a federal prison that they'll have to feed him through a pipe."

"The grand jury is ready to act?" MacKenzie asked. He seemed the calmest man in the room.

"We'll need a few days to present today's evidence," Smallwood said. "If Patrolman Hager dies, that'll mean adding another charge."

"Hailey didn't shoot anyone," Dave said.

"No, he conspired to bring about the shooting," the Attorney General said. "And if the patrolman dies it becomes conspiracy to commit murder."

"Mr. President," Dave said, "I don't claim to know what happened. But there were rumors that the Bureau would have its agents start the shooting. And I think the first shot was fired from an upper window of a warehouse on Fourteenth Street."

"So Hailey planted a man in the warehouse," Barney said.

"Or the Bureau or the Secret Service or someone else did," Dave replied. "We've got to find out what did happen."

"I think what happened is fairly clear, Dave," Charlton MacKenzie said gently. "A group of radicals came to Washington looking for trouble and they deliberately provoked a confrontation. Perhaps they got more trouble than they'd counted on. It behooves us to determine what laws they have broken and to take appropriate action. And I think public opinion will demand that we do."

"But what about the agents provocateurs?" Dave demanded. "Don't you think the President ought to know about that?"

"I think that as a practical matter," MacKenzie replied, "it's unlikely that the U. S. Government will care to reveal—should it be the case—that its own agents provoked a gun battle with the marchers."

"All right," Dave said, "but I still say the President should know if this is the kind of game the Bureau is playing."

"Yeah, I'll check into it," Barney said vaguely, confronting an old question—who polices the police?

The President turned back to the television screen. There were scenes of firemen shooting water into fiery storefronts and of teenagers pelting them with rocks. There was a report that the soldiers had arrived and cordoned off a forty-block area. Finally, there was an interview with Elijah King.

"The pigs opened fire without warning," the young black shouted. "It was genocide and that big lying cowboy in the White House was behind it."

Barney's fist crashed down onto his desk and the Attorney General jumped to his feet in rage.

Oh shit, Dave thought. My people.

The newscast ended a minute later and Barney Newfield, his face dark and furious, rose and silently left the room.

A Man's Own Fortunes

1

By mid-September the campaign was upon them. The President was not a candidate but he and his program were the main issue in hundreds of congressional elections. Everyone knew this, and Barney Newfield and the men around him unashamedly put aside the business of government to devote themselves twenty hours a day to the business of politics. Dave devoted his days to grants that should or should not be made, candidates who should or should not be helped, and his nights to speech-writing, for the President had agreed to deliver six "non-political" speeches in the final weeks of the campaign. The speeches came at Dave one after another, like bulls at a weary matador, and only through night after sleepless nights of Scotch and coffee and naps on his sofa was he able to meet the deadlines. If Hailey's march had pulled him and the President apart— and it had, Dave had no illusions about that—the speeches drew them back together. The first of the speeches, on the New Cities, delivered a week after Hailey's march, was hailed in a New York *Times* editorial as "a noble and historic statement." When Dave read the editorial and saw Barney grinning all morning about it, he thought, most humbly, "God bless you, New York *Times*, God bless you."

"Elias, baby, how are you?"

Just to hear his friend's voice made Dave feel better, midway in an endless stupor of a day.

"Cool, daddy, cool."

"I hear you're cleaning house at Labor."

"We've made the bureaucrats sweat a little," Elias laughed.

Dave smiled into the telephone but he was not smiling inside where it counted. Elias had gone to Labor, and they were in different orbits now. Instead of talking to Elias twice a day as he had in their New Cities days, they spoke perhaps once a week.

"What's up?" Dave asked, glancing at his watch.

"It's this job training program for addicts," Elias said. "We've got to go ahead on it."

"I can't, Elias. I can't touch it till after the election."

It was a twenty million dollar grant for job training for three thousand drug addicts in Harlem. It was a fine program but it was, in the political patois, a nigger grant. The administration was already out on a limb with the blacks and couldn't touch this program until after the elections.

"That's too late, Dave," Elias protested. "The beauty of it is the academic credit from Columbia, but they won't wait till mid-November."

"I'm sorry," Dave said. "That's how it is. You'll just have to work it out if you can."

"Yeah," Elias said wearily. "Okay." He understood the problem, but he was at Labor now and his priorities were no longer Dave's or the President's.

Governor Holbrook was angry. Governor Holbrook was mad as hell. Governor Holbrook was a short man, near sixty, once handsome and vibrant, now a stocky, bejowled old pol from the whistle-stop era running scared against a handsome young challenger from the time of television.

"My state deserves a New City," the governor repeated. "My state has the plans and the know-how. Do you deny that?"

"No sir," Dave said softly. It was sometime in midmorning and he buzzed to Mrs. Gill for more coffee. He'd not slept the night before and there was a buzzing in his right ear.

"Then why won't you give me a straight answer, boy?" the governor demanded.

"As I said, Governor, the Corps of Engineers is surveying many proposed sites . . ." He recited all the pious lies. In truth, they knew where the first New Cities were going, but they weren't about to announce the decisions until after the elections. Better to leave all fifty states with a ray of hope than to please five and infuriate forty-five others.

The governor needed a Yes or a No. A Yes would be some prime-quality pork to take home from Washington, and even a clear-cut No might be turned around to good advantage. But he was getting no help in the White House. He had backed the wrong man for Vice-President two years earlier and the right man hadn't forgotten.

"Look, boy, I know what the President will do with those Corps of Engineers reports. He'll throw them out and put the New Cities where he damn pleases."

Quite so, Dave thought.

"I need help," the governor said angrily. "If you can't give me a New City, at least you can say the President is impressed by our plans."

"I'll talk to the President about it," Dave said.

"You'll talk to him!" the governor shouted. "Damn it, why can't I talk to him?"

"His schedule, Governor . . ."

"Damn his schedule! I've half a mind to march in there . . ."

You do that, mister, and the Secret Service will drag you kicking and screaming to St. Elizabeth's . . .

"I've heard about you and these cute deals you've been making with the radicals . . ."

"You've been misinformed, Governor."

The governor left, white-faced, hating Dave for making his status with the Administration perfectly clear. Dave sighed and wondered which "cute deals" the governor had heard about. His talk with Hailey before the ill-fated march? His meetings with Rivera? Or his negotiation with Hailey and Elijah King about the New Cities? Whatever it was, he knew he'd hear more about it.

He should not have read the memo from his friend at Justice. He did not have to read it, since it had nothing to do with the elections. But he read it because his friend was trying to improve the federal prisons and he'd attached a note: *Dave, this is the kind of thing we're trying to stop but we must have money.* So Dave read the memo and then he dropped it to his desk and sat for a minute with his eyes closed.

The memo concerned one John Franklin Cranshaw, a young

pacifist who'd been sent to a federal prison for refusing the draft. It happened that Dave had met Jack Cranshaw, as he'd been called, several years before when he'd been visiting Roy Hailey's slum project in Cleveland. He remembered Cranshaw, a soft-spoken, baby-faced kid who played the guitar and talked about Thoreau. Now, after several years in the anti-war movement, Jack Cranshaw was in prison and had become a model prisoner. He worked in the prison hospital and taught remedial reading to other prisoners at night.

On a recent Saturday afternoon Jack Cranshaw walked into the prison laundry room where a dozen black prisoners were getting high on pep pills smuggled from the prison hospital. The blacks grabbed him and tore off his uniform and stuffed his underpants into his mouth. Then they spread-eagled him over a clothes dryer, gangraped him until his anus was a bloody pulp, until the tip of his intestine hung out, until finally they tired of the sport and stumbled away. Eventually Cranshaw's cries caught a guard's attention and was taken to the prison hospital, where two days later he hanged himself from a light fixture.

In time, Dave forced the prison scene from his mind, but it was replaced by other scenes, image after image of the horrors in America. He saw the five thousand children described in another memo, whose pregnant mother had caught German measles in a 1965 epidemic and had been born deaf and almost blind, who could not be taught in public schools and were not being taught by anyone now for want of money. He saw old people who went hungry at the end of each month so they could afford the pain-killing drugs the drug companies sold for a four-hundred percent profit. He saw coal miners who choked to death with black lung and other miners who died more quickly in cave-ins because no one gave a damn about their safety. He saw Vietnam veterans, maimed and forgotten, in crowded, hopelessly understaffed hospitals. He saw children in the South with bodies infested with worms, and children everywhere whose minds were being stunted by wretched schools, children North and South condemned at birth to a life of poverty and ignorance amid the greatest wealth the world had ever known.

He saw these and other scenes until with a stifled cry he forced them from his mind and returned to the papers on his desk. If you gazed too long into the abyss you would go mad.

Another pressure struck closer to home.

Early Sunday morning, Dave and Eleanor were awakened by a loud blast, the clatter of breaking glass, then the squeal of automobile tires. Dave threw on a robe and rushed outside, to find that the picture window on the house next door had been shattered. The house belonged to a pompous doctor named Page whom Dave had met once or twice. Lights were on in the house and Dave knocked on the front door.

"Someone shot at us," Page's wife cried when she opened the door. "They shot through the window."

Page put down the telephone and looked at Dave suspiciously.

"Anything I can do?" Dave asked.

"Not a thing," Page snapped. "I've called police. Not a thing you can do."

"Okay, goodnight," Dave said, and went back home.

But later that morning, as he and Eleanor were having breakfast, Dave answered the doorbell and found Homer Rouzer, the deputy chief of the Secret Service, on his doorstep.

"Mornin', Mr. Hyer," said Rouzer, a lean, homely, competent Mississippian.

"Morning, Chief. What's up?"

"Well, might be a little trouble," Rouzer drawled.

"What kind of trouble, Chief?"

"That shootin' next door."

"What about it?" Dave asked patiently, knowing there was no way to hurry Rouzer.

"That fellow Page told the po-lice there weren't nobody who'd be shootin' at him, so it must've been somebody shootin' at you."

"He's crazy."

Rouzer scratched a leathery cheek. "Well, Ah don't know," he said. "Could be somebody shootin' at you and hit him by mistake. Don't forget all them letters you got after that last speech you made."

Dave frowned. Two weeks earlier, he'd spoken to a Press

Club luncheon about the New Cities. His speech was reported in the papers, and because he spoke of the benefits for Negroes, he got the usual flurry of hate mail, which he'd routinely forwarded to the Secret Service.

"I'd forgotten that," Dave admitted. "What do you think we ought to do?"

"We oughta put some men here for a spell, till we've checked it out."

"My wife won't like that."

Rouzer pursed his lips. "It's her 'n your little girl we'll be tryin' to protect."

"Yeah," Dave said. "Come in and sit down while I talk to her." He went to the kitchen and told Eleanor the news. Her face went white—from anger, he knew, not fear.

"I'll take Sally and go home this afternoon," she declared. By home, she meant her parents' home in Connecticut.

"I don't think you should," he told her.

"Shall I stay here and be shot at?"

"Eleanor, it's probably some drunks who shot up Page's house at random. But if anyone did want to harm us, the Secret Service can protect us easier here."

That was part of it, and also he didn't want Eleanor's parents thinking that being married to him involved being shot at; they were already cool to him because of her unhappiness in the past year.

"Protect us how?" she demanded. "Put soldiers on the lawn? Is this how we're to live?"

"There won't be any soldiers, Eleanor," he said evenly. "Come on, just talk to the man."

Rouzer was good with Eleanor, calm and reassuring. "You'll never know our men are there, Miz Hyer," he promised. "But they will be, an' if you want to go anywhere, they'll go right along with you."

"Where will they be?" Eleanor asked.

"Oh, they might be parked down the block. Might be strollin' by. If it went on a spell, we might see 'bout rentin' a house nearby."

"My God," Eleanor exclaimed. "How long could it go on?"

"Don't you worry now," he told her, embarrassed at his slip. "You let us do all the worryin' for you."

Eleanor gave him a faint smile and went to see about Sally. Dave and Rouzer discussed the details of the surveillance for a few minutes. Rouzer explained that the Secret Service would immediately begin to check Dave's hate letters against its lengthy list of Klansmen, Minutemen, and assorted crackpots who were believed to be potential assassins.

"How many are on your list?" Dave asked.

Rouzer scratched his cheek reflectively. "Oh, maybe two, three thousand," he allowed. "That's the rightwing types. Ah reckon they're the ones who'd be gunnin' for you."

Billy Doyle sat down, frowning and shaking his head as he pulled two clippings from his pocket.

"David, I'm bothered about these," he said. "I've had a hundred readers write me and ask why I haven't told them about this. I don't know what to do except come to you for an explanation."

He handed Dave the clippings, two columns written by a far-right former congressman and published in *Human Events*. The first repeated the charge that Dave had threatened Colonel Molina, and phoned the President from Caravelas threatening to resign unless Rivera was protected. The second hinted that Dave was deeply involved in a plot to help Rivera escape from captivity.

Dave glanced at the clippings and put them down on his desk.

"I've seen these, Billy."

"What do you say about them?"

"Well, we've already discussed the first one. And the second one, about a plot to free Rivera from prison, is utter nonsense. What could I do to free him?"

"I don't know," Doyle admitted.

"Billy, I think the real story here is how these things spread," Dave said, with more self-assurance than he felt. "Those charges first appeared a month ago in the *Thunderbolt*, which you know is a hate-sheet, pure and simple. Now they've been dressed up a bit and printed in *Human Events,* which isn't exactly an unbiased observer of this administration."

"But the question isn't where they appeared," Billy Doyle said softly. "It's whether they're true."

Dave spread his hands. "What more can I say? These are baseless charges, started by the ultra-right for political purposes. They want to use me to get at the President. So far, these charges don't matter, because nobody but True Believers read these sheets. But if you print them it will matter because millions of people trust what you tell them."

Doyle did not answer directly. "I did some nosing around at the CIA," he said, "and I heard there might be something afoot to free Rivera."

"That may be," Dave said, "but I know nothing about it."

Doyle shook his head wearily. "What are we coming to, David, when people in the CIA are trying to free a captured Communist terrorist?"

Why not, Dave thought, they captured him in the first place. The CIA giveth and the CIA taketh away.

"You know the kinds of problems we have over there," he said.

Doyle rubbed his chin with the back of his hand. "I'm not going to write anything yet, but I'll be honest and tell you I'm bothered by all this."

"I'm bothered too," Dave said with a smile. "It's me they're after."

"I think it's oversimple, David, to say that people are just using you to get at the President," Doyle said. "People might have legitimate doubts as to whether your authority is too great for a man of your age."

Dave guessed that was what Doyle felt and he didn't see much he could do about it. "I have very little authority, Billy. I'm just an instrument of the President."

"But the President is a hard-pressed man," Doyle replied. "Perhaps the President's instrument takes on a life of its own."

"Not often."

"You have to be careful, David," Billy Doyle mused. "It isn't that power corrupts, but that it tends to excite men, particularly young men. Confuses them, intoxicates them, makes them rash. Not many men know how to handle power."

Dave said nothing.

"Harry Hopkins was one who could handle it," Doyle went on. "You know about Harry?"

"I've read Sherwood."

"Harry was a kind of genius," Doyle said. "Course, he had to be, to survive with FDR."

"I've never claimed to be a genius," Dave said.

"Not many are," Billy Doyle said. "Not many are."

Doyle left, mollified for the time being, but Dave was bothered by his attitude and he was more bothered when O. B. Perkins came to his office that evening and handed him a brief wire-service story.

CONGRESSMAN A. B. HARDY, REPUBLICAN OF SOUTH DAKOTA, CHARGED TODAY THAT PRESIDENTIAL ASSISTANT DAVID HYER HAS HELD SECRET MEETINGS WITH NEGRO MILITANTS IN WHICH HE PROMISED THAT SOME OF THE ADMINISTRATION'S PLANNED NEW CITIES WOULD BE ALL-NEGRO. HARDY CHARGED THAT HYER MADE THE ALLEGED AGREEMENT IN SECRET MEETING TWO MONTHS AGO WITH MILITANT NEGRO LEADER ELIJAH KING AND WITH ROY HAILEY, THE NOW-JAILED WHITE RADICAL.

That was all. Hardy had the honor of being the farthest right of the four hundred and thirty-five members of the House, and his frequent charges against government officials didn't rate much attention.

"Well, what do we say about this one?" O.B. asked, giving Dave his sleepy, skeptical gaze.

"Obviously, we deny there's any deal to make the New Cities all-black," Dave said. "If necessary, we confirm that I talked with King and Hailey about the New Cities, just as I've talked with dozens of other people about them."

"Does the President know about this?"

"About what?"

"About you meeting with these birds," O.B. drawled.

"Of course he knows about it. What kind of wisecrack is that?"

"Don't get hot, pal. I've got to get the story straight."

"Okay, you've got it straight."

"Fine, pal," the press secretary said. "Thanks a million."

Hardy's charges were not carried in the New York or Washington papers, but Dave knew they would surface in the South and the Midwest, would circulate on the rightwing underground, would be clipped and mailed to certain political leaders and be inserted in certain files. It was hard to think that at some point in the campaign they would not be used by the opposition. There was not much he could do. He could call in a friendly columnist and encourage a favorable column, but that sort of thing often backfired—once the Washington pack smelled blood, they all started after you. Better to keep quiet and wait. Perhaps it would die down. But he could not be hopeful and as he pushed on with his speechwriting it was with the uneasy feeling of a man waiting for the other shoe to drop.

2

"Gee I'm glad to see you," Brenda said. "How about some sherry?"

"Well, it's almost noon," Cathy grinned. "What've you been up to out here?"

"Oh, I planted a couple of trees," Brenda said, "but mostly I've just been visiting with Mama and Sis. I finally ran them out today."

"Been swimming?"

"Just once," Brenda admitted. "I get so sick of those Secret Service guys following me everywhere. The only privacy I get is if I stay here at home." Brenda rolled her eyes helplessly. "What about you—you out here writing a story?"

"Yeah, I'm visiting Berkeley and S. F. State, trying to figure out what the radicals are up to."

"What are they up to?" Brenda asked. "Trying to put my husband out of a job?"

"I think so," Cathy admitted.

"Power to 'em," Brenda giggled. "Hey, did you know I went to S. F. State for a year, back in the Dark Ages? But we didn't think anything about politics back then. Just guys."

"They're still thinking about guys, believe me," Cathy said. "How far is State from here? I got to go over there this afternoon."

"Just six blocks," Brenda told her. "What's happening?"

"Oh, the regents fired a professor, so the kids are having a protest rally and the administration may call in the cops. The usual chaos."

Brenda poured them both more sherry and looked out the window at the two Secret Service men sitting in a car parked in front of her mother's house.

"My bodyguards," she sighed. Then she looked at Cathy and grinned. "Say," she said, "I've got a heck of an idea."

Her plan was irresistibly daring. They would ditch the Secret Service and go to a little Italian restaurant near the university for lunch. Eluding her guards proved not to be hard. Brenda knew, and they didn't, that the basement of her mother's house was connected to the basement of the house next door ("My old man and the guy next door had this plan for a two-family bomb shelter," she explained, "so if the Ruskies attacked it'd be us and the McCardles against the world") and from next door they could slip down the alley. Keeping Brenda incognito was not hard either. She had bought an expensive wig which, along with a huge pair of dark glasses, transformed her from America's most famous strawberry blonde into a stunning but anonymous brunette.

"Well, dearie, I'm not going to celebrate my freedom with sherry," Brenda said as they slipped into a booth at the back of the dark, small restaurant.

"Two martinis, please," Cathy told the waitress.

"Extra dry," Brenda added. "Say, honey, where's all your customers?"

The waitress waved a plump hand toward the front door. "Since them kids started all that trouble at State, people's afraid to come around here," she said, and shuffled off toward the bar.

"Well, it's kinda nice to have the place to ourselves," Brenda said. "Oh, Cathy, you don't *know* how good it is to get away from those gumshoes."

"Yeah, I guess it gets on your nerves," Cathy said.

"And they are so *square*," Brenda said. "The other morning I invited one of them to come have coffee with me. 'Wait a minute, till I get my partner,' he says. Did he think I'd seduce him?" She shook her head and laughed. "I guess they're afraid of Barney. As if *he* cared what I did."

"You're Caesar's wife," Cathy said. "Got to be above suspicion."

"Yeah, that's me, Caesar's miserable wife. Lord, Cathy, people think it's so glamorous. But all I do is meet people I don't want to meet and go places I don't want to go. The things I want to do, I never get to. And, oh, those biddies from the society pages, sniffing around everywhere. I can't scratch my fanny without Betty Beale writing a column about it."

"Caesar's wife," Cathy mused, sipping her martini.

"That's not what Eddie Gooch calls me," Brenda giggled. "He calls me the Sheriff's Girl."

"What's that mean?"

"Oh, it's the punch line of one of Eddie's dirty jokes—a cowboy says 'You don't screw with the sheriff's girl.'"

"What's gonna happen to him?" Cathy asked.

"To Eddie?" Brenda asked. "Nothing. Eddie could steal the Washington Monument and Barney would stick by him. That's how Barney is. You've got to give him your heart on a platter, but if you do, he'll take care of you."

"Waitress, bring us two more," Cathy called. "You're not in any rush, are you?"

"Me in a rush? No, sweetie, Mama's as free as a bird. Till tomorrow morning, when I've gotta make my Smokey the Bear speech to the Northern California Daughters of Calliope."

"To who?"

Brenda fluttered a hand in exasperation. "Some congressman's wife is the Chief Daughter. It's a bunch of do-gooders." Brenda sighed. "Me, I was always a do-badder. You were right in that article you wrote. I'm just a swinger. Never wanted to be anything else. They can write on my tombstone, Here Lies Brenda, She Swung When She Could."

Brenda stared glumly into her martini glass, as if it were a crystal ball in which she glimpsed a future devoid of swinging.

"Oh, Cathy," she cried, "change places with me. I'll be a reporter and you can have this First Lady bit. How 'bout it?"

"No thanks," Cathy said. "Hey, tell me about Sharon Flatt's wedding."

A smile returned to Brenda's face. "Oh, it was a dream," she said. "Biggest thing that ever happened in West Virginia. They're gonna be so happy, once Winnie gets the hang of married life."

"It got plenty of publicity," Cathy said.

"Well, it should," Brenda said. "It's kind of inspirational that a sweet little typist can still marry a nice young millionaire."

"And have the President give away the bride," Cathy added.

"Yeah," Brenda said, her smile widening. "The dear boy had tears in his eyes."

"I saw where one of the society writers gave you credit for bringing the happy couple together," Cathy said.

Brenda batted her blue eyes contentedly. "Well, you know what the Good Book says, dearie," she replied. "Blessed are the matchmakers, for they shall inherit their husbands."

Cathy returned her smile; she was feeling good. She had no desire to go watch cops and kids yelling at each other that afternoon. "These martinis are kind of watery," she said. "I think I could stand another."

"Speaking of young romance," Brenda said when the waitress had gone, "how are you and Davey getting along?"

Cathy glanced sharply at Brenda. "What do you mean?"

"No secrets from Mama," Brenda said. "Mama knows everything."

In fact, Brenda's question was based on a hunch, but an educated hunch. Although hailed as one of America's sexiest women, Brenda was one of the few married people she knew who was unwaveringly faithful. This fact gave her, like a teetotaler at a drunken party, special insights into the weaknesses and waverings of others.

Cathy's frown loosened after a moment into a resigned smile. She guessed it was silly to think there could be any secrets in Washington. "I still see him once in a while," she said. "But I don't think I will much longer."

"I'd of never picked you two for a pair," Brenda said. "How'd you get together?"

"I don't know exactly," Cathy admitted. "I'd just broke up with another guy, that was one thing. And it may not make much sense, but Dave is such a machine in his work, such a computer click-click-click, that I sort of wanted to see if he was human."

"Oh, Davey's plenty human," Brenda said. "But he's changed a lot in the last year or two. When I first knew him, he was just a sweet kid. Eager and idealistic and all. Maybe he's still that, but he's gotten harder, sort of cynical." Brenda paused and fiddled with a spoon. "I guess working for Barney long enough would do that to anybody. But Davey has changed, got more independent. Him and Barney are always going to the mat about something. Sometimes I think Davey's got too independent for his own good."

"Maybe he thinks that's what the President needs from him," Cathy said. "Dave's awful smart. I guess that's really the main thing that got us together. I've learned so darn much from him, and it shows in my writing."

"What does he do, give you hot tips?"

"Not so much that," Cathy explained, "as telling me what questions I ought to ask, making me dig deeper into things."

"Why do you say it won't go on?" Brenda asked.

Cathy's thin shoulders jerked impatiently. "There never was any future to it," she said. "He had his fling and I had mine, but, you know, it ain't no big production."

"You kids," Brenda said wistfully. Then, "Does Eleanor know about it?"

"I don't think so," Cathy replied. "But I didn't think *you* knew about it."

Brenda winked across the table delightedly. "Maybe I'm a better reporter than you are," she said.

"What's she like?" Cathy asked. "His wife."

"Oh, Eleanor's fantastic," Brenda said. "Beautiful and smart and sweet." Brenda smiled ruefully. "I hate her. She's so damn slender and graceful—whenever she walks in I always feel like Elsie the Cow."

"He never talks about her," Cathy said.

"I think Ellie's been giving him a hard time," Brenda told her. "I can remember when Davey and Ellie were first married, five or six years ago. We'd see them at parties and they'd walk in and everybody'd just stop and stare. There was Davey, twenty-five or so, handsome and bright as hell, and Ellie on his arm, so damned gorgeous it made you want to cry.

"The only trouble was, neither one of them is exactly modest. They were always like Dick and Liz on the same stage, both fighting for the spotlight. And she usually won. But then they got to Washington and except for that one movie poor Ellie's stuck out in suburbia. Dave never gets home till midnight, and when he gets home, I don't think she exactly meets him with open arms."

"So along comes Cathy Quinn, Girl Reporter," Cathy said.

Brenda fluttered her false eyelashes. "A girl's got to take it where she can get it," she said. "Let's order. How about some spaghetti, and a bottle of Mountain Red, for old time's sake?"

It was past three when they left the restaurant. The sudden glare of the sun made Brenda dizzy, and she grabbed Cathy's arm for support.

"I believe Mama is a little tipsy," she said. She was only dimly aware of the shouts and sirens at the other end of the block, near the university. Then the shouts came closer and she looked up and saw dozens of people running toward them. A window was shattered nearby.

"What's happening?"

"They're arresting people," Cathy said. "Come on, let's get out of here."

They began to walk rapidly toward the other end of the block, away from the university, but as they neared it two police cars raced up and a dozen county patrolmen formed a wall across the intersection. Brenda and Cathy instinctively backed away from the police, and they became part of the crowd trapped in the block. Most were kids, but a few were older, bespectacled types who looked like professors. The young people huddled together; one girl wept and one boy was cursing the police.

A black bus stopped in the intersection. A boy with a beard tried to dart past the police line and was tackled by a trooper and beaten with a billyclub.

"*YOU ARE ALL UNDER ARREST*," a trooper said with a bullhorn. "*ENTER THE BUS PEACEFULLY OR FACE ADDITIONAL CHARGES.*"

"Jesus Christ," Brenda said. "I've got to tell them who I am."

The police line was forcing the crowd toward the bus. Brenda shoved her way past the kids to the one with the bullhorn. "Hey, you're making a mistake," she told him. "I just came out of a restaurant over there."

"We got orders. Everybody in the street goes."

"I'd better tell you who I am."

The policeman's eyes were bright with scorn. "I don't give a fuck who you are, sister. You're just another troublemaker. Now get your ass in that bus."

When she started to speak again he jabbed her in the stomach with the end of his club. Brenda doubled over, feeling sick. Cathy pulled her back.

"Maybe we better get on the bus," Cathy said. "There'll be somebody at the other end we can explain things to."

Moments later, Brenda stared in disbelief through the wire-mesh windows of the bus as it jerked through the familiar streets. Around them, the kids were singing "We Shall Overcome" and "Give Peace a Chance."

"Jesus Christ," Brenda said numbly. "This can't be happening. Oh, God, Barney'll kill me!"

3

After they had ridden a long way, the bus passed through some gates. Two other buses were behind theirs. The kids were no longer singing.

"What's this?" Cathy asked.

"I think it's the prison farm," Brenda said. "What'll happen here?"

"They'll probably book people and let them go on bond," Cathy said.

"I don't know what to do," Brenda whispered.

"You'd better tell them who you are," Cathy said.

"I'm afraid to," Brenda said. "I'm afraid it'll cause a stink and get in the papers and then I don't know what Barney'd do. You see what I mean?"

"Yeah," Cathy said.

"What if I just went on through this and didn't give my right name?" Brenda asked. "You think I'd get away with it? Do they check?"

"Usually they don't," Cathy said. "If nobody recognized you, you'd probably make it."

"What about you?" Brenda asked. "Can't you tell 'em you're a reporter?"

Cathy's face was a tight little knot. "Hell no," she said. "I'll play their silly game." Then she added, "Brenda, you do what you think is right for you. It may not be what's right for me."

The bus jolted to a halt in front of an old brick building surrounded by a high wall.

"Okay, everybody out," the driver called. "Men to the left, women to the right."

"Stay close to me," Brenda whispered.

"Don't worry," Cathy said.

Deputies divided the men and women into separate groups. There were about a hundred men and perhaps forty women. Most of the women were young, and wearing jeans and sweat shirts; Brenda, in her miniskirt, felt the cool wind blowing off the ocean.

There was a scuffle among the men. A middle-aged man in a cord coat tried to speak to the deputy in charge. Another deputy pushed him back into the crowd. The man in the cord coat pushed back, and the deputy swung a pair of handcuffs against the side of his head. The man fell to the ground and lay still.

"All you creeps pay attention to this," the chief deputy shouted. "This man there just got a new charge against him—assaulting an officer."

"Okay, you women come on dis way," a young Negro deputy said. "Single file, no talkin'. We going to de yawd."

"What's that?" Brenda whispered, but Cathy only shrugged.

They entered the brick building, flanked by a half-dozen grinning guards, marched along a corridor, then went out a heavy iron door into an asphalt-covered courtyard about the size of a basketball court. It was closed on one side by the building and on the three other sides by a high chain-link fence. A chill breeze blew across it from the distant bay.

"Okay, dis here de yawd, where you gonna be a spell," the Negro deputy said. He was thin and had two gold teeth. "Line up in two lines, a arm-length apart."

The women shuffled about awkwardly until they had made two lines.

"When do we post bail?" a red-haired girl in the front row demanded. She had the peace symbol stenciled on the back of her denim jacket.

"No talkin'," the Negro said.

"You've got to tell us when we post bail," the girl snapped.

The Negro slapped her across the breast with his billyclub.

"You white whores keep quiet," he barked. "Now everbody lay down, on yo' stomach, hands up over you' heads, faces to de left."

The two lines of women hesitated and the deputy raised his

club menacingly. *"DOWN, FAST,"* he shouted, and the women lay down on the cold asphalt.

Cathy could see Brenda, her lime-colored dress already smudged by the dirty asphalt. Brenda, looking to her left, could see the redheaded girl who had been hit by the guard.

Brenda could not believe this was happening. She shut her eyes and told herself it was a nightmare, but when she felt the rough asphalt against her cheek she knew it was not. She had a headache from the martinis and wine, and she had a terrible feeling that she had done something wrong. She shouldn't have fled the Secret Service. She shouldn't have gotten high at lunch. Somehow it seemed she was at fault, not the police, and if this story got out it would embarrass Barney and lose the elections and it would be her fault. She knew this was hostile political territory for Barney and she was afraid of these men. She thought the only thing she could do was to bluff it through on her own, somehow get out of here without being recognized. She knew she could do it. Then Barney would be proud of her. She only had to keep her head. And she had Cathy to help her.

"Any you creeps got a camera, set it out in front of your head," a guard shouted, this one with a gruff Southern voice. "We find a camera later, we'll smash it and yore head at the same time."

"Don't nobody move," another yelled. "We shoot to kill."

At first, Brenda did not mind lying flat. It gave a sense of privacy; she would lie very still and it could not be long until they would be freed. Soon, she lost all sense of time. It was dark, she guessed it was about nine; some of the women had asked about food and the guards had laughed at them.

"Hey, Joe Bob, the Commies want some food," one shouted.

"Let the creeps starve," another said angrily. "God damn 'em, I never got no education, and they git one handed to 'em and all they do is start riots."

The taunts and insults continued intermittently through the night. Slowly, the guards began to take on individual aspects. The Negro was bitter that he had no education. The Southerner had been in Vietnam and blamed students and demonstrators for the death of his buddies there. A third, an older man, wandered among the women making dirty remarks.

The fog swept in around eleven and the night became damp and piercing cold. Brenda shivered and bit her lips to keep from crying.

"We're freezing," one girl complained.

"I gotta nice warm bed at home, honey," the older guard said. "How'd ya like to come there?"

"They ought to put all these liberal Communists in concentration camps," the Southerner said. "They don't belong in America."

At midnight, the guards changed, and the women were allowed to stand and walk around. Later they were taken inside, into a large bare room with wooden benches, and given paper cups of black coffee. They sat on the benches, under a bare electric light, unable to sleep, through the night, until finally they saw the first glow of dawn through the barred windows. By then they were too tired for questions or demands, and the guards were too bored to taunt them.

Just before dawn, the red-haired girl began to sob. Another girl comforted her.

"They're trying to break us, Lou. Don't let them break you."

The red-haired girl wiped at her eyes. "I was in jail for thirty days last Christmas," she whimpered. "I don't think I can do it again. I don't think I can."

They were given another cup of coffee at 5 A.M., and two clerks arrived and began to take their names. That seemed a sign of progress, and their spirits rose a little. Brenda winked at Cathy.

Cathy gave her a smile and continued to watch the scene around her with narrowed eyes. She had survived the night without complaint. She was tired and cold, but she observed her captors with the sweet hatred of one who is certain of revenge. From the moment she had seen the first police, something had changed inside her, the girlishness of lunch was gone, the tipsiness too, and she became her cool professional self. Her eyes saw every face and movement, her ears heard every curse and threat, and through the long cold night she recited them in her mind until each detail was etched on her memory. She knew now in the first soft light of dawn that it was all there—the story of the decade had dropped into her lap. When finally a fat deputy announced that they would each be allowed a phone call, a faint smile lit Cathy's face, and visions of a Pulitzer danced through her head.

4

Dave's day did not begin well. Ever since Billy Doyle's visit to him and the Congressman's charges that he was making deals with black militants, he had been waiting for that other shoe to drop. Now it had dropped twice in two days.

The day before, he had seen the new issue of *The Reformer*, a leftwing weekly with a circulation of a hundred thousand. Its "Washington Notes," written by a man named Thomas Swann, led with this item:

"Word has leaked that Davey Hyer, the Newfield administration's Little Mary Sunshine, was on the scene when the CIA captured revolutionary hero Alberto Rivera in Caravelas. Just what Davey Boy was doing there, so far from his home in the segregated Virginia suburbs, isn't clear, but indications are he was sent to make sure the CIA didn't bungle the job. If that's true, or anything like that, we need to know more about this slick-talking young 'liberal' and his role in the administration's vicious counterrevolutionary policy. It should be noted, too, that Hyer was present when FBI undercover agents fired upon peaceful participants in the Free Rivera March earlier this month. The evidence indicates that Hyer, this so-called 'liberal,' is in fact the administration's ace hatchet-man."

Dave had almost laughed. It was such a monstrous lie that it defied rebuttal. Swann had sought an appointment with him a couple of weeks earlier and Dave, after checking with O.B., had turned him down. "He's a radical rat," O.B. had said. "Don't waste your time with him." Now Dave wondered if he might have done better to talk to Swann, and he wondered too if O.B. had deliberately given him bad advice. There was no way to know. Dave was bothered by the sharply personal tone of the attack, by the sense that this Thomas Swann hated him with the intensity that radicals often reserved for liberals. Dave learned that Swann, in the year he had been writing for *The Reformer*, had pulled so many hatchet-jobs like this that few people paid attention to him. Yet Dave knew too that people in Washington believed what they wanted to believe.

Now, on Saturday morning, he was greeted with an even more serious item in the Evans-Novak column. "David Hyer," it said, "President Newfield's bright, New Leftish speechwriter and troubleshooter, is caught in a mounting crossfire of criticism. Conservatives are angry at reports that Hyer has been dealing with black militants to shape the New Cities along separatist lines, while liberals are miffed at Hyer's alleged role in the recent shoot-out between police and radical marchers in the Nation's Capital."

Dave hadn't been aware that he'd been caught in any cross-fire of criticism—but he would be now. He knew that Novak and O.B. were old friends, and he guessed that O.B. had planted this one. Good old O.B.

He was mulling over these attacks as he sipped his breakfast coffee, wondering what he might do to offset them, when the phone rang.

"I'll get it," he told Eleanor, and walked to his study.

"Long distance collect to Mr. David Hyer from Miss Catherine Quinn in San Francisco," a metallic voice said. "Will you accept?"

"Yes," Dave said, and shut the door of the study.

"Dave, listen close," Cathy said, her voice low and deliberate. "I'm calling from the county prison farm in San Francisco. I got arrested yesterday by mistake when police grabbed everybody in sight after a demonstration at the S. F. State campus. I've been in jail all night and now they're letting us out on $500 bond."

"You need money?" Dave asked. He was annoyed that she'd called him at home, but he found the picture of Cathy in jail all night rather amusing.

"Listen," she said. "That's not all." Her voice lowered. "B. is with me."

"Bea? Who's Bea?"

"The Lady. The Sheriff's Girl."

"What?"

"Yeah, that's right . . ."

"Are you playing games?" he asked sharply.

"God damn you, listen. It's Miss Jackson."

"The maiden name?" he asked.

"That's right."

"Why didn't she tell them who she was?" he demanded.

"It happened too fast," Cathy said. "Then she was afraid."

"And nobody's recognized her?"

"That's right," Cathy said. "Now will you do something?"

"Yeah," he said quickly. "Just keep her quiet. I'll have somebody there inside an hour."

Who? That was the next question. There was not time for someone to fly out from Washington. Who did they have in San Francisco that they could trust to handle this mission and to keep the secret thereafter? When it came to a showdown, a President has precious few people he can trust—which is why the Eddie Gooches of the world endure.

Dave called the President. As he dialed he was angry and shaken, angry at the California police and fearful of the possible consequences of this thing, yet he felt too a certain grim satisfaction that at least someone else was having some problems for a change.

The President cursed only once when he heard the story, then he was all business.

"We've got to get them out of there fast," he said. "Who have we got? What about that bald-headed judge? Happman?"

"He'd cause too much attention," Dave said. "Any of the party leaders would. I'm thinking about a lawyer named Finney who worked on the campaign. A young guy. You remember him?"

"No."

"Well, I trust him. He may be our best bet. We haven't got many friends out there."

"You're betting your ass on him, kid."

"I think he's okay," Dave said.

"Okay," the President said. "Call him. Tell him to get moving."

"Right."

"And look," Barney continued. "Get a plane to the nearest airport. Tell Finney to get them aboard it fast. I don't want them to talk to anybody. I don't want that Cathy kid within a mile of a telephone. You think she's already called her office?"

"I don't think she'd call from there," Dave said.

"Well, bring her ass straight here," Barney snapped. "We've got to have a talk with her!"

By the time Finney called to say he had bailed the two women out uneventfully, Dave had spoken to Brenda's mother. When Brenda had not come in that night, her mother had said nothing to the Secret Service—in earlier years Brenda had spent her share of nights out, and her mother thought it wisest not to sound any alarms. Dave invented a story to explain to the Secret Service why Brenda had slipped back to Washington, and another to appease the Northern California Daughters of Calliope. Then he and the President and O. B. Perkins met in the President's office to wait for the two women.

"What the hell was she doing out loose with that girl reporter?" Barney demanded.

"I don't know," Dave said.

"She's *your* pal, ain't she?" Barney said.

"I know her," Dave replied, fearing that in the President's mind he was bearing some of the blame for this episode.

Brenda and Cathy arrived at the White House in early afternoon.

Barney rose and greeted Brenda with a kiss—this for Cathy's benefit.

"You go up and get some rest, honey," he told her. "You take yourself a nice long nap."

Brenda smiled weakly and left the room. The President turned to Cathy.

"Sit down, little lady," he said. "You know Dave and O.B., don't you?"

Cathy nodded suspiciously.

"How about some soup?" Barney said. "Or maybe a drink?"

"No thanks," Cathy said. "We ate on the plane."

"Cathy, I'm mighty upset by this thing," the President said, "and I wish you'd tell me just what happened."

"There's not much to tell," Cathy said, and outlined the episode.

"That's awful," Barney exclaimed when she finished. "That's the kind of thing we're trying to stop."

"It's bad," Cathy agreed.

"If this had to happen," Barney said, "it's a good thing you were there. I don't know what she'd of done without you."

"Yeah," Cathy said.

"You sure you don't want to go upstairs and take a nap?" he asked.

Cathy shook her head, never taking her eyes from his face. "I've got to get back to my office," she said.

"To your office?" Barney said. "You better go home and get some rest."

Dave listened resignedly. This game was called Barney Plays Dumb.

"I've got a story to write," Cathy said impatiently. "So if you'll excuse me . . ."

"A story?" Barney asked. "What story?"

"A story about what happened last night," she cried in exasperation.

"About you being arrested?" Barney suggested.

"About me and your wife being arrested," she said. "About what those dirty bastards do to people."

The President's mouth fell open. "You mean you'd do that to Brenda?" he asked incredulously.

"I'm not doing anything to her," Cathy snapped. "Those animals out there have already done it. I'm just reporting what happened."

O. B. Perkins jerked his thumb at Cathy. "Wasn't everything between you and her off the record?" he asked.

"When we were eating lunch it was," Cathy said. "But not after we got arrested. That's public property."

"Cathy," the President said, "have you thought what your story would do to Brenda?"

"I don't think it'd do anything to her, Mr. President," the girl said. "She didn't do anything wrong. She was an innocent victim. Look, you say you want to stop this police-state stuff. Well, so do I. And this story will help. It'll show what the cops are doing to people. I think it makes your wife look pretty darn brave."

"Cathy," O.B. said in his gentlest voice, "that's not how it'd come out. People are always looking to think the worst about a pretty woman like Brenda. Most people would see everything the worst way they could. They'd say why did she slip away from the Secret Service? And how much had she had to drink? And what was she doing down there with the hippies? And what did the cops do to her all night? And why didn't she say who she was? And a dozen other things. It's like if a woman's been raped, Cathy. It isn't her fault, but people still smirk at her and think maybe she asked for it."

Cathy shook her head. "That's not how I'd write it," she insisted. "And I can't help it if people have dirty minds."

"But you can help it about this story," the President said. "Cathy, you may not know it, but Brenda's pretty high-strung. Sometimes she drinks more than's good for her. If this thing gets out, it may hit her pretty hard."

"Look, Mr. President, I can't help that," Cathy declared. "I'm sorry this happened. But it's a hell of a story and it's my job to write it."

"Why don't you just write it about yourself and leave her out of it?" O.B. asked.

"Then it's no story," Cathy said.

"You want that Pulitzer pretty bad, don't you?" O.B. snapped.

"As bad as you wanted yours, mister," Cathy snapped back at him.

"I know some people on the Pulitzer Advisory Board," O.B. said, "and I don't think . . ."

"Well, now, you're a young girl and you're gonna win lots of prizes," Barney injected smoothly. He and O.B. were slipping into the Mutt and Jeff routine—O.B. playing the heavy and Barney the good guy.

"You and me disagree on how much trouble this story would cause," Barney said, "but I've been in politics longer than you, so let's pretend I'm right."

"Then I'm sorry," she said, "but I'm not in politics and I've still got to write my story."

"Why?" Barney asked softly. "Why do you have to write it?"

Cathy leaned forward, weary and deeply serious. "Because in my business the worst thing you can do is to start writing what the politicians want you to write, even a President. Because if you prostitute yourself once, you'll be a whore the rest of your life, like old Billy Doyle and all those stupid columnists. I'm sorry if anything I do hurts Brenda, but it'd hurt me worse if I sold out now."

"Nobody's talking about you selling out," the President said. "We're talking about using some judgment, some restraint. We're talking about you looking at the big picture instead of just a piece of it."

"What big picture?" Cathy asked.

"This country, Cathy. What happens in this country. Listen, you're too young to remember, but it hurt Kennedy when there was all those stories about people pushing each other in swimming pools. And it hurt Lyndon when they wrote about him tooling around the ranch with a beer in his hand. And it's gonna hurt me if people think my wife slipped away from the Secret Service and went down to some riot and got arrested with a bunch of hippies."

"Mr. President," Cathy said wearily. "They were just ordinary Americans and the cops came up and . . ."

"Okay, Cathy," he said, "but I'm talking about what people would think. And I don't mean it'd hurt me, Barney Newfield. To hell with me. I mean it'd hurt the administration. Hurt those bills we're trying to pass, the things we're trying to do for people."

"I can't think about those things, Mr. President," she said. Dave caught the first note of uncertainty in her voice. "I just tell what happened."

"You've got to think about those things," O.B. injected. "This ain't Podunk you're covering now, it's the United States of America, and you've got some responsibility for what you write."

"To make it true," Cathy said.

"To make it responsible," O.B. pressed. "To think what it does."

"No," Cathy insisted. "To make it true and not to speculate on who it does what to. That's when I stop being a reporter and become a politician."

"Oh, crap," O.B. said sharply. "You think you can shut your eyes and win your prizes and screw what it does to the elections and to the administration? Just so the little girl gets her glory—is that it?"

"Listen, mister," she replied, "don't you lecture me. You're just another press agent as far as I'm concerned."

"Yeah?" O.B. said. "Well I'm trying to help this country in my job. What about you?"

"Mr. President," Cathy said, "there's no use going on with this . . ."

"Let me ask you something else," O.B. persisted. "You covered the police beat up in Boston, didn't you?"

"Yeah," Cathy said sullenly.

"Yeah, and you know how to talk to cops," O.B. said. "So why didn't you get Brenda out of this mess when the cops first showed up?"

"I told you, it happened too fast," Cathy declared.

"Oh, bullshit!" O.B. roared. "You could have got her out before you got onto the bus or after you got off the bus or anytime during the night. All you had to do was wave your press card."

"She didn't want to take any chances," Cathy said.

"You could have said she was your sister and they'd have waltzed you both out the door," O.B. said.

"That wasn't my job," Cathy said. "I told her to do what was right for her and I'd do what was right for me."

"In other words," O.B. pressed, "you let her get crucified while you sat there licking your chops about your big story."

Cathy stood up and shook her fist at him. "I don't have to take that from you!" she shouted.

O.B. rose and faced her. "Yeah?" he declared. "Then tell me you couldn't have got her out of it, if you'd wanted to, before you ever got on that bus."

Cathy sank back down and shut her eyes.

"Jesus Christ," O.B. continued. "Brenda thought you were her friend. And the first chance you get, you stab her in the back. You talk about prostituting yourself. What kind of whoring is that?"

Cathy began to sob. "God damn you, leave me alone," she said.

Barney was watching her coolly. Now it was his turn again.

"O.B.," he said quietly, "why don't you go out and see that Finney fellow while me and Dave talk to Cathy?"

When the press secretary had gone, the President said, "Cathy, if O.B. gets a little riled up, it's just because he's loyal to me. He knows you want to do what's right. This isn't easy on any of us. I've got to think about Brenda and about the elections too."

"And I've got to think about my story," Cathy said, beginning to regain control of herself.

"Okay, let's talk about your story," he said. "You know what I want—I want you to leave Brenda out of it. If you do, you lose your big scoop and a lot of publicity. Okay, I understand that. But there are other stories, Cathy. Me and Dave and O.B. can get you an awful lot of stories."

"I don't need any help getting stories," she said sullenly.

"Don't you?" the President asked. "I thought Dave here had been giving you a little help lately. It never hurts to have somebody open the doors for you."

"I'm not making any deals," she said.

"Sure you're not," Barney said. "I'm just telling you that we help people who help us. You know, Cathy, I'm afraid O.B.'s right—people are gonna wonder why you didn't help Brenda out. It might even look to some people like you took her down there hoping something like this might happen."

"That's not true," Cathy said. Or was it? She knew that as they had walked to the restaurant she had thought of taking Brenda onto the campus, thought there might be a story in her reaction to the demonstrations.

"Your father's a longshoreman up in Boston, isn't he?" Barney asked. "About to retire, I hear."

Cathy nodded wearily.

"I was talking to the head of the longshoremen up there," Barney said. "They've got a spot open for a vice-president. Pays pretty good. How much was it, Dave?"

"Twenty-five thousand," Dave said, and Cathy looked at him for the first time that afternoon. She did not seem to recognize him.

"A good job for a fellow who's worked hard all his life," Barney said.

"I don't care if you make the old fool ambassador to Spain," Cathy said. "It's nothing to me."

"Might make things a lot easier for your mother," Barney said.

Cathy sat up straight in her chair, her eyes bright with anger and frustration.

"If you're gonna buy me off," she said, "you're gonna have to do better than that."

"Nobody's buying you off," Barney said. "We're just trying to figure what's best for all of us. Listen, Cathy, there's a big story coming up that I'm gonna tell you about in confidence. Leon Kerkelot's been negotiating with the Chinese, all top-secret, for six months. We're about to make a deal with them."

He paused and the girl looked at him sharply. "What kind of a deal?" she asked.

"Diplomatic relations," he said. "Trade, cultural exchanges, the whole works."

"What about Taiwan?" she asked.

"Leon's got a twenty-year plan where it gets neutralized," Barney said.

"When's all this happen?" she pressed.

Barney shrugged. "Couple of months, maybe. After the elections, so they don't say it's political. Look, I want you to have this story. Exclusive, as soon as we can let it go. You want a Pulitzer? There it is."

"You mean a leak?" she asked. "Or an interview?"

"An exclusive interview."

"No prior leaks?" she asked. "The whole thing for me?"

"That's right," he said. "What do you say?"

"I want the job for my old man too," she said. "And I want other stories, plenty of them."

"You'll get them," Barney promised.

"Okay," she whispered, her face suddenly lined and old. "Okay."

She stood up and stared at Barney as if she'd only seen him for the first time. "God damn you," she said finally, then she walked quickly out. The President watched her go, and his face, too, was weary.

Dave followed Cathy out and caught up with her in the hallway. "You did the right thing," he told her, not sure if he meant it or not.

She turned on him furiously, her eyes wet and glowing. "I hope I never see you again," she said, and ran awkwardly down the corridor and out the door into the lobby.

Dave shrugged and walked back to the President's office. O.B. had returned. "I've got a couple of good stories to give her," he was saying.

"Yeah, give her something fast before she changes her mind," Barney said.

"I didn't know Leon had reached an agreement with the Chinese," Dave said.

"He hasn't yet," Barney admitted. "We may have to now."

Dave laughed helplessly. The President stood up and stretched. "I like her," he said. "She's a tough little cookie. For a while there, I didn't think she'd crack."

Brenda called that night, just before he left his office.

"I'm not interrupting anything, am I?" she asked uncertainly.

"Of course not, Brenda. How are you?"

"Oh, I'm okay I guess. A little stiff is all. It's *him* I'm calling about."

"What about him?"

"Dave, listen, he's so mad at me now he won't talk to me, but somebody's got to tell him how it is out there."

"What do you mean?"

"Dave, it's like . . . like Hitler or something. The way they're treating people. Can they do that in America?"

"Yeah," he said. "They can."

"He's got to do something to stop them, Dave," she said. She started crying. "You've got to talk to him, make him do something."

"I'll try to," he said. "And you talk to him, too, Brenda. We've all got to talk to him, all we can."

5

The weekend in New York promised to be a pleasant interlude in the campaign, if not exactly the interlude that Dave and Leon Kerkelot had hoped for.

They had for a month been trying to persuade the President to deliver a major "peace speech" at the UN. Leon stressed the impact the speech might have on world opinion, and Dave reminded the President of the public acclaim for Eisenhower's great peace speech in 1953 and Kennedy's at American University ten years later. But Barney would not be persuaded; he read the national mood differently and accepted Charlton MacKenzie's counsel that a peace speech would be seen as softness toward the Communists and thus would backfire politically.

But it was necessary for the President to deliver some speech in New York City, so at MacKenzie's urging he accepted an invitation to address a dinner meeting of the National Executive Council in mid-October. His topic would not be peace, but fiscal integrity, and Dave wrote the speech without joy—"A classic piece of sanctimonious crap," he confided to his wife on the night he finished it.

The dinner was on Sunday evening, and the President and his entourage flew up Saturday noon and checked into the Plaza. Dave hurried across town for a late lunch with the ad executives who were handling the party's television campaign. Some last-minute changes had been ordered by the President, mainly involving fewer black faces and more praise for law-enforcement agencies. When one of the younger ad men objected, Dave cut him off impatiently. "Can't you see the difference between shadow and substance?" he demanded, with more conviction than he felt.

After the meeting he returned to the hotel. The President, for security reasons, had the entire fourteenth floor, with a majestic suite overlooking Central Park, and the rest of them had suites on the floor below. It was a lovely autumn afternoon, with cool air blowing in off the park. Dave wished he had time to take a walk. Instead, he hurried to the President's suite to report on his session with the ad men.

Barney was lounging in a gold and white Louis XVI chair, drinking a Bass Ale and talking to Eddie Gooch. Barney was in a good mood, and for good reason. His meeting that evening with a dozen Democratic leaders would break up at eleven, at which time, a dozen blocks away, Miss Agnes Cummings, twenty-four, the lovely and much-acclaimed star of *Sigmund*, a new musical based on the life of Freud, would slip out the stage door, enter a waiting car, don dark glasses, and be driven by Eddie Gooch to the Plaza, where she would ascend via a service elevator to the President's suite. In the morning, Eddie would drive her back to her apartment in the Village. This procedure had been followed several times in several places since the President had met Miss Cummings when she sang at a White House dinner two months earlier.

Brenda had not come to New York. Barney was still furious with her about the San Francisco episode, even though the secret seemed safe. Brenda had been drinking heavily, and earlier that week Dave had nursed her through the final stages of one binge, an episode that left him shaken and depressed.

He had a beer and briefed the President on the meeting with the ad men, and also on the backgrounds of the officers of the Executive Council. Eddie Gooch listened, guzzling his beer and belching occasionally, and Dave left as soon as he could. In the weeks since Eddie's trouble, they'd had little to say to one another, and Eddie's unconcealed hostility got on his nerves.

"Do you want me to come to that meeting tonight?" he asked the President as he was leaving.

Barney shook his head. "Just a bunch of dirty old politicians," he said. "Go see a show or get laid or something."

Dave was annoyed at being left out, but there was nothing to be done about it. Barney had been cool to him ever since Hailey's march had become a riot, but the work on the campaign speeches seemed to be bringing them back together, and if the elections went well he thought everything might be all right.

The Oak Bar was cool and quiet in the late afternoon. Dave arrived ten minutes early and took a seat beside the row of windows overlooking Fifty-ninth Street and the park. He ordered a drink and, as his eyes adjusted to the dimness, looked around the room. Two men were sitting at the bar, and a young couple was huddled together at a table near the door. The bartender, elegant in his gold jacket, was polishing glasses, and the three waiters were putting bowls of peanuts and dark green bottles of mineral water on the tables. It was a pleasant bar, and he thought for a moment of the places he'd really enjoyed drinking in his life. He thought of Van's Place, a big noisy tavern a mile from Priest Lake, in northern Idaho, where he'd gone on Saturday nights the summers he worked for the Forest Service, gone to drink icy Lucky Logger beer, to pick up nurses from Spokane, to whoop with drunken pleasure at midnight when the string band played *Won't You Come Home, Bill Bailey?* and *Squaws Along the Yukon.* A good place, and two good summers. He thought too of Clara's, the old stone Clarmont Restaurant at the edge of the mountain in Monteagle, Tennessee, where they'd go when he was in college, to sit out under the dogwoods on spring afternoons, drinking Budweiser and arguing about Yeats and Eliot. And he thought of Louie's Place in Austin, a crowded tavern where he'd spent his afternoons during his summer term at the University of Texas law school, drinking Lone Star with Pi Phis and Thetas and listening to Brubeck on the juke box. It seemed incredible that less than ten years had passed since then.

Jack Frazier, tall and elegantly attired, paused and blinked his eyes as he entered the bar. Dave waved, and Frazier strode across the room to join him. Dave didn't know why Frazier wanted to talk to him, but Frazier was someone he was always glad to see. He had been an Assistant Secretary of Commerce under Kennedy, and in the first Johnson year, and then he had returned to New York to become a partner in a law firm. Dave had called him in to help write the tax-reform bill, and they kept in touch by phone. Frazier was a shrewd and sophisticated man, from an old Boston banking family, and Dave admired him.

"Look, Dave, I won't beat around the bush," Frazier said in his clipped, nasal Boston accent, after a minute of smalltalk. "We've got three times the work we can handle. We've got to expand the firm. What we need most are men who understand Washington."

"We need those too," Dave said.

"We can pay more," Frazier said. "Look, what I'm saying is that when you're ready to make a move, I wish you'd give us a chance to make you an offer."

Dave didn't answer. His problems were too much of the present to have allowed him much thought of the future.

"What's your plan?" Frazier pressed. "How long are you signed on for?"

"I don't know, Jack," Dave admitted. "I'm obligated at least through the presidential election. I don't know about after that."

"After that you'll be worn to a nub," the older man said. "I know that job. Nobody can take that pressure more than three or four years. Maybe less."

Dave laughed silently. Maybe less.

"You don't think you might leave before the election?" Frazier asked.

Dave studied the lawyer's craggy, confident face. Were there rumors circulating about him and Barney? He wished he knew, but he didn't know Frazier well enough to ask.

"Anything can happen, Jack. The finances are tough and the home life is impossible. But I've got no plans to leave."

"What are you guys paid now?"

"Thirty-five."

"God, that's a crime. We could start you as a partner at seventy-five or eighty, and you'd be over a hundred soon."

"If I do practice law when I leave, it's going to be real law. I could make a fast bundle by trading on my contacts, but that won't pay off in the long run."

"I couldn't agree more," Frazier said emphatically. "You know our firm, Dave. That won't be a problem."

"No, I don't guess it would be the problem."

"What is the problem, Dave?"

Dave shook his head. "I guess just letting go. You know the story. This job is ruining my health and my finances and my marriage, and I can't imagine being anywhere else."

Frazier nodded. "Yeah," he said. "The withdrawal pains are rough."

"Don't you ever miss it?"

Frazier frowned at the thought. "I did for six months or so," he said. "But, you know, when I went back one day I found a guy in my old office doing my job and getting my ulcers, and I decided they could manage it without me."

"But could you manage without them?" Dave asked.

"I manage damn well. I play tennis twice a week, and take the kids for a bike ride on Sundays, and eat in good restaurants two or three nights a week, and spend a month at the beach in the summer. Listen, I like living a normal life."

Dave nodded, but he was thinking of the New Cities and the minimum-wage bill and the draft-reform bill and the struggle in Caravelas.

"I know what you're thinking," Frazier said. "About all that power and all those big things you want to do, and how up here you'd just be another Wall Street lawyer. Right?"

"Yeah."

The lawyer sighed. "What can I say? You've been in about a year, right? Well, I remember in '61, I felt the same way. We'd won the election and we were the best people with the best intentions and we were going to shape up this country. Oh, God, did it all look easy. New Frontiers. So I went in like a pistol and busted my ass for two years and one day my wife said she was going to divorce me. So I quit. And you know, they got along without me fine. And I got along without them."

Dave stared at the shiny black tabletop. The waiter brought them a bowl of pretzels. Frazier finished his daiquiri.

"All I'm saying, Dave, is that at some point in time you cross a line and you say, 'I can't save the world; I'd better save myself.'"

"I know it," Dave said. "I just haven't crossed that line. Maybe I see it up ahead, but I'm not there yet."

"When you do, let me know," Frazier said, rising abruptly.

"I will," Dave promised. They shook hands and the lawyer left.

It was six and Dave realized he had nothing to do for the evening. He walked down to Sardi's and drank two beers and had the Veal Cutlet Catledge for dinner. No one he knew came in. As he was having coffee, he overheard Vincent Sardi saying to a man at the next table: "What happened to Pete? I'll tell you what happened to Pete. He had his hand in the till, which is a weakness among bartenders, practically a tradition, but he was very popular with the waiters. Then he made his mistake. He dipped into the tip fund, and that lost him his support and I canned him. I hear he's working somewhere in the Village now."

After dinner, Dave tried a couple of boxoffices, and got a ticket to one of the season's top musicals, but it seemed pointless and somehow wasteful, and after twenty minutes he walked out. He went to the Algonquin for a drink, but seeing the young couples there only increased his loneliness and, knowing nothing else to do, he walked back to the Plaza, bought some magazines, and was in his room by eleven. After a while, it occurred to him that the President was probably already enjoying the favors of Agnes Cummings, just overhead, and that only increased his restlessness. But Eleanor was coming up the next morning, and it would be a busy day, and so he soon cut off the light and went to sleep, finding some consolation in the thought that at least it had been a sane, sober, problem-free evening.

Eleanor arrived the next morning for a brief holiday. Her visit was a celebration, a treat they were allowing themselves because the Secret Service had solved the mystery of the shotgun blast through their neighbor's window and had removed the agents who'd been guarding their house.

The agents had been as unobtrusive as Rouzer had promised. Eleanor was never sure who or where they were—and she scrutinized each passing postman, repairman, and pedestrian closely—but if she backed her car out of the driveway, a black sedan would fall in behind her and stay close until she returned home. She seemed secure, and yet the thought of snipers and bombers, once planted in her mind, rubbed her nerves raw. Dave, knowing this, made arrangements to come home by eight or so each night, so they could have a drink and dinner together before he retired to his study for his nightly bout of speech-writing. For a time, the frictions between them vanished; he felt a protectiveness toward her and a sadness that he had brought this new pain into her life. The first night, he tucked her in bed and kissed her before returning to his study, and every night after that she sat in his study reading until he was ready to come to bed.

The ordeal ended with a call from Rouzer on a Wednesday morning.

"It's all over, Mr. Hyer," he announced.

"What happened?"

"Well, seems it never was you they was shootin' at," Rouzer said. "It was that fellow, Page, next door. The long and short of it is, Page had him a lady friend and the lady friend had a husband and it was the husband who done the shootin'. Page just thought he'd blame it on you, you bein' a politician and all."

"That dirty son of a bitch."

"It was a nasty trick," Rouzer agreed. "Specially the way it scared Miz Hyer."

"I'm going to get that bastard."

"Well, now, Mr. Hyer, Ah thought about that, but all you could get him for, legally, is givin' false information to the po-lice, and that might be hard to prove."

"Yeah," Dave said.

"But Ah had a talk with your po-lice chief out there," Rouzer continued, "and Ah think that fellow Page is likely gonna move somewhere else pretty soon."

"You've done a hell of a job on this," Dave said. He meant it; the next day he put a glowing letter in Rouzer's file.

"Glad to be of service," Rouzer said.

When he told Eleanor the news that night, she laughed until her laughter turned to tears. He stroked her hair. "Sweet Ellie," he said. "My brave soldier."

"That awful little man Page," she said, starting to laugh again.

"With a jealous husband shooting at him. Do you know he tried to talk fresh to me one time, at the drugstore?"

"I ought to shoot that bastard."

Eleanor looked at him, her eyes sparkling with tears, and put her face close to his. "No," she said. "You ought to thank him. This is the best week we've had all year."

Now, Sunday noon, they went down for breakfast in the Palm Court. Eleanor looked grand—her smile radiant, her hair a richer gold than the October leaves—and Dave felt the old pride as the maitre d' led them to a table and he saw men staring at her.

"Eleanor?" a woman said.

They paused and Ellie blinked at a dumpy woman who was sitting with a small, bald man.

"Eleanor?" the woman repeated uncertainly. "You wouldn't remember me, but . . ."

"Of course I remember you, Madeline," Eleanor said warmly, taking the woman's hand. "How could I forget after those two months in Montana?"

She introduced Dave, who nodded at the woman and her husband. "Madeline was the most wonderful make-up artist M-G-M ever had," she explained. "How's your son?"

"Oh, he's almost through medical school," the woman said. "Do I hear you've made a new picture?"

"And I may do another," Eleanor said happily.

"Oh, you should," the woman exclaimed. "You've got too much talent not to use it."

Eleanor gave the woman a hug and they went on to their table.

"You ought to be the politician," he said.

"She was a damn good make-up woman," Eleanor said. "When she was sober."

He ordered two Bloody Marys and glanced contentedly around the Palm Court. Within its bright circle of palms and mirrors, around its small, marble-topped tables with their pale pink tablecloths, two hundred of his affluent countrymen were enjoying two-dollar drinks and five-dollar breakfasts, and the sound of their laughter and the clink of their silver became a low, happy hum that relaxed and pleased him, like the sound of surf or of birds at dawn. He loved this place; it was a sign of weakness, but he loved it.

A couple across the room had their daughter, a girl of six or so, with them, and he wished Sally was there. He wanted her to grow up knowing places like this.

"What are you smiling at?" Eleanor asked.

"That little girl over there. I wish Sally was here."

Eleanor frowned—bringing her daughter to New York was not her idea of a holiday. Dave told her about Jack Frazier's offer.

"Are you interested?" she asked.

"It's a good law firm," he said. "I could make a lot of money."

"Would we have to live in Manhattan?"

"We could live anywhere we wanted to," he told her. "Do you think you'd be happy up here?"

"Dave, I'd be happy almost anywhere if you'd make some time for me," she said.

A pianist and violinist began a lively if improbable rendition of *Seventy-six Trombones*. Dave ordered another Bloody Mary and they talked about Sally's progress in nursery school until breakfast came.

"Dave," she said, midway through the meal, "why is that man writing those things about you in *The Reformer?*"

"Where'd you see that?"

"Somebody mentioned it," she said, "and I read it at the newsstand."

"He's just a hack trying to make a name for himself."

"Can't you sue him?"

"No."

"I don't understand it," she said angrily. "Aren't you both liberals?"

"No, I'm a liberal and he's a radical."

"What's the difference?" she asked impatiently.

"Radicals are more pure in heart," he said.

"It's not funny," she cried. "You work so hard and all you get is this abuse. We could be so happy if you had some other job."

He reached out and touched her hand. "Don't worry about my critics," he told her. "I'm not."

They returned to their room and made love—how long, he wondered, since they'd made love in the afternoon?—and later they went up to the President's suite for a drink.

About a dozen people were there: Eddie, O.B., Leon, Mac-Kenzie, an editor from the *Times,* two senators and their wives, the president of the Business Executive Council. The President gave Eleanor a hug when she entered, and she moved easily among the men, accepting their attention as her due.

"Dave, did you hear about Congressman Whitelaw?" the senator from Tennessee asked.

"No sir, what?"

"Poor fellow had a stroke yesterday, down in Nashville," the senator said. "Don't look like he'll run again now."

"That's too bad," Dave said. "What happens if he steps down?"

"They have to hold a special election in thirty days," the senator told him. Dave wondered if he'd be hearing again from his friend Elton Carr.

It was a lazy, gorgeous afternoon, and they laughed and drank until the shadows of early evening began to fall across the red and orange foliage below them. Then it was time to change and drive across town to another hotel for the business executives' dinner.

The dinner proved not unpleasant. Dave and Eleanor sat at a table with four of the younger executives and their wives. The talk was friendly, the food and wine were excellent, and the President's speech was warmly received. Barney was a formidable figure in a tuxedo, and he delivered his promises of fiscal prudence with all the thundering sincerity he might, on another night, devote to the New Cities or to world peace. Dave, having written the speech, knew what a windy affair it was, but somehow Barney's delivery gave it an illusion of substance, and the businessmen rewarded him with a standing ovation when he finished. Magic, Dave thought, magic.

"Dave, we're all going for an after-dinner drink," one of his hosts said. "Will you and Eleanor join us?"

"Sure," he answered, warmed by the wine and the applause. "Fine."

They went to a private club on the fortieth floor of the Pan Am Building. A large, elegant room was reserved for them, and from its windows they could see a million lights burning beneath them, towers of light upon a field of light, racing toward the dark wall of the river.

The wives gathered at one end of the room and the men at the other, drinking brandy and smoking cigars. One of the young executives, a bright, confident fellow who'd been a Rhodes scholar, outlined a proposal for the government to give tax credits for job-training programs by industry. Dave asked polite questions, but he was not interested in the plan—he wanted government to train the unemployed, not industry. Later, they talked about the New Cities, the economy, and the coming elections in a careful, non-partisan way. Neither side wished on this occasion to offend the other, so when they reached the inevitable points of disagreement, they would side-step them with a joke, a shrug, or another drink. Dave was aware, and he knew his hosts were too, that they were among the small group of men who would be running America for the next thirty years, and whatever their philosophical differences it was wise to have lines of communication to the enemy camp.

Dave excused himself to go to the bathroom, and as he left their room he noticed a small bar directly across the hall. The room was empty except for the bartender, a husky young man in a white coat.

"Quite a view," Dave said.

"It is indeed, sir," the young man said.

"Could you fix me a Scotch and water, and put it on our bill across the hall?"

"You bet, sir. Cutty Sark?"

"That's fine," Dave said. "You work here regular?"

"Yes sir, two years now." He was a good-natured, rather stolid young man, and he poured the drink with style and precision.

"You like it?" Dave asked.

"They're very fine employers, sir, and we get a good many benefits. And you know, sir, I like bartending. I think of it as a skill, like pharmacy. You have to blend your ingredients just so."

"What do you drink yourself?" Dave asked.

The young man grinned. "Funny thing, sir, but I've never cared for drink. But I like to see other people enjoy themselves."

Dave smiled and picked up his glass. "Well, thanks for the medicine," he said, starting back to his party. "Good luck to you."

"The same to you, sir," the young bartender said.

Dave had almost finished a Scotch, and was thinking they should leave, when one of his hosts, the Rhodes scholar, said:

"Did you hear about that man Rivera, down in Latin America?"

"You mean that story in this morning's paper?" Dave said. "It's not true."

"Yes, I saw that," another man said, a short man with red hair "Something about a political deal."

"What happened," Dave explained, "was that the Republican National Chairman charged there was a deal to free Rivera after his trial. But it's a lie."

"No, no, I don't mean that story," the Rhodes scholar said. "I mean the report that just came on the radio."

"What report?" Dave asked.

"I understood them to say he'd been shot."

"Shot?" Dave asked. "Killed?"

"I believe so," the Rhodes said.

"Oh, I thought you meant the newspaper story," the redhead said.

"No, I just heard a radio bulletin," the Rhodes explained patiently. "The bartender's got a radio."

"You can't get away from these little transistors nowadays," the redhead complained.

"Our ingenious Japanese friends," the Rhodes said. "You know they've got one for four dollars now?"

"I'll bet they don't last," the one with the red hair predicted.

Dave excused himself and crossed to the bar.

"Do you have a radio?" he asked the bartender.

"Yes sir," the young man said. "Hope I haven't been playing it too loud, sir."

"No, no. I want to hear the news."

"Sure thing, sir, I been trying to get some ball scores myself."

He pulled the tiny radio from under the bar. He twisted the dial and they heard snatches of Sinatra, a sermon, a Geritol commercial, Mozart, another sermon, and Johnny Cash before a newscaster's somber voice said:

"According to Caravelian government sources, the legendary guerrilla leader was shot while trying to escape. He was said to have died instantly."

That was all. Dave moved to the end of the bar and stared down at the city lights. He had no particular feeling, except one of helplessness. One of the newscaster's phrases stuck in his mind. Trying to escape. He thought of it a moment. Wasn't almost everyone trying to escape, to something or from something? Trying to escape from the past, or the present, or the future? Rivera was one of the few men he'd ever met who wasn't trying to escape.

"I beg your pardon, sir," the young bartender said. "Would a drink help?"

"Maybe it would," Dave said. "What's your best Scotch?"

"The twenty-five-year-old Chivas is awfully good, sir."

"Then give me a double. My friends will pay for it."

The young man poured the drink. "There you are, sir."

"Thanks."

"If I may ask, sir, did you know this fellow they killed?"

"I'd met him," Dave said.

"Then I know how you must feel," the young man said sympathetically. "I remember how I felt when they shot Senator Kennedy. I felt like I'd lost somebody in my own family, even though I only met the senator once, when he came campaigning in my neighborhood. I shook his hand, right there on Queens Boulevard. He was a good man, Senator Kennedy was."

"Yes, he was," Dave said.

"Was this Rivera a good man?" the bartender asked.

"I think he was."

The bartender nodded his head. "It seems like it's only the good ones they kill," he said finally.

The last drink hit him on the ride back to the Plaza. By the time they got into bed his head was spinning. He put his hand on Eleanor's arm.

"Let's make love."

"We did this afternoon," she said. "I'm tired."

"Come on," he said impatiently, and pulled her toward him.

"You're drunk," she said. "Leave me alone."

He put his hand between her legs and after a moment she relaxed. "All right," she said. "Do it."

"You do that first," he told her.

"I don't want to."

"Damn you, do what I say." He grabbed her by the hair and pulled her to him until she did what he wanted, but only moments after she began he passed out, and she turned away from him and wept silently into the pillow.

When he awoke she was closing her suitcase. His head ached and scenes from the night before were coming back to him. She picked up the suitcase and started for the door.

"Where you going?" he asked, pulling himself upright in the bed.

"Home."

"Wait a minute," he said. "Let's have breakfast."

"No thanks."

"Then let's talk."

"About what? What a great lover you are?"

"I was drunk. I'm sorry."

"You've been drunk too much lately," she said.

He didn't answer. He'd been drinking too much for months. He'd blamed it on the campaign, told himself that whiskey was the fuel that kept him going.

"Don't tell me your excuses," she said. "I don't care if you drink yourself blind. But I won't have you getting rough with me when you do."

He shook his head miserably. "I'm sorry," he said again. She opened the door, then looked back at him.

"Why do you spoil things?" she asked gently. "You can be so nice, Dave."

Before he could answer she was gone.

6

Billy Doyle's column appeared on the Tuesday after their return from New York. He began by saying he wrote more in sorrow than in anger. It pained him, he said, to criticize a young man who shared many of his own liberal beliefs. Yet a strange sickness, he said, had spread among many of the liberals of the new generation. They saw only the worst in America. They rejected known cures for unknown experiments, preferred confrontation to conciliation. They developed strange, romantic fascinations for men like Guevara and Rivera, Roy Hailey and Malcolm X, who were, after all, little more than common criminals. They denied freedom of speech to great Americans like Hubert Humphrey, forgetting that men like Humphrey and Richard Daley and Lyndon Johnson had been fighting for liberal causes before they were born. In their innocent desire for "peace," they forgot the lessons of Munich, that appeasement can only bring disaster, be it in South Vietnam or in Caravelas.

When such views were limited to a few bearded misfits or black fanatics, Doyle wrote, they were of small importance. But he was writing this column because he had become painfully aware that a man who held many of these confused views was today sitting at the right hand of the President of the United States. He had known David Hyer for nearly five years, said the columnist, and had the highest admiration for his intelligence, his energy, his idealism. And yet, in recent months, he had heard increasing reports that David Hyer was afflicted with the New Left sickness. And in talks with Hyer, and with others high in the government, he had become convinced that the reports were true. It was known, for example, that Hyer had been present in Caravelas when Rivera was captured and had overstepped his authority to intervene on the prisoner's behalf.

It was reliably reported that Hyer had met secretly with extremist leaders Roy Hailey and Elijah King, and encouraged them to expect black control over the New Cities. And it could be said on the highest authority, Doyle added, that no such commitment was authorized by President Newfield.

A President must rely on many men, Doyle said, and it is good for him to have lines of communication to all segments of American thought. Yet a President, who holds vast and awesome powers, must be exceedingly careful not to share his power with men who are unprepared to wield it wisely. A dangerous trend in recent years was the concentration of power in the White House, often to the exclusion of the cabinet. Certainly such a policy would be unwise in an administration which possessed such experienced figures as Charlton MacKenzie, Warren Cutliff, and J. Wesley Smallwood. I cannot escape the belief, however painful, Doyle concluded, that President Newfield would do himself a favor—and perhaps do David Hyer a a favor—if he sharply curtailed the authority granted to his idealistic but ofttimes misguided young speechwriter.

The idealistic but ofttimes misguided speechwriter managed a grim smile as he read the column. Poor old Billy Doyle—how he had suffered through that one. Dave wondered about that "it can be said on the highest authority"—had Doyle talked to the President, or was O.B. talking for him? Dave took the flattering mention of Smallwood to mean the Attorney General had somehow assisted with the "background" for the column— that was usually the way it worked.

In a way, Dave was relieved to see the column. The other shoe had dropped, and dropped hard, but now it was done. It was bad, but there had been a lot of good columns and articles before it, and not even Billy Doyle could undo all that with one blast. Dave would either ride this out or not. Doyle, the semi-official spokesman of the American political establishment, had read him out of the ranks. There only remained to see whether the President would heed his advice or ignore it. For an instant (my New Left sickness, he thought) he was not sure he cared. Something had changed in him after

Rivera's death. After a year of giving all he had for Barney Newfield, he was tired, he felt moments of despair, he wondered if it was all worth it, or if it mattered. Yet he knew that, whether or not his work mattered, his reputation did. He had to survive—and as gracefully as possible. He did not want to give his enemies the satisfaction of seeing him defeated, or seeing him cringe under fire.

At the staff meeting that morning the President joked about it—"When you finish those speeches, Dave, your new assignment is emptying the wastebaskets"—and they all laughed, although he thought Eddie Gooch and O. B. Perkins were not so much laughing as smiling.

That was all. A few officials seemed that week not to return his calls so quickly as before, but that was probably his imagination. He knew people were gossiping, but he did his work as always, juggled appointments and phone calls, worked on speeches, and if his influence with the President was any less, he did not know it. Perhaps he was more restrained now, in his advice to the President, but he blamed that on the demands of the political campaign. Yet he wondered. He knew the old equation in government—you trim your sails to protect your "effectiveness," and in protecting it you lost it.

Friday morning was clear and lovely. The autumn air hinted of football games, girls in bright sweaters, hunting trips, burning leaves. As Dave rode to work the trees along the parkway were a brilliant red, gold, and orange. He marveled that in this glorious season millions of Americans could care which old men occupied some obscure offices on Capitol Hill. His job was to make them care, and he was not sure he cared any more. His intellect did, but his emotions were beginning to flag.

He had plenty to do that day. Barney was visiting a New City site in the morning, and returning to the White House to address a luncheon for the wives of administration officials. Dave would draft remarks for those two events, then continue work on the final campaign speech. One of the guests at the luncheon would be his wife; he had urged her to drop by his office beforehand, but she had been noncommittal. He and Eleanor had barely spoken since the New York trip; if she had seen the Doyle column she hadn't mentioned it. He didn't much care. His wife was one of several problems he had decided to put out of his mind until the elections were past.

Leon Kerkelot was frowning as he dropped into the chair beside Dave's desk. He ran a hand nervously through his hair.

"You're sure you have a minute?" he asked.

"Sure, Leon. The President's talking to the Democratic ladies and I'll talk to you. What's on your mind?"

"You know I'm having Dean de Villers from Cal Tech in to see the President today?" Leon asked.

"At five-thirty, if all goes well," Dave said.

"Yes. What I wondered, was if you know anything about the President's rather mercurial state of mind today. The Dean is primed for an eloquent cut-the-defense-budget plea, but I hate to waste it if the President is going to tune him out."

"No, today's a good day," Dave said. "He's pissed at the Air Force about those new cost overruns. And otherwise he's pretty happy because he lucked into an eagle on the fifteenth hole at Burning Tree yesterday."

Leon sighed and shook his head.

"Is your guy pretty sharp?" Dave asked.

"Very."

"Then why don't you suggest that if he just happened to mention the subject of golf—beautiful day for it, or something— it might warm the cockles of the President's heart?"

"I will," Leon agreed.

"Good," Dave said. "Now, what other problems can I solve for you?"

Leon frowned and gestured awkwardly. "Dave, what about all this nonsense I've been reading?"

"Just newspaper talk."

"Is there anything I can do?"

Dave thought a moment. "Here's an idea, Leon," he said finally. "You and Dean de Villers take a walk through Lafayette Park holding hands—that'll take their minds off me."

Leon's laugh was forced. "Another thing, Dave," he said.
"What?"

"This is difficult—do you remember that meeting of party
leaders in New York?"

"Sure."

"Apparently some of those men complained rather angrily
to the President about the role you've been playing."

"Like what?"

"Understand, Dave, I wasn't there. But I'm told there were
references to your trip to Caravelas. And also to your talks with
the blacks about the New Cities."

"The Billy Doyle bit," Dave said.

"Yes, but this was before Doyle's column."

"Three days before," Dave said. "Forgive my paranoia, Leon,
but I don't think the two events are unrelated. But go ahead:
What did the President say?"

"You know how he is—he didn't say anything. Just listened.
If he hasn't spoken to you about it, probably he intends to
ignore it. But I thought you should know."

"I appreciate it," Dave said. "Did you hear if they made any
specific demands—this-boy-must-go—or just bitched in general?"

"I didn't hear of any demands."

"That figures," Dave said. "They had Billy Doyle to make
their demands for them."

"It appears so," Leon said.

"The most interesting question, Leon, aside from the small
matter of my political future, is who's behind it. Anyone can
leak a column to Doyle, but very few people have the clout
to stir up three or four major party figures to complain to
the President about such a minor issue as me." Dave raised
his hand and solemnly pointed in the direction of Foggy Bottom.
"In fact, I'd say the finger of suspicion points at our distinguished Secretary of State, Mr. MacKenzie."

"I agree," Leon said. Dave wondered how much more Leon
might know, and where he'd gotten his information, but those
were not things for him to ask.

"And I would further say," Dave continued, almost enjoying
it, "that an alliance between Charlton MacKenzie and Billy

Doyle is altogether probable, since Billy Doyle considers Charlton MacKenzie the greatest American since Herbert Hoover—I mean, Hubert Humphrey. Forgive me, Leon, I'm getting delirious."

"Your sense of humor is remarkable."

"It is my rock and my foundation," Dave said gravely.

It was easy to joke with Leon, but when he was gone Dave thought hard. MacKenzie was a formidable adversary, one who wouldn't move unless he thought the time was right.

Dave decided he had to talk to Barney. If party leaders were shooting at his back, he deserved to know who and why. And if MacKenzie was behind it, let him come out into the open. The more he thought of it, the more his anger increased. He hadn't busted his ass for Barney Newfield for five years to be treated like this. He jumped to his feet and hurried down the hallway to the President's office.

He strode past the secretaries' desks, to the President's door; he tried it, as he always did, and found it locked, as it rarely was.

"He's got someone with him," Mrs. Purvis called.

"Who is it?" Dave asked.

"He may be a few minutes," the secretary said vaguely.

"I'll wait," he said impatiently.

Dave picked up an afternoon paper and leaned against the doorway. Just then, the President's door opened and Eleanor stepped out, her golden hair loose about her shoulders.

Her eyes widened when she saw him, then she smiled. "Hello," she said.

He looked at her in confusion, then he thought of the secretaries watching. "How was the luncheon?" he asked her.

"Fine," Eleanor replied. "Then the President brought some of us back and showed us the New Cities plans."

Dave nodded. He didn't see any other women around.

"Are you going in?" she asked.

"No," he said. "No. I'll walk you out."

They walked down the hall and through the lobby without speaking. Outside he turned and took her arm.

"What the hell is going on?" he demanded.

"What do you care?" she replied, then she shook free and walked briskly toward Pennsylvania Avenue.

David Hyer returned to his office in confusion. He was not even sure he wanted to know what Ellie had been doing in there. Yet could he help but know? He knew Barney. He knew Eleanor. He knew the locked-door game. He knew two and two but he was afraid of four. He had been ready to confront Barney over his political crisis, but he did not know how to deal with this. He could walk out and never come back, or he could pretend it had never happened, but he did not think he could talk about it. Barney always found your weak spot, always broke you one way or another.

Just then the President buzzed. Dave grabbed the phone. "Come in here," Barney commanded.

Dave walked slowly back to the President's office. He assumed this had to do with Eleanor, that Barney was forcing a showdown. But when he entered the office, he found Secretary MacKenzie and Attorney General Smallwood with the President.

"Sit down," Barney said briskly. "The Attorney General's just brought over the indictment of this Hailey character. Justice puts it out at noon tomorrow and I want you to rewrite my speech for tomorrow night. I want to say how it's these radicals like Hailey who're standing in the way of progress, and we're not gonna put up with it."

"How do you mean?" Dave asked. He was struggling to refocus his mind from his wife to this thing about Roy Hailey.

"There's a feeling, Dave," Charlton MacKenzie injected softly, "that the administration has not sufficiently dramatized its commitment to law enforcement. These indictments, plus a presidential statement, will make our position perfectly clear."

"What are the indictments for?" Dave asked.

"It's all in here," Smallwood said. He held up some papers and Dave went over and got them.

He skimmed the indictment. It charged Roy Hailey, Elijah King, and six others of conspiracy to riot in connection with the Free Rivera march. As Dave read the indictment, he felt the mood of the three older men, the anger, the indignation, the determination, and he knew this was a time to remain silent. Yet when he finished the indictment, and saw the smug smile on the Attorney General's face, he was struck again by the thought that Roy Hailey was a better American than J. Wesley Smallwood could ever dream of being.

"Two things bother me about this, Mr. President," he said. "First, it's a weak case because no one knows who started the shooting on Fourteenth Street. Second, there's the whole question of the constitutionality of the law."

"Mr. Hyer," Smallwood said indignantly, "can you really believe there's any question of who started the riot? These people wanted trouble and they got it. And now they're going to get some more."

"Dave," MacKenzie said, "your point about the constitutionality of the law is well taken. Eventually, the courts will settle that question. But in the meantime, this case will make the point we wish made, that this administration will not tolerate radical agitation that leads to riot."

"Say," the President injected, "aren't you the guy who told me we ought to isolate the radical leaders?"

"Yes sir," Dave said. "But I meant political isolation, not trying to send them to prison on trumped-up charges."

"I take strong exception to that remark," the Attorney General snapped. "Mr. President, I was under the impression that this matter was all settled and we were here to explain it to this speechwriter."

"It is settled," the President said. "Dave, I want a first draft tonight. Strong and quotable. Tell 'em we're not gonna stand for anarchy. From now on, the radicals are up Shit Creek without a paddle. You got it?"

Yeah, I've got it, Dave thought. It's called law 'n' order, and now you're running on it. And maybe we're all up that creek without a paddle.

But there was no use arguing further, not with MacKenzie and Smallwood there, so Dave rose. "Okay," he said, "I'll see what I can do."

Back in his office, he reread the indictment, then he put a sheet of paper in the typewriter. In his desk drawer, he found scribbled on a sheet of yellow paper a quotation from

Carl Sandburg that he'd meant to include in one of Barney's speeches. It said:

> *Across the bitter years and the howling winters*
> *The deathless dream will be the stronger*
> *The dream of equity will win.*

That was the kind of thing they'd used in other campaigns, but it would hardly fit in the speech at hand. He sat looking out his window at the radiant blue sky. A burst of wind sent showers of leaves twirling gently to the ground. It seemed to Dave that they had reached the end of something, all of them, he and Barney and the administration and the country. The thought saddened him, but he no longer believed he could do anything about it. He got up and walked to the President's office.

"Yeah? What is it?" Barney growled.

"This speech," Dave said. "I can't write it. Maybe O.B. can do it."

Barney's face showed his anger. "Look, kid," he began, "there's some things you and me better get straight."

"I agree," Dave said. "But the best way to get them straight is for me to give you my resignation."

Barney's mouth dropped open in surprise. Dave watched coolly, relaxed now—suddenly he felt good, as if a load had been lifted from him. He almost smiled; this was one of the few times he had ever seen Barney at a loss for words. People did not quit Barney Newfield—he quit people.

"You sure that's what you want to do?" Barney asked finally.

Dave noted that Barney raised no objections. Perhaps he was relieved. Perhaps he'd hoped for this. Dave would never know and he no longer cared.

"It's not just this speech," Dave said. "It's a lot of things. Mainly, it's time I got out and did something on my own."

"Like what?" Barney asked, a hint of scorn in his voice. Where did you go after you had worked for a President? It had to be downhill, and they both knew it.

"I've got some offers from law firms," Dave said. "I'll make up my mind this afternoon so O.B. can announce it at his four o'clock briefing."

"What's your hurry?"

"Leaving's painful," Dave said. "I'd just as soon get it over with. But I'll keep working until after the election, if you want me to."

Barney sidestepped. "You thinking about going down to Nashville and running in that special election?" he asked.

In truth, the idea was in Dave's mind, but he had not yet had time to think it through.

"I don't know," he said. "Possibly."

"I remember one time you said if you ever wanted to tell me to kiss your ass, you'd go run for Congress," Barney said. "That what you're telling me now?"

"No sir," Dave said. "Not at all."

Barney stared at him curiously.

"But I would like to say, as strongly as I can, that I think these indictments are wrong, and our military involvement in Caravelas is wrong, and whatever their short term advantages, they'll hurt you in the long run."

Barney's eyes narrowed. "If you feel so strong about it, why are you leaving?" he asked.

"I did what I could," Dave said. "It hasn't seemed to matter much."

"Let me tell you something," Barney said. "I know how you stand on things and who agrees with you. And I know what Smallwood thinks and who his people are. What I've got to do is build a program that can get both sides behind it. Nobody's gonna like it all, but they'll like enough of it to support me. The trouble with you liberals is, you want the whole pie, you don't want to share anything with anybody else. But that ain't how this country works."

"I understand that," Dave said. "But there are limits to what is acceptable, and men like the Attorney General will try to push you past those limits."

"Well it's not your worry any more," the President said. "You can go make yourself a pile of dough trading on the name I gave you."

"I think you got your money's worth," Dave shot back.

Barney broke into a grin. A great deal could be read into

his grin, more than Dave wished to consider. He stood up. He wanted to keep this on his own terms.

"I owe you a lot," he said evenly. "I'd never deny that."

Barney stood up too, his face cordial now, and came around from behind his desk. "Well, you did me a lot of good," he said. "Probably you're smart to get out on your own. Good luck."

He put his arm around Dave's shoulders and piloted him toward the door.

"Thanks," Dave said. "Good luck to you." Then he was out and the door had closed behind him.

Back in his office, he felt better with each passing minute. He did not delude himself that he was a hero, that he had taken a splendid stand on principle. Probably he had gotten out just in time. But that was something—he'd called the shots. And it would be friendly, publicly at least. He and Barney would say glowing things about each other. That was how it was done. He wanted the President's blessing, and the President certainly didn't want his ill-will. If nothing else, he knew too much.

He felt no bitterness toward Barney. He understood what he was doing and why. He just no longer wanted to be part of all those necessary compromises. He did not regret the years with Barney, but neither did he regret that they were over. He knew that in this past year he had pushed Barney too hard. He could see how each incident, Rivera and Hailey and the Gooch affair and the others, had irritated Barney, angered him, finally made this parting inevitable. Yet he did not think he would change much. You were what you were and you did what you had to do.

Now he had to decide what to do next. He needed money and he needed prestige, so his step down would not be too great a step, so his enemies could not gloat at his fall. The only alternatives, really, were to join a blue-ribbon law firm, to take a corporation job, or to run for office. And with the limited time he had, there were only two choices. He could join Jack Frazier's firm (or a dozen others, but Frazier's was as good as any) or he could return to Nashville. The special election for Congress was set for early December.

He had scorned the congressional race when Elton Carr had suggested it that summer, but things had changed and it was more tempting now. He could be his own man, build a political base, be free to speak out on national issues, lay the groundwork for a Senate race—and, yes, tell Barney Newfield to kiss his ass if he felt like it.

The trouble was that he was weary of politics, and the prospect of throwing himself headlong into a hectic, month-long campaign seemed more than he could endure. With a month's rest, perhaps, but now he was sick of politics, burnt-out.

New York was more alluring. If he joined Frazier's law firm, a dazzling future would spread out before him. He would be a rich man by the age of forty. He would win the independence that only money can buy. And with that money and independence he would—at the right time, at the right place—re-enter the world of politics. Power was his goal, but he saw now that the only real power was elective power, the power that comes from the people. And he could get that—his prospects were as good as those of any man his age in America. The year in the White House had given him a political celebrity that was priceless. While he was making his fortune, he would also be building a political base. He would write for the right magazines and appear on the right television programs. He would befriend the New York party leaders—speak at their fund-raising dinners, serve on their advisory committees. Then, in a decade or so, with money, celebrity and party support, he would inevitably be called on to run for a major office, for senator or governor. And he would run and win.

Yet even as he thought on it, doubts began to gather like dark clouds. If he went with Frazier's firm, would they let him practice law? Or would he be their "Washington man," their string-puller, their $100,000-a-year lobbyist? Wasn't that what they wanted him for? And if he did that, wouldn't he still be Barney's man, but now Barney's man flying to Washington twice a week to wheedle favors from men he'd once given orders to? How long could he keep his liberal support if he became a corporation lawyer? Most of all, he wondered what ten years of Wall Street, ten years of eating in expensive restaurants, drinking in expensive clubs, serving expensive people, would do to him, do to his body and do to his soul. How long could you work for the fat cats and not become one? If, finally, the opportunity for political office came, would he be too soft to want it or deserve it?

New York held out to him, literally, the best life in the world—the best shops for his wife, the best schools for his children, the best clothes and cars and theaters and clubs for himself. Part of him lusted for that rich, sweet life. It was all so easy, all there for the taking. Perhaps that was why he hesitated: half a lifetime had taught him that the things that came easily were rarely worth having.

He decided.

He seized the phone and two minutes later was talking to Elton Carr in Nashville.

"Elton, I'd like to talk about the congressional race."

In the few moments it had taken to place the call, he had been filled with feverish excitement. His doubts were gone. He was thrilled by the challenge of a campaign, by the scent of combat ahead. He wanted to fly to Nashville that moment, to put himself before the voters, to win their approval, their support, their affection.

But now, speaking with the state's most influential Democrat, he restrained his enthusiasm.

"You thinking about running, Dave?"

"I've been thinking about it ever since we talked this summer. Back then, I didn't see how I could leave here. But now I can. It boils down to this—if you think I've got a chance, I'll announce."

"Well, Dave, a bright fellow like you would have a chance in any race. Course, it's going to be a tough one."

"How's it shaping up?"

"Did you know Tom Carver's announced?"

"That silly bastard?" Dave said. "We were in law school together."

"He'll have a lot of money behind him. But I'd say Larry Houston is the real front-runner right now."

Dave had met Larry Houston once or twice. He was a hardware store owner who served on the City Council. He was forty, honest, unimaginative, and a hard worker.

"I ought to be able to handle Houston," Dave said.

"Well, you'd look better on television, and you'd be a better speaker. Course, in an off-year election, we're dealing mainly with the bloc votes, and Larry's got a lot of support locked up. He's mighty close to the labor people—goes to their parties, knows their wives and kids. And he's picked up black support, working for them in City Council."

"He doesn't know anything about national issues, does he?" Dave asked.

"I guess not," Elton Carr said. "But about the only big issue in this campaign will be where the new Interstate goes through town. Oh, and there's been some demonstrations out at Fisk, but that's not much of an issue—even the blacks say that's got to be stopped."

"Elton, if I came down there and ran a good race, ran hard as hell, could I take Houston?"

"Hard to say, Dave, I'd of been more optimistic back this summer, but after you said you weren't interested, a lot of people moved on over to Larry. I don't want to discourage you."

A God damned City Councilman, Dave thought.

"Let me think about it, Elton, and I'll get back to you," he said.

In the next hour, he called the two smartest politicians in Nashville—the editor of the *Herald* and a judge he knew—and neither said what he wanted to hear. So that was that.

He wasted no time in mourning. If you didn't get your first choice, you took the second. He called Jack Frazier, negotiated a moment, and got what he wanted—$85,000 the first year, with a month's vacation at the start, and an understanding on the kind of cases he would handle.

Then he made a local call.

"Hello?" she said in the hesitant, breathless voice she used for answering the phone.

"Eleanor? I'd like to talk a minute."

"I don't want to talk about this afternoon," she said sharply.
"Neither do I."

"Then what do you want?"

"To tell you I just quit."

He heard her gasp, then a pause.

"Because of me?"

"No," he said. "Because of me."

"What are you going to do?"

"Join that law firm in New York."

"What about us?"

"I thought we might try to pick up the pieces," he said.
"I might be easier to live with up there."

"I'd like to pick up the pieces," she said softly.

"Good," he said. "That's good. I'll be home in a couple of
hours."

He went across to check with O.B. about the announcement.
When he entered the press secretary's office, he found O.B.
on the phone, his back to the door.

"Listen, Tom," he was saying, "this guy was never a pol.
He's a fucking *poet*. He put pretty words together, that's all.
If you wanta write Davey Hyer's obit, you just say, 'Here lies
a speechwriter who got in over his head.'"

Dave started to leave, but as O.B. hung up the phone he
swung around and saw him.

"Well, good buddy, what can I do for you?"

"You have that announcement?"

"Sure. You want to see it?"

"If you don't mind."

"Be my guest," O.B. said, and held out some papers.

Dave skimmed them. The President's statement praised his
departing aide, but not quite as effusively as was customary in
these rituals. Reporters would know the difference.

"Look okay?" O.B. asked, not quite hiding his smile.

"It's fine," Dave said and left the room.

After O.B. put out the announcement, Dave began getting
calls. The *Times'* White House man tried to pin down a rift
between him and the President, but Dave stuck to his story—
he had resigned for "personal and financial reasons." When

the reporter asked about his new salary, Dave told him, not for attribution, that it was "around $100,000." That would impress the locals. O.B. and Eddie would be busy passing word that he'd left under a cloud, and there'd be plenty of people eager to believe it. But talk of a $100,000 salary would do much to quiet them. Money was the one thing people in Washington always understood.

Friends called to wish him well. Elias called, and Leon Kerkelot and Steve Vale and Sid Frankel, and even Charlton MacKenzie. "I hope I shall be seeing you often," MacKenzie intoned. Dave thought: Not if I see you first, Charlie, but he bade MacKenzie a polite farewell.

An editor of a large publishing house called, and said Dave could name his price if he would write an insider's account of the Newfield administration. Dave put him off; a book was part of the arsenal of celebrity, but he must plan his very carefully.

At six-thirty he turned on his television set to see if his resignation had made the evening news. It did briefly, but the program began with a far more important story. Rebels in Caravelas had overrun the ROC army base at Leticia and were fighting in the outskirts of Johnstown.

Later in the show, there was a film of Barney's tour that morning of the New City site in New Jersey. He'd flown up by helicopter, and two dozen dignitaries had waited for him in the middle of a huge meadow. His helicopter hovered fifty feet above them, then suddenly out came Barney, clinging like a damn acrobat to the revolving ladder in the copter's belly. He hung there, graceful, grinning, waving happily, until the helicopter gently lowered him to ten feet above the ground. He dropped the rest of the way, sure-footed as a cat, improbable as a Martian, and he was still laughing as he shook hands with his startled hosts. Then the camera followed his tour of the site, with close-ups as Barney marched around eagerly, peering at hills and valleys, rivers and woods. Dave knew that in his mind's eye Barney saw a street here, a school there, saw houses rising before him in the glorious future of his imagination.

Barney and his beautiful dream, his shining towers. Dave

wondered how much of the dream would be left in a year or two, after it had been whiplashed by the bureaucrats, the Congress, the militants, the mayors, the contractors, the unions, and all the others. Dave wondered, too, more urgently, if Barney was on the brink of a major commitment of troops in Caravelas.

But those were not his worries now. He had a new life, new challenges. And he would meet them with his eyes open. The question was whether you used Wall Street or Wall Street used you. He understood the system now; it offered vast rewards if you would accept its values, serve its ends. The system broke men, but if you were tough and shrewd enough you could break the system, use it, make it work for you. That was what he would do.

He sat for a last quiet moment in his White House office and watched the President's televised figure leap back into the helicopter, watched the helicopter shoot away until it was only a dot on the horizon, and suddenly he felt an old, good feeling race through him, warming his body like whiskey, the feeling of being alone, of being on his own. He had known that feeling many times before. He had known it at twelve when he arose before dawn on winter mornings to throw his paper route. He had known it at seventeen when he'd hitch-hiked a thousand miles to enroll in a college he'd never seen. He'd known it at twenty-four when he was public defender challenging the district attorney's men. Now he was on his own again and he felt the old pride and the old joy return. He knew now that he would always be alone, that he would live a life of temporary alliances, that his sweetest victories would always be private victories. He was going after the top prizes now and there would be dangers, but he did not think he would fail. He would be on the outside now, starting over, but he would fight back to the top. He had come too far, from so near the bottom to so near the top, to be stopped. He would be back, he was sure of that. He would be back.